Highest Praise for John Gilstrap

DAMAGE CONTROL

"Powerful and explosive, a kick-ass read, unforgettable. If you like Vince Flynn and Brad Thor, you'll love John Gilstrap."
—**Gayle Lynds**

THREAT WARNING

"A character-driven work where the vehicle has four on the floor and horsepower to burn. From beginning to end, it is dripping with excitement."
—**Joe Hartlaub, *Book Reporter***

"*Threat Warning* reconfirms Gilstrap as a master of jaw-dropping action and heart-squeezing suspense."
—**Austin Camacho, *The Big Thrill***

HOSTAGE ZERO

"Jonathan Grave, my favorite freelance peacemaker, problem-solver, and tough guy hero, is back—and in particularly fine form. *Hostage Zero* is classic Gilstrap: the people are utterly real, the action's foot to the floor, and the writing's fluid as a well-oiled machine gun. A tour de force!"
—**Jeffery Deaver**

"This addictively readable thriller marries a breakneck pace to a complex, multilayered plot. . . . Exceptional characterization and an intricate, flawlessly crafted story line make this an absolute must read for thriller fans."
Publishers Weekly (starred review)

NO MERCY

"*No Mercy* grabs hold of you on page one and doesn't let go.
Gilstrap's new series is terrific. It will leave you breathless. I
can't wait to see what Jonathan Grave is up to next."
—**Harlan Coben**

"The release of a new John Gilstrap novel is always worth
celebrating, because he's one of the finest thriller writers on
the planet. *No Mercy* showcases his work at its finest—taut,
action-packed, and impossible to put down!"
—**Tess Gerritsen**

"A great hero, a pulse-pounding story—and the launch of
a really exciting series."
—**Joseph Finder**

"An entertaining, fast-paced tale of violence and revenge."
—*Publishers Weekly*

"No other writer is better able to combine in a single novel
both rocket-paced suspense and heartfelt looks at family and
the human spirit. And what a pleasure to meet Jonathan Grave,
a hero for our time . . . and for all time."
—**Jeffery Deaver**

AT ALL COSTS

"Riveting . . . combines a great plot and realistic,
likable characters with look-over-your-shoulder tension.
A page turner."
—*The Kansas City Star*

"Gilstrap builds tension . . . until the last page, a hallmark of
great thriller writers. I almost called the paramedics
before I finished *At All Costs*."
—*Tulsa World*

"Gilstrap has ingeniously twisted his simple premise six ways from Sunday."
—*Kirkus Reviews*

"Not-to-be-missed."
—*Rocky Mountain News*

NATHAN'S RUN

"Gilstrap pushes every thriller button . . . a nail-biting denouement and strong characters."
—*San Francisco Chronicle*

"Gilstrap has a shot at being the next John Grisham. . . . One of the best books of the year."
—*Rocky Mountain News*

"Emotionally charged . . . one of the year's best."
—*Chicago Tribune*

"Brilliantly calculated. . . . With the skill of a veteran pulp master, Gilstrap weaves a yarn that demands to be read in one sitting."
—*Publishers Weekly* **(starred review)**

"Like a roller coaster, the story races along on well-oiled wheels to an undeniably pulse-pounding conclusion."
—*Kirkus Reviews* **(starred review)**

SCOTT FREE

"Gilstrap hits the accelerator and never lets up."
—**Harlan Coben**

EVEN STEVEN

"Gilstrap has an uncanny ability to bring the reader into the mind of his characters."
—*The Denver Post*

DAMAGE CONTROL

A JONATHAN GRAVE THRILLER

JOHN GILSTRAP

PINNACLE BOOKS

Kensington Publishing Corp.

www.kensingtonbooks.com

PINNACLE BOOKS are published by

Kensington Publishing Corp.
119 West 40th Street
New York, NY 10018

All Kensington titles, imprints, and distributed lines are available at special quantity discounts for bulk purchases for sales promotions, premiums, fund-raising, educational, or institutional use. Special book excerpts or customized printings can also be created to fit specific needs. For details, write or phone the office of the Kensington special sales manager: Kensington Publishing Corp., 119 West 40th Street, New York, NY 10018, attn: Special Sales Department; phone 1-800-221-2647.

PINNACLE BOOKS and the Pinnacle logo are Reg. U.S. Pat. & TM Off.

ISBN-13: 978-0-7860-2493-3
ISBN-10: 0-7860-2493-3

First printing: June 2012

10 9 8 7 6 5 4 3 2 1

Printed in the United States of America

JUN 2 6 2012

For Chris

CHAPTER ONE

Pacing her huge office high atop the Crystal Palace Cathedral in Scottsdale, Arizona, Reverend Jackie Mitchell checked her watch for the fifth time in half as many minutes. Three-oh-five. The unpleasantness was supposed to have ended an hour ago. Mr. Abrams had promised that she would know that her parishioners were safe within moments of the rescue's final outcome.

As soon as we have anything to report. That's how he'd put it. *As soon as we have anything to report.*

She tried not to worry—Abrams had assured her that everything would go well, that it *had* to go well—but given the stakes, it was hard not to harbor doubt.

Certainly, the children would be traumatized emotionally, and perhaps the adults as well, but that was to be expected under the circumstances. They'd been taken hostage. Of course there'd be trauma.

Jackie refused to dwell on the events that had brought her to this point. That was the past, and the end was finally in sight.

Abrams had *sworn* that this would be a seamless operation. Without that assurance, she'd never have gone along.

In the end, Jackie knew that the Lord would forgive her. The Crystal Palace was a testament to Him, after all. He had to understand. Why else would He have led her here? This . . . *opportunity* had come at too fortuitous a time for it to be anything but guidance by His hand. Abrams's call had been a sign, a clear message that the Crystal Palace was destined to survive despite all the tests and the scandals. God knew Jackie's heart.

We are all sinners. It's God's greatest desire to forgive us.

And forgive her He would.

When the phone rang, Jackie let out a yelp. She turned from the window and its panoramic view of Arizona's rolling hills and walked across the plush baby-blue carpeting to her six-by-eight-foot glass-topped desk to lift the receiver from its cradle.

"God bless you," she said. It was her standard greeting for any caller who got past her assistant.

"Would've been nice if he did," Abrams said. With his thick New England accent, there was no need for him to introduce himself. "Unfortunately, it's as bad as it can get."

CHAPTER TWO

Jonathan Grave ignored the drop of sweat that tracked down his forehead and over the bridge of his nose. It made no sense to wipe it away when there'd just be another to follow. What was it about jungles, he wondered, that made them so attractive to bad guys? Perhaps it was a kind of insect-borne mass psychosis.

The same variety of sickness that kept bringing him back to the stifling heat time after time. He'd long ago stopped telling himself that he'd get used to it after a while. He concentrated instead on getting past it, and he did that by focusing on the misery of the people whose rescue was his responsibility.

The bud in Jonathan's left ear popped to life. "Scorpion, Mother Hen," said the voice that had guided him through way too many difficult moments. "The satellite picture just refreshed. You have what appears to be a squad of five soldiers approaching your location from the west. I've only got heat signatures because of the canopy."

Jonathan pressed the transmit button in the center of his ballistic vest. "Range?"

"Close. Quit talking."

They moved cautiously, but still made too much noise. His mind raced to make some sense out of it. They could not be reinforcements because no one outside his very small circle knew he was here. That made them bad guys until proven otherwise, and their presence made this operation vastly more complicated.

"I see movement but no faces." Jonathan heard Boxers' unmistakable growl through the same earpiece. Closer to seven feet tall than six, with a girth that made him look bulletproof, Boxers had been born as Brian Van de Meulebroeke, and had been Jonathan's right-hand man from back in their days in the Unit when they'd toiled under the supervision of Uncle Sam and his surrogates. His position on the opposite hill gave him a good view of Jonathan's location. "Looks like they might be here for the same reason we are. They're taking positions next to you."

Jonathan acknowledged by tapping his transmit button once to break squelch. They might be in the same place, Jonathan thought, but he doubted that they were here for the same reason. Jonathan's plan was to let a group of kidnappers take a bag loaded with three million dollars in return for leaving behind their hostages. Now it seemed that there'd be competition for the money.

"One is very damn close to you, Boss," Boxers went on. "I give it twenty feet of separation, and he's settling in. There's enough brush between the two of you that as long as you don't sneeze, you'll be invisible." After about ten seconds, Boxers finished with, "I've got his range dialed in. If he makes an ugly face, I'll take him out."

In Boxers' world, there were no problems so great

that they couldn't be solved with the appropriate application of firepower. In this case, the firepower in play would be Hechler and Koch's HK417, a lightweight cannon chambered in 7.62 millimeter that could send ten rounds per second downrange with needle-threading accuracy. As far as Jonathan was concerned, it was the best marksman's rifle since the M14, and he had every confidence that as long as Boxers was within a thousand yards (he was actually within a quarter of a thousand yards), his closest visitor posed no physical threat.

But why had he been joined by soldiers, and where had they come from?

His earbud popped again. "Look sharp, guys," Mother Hen said. "I've got vehicles approaching from the south. Looks like a school bus followed by an SUV. School bus, maybe, but definitely not a late model. Estimate a half mile from the drop."

Moving carefully, Jonathan flexed his shoulders and prepared himself. With his back braced against a leafy, foul-smelling tree and his elbows braced against his raised knees, he pressed his M27 carbine into his shoulder and scanned the area through his scope.

The backpack with the ransom remained at the base of the tree where he'd placed it twenty minutes ago, at the edge of the rutted path that looked more like a hiking trail than the road that it was supposed to be. The same canopy of leaves that trapped the humidity to the ground also filtered out much of the sunlight, casting this part of the world in a kind of perpetual twilight during the day. He'd done his best to make the backpack stand out in a shaft of light.

The instructions for this op were as simple as they were objectionable. Jonathan was to be a bagman. He and Boxers were to allow the bad guys to collect their millions and get away. In return, the bad guys would release their hostages, four adults and six children aged fifteen to seventeen. Jonathan knew little about their condition, but after a week in captivity, mobility was not going to be their long suit.

If Jonathan had been allowed to write the script, this drop-off would have been made in the wide-open desert regions of northern Mexico, where everything and everyone would be in the open, but the bad guys had insisted on a jungle transfer in the south. That was a mistake that played to Jonathan's strengths. While the wide vistas of the north played to their paranoia of not being able to get away quickly, this kind of thick foliage screamed ambush opportunity.

Accordingly, he and Boxers had poised themselves for a classic ambush, to be sprung if the kidnappers decided to break the rules. As long as they drove into the clearing and off-loaded the hostages to be counted, they would be allowed to pick up their ransom and drive away in the follow car, leaving the bus behind. Just about any other scenario would result in a very, very bad day for the kidnappers.

Then these new guys showed up. If they started shooting, the kidnappers would panic, and then there'd be a bloodbath.

"I've got eyes on the precious cargo," Boxers said into his radio. He was in position to see the approaching vehicles before Jonathan could. "I can't count heads through the windows, but it looks like a full load."

Jonathan acknowledged with a tap on his transmit button.

Ten seconds later the flat nose of an ancient bus turned the sweeping corner into the kill zone, its engine wheezing like an old man. To his right, he heard the interlopers reacting with movement. "It's here," the close one said in Spanish, perhaps into a radio, or perhaps just to himself. From this range—call it fifty yards—Jonathan could see the silhouette of the driver, even though he couldn't make out his features.

"Looks like the follow car is hanging back," Boxers advised. "It is an SUV, and it appears to have only a driver inside."

The newcomers had fallen silent. As Jonathan settled behind his rifle scope to track the action in and around the bus, he tried to ignore the tingle in his spine that told him trouble was coming.

"They're going to kill us, aren't they?" Allison asked.

If they don't, I might, Tristan didn't say. He'd been handcuffed to her for nearly five days now. What was that, a hundred twenty-five hours? That's how many hours she'd been whining. Honest to God, it didn't matter if he was trying to sleep or if he was in the middle of a conversation with someone else, Allison Bradley never shut up.

This ordeal had offered up too many cruel twists to even keep up with anymore, but none had been crueler than the kidnappers' decision to handcuff him to Miss Bubbly Cheerleader-Turned-Doomsayer. For five long days, they'd done *everything* together—including the humiliation of biological chores—and at every turn, Allison had featured herself at death's door. They were all scared, for God's sake.

"Seriously," she repeated, "I think they're going to kill us."

From behind: "Allison, shut up!"

For an instant, Tristan thought that he'd inadvertently spoken his thoughts aloud. Instead, the words had erupted from Ray Greaser, who, back in the world, had been Ken to Allison's Barbie, the clichéd quarterback-cheerleader Homecoming royalty. The resulting photo in the yearbook exuded the kind of perfection that every high school student dreamed of, yet Tristan would never achieve. He told his friends that the photo looked like an Aryan recruitment poster.

"Don't tell me to shut up!" Allison snapped. "In fact, don't even *speak* to me."

"*Cállate*," snapped the nameless man up front with the machine gun. *Shut up.*

Great, Tristan thought. *Now I'm channeling a terrorist.*

Like all of the gunmen on the bus, the one up front wore military fatigues, but of a style that Tristan didn't see in the States anymore. The green and black camouflage appeared more as smears of color than the precise digital patterns of modern warriors. The clothes didn't matter as much as the rifles, though. Or the pistols. Or the hand grenades.

Tristan sensed that this was the beginning of the end. After all the days and nights of anger and agitation among these murderers, the past twelve hours had brought a lighter mood. Whatever the endgame was, it had apparently been achieved because the guys with the guns had been a lot more cheerful.

Assholes. Every time he thought about what they'd

done to Mr. Hall and Mrs. Charlton, he wanted to kill them. He wanted *somebody* to kill them. Especially for Mrs. Charlton.

The bus slowed by half—if that was even possible, given the snail's pace they'd been traveling for the last three hours—and as it did, the terrorists became more agitated.

"We're almost there," one of them said in Spanish. "It should be just around this curve."

"What are they saying?" Allison asked. Why she'd decided to come on a trip to rural Mexico without knowing a word of the language was beyond Tristan.

He ignored her. A better option than punching her.

The bus took the curve at slower than a walking pace, its engine screaming and transmission rattling as if someone had thrown rocks in the gearbox. Finally, they stopped, and the men with the guns started moving and chattering quickly.

"They're saying we're here," Tristan translated, hoping to get ahead of the inevitable question. " 'Positions, everyone.' "

"What does that mean?" Allison whined.

"How the hell do I know? They're not talking to us."

"I see it," said the driver, pointing through the windshield to a spot ahead of them.

The other five terrorists abandoned their spots among the hostages and surged forward to get a look. In Tristan's mind, the gunmen were essentially one person. He'd made an effort to avoid eye contact, or even to look at their faces. He knew that if he ever came out of the other end of this thing alive, he didn't want their malignant eyes haunting his dreams. He prayed that

there'd be some kind of hypnosis he could undergo that
would erase this nightmare forever.

"Get ready to take your positions," said the gunman
who'd staked out the front of the bus as his own territory. Tristan figured that guy to be the one in charge because he was the one who gave the most orders. "Keep
watch for any sign of soldiers or police. Are you ready?"

The answer came more as an enthusiastic roar than a
verbal response.

The bus rocked as four soldiers streamed out of the
fanfold front door and formed a circle around the vehicle. They kept their rifles at their shoulders, pointed out
toward the jungle. Seated where he was on the right-
hand side of the bus, Tristan couldn't see any details of
what they were doing, but he noted that everyone in the
bus had stopped talking.

If it hadn't been so quiet, he probably would not
have heard the *tick* of the windshield breaking and the
wet *thwop* of the driver's head exploding as two distinct sounds.

CHAPTER THREE

Jonathan tightened his grip on his weapon as the bus's folding door opened and four armed men rushed out. All of them wore ancient M81 woodland cammies, and were armed with MP5 submachine guns, no doubt courtesy of a happy gun store owner in Texas. They moved with choreographed precision that demonstrated they'd been trained, albeit to a level that didn't concern him much. The four took up defensive positions on each corner of the bus, and waited while a fifth guy—the driver of the van—hurried forward to join them. The bus driver remained in place behind the wheel.

With everyone in position, they held for a few seconds, and then the fifth guy moved forward, his weapon pressed to his shoulder, his eyes scanning for threats. He clearly had spotted the backpack.

He'd walked maybe a half dozen steps when a high-caliber rifle shattered the silence of the afternoon and brains spattered the interior of the bus's windshield. The shot came from the guy on Jonathan's right, and half a second later, he heard the whip crack of Boxer's incoming round as it sheared the shooter's head from his shoulders.

Then the world erupted in gunfire.

In the space of a heartbeat, the five kidnappers opened up on the jungle, firing randomly at targets they couldn't see. Farther away on Jonathan's right, the rest of the newly arriving shooters returned fire, proving that whatever their skills might be, marksmanship did not rank among them.

Jonathan fired a three-round burst and dropped the terrorist at the right front bumper. Two seconds later, he was under fire from his right, his position being raked by the late arrivers. He slapped his transmit button. "I'm under fire," he said.

He'd barely released the transmit button when Boxers started stitching the area with .30-caliber rounds. Whoever they were, they didn't have the stomach for a protracted gun battle. As loud as they had been coming in, they made a hell of a lot more noise as they ran away.

In a perfect world, Jonathan would have caught them in a cross fire to keep them from escaping; but today those people were just a distraction. His real targets were down there on the ground below.

Jonathan's worst nightmare would come true if the soldiers on the ground turned their attention to the bus. In the twisted logic that was hostage negotiation, they had every right to do so. They no doubt felt both betrayed and doomed. It only made sense to take the hostages with them.

As if on cue, two of them turned their weapons on the bus and opened fire. Boxers was already a beat ahead. Jonathan couldn't hear the Big Guy's rifle, but he recognized the marksmanship. On the far side of the bus, a spray of blood marked the demise of one gunman, and before his buddy could even react, he, too, dropped dead.

Jonathan went to work, too. He killed the bagman first, with a double tap to the chest, and then he moved to the two on his side of the bus, killing them with two shots apiece.

Then it was done. All the bad guys were dead, and the whole gun battle had lasted less than ten seconds.

Half a tick later, Boxers nearly shouted over the radio, "What the hell's going on, Boss?"

Jonathan pressed the transmit button to respond, but froze when he heard more gunshots. These seemed muffled compared to the others, and they were followed immediately with the sound of screaming.

"Shit!" he spat on the air. "There's a shooter on the bus."

Tristan had never seen so much blood. The spray of bone and brains went everywhere, misting the windows pink. An instant later, the world outside erupted in gunfire. He looked out the side window and saw the soldiers or the kidnappers or whatever the hell they were shooting long blasts of machine gun fire into the jungle.

"They're going to kill us!" Allison screamed.

And then the guys outside spouted blood and fell to the ground.

Paul McDaniel, another jock, shouted, "Get down!"

and then the loudest bang Tristan had ever heard startled everyone into silence. And there was more blood in the air. Tristan could taste it.

People started screaming. Danielle Taylor was next. Tristan had never gotten to know her very well, but she smiled a lot. He'd wished several times that he could have been handcuffed to her instead of to Allison. The soldier at the front of the bus knew none of this, of course, as he pressed his rifle against the side of her head.

"Please don't," Danielle begged. "I—"

The kidnapper pulled the trigger.

At least she died fast.

What surprised Tristan the most was the clarity of it all. It was as if time had slowed to a heartbeat every five seconds. As the gunman strolled casually down the center aisle, Tristan's brain recorded every detail. The muzzle flashes. The way people just went limp when their souls were blasted out of their heads. Always a head shot, always a dead body.

With Danielle gone, the soldier pivoted and leveled his rifle at Ray Greaser. Tristan had never liked Ray, but right now, he felt like a brother. He started to cry when the rifle turned to him. "Please don't," he said.

Good guys never pleaded for their lives in movies, Tristan thought, yet everybody pleads when their time comes. Even as his heart hammered in his chest hard enough to break a rib, Tristan wondered what he would do when his time came.

This was so unfair. They were all handcuffed together, and the soldier with the rifle could move as fast or as slowly as he wanted. Every advantage lay with the murderer. That just wasn't right.

The soldier was about to kill Ray when someone yelled, "Hey, asshole!" It was in English, and when the gunman pivoted and pointed his gun at the shouter, Tristan was shocked to realize that the words were his own.

But they were, and he was already in for a dime. Now it was time to be in for a dollar. "You don't have to do this," he said in Spanish. As the words left his mouth, he caught movement off to his right, outside the bus.

"Yes, I do," the soldier said. He murdered Ray, and then his gaze followed Tristan's. First his eyes, then his head, and finally his rifle. Someone was storming the bus.

The gunman flipped a switch on the side of his rifle. Tristan knew he was going to die now. He hooked his free hand around Allison's neck and he pulled her to the floor.

The shooting became insane.

"Give me covering fire on the hill," Jonathan said into his radio as he sprinted toward the vehicle full of precious cargo. Whoever took the shot at the driver had screwed up everything, and the penalty was death.

An instant later, Boxers opened up, raking the trees above and behind Jonathan with bullets. If the shooter was still there and they didn't kill him, they would make him go to ground, which accomplished more or less the same goal.

The sound of the gunfire must have startled the killer on the bus, too, because he stopped firing at the hostages and looked out the far side window toward Boxers' location.

The distraction lasted for only a second or two, and then the shooter returned to his executions. Jonathan knew from sound alone that he was firing big ammunition—probably 7.62 millimeter—and he knew from experience how much damage they could do to the human anatomy. God only knew how many PCs the shooter had already killed, but Jonathan aimed to stop him.

As he closed the distance, he let the carbine fall against its sling and he drew his Colt 1911 .45 from the holster on his thigh. At this range, any bullet he fired from the carbine would pass completely through the man he intended to shoot and then go on to endanger the people behind him. Besides, the Colt was the best weapon ever made.

He was still ten yards out when he identified his target, but he didn't have a clean shot. Too many heads bobbing in and out of the sight picture. Even from out here, he could see the blood on the windows and the walls of the bus. He could also see the holes through the sheet metal that marked the paths of the bullets that had exited their victims. The gunman was walking down the aisle, front to back, casually taking aim at hostages' heads and blowing them away. For Jonathan, the worst of it all was the lack of screaming inside the vehicle.

People screamed only when they thought they had a chance to live.

The movement must have caught the gunman's attention, because when Jonathan was still thirty yards out, the guy opened up on full auto inside the bus. It was a slaughter.

The gunman turned as Jonathan leaped through the open door and dove on his belly. The shooter followed him with his own weapon. a stockless AK with a banana clip. Jonathan saw in a blink that the bad guy's aim was off by half a foot, and that would be his last mistake.

The AK launched its massive bullets at two thousand three hundred feet per second. At this range, the boom was beyond deafening. The sound pressure hit with a force all its own.

Jonathan's mind recorded all of the sights and the noises as a matter of instinct, dismissing everything so far as inconsequential. He had lives to protect, and to do it he had to kill this asshole or die trying. As he hit the floor on his right side, he slid across the blood-slick grooved rubber matting and came to rest with his head nearly touching the foot of the dead driver.

Before the AK could cycle for a second burst, Jonathan's hand flexed and his pistol barked. The angles were all wrong for a reliable one-shot kill, so he took out the shooter's knee with the first shot to get him falling. A quarter second later, the collapsing terrorist spread his arms just wide enough to expose his chest, and Jonathan drilled his heart. Just for good measure—in case the bad guy was wearing body armor Jonathan couldn't see—he launched a final round through the bridge of the shooter's nose. Three shots in just over one second, and the world had one fewer terrorist to worry about.

Then there was silence. Even as Boxers hammered away at whatever targets he could find outside, nothing moved in the interior of the vehicle. This was where there should have been unbridled panic, punctuated with screams of terror and cries for help. Instead, he heard only the pounding of his own heart.

He stood cautiously, his weapon at the ready. The metal floorboards were slick with blood. Windows and seats had been shredded by bullets, their occupants contorted into postures that were only possible in death. At first glance, Jonathan counted seven bodies, five teens and two terrorists. He neither knew nor cared what the numbers outside tallied up to.

Jonathan pressed the transmit button in the center of his vest. "Big Guy, I need you in here now." They usually tried to keep emotion out of their voices on the radio, but he heard the leaden dread in his own.

"Listen up!" he yelled. "I am an American and I am here to take you home. Can anybody hear me?"

He moved methodically down the center aisle, weapon ready but his finger out of the trigger guard. He moved seat by seat, scanning the carnage, observing the way the terrorists had bound them together. In the very back, two of the hostages—both boys—sat bolt upright in their seats, one with part of his brain exposed, and the other with two holes in his chest.

The entire bus shifted as Boxers mounted the steps. "Holy shit."

Jonathan turned to the man he'd served with for so many years. It was time to say something, to give an order. But he felt frozen. He'd had ops go bad in the past, but nothing like this. "What the hell happened? Who opened fire?"

"Are they all dead?" Boxers asked.

"I've only done a primary," Jonathan replied. In a

primary assessment, you look for the obvious—weapons and people who are wounded. The secondary assessment looks for more detailed signs of life. Here, today, that seemed like a waste of time. "How secure is our perimeter?"

"I saw them running," Boxers said. He grabbed the dead driver by his collar, pulled him onto the floor, and slipped into his seat. "We're getting out of this clearing," he said. "We're too good a target." He restarted the engine, threw the transmission into gear, and popped the clutch.

As they lurched forward, Jonathan sat heavily on the edge of a seat. "Where are you going?" he yelled. If they were getting away, he expected them to be going backward.

"The money," Boxers said. "Ain't no way I'm leaving that much cash for the bad guys."

He raced forward for thirty yards and jammed the vehicle to a stop. For a guy of his size, he moved with impressive speed, slapping the transmission into neutral and then heaving himself out of the seat, down the steps, and out the door. By the time Jonathan could gain his balance to provide cover, the Big Guy was already back at the foot of the stairs, the green-and-blue backpack dangling from his hand. Within ten seconds, they were moving again.

He jammed the stick shift into reverse and popped the clutch. As they lurched backward, he yanked the wheel hard to get them turned around, and then he shifted into second gear and gunned it. They tore down the road that the bus had come in on, and after they turned the corner and disappeared from the established shooting lanes, Jonathan surveyed the carnage. Wherever he looked, all he saw were corpses. He'd let all of them down.

"You okay, Boss?"

Jonathan looked up to see Boxers' eyes in the mirror.

No, he was not okay. Okay wasn't even within the same emotional solar system as where he was. Someone somewhere had deliberately sabotaged this mission, and whoever it was, was going to pay dearly, so help—

Somebody moaned. At first, it was barely audible—so low that Jonathan thought maybe he'd imagined it. But Boxers clearly had heard it, too. Then it became louder, before it became a scream: "Get it off me!"

The bodies on the floor in the seat behind him moved.

"Box!" Jonathan yelled. "Stop the bus!"

Tristan couldn't breathe. He felt as if he was trying to climb out of a hole in his mind, but something was holding him down. Some*one* was holding him down. Trying to crush his head, pressing it into something hard and lumpy.

And wet.

He tasted blood.

As consciousness returned, so did awareness. Memory of what had happened. The shooting. The brains and the blood.

Like the blood he could taste.

He opened his eyes, and there was Allison, staring at him. Unblinking. Dead.

He heard himself screaming before he knew that the voice was his. But once he did know, he wanted to make sure that it could be heard. Allison was dead and she was bleeding into his mouth.

Horror flooded his veins. He needed to get her off him. He tried to push, but his hands wouldn't work. They couldn't be separated anyway, he remembered because they were tied together with a steel chain. Screaming seemed to be the only thing he was capable of.

Then she moved. Dead Allison moved. Her eyes never blinked, but she somehow heard him, and she was levitating away, pulling him with her by his wrist.

An instant later, in a transition he never saw, a man's face appeared where hers had been. It was a hard face, but the blue eyes looked friendly—serious, but friendly. Another man stood behind him, but Tristan wondered if he was hallucinating. The second man was huge.

The face up close was saying something to him. His hands were on Tristan's shoulders and they were shaking him. "Easy now," the man said. "You're safe. It's over. You're going to be okay."

He spoke English. Tristan felt as if he hadn't heard English in months. As his eyes focused, he saw that the man wore a uniform and that he dripped weapons. Another jolt of panic shot thought him and he tried to pull away.

Damned handcuffs.

"Tristan," the man said. "Tristan, listen to me. Come on, son, pull it together. You're okay. You're going to be just fine. We're here to take you home. We're the good guys, okay? The bad guys are all dead. You're safe."

Was that possible? Who was this man? Nothing made sense.

But he felt himself gaining some control. He spit to get the blood out of his mouth.

The man with the blue eyes said, "Are you all right? Are you hurt?"

Didn't he just say that I was fine?

"I don't think this blood is yours," the man said. He started to lift Tristan's T-shirt, and Tristan pulled away.

"No," he said. What the *hell* was going on here?

"Son, settle down. I'm only checking to see if you've been shot."

Really? Wouldn't I be the first to know if I'd been shot?

"His color's good," the big man said. "He moves good. I think he's fine. I'm getting us out of here." As he spoke the words, the bus's engine started to make a screeching sound, and the big man yelled, "Shit! The engine's been drilled, Boss."

Blue Eyes lifted the T-shirt again, and this time Tristan let him. "Did you kill the follow vehicle?" he called over his shoulder.

The driver said something that Tristan couldn't understand, and then the bus stopped again.

"I don't see anything," Blue Eyes said. He let Tristan's shirt fall back into place. Blue Eyes reached into one of his many pockets and pulled out a tiny key.

"Tristan, I want you to listen to me."

"How do you know my name?"

"I know all your names," the man said. "My partner and I are here to rescue you, to take you home."

"What home?" Tristan asked. "Like, *home* home? In Scottsdale?"

The man smiled. "That's the one." As he spoke, he slipped the key into the handcuff on Tristan's wrist. As the bracelet fell away, his wrist started to throb. "One more."

The driver yelled, "Boss, we gotta go!"

As Tristan's eyes followed his rescuer's hand and the key down the shackle on his ankle, he noticed for the first time how much blood there was on the floor. He was wet with it. As that shackle also fell away, something tightened in his belly. It was the same panicky feeling from the other day when the gunmen first stormed their bus in Ciudad Juárez.

"Look at me, Tristan," the man said. "Look at *me*, son."

Tristan raised his eyes to meet the blue ones. The man smiled. "You're going to have to trust me, Tristan. I want to get you out of here, but first I want you to make me a promise."

"Who are you?" Tristan asked. His brain was starting to work again, and that seemed like a really important question.

"We'll get to that later, I promise," the man said. His big partner had somehow disappeared from view. "Will you make me a promise?"

Tristan nodded. "Yes. Sir."

Another smile. "Okay. I'm going to help you stand, but then we're going to hurry out of here. I don't want you looking around."

"Why?"

"Promise me."

Tristan craned his neck and turned his head to see what the man was trying to hide, but Blue Eyes was too quick. A countermove for every move.

"What are you going to do to me?"

"With you," the man corrected. "I'm going to help you get out of the bus."

Tristan pulled his legs up under him and started to stand. "I can do it myself."

The man put a hand on his shoulder and pressed him back down. He was stronger than he looked. "I know you can," he said. He took a deep breath, and the eyes turned sad. "Your friends are all dead, son. You don't want to see that. That's not how you want to remember them. Just look straight ahead and we'll get you out of here."

The knot in his gut tightened. "They're *dead*? All of them?"

The man pressed his lips into a kind of pout. "I'm afraid so, Tristan."

"How?"

"Scorpion!" the driver yelled, louder this time. "Can we save the counseling for later, please?"

Blue Eyes—Scorpion?—stayed focused on Tristan. "We're going to go right now."

With that, the rescuer grabbed the front of Tristan's T-shirt in both fists and lifted him to his feet. As he rose, Allison's head thumped against the floor of the bus, where she launched a spray of blood spatter from the gathering puddle.

"She's dead," Scorpion said. "She can't feel anything. Just keep moving."

Scorpion half carried Tristan as he stumbled down the center aisle of the bus. He stepped over what was left of the terrorist who had shot everybody, and he bumped up against Danielle, whose head was mostly gone. Scorpion seemed to sense when he was about to freeze because he pulled harder to drag him along.

Tristan tried to do as he was told—to look straight ahead—and he understood why he was supposed to do it. But the temptation proved overwhelming. When he finally got to the top of the stairs, he dared a look backward.

It was too awful to comprehend. Truly, they were all dead. These people who had shared this awful experience with him over the past week had all been mangled by bullets. None would ever speak again. Blood was *everywhere*. He didn't know how that was possible.

But he knew he was alone now.

What about their parents? Who's going to tell them?

"Keep going, Tristan," Scorpion said. The rescuer planted his hands in Tristan's armpits and nearly carried him down the stairs from behind. His rifle hurt as it pressed against his back.

Tristan stumbled on the last step and lost the flip-flop from his left foot. He watched it fall onto the grassy road cut, and as he reached for it with his toes, he saw—really *saw* for the first time—how bloody his legs and feet were. He could only imagine about the rest of him.

His stomach flopped, and he retched, but he hadn't eaten in days. Nothing but bile came up.

The driver looked even bigger up close than he did at a distance. He was positioned just outside and in front of the door, his rifle pressed to his shoulder as he pointed the muzzle uphill.

"We're ready," Scorpion said, and an instant later, the man's grip switched from the front of his T-shirt to the waistband of Tristan's shorts—at the small of his back—and he jerked the pants up in kind of a power wedgie. Scorpion's other hand pressed against the back of Tristan's head, bending the boy into an inverted L. He maintained that position as they fast-walked across the rutted roadway to a rusty beige Toyota SUV.

Once at the vehicle, Scorpion opened the back door with the hand he'd moved from his head, and then Tristan found himself landing hard on the torn fabric of the bench seat. "On the floor," he commanded. "Stay there till I tell you to get up."

CHAPTER FOUR

With the PC secure in the backseat, Jonathan swung his M27 to his shoulder to cover Boxers as the Big Guy tossed his ruck into the backseat, slid into the driver's seat, and started the engine. "First thing to break our way," Boxers announced. "Keys were in the ignition."

Jonathan opened the door to the shotgun seat, tossed his ruck on top of Boxers', and they were moving even before he got the door closed. A few seconds later, after a violent J-turn, they were on their way, spewing a rooster tail of dust behind them.

"You okay, Tristan?" Jonathan shouted. When he didn't get an answer, he looked behind him into the backseat, where the kid sat in a fetal ball on the floor behind Jonathan. Tall and lean to the point of skinny, the kid was all arms and legs. Filthy and sweaty and blood-smeared, Tristan Wagner's exhausted expression gave him the look of an old man in a teenager's body. Good thing he was crouched on the right side of the floor. If he'd been on the left, Boxers might have crushed him as he launched his seat back to make room for his legs.

The boy appeared to have slipped into that non-place that so many PCs—precious cargoes—retreated to as they grappled with the challenge of understanding the unthinkable.

"Tristan?"

The boy's eyes rocked up to meet Jonathan's. They were a shade of green that Jonathan associated with cats, not people. He looked ready to cry.

"It's almost over for you, son," he said. "I'm sorry for your friends." He hoped that that last part hadn't sounded like a throwaway line. He truly was sorry that they'd been killed, and he truly felt for the emotional grater that lay ahead for the kid. More than that, though, he wanted to keep the reality first and foremost in Tristan's mind. Jonathan had seen too many rescued hostages slip into crippling denial. No matter how awful the truth might be, it was Jonathan's experience that embracing it early on caused far less emotional trauma in the long run than did the slide into delusion.

As Tristan pressed his hands to his eyes and started to cry, Jonathan turned around to face forward.

"You want to tell me what the hell just happened up there?" Boxers said.

"I have no idea," Jonathan said. "You got eyeballs on the guys who joined us. What did you see?"

"Looked like army to me," Boxers replied. "Maybe police, I have a hard time telling them apart."

"They fired the first shot, right?"

"That's the way I saw it. They took out the driver, and then everything came unzipped from there."

Jonathan tried to pull the details into some kind of recognizable form. No one was even supposed to know that they were here.

He'd been contacted the usual way, through a blind email address via a reference from another client. After the security checks were completed, and funds had been deposited in Security Solutions's offshore account, Jonathan had made contact, via an untraceable prepaid phone, with a Beatrice Almont, who turned out to be the lawyer for the Crystal Palace Cathedral in Scottsdale, Arizona.

The name sounded familiar to Jonathan, and a quick Internet search reminded him that the Crystal Palace was spiritual home to Reverend Jackie Mitchell, a fire-and-brimstoner whose preachings were beamed throughout the world to her million-plus-member congregation.

Ms. Almont obviously had no experience in dealing with the likes of Jonathan, whose line of work made most officers of the court pretty damn jumpy. Under the circumstances, though, she didn't have much choice.

Tristan and his friends were missionaries from the Crystal Palace, sent to Mexico to help with recovery from a recent earthquake. The very thought of it angered Jonathan. These missionary trips with children were just extended photo ops as far as he was concerned. In the grand scheme of things, what could a bunch of kids possibly contribute that would be worth the risk of sending them into the lawless land of diseases and bad medical care? And after doing so, how could the so-called responsible adults claim to be shocked when things go horribly wrong? Dangle a carrot in front of an alligator's mouth for long enough, and sooner or later it's going to snap at it.

In the case of the Crystal Palace missionaries, fate struck swiftly. Less than half an hour after the busload of innocents had crossed into Mexico, gunmen stormed aboard as it was waiting at a traffic light in Ciudad Juárez. The speed with which the ransom demand had arrived in Reverend Mitchell's email told Jonathan that there was nothing random in this human seizure, and the efficiency of the kidnapping and the subsequent extortion left little doubt in Jonathan's mind that it was a well-planned operation executed by well-trained, well-funded professionals. In that part of Mexico, that meant Felix Hernandez was involved. The fact that the hostages were subsequently transported over a thousand miles to their current location closer to the Guatemalan border than that of the United States hinted at a cooperative deal between drug lords that meant more trouble for the Mexican government.

The terms of the ransom could not have been simpler: Pay the money, get the hostages back. Done and done. Any attempt to involve the police or the army or the United States government would result in the summary execution of every hostage.

In his initial conversation with lawyer Almont, Jonathan had felt compelled to be blunt, lest she not understand the seriousness of the hostages' plight. "There's good news and bad news when dealing with the Mexicans," he'd said. "The good news is, the drug cartels have reduced kidnapping to a business. They don't bluff, and they don't jerk you around. You give the bad guys the cash, and they let their hostages go. If they didn't, people would stop negotiating with them, and they'd lose a major revenue stream."

"You're assuming that this is drug related," Ms. Almont said. "That isn't necessarily the case."

Jonathan's research showed that she was a corporate

lawyer, more used to negotiating lease terms than ransom payments. Her voice didn't exactly tremble, but the stress was plain. "They were taken in Ciudad Juárez," Jonathan explained. "If it's violent, and it's in Ciudad Juárez, the drug cartels are involved."

"You sound experienced in these things."

"I'm assuming that's why you called me."

He sensed that she was marking time in the conversation, perhaps to wrap her head around it all. "You said there's good news and *bad* news," she said after a few seconds of silence.

Jonathan thought it was obvious, but apparently not. "Like I said, it's a business for them. For the intimidation side of the equation to work, they have to show no mercy when the ransom fails to appear."

"You mean they kill the hostages."

"I mean, they make a show of killing them as violently and with as much gore as possible before dumping the bodies in a public place in plain sight of dozens of witnesses who know better than to have seen anything. Ciudad Juárez saw four thousand murders last year, all of them carried out by the cartels."

"Four *thousand*! Why haven't I heard about these?" Ms. Almont asked.

"The newspapers won't write about them," Jonathan said. "A few of the stories get printed, but mostly they get quashed by the editorial boards."

"I guess they don't want to scare off all the tourists," she guessed.

Jonathan laughed. "Clearly you've never been to Ciudad Juárez. No, that's why they quash the stories about the growing number of murders in Aruba and the

Mexican Riviera. Bloodbaths and spring break make bad partners. The reason they suppress the stories in the northern areas is to keep their own families from being targeted."

He could hear the shock in the lawyer's voice. "Is it really that bad? The cartels are running the newspapers?"

"And the television stations and the police force and the army. Well-orchestrated intimidation is a powerful weapon, Counselor."

"So, are you suggesting that we pay the ransom? I thought you specialized in hostage rescue."

"I specialize in returning hostages to their loved ones," Jonathan corrected. "If I can accomplish that by paying off the bad guys and not get shot at, I'm happy."

"And you think that will work?"

"I think we need to plan that it will," Jonathan hedged. "But we prepare for the possibility that it won't. They may be businessmen, but they're also murderers."

"That's why we need you," she said.

"Whether you need me or not is your decision. I'm telling you what we bring to the table."

"And I'm just supposed to trust you with three million dollars? I don't even know who you are."

While Jonathan understood her hesitation, he didn't have patience for it. "You called *me*, Counselor," he said. "Not the other way around. Hire me or don't hire me. Just don't waste my time." One fewer opportunity to put his life on the line for strangers wouldn't bring a tear to his eye.

Almont said, "I've never been in a position like this

before. Everything I know tells me that this is a matter for the State Department and the Mexican police."

"And I'm telling you that's the biggest mistake you can make. Word travels at the speed of light, and bullets aren't a whole lot slower. Do not expect hesitation from these people, and don't expect mercy."

The lawyer took her time weighing options. "How do I know you're really the best?"

"You've seen my fee," Jonathan said, "and I assume you heard about me from someone you trust. The fact that I'm still alive to be talking to you must say something."

"I don't even know your name."

"Sure you do."

"Scorpion is not a name. It's a cartoon character. You could be anybody."

Jonathan reached the end of his patience. "Okay, Ms. Almont, I'm done with you. If I get word in the next two hours that my fee has been deposited in my account, I'll get back in touch with you. If I don't, so be it. Either way, best of luck."

Then he hung up. Twenty minutes later, he heard from his bank. Four days after that, here they were on the tail end of it all, and the kidnappers had won on every count.

And now this.

"You know, we've still got a perfect record," Boxers said. "For rescues."

Jonathan appreciated the effort to make today's outcome somehow less shitty than it really was, but he wasn't buying.

Boxers read his expression for what it was. "I'm

serious. They executed the hostages before we were even part of the game. That's not on us."

Then Jonathan understood that the Big Guy wasn't trying to make Jonathan feel better; he was trying to make himself feel better.

"Something to talk about over some scotch when we get back to the World," Jonathan said.

"Can't happen fast enough for me," Boxers growled.

Jonathan's earbud popped, startling him. "Scorpion, this is Mother Hen. There's a problem. A big one."

Jonathan exchanged looks with Boxers, whose radio carried the same traffic as his. The law of averages mandated that *something* start going his way. He pressed his transmit button. "Go ahead."

"SkysEye is picking up heat signatures from people gathered around your first-stage exfil site."

A big problem indeed. "I need more than that, Mother Hen. What are you telling me?"

From the backseat: "Mother *Hen*? Who the hell is that?"

"I think I count ten people," she replied. "Maybe eight, maybe twelve. With the four-minute refresh rate, it's hard to tell. It looks like they're setting up an ambush around the vehicles."

Boxers brought the Toyota to an abrupt halt. "We're less than half a mile away," he said, answering Jonathan's unasked question.

"Less than half a mile from what?" asked Tristan. "What's happening?" He couldn't hear the radio traffic, but apparently he could read body language.

It was official now: everything about this mission

had come unzipped. And whoever was pulling on the zipper was damn good at his job.

Jonathan said, "Stand by, Mother Hen." To Tristan, he said, "Stay put. Big Guy, let's chat outside."

They exited their respective doors and joined up behind the trunk. "Somebody's gonna die," Boxers said. "A trap? Somebody set a *trap*? Actually, that's *two* traps. In less than a half hour. What the hell's goin' on, Dig?"

Jonathan's mind screamed to find an answer. Whatever was going on, the perpetrators had jammed them up big time. Jonathan and Boxers had no legal authority to be where they were in the first place, and they'd just left a field littered with bodies. That in itself wasn't a big deal, provided they could get out of the country quickly. They'd stashed a Gulfstream G550 corporate jet at the hacienda of Rudolfo Gutierrez for just that purpose, but to use it, they had to get to it, and for that they needed the stashed SUV.

"They knew that we'd need the vehicles," Jonathan said, "and they knew precisely where we'd stashed them. How is that possible?"

"There's only one way," Boxers said. "Somebody sold us out. What do you bet I can talk one of the trap-layers into telling us who?"

"We're not engaging them."

Boxers recoiled. "Come again?"

"I said we're not going to engage. Not with those odds, and not with the PC in tow."

"Who said I was goin' to tow him along?"

Jonathan knew that Boxers was just blowing off steam. Their mission began and ended with protecting the PCs and returning them to their homes. This wasn't the time to pick a fight, even if the fight had been picked for them first.

"We don't need the vehicles anymore," Jonathan said. "When we planned this, we thought we were going to have a bunch of PCs. Now we're down to one, and we've already got a vehicle. That'll be fine."

Boxers dropped his voice to a whisper. "No, it won't. Our supplies are all there. Our IDs. Shit, half our ammo. We can't just leave all of that."

"We'll have to," Jonathan said. There was no sense arguing the point. No way was he going to lead a party this size into a dozen guns. Certainly not when they were already lying in wait. Suicide was not on the agenda.

"I don't think this piece of shit has enough fuel to get us to Gutierrez's place," Boxers said. "And I'm guessing that gas stations will be hard to come by."

"We can't use the Gulfstream anymore, either," Jonathan said. The depth and desperateness of the situation was just beginning to hit him. "If they know about the ransom drop, and they know about the first-stage exfil site, we have to assume that they'll know about the Gulfstream. We can't risk it."

Boxers' eyes narrowed as he processed the ramifications. "Look, Dig—*Scorpion*—let me put something on the record here. I am not retiring in Mexico. This place is a cesspool."

"I agree on both counts," Jonathan said. "But I'm not dying here, either. We have to figure out another way."

"It's a thousand friggin' miles," Boxers said.

"So, clearly, we're not walking. We need to think of something else." He pressed his mike button. "Mother Hen, Scorpion."

"I'm here."

"We've got a pretty significant change of plans here." As he detailed all of the careful planning that now was meaningless, Jonathan tried to shake away the growing sense of dread that blossomed in his belly.

CHAPTER FIVE

At four-thirty, the food court outside the Cineplex in Tysons Corner Center in Vienna, Virginia looked more like a school cafeteria than a public eating place. Kids by the dozens crammed the tables, jamming their faces with the fried crap that passed for food these days, while talking way too loudly about triumphs and crises that mattered only to them. Perhaps if these urchins spent more time in school instead of enjoying three months of sanctioned truancy every summer, the future wouldn't look so bleak.

Trevor Munro believed to his core that Hell must surely have a food court.

Munro wasn't here for the food. He'd already had his meal for the day, lunch in Langley with the DCIA in the director's private dining room on the sixth floor. It was becoming his regular dining venue now that his star had finally begun to rise again.

This one last thing—the business in Mexico—was the final detail that should earn him his own office on the sixth floor. Like so many triumphs, though, this one would come with its measure of indignity. Pausing at the top of the escalator, he adjusted his tie and patted the wings of his collar with a thumb and a finger, just to make sure that they lay straight. Image mattered.

He found Jerry Sjogren right where he said he'd be, near the movie ticket kiosk. Somewhere in his mid-fifties, Sjogren was thick of middle and mostly gray, with an aura about him that shifted between grand-fatherly and predatory, depending on his audience. Munro knew the predatory persona to be the real one, because he understood what the man did for a living.

"You're late," Sjogren said when Munro came within earshot. If there was such a thing as a redneck New England accent, Sjogren had one. "Want to grab some lunch?"

"Your time is bought and paid for," Munro said. Neither man offered to shake the other's hand. "And no, I don't want lunch. Let's walk."

"Oh, that's right," Sjogren joked. "If a restaurant doesn't have crystal glasses and linen tablecloths, you won't eat in it."

Munro led the way to the elevator that would take them down to the first floor of the mall. They waited in silence for the car to arrive, and then for it to disgorge another gaggle of children. As two more kids—a boy and a girl, each maybe fifteen—tried to board with the men, Munro turned on them. "This elevator is closed," he said. "Use the escalator."

"Screw you," the boy replied. Then he got Munro's glare and he backed off. He and his girlfriend were al-ready walking away when the doors closed.

"Way to keep a low profile there, Trev. Terrorizing children. Make you feel big?"

Sjogren knew damn well that Munro hated the diminutive form of any names—Billy, Bobby, Tommy—

but that he particularly hated changes to his own. He chose to ignore the affront. "It's not about feeling big, Sjogren. It's about feeling fulfilled. And fulfillment for me comes when I hear a report from my very expensive contractors that they've completed the job that I hired them to do."

The elevator doors opened again, and they stepped out to stroll the mall.

"Interesting you put it that way," Sjogren said. "Normally, when people pay a lot of money for expensive contractors, they know enough to stay out of the contractor's way so that he can do his job."

Munro's stomach flipped. "What are you telling me?"

Sjogren recoiled. "Holy shit, I thought you knew." He laughed. "It was a cluster fuck of major proportions. Hostages dead, money gone, and your guys still alive and on the run."

Munro's emotional shield faltered. He pointed to the right, toward the door to the parking lot. The conversation had turned to one that demanded more privacy.

When they were outside, Munro opted to keep them walking, despite the thick humidity and blistering sun. "How is that possible? How did you let it go so wrong?"

"I didn't let anything go wrong," Sjogren said with a laugh. "You wanted me to find out who killed your friend, and I did that. I even got you names—Harris and Lerner, though I'd be shocked if that was their real names. You asked me to arrange a way to snare them, and I did that, too. I even found a church to play along— and I gotta tell you it's scary how really frickin' easy that was. Everything I touched went fine. If I'd had my way, Harris and Lerner would both be dead now, and the dear little darling kids would be home, or at least on their way."

Sjogren paused. Munro knew he was waiting for a reaction, but he wasn't going to give him the satisfaction. One of the problems with ceding wet work to contractors was the lack of respect. The better they were at their jobs, the worse the problem became.

Sjogren pressed his attack. "Things didn't start coming apart until you had to go all Machiavellian and kill the kidnappers—who, by the way, worked for Felix Hernandez, about the most disturbed and disturbing asshole on the planet. I thought that's the guy whose dick you were trying to suck in the first place."

This time, Munro had to stop. It was just too much to process while walking. "Felix didn't care about them. I had his blessing."

Sjogren laughed again, causing Munro's ears to burn. Everything was funny to this guy. People who laughed too much died early in Munro's world

"Felix now, is it?" Sjogren mocked. "So you two really are butt buddies. I'd heard that, but I didn't believe it. I didn't think that even you Agency guys were stupid enough to go to bed with the likes of him." He poked Munro with his elbow. "You know, Trev, friendships like that can be hard to survive."

"*None* of the hostages survived?" Munro asked. It seemed impossible. "Have you verified that?"

"One or two might have," Sjogren said. "My guy on the ground—an army captain named Palma—told me there were thirteen dead on the ground, including the kidnappers and two of Palma's own guys, but a full count is complicated by the fact that we don't really know what the starting numbers were. We know that your butt buddy's goons killed a couple before the bus ever got to the jungle, but since you insisted that the goons die first, we don't know who or how many. The only kid missing is a seventeen-year-old named Tristan Wagner. Stupid name, yeah, I know. The four chaperones are missing, too, but like I said, they might have been killed before. I haven't looked it up in the dictionary, Trev, but I'm pretty sure this set the new definition for a cluster fuck."

Profanity notwithstanding, Sjogren's larger point was spot-on. But what seemed so shockingly simple to that beefy boor—getting the Crystal Palace to go along with the scheme—turned out in the end to require a great deal of heated last-minute negotiation.

The original plan had called for Hernandez to keep the ransom—three million dollars. Then, the right reverend Jackie Mitchell changed the rules at the last minute. She decided that for the kind of risk she was taking, her own three million was not enough. She needed the ransom, too, for a total of six mill. Any less, she said, and she'd go to the FBI. She'd take some heat, she reasoned, and might even face jail time, but she rolled the dice that it would all go harder on Munro than it would on her.

As with any good game of brinksmanship, it's impossible to tell when the other party is bluffing. As a longtime veteran of such games, Munro sensed that she was serious. Given all the scandals she'd endured in the last year or so, she'd been coming from a very weird psychological starting point. Under the circumstances, such self-destructive behavior was well within the bounds of reason.

In the end, he'd had no choice but to blink.

Getting Hernandez to agree took some work, as well, but it turned out that settling the debt owed to him by Harris and Lerner—Munro was likewise willing to bet those weren't their real names—was worth the three million dollars. Unfortunately, Felix's largesse did not extend to the soldiers who'd done the kidnapping in return for a share of the payment. They would be angry when they found out that there'd be no payment for their efforts—angry enough to pose a security risk to Felix. Therefore, they had to die, too.

Now, after all that, Munro had nothing to show for all of his efforts but collateral damage. Worse, if Sjogren knew these details from his people on the ground, then Hernandez must know as well, and he'd be furious.

"What are you going to do to fix this?" Munro asked.

"What am *I* going to do?" Sjogren said, aghast. "I'm going to call it a day and watch the fireworks. The question is, what are *you* going to do? You screwed the pooch big-time on this. Not only are Harris and Lerner still out there—now they know they're being hunted. You don't have a clue who they are, but depending on who they might talk to, they'll find out who you are. Or maybe they'll just figure out how totally screwed up the Crystal Palace folks are. Oh, yeah, and let's not forget what's going to happen when all those big parishioners get wind of what you did with those little parishioners. Of course none of that will matter if Hernandez gets to you first." Another laugh, this one heartier than the others. "Hell, Trev, I get nervous just standing next to you."

"We can't let them get back into the country," Munro said, the barest outline of a plan forming in his mind.

"How's that?"

"If we can keep them in Mexico, we can keep this contained. If they cross the border, it will be too late."

"You don't even know who you're looking for. How are you gonna do that?"

"I'm going to trap them," Munro said. Just like that, the plan became fully formed in his head. As he walked away from Sjogren, he said over his shoulder, "You're still in this. Keep a phone nearby in case I need you."

Mother Hen—a.k.a. Venice Alexander (it's pronounced Ven-EE-chay, by the way)—sat in her office on the top floor of the converted firehouse in Fisherman's Cove, Virginia, watching helplessly as the nightmare unfolded. Her official job title was something like director of operations for Security Solutions Inc., the private investigation firm that served as the cover for Jonathan Grave's hostage rescue shenanigans. When the boys weren't out saving lives, she in fact managed seven investigators, who each ran as many as eight different investigations simultaneously. The legitimate side of the business earned a fortune—not that Jonathan needed it—and numbered among its clients some of the biggest corporate names in the world. Few of the staff on the overt side of the business understood the covert side—or if they did, they had the good sense to keep their suspicions to themselves.

Routine investigations, though, could never hold

Jonathan's attention. He lived for the adrenaline rush of the rescue missions. When he was away on an op, it fell to Venice to manage whatever intel they could get, and to troubleshoot things when they went wrong.

Right now, things were going very, very wrong. And she'd sent for reinforcements.

When Gail Bonneville arrived in the War Room— the high-tech teak conference room that was decked out with every techno-toy imaginable—her hair was still wet from the shower that Venice's call had interrupted. Even disheveled, Gail had an air of athletic grace about her that always thrummed a pang of jealousy in Venice, whose constant battle with the same thirty pounds had once again turned to a losing one.

"What's wrong and how bad is it?" Gail asked as she helped herself to one of the ergonomic chairs that surrounded the massive table. As she spoke, she lifted a panel in the table to reveal a computer screen, slid out a keyboard, and logged in to her account.

"All the hostages but one are dead," Venice said. She took a couple of minutes to fill in the rest of the story.

A former member of the FBI Hostage Rescue Team, and a retired sheriff of a small community in Indiana, Gail Bonneville had a law degree and a PhD in criminology. After one particularly difficult op in West Virginia, she'd decided that extra-legal door crashing didn't suit her, and she'd assumed official control of Security Solutions's legitimate side. She kept her finger on the pulse of the covert side, but she no longer put herself in the position of perhaps having to shoot people whom she had no authority to kill.

As Gail listened to Venice fill in the details, the space between her eyebrows folded into deep furrows.

"How's Digger holding up? He's never lost a hostage, has he?"

Venice gave a look that said, *Are you kidding me?* "You might have noticed that Dig doesn't exactly bare his soul to me."

"To anyone," Gail acknowledged. She sat back in her seat and scowled even deeper. "I don't understand how this is possible," she said. "The entire population of people who knew about this is either in this room or in Mexico getting shot at. How could their plan have leaked out?"

"That's why I called you in," Venice said. "None of this adds up. I thought of Reverend Mitchell at the Crystal Palace and whoever is advising her, but that doesn't make sense, either. Even if she had reason to betray us—and why would she when the mission is to rescue her parishioners?—Digger never divulges operational details to a client. To prevent this very scenario."

"Like I said," Gail concurred, "we're witnessing the impossible. You and I haven't leaked anything." A pause. "Right?"

Venice's ears turned hot. She'd known Jonathan since she was a little girl, and she'd been his right hand for nearly as long. Gail was the newcomer, and while she was Jonathan's regular bed partner—who the heck knew where their relationship stood these days?—how dare she question—

"I'm sorry," Gail said, clearly interpreting Venice's glare for what it was. "Of course you didn't. Boxers doesn't say two hundred words a month about anything, and he'd cut out his tongue before he talked about an upcoming op, so he's out, too."

Venice didn't like the remaining implication any better than the veiled accusation against her. "Are you saying that Digger sabotaged himself?"

Gail held up a hand. "I'm not suggesting that he did it on purpose, but you know how Jon can be when he gets into his gamesmanship mode. Remember how we first met?"

Gail had a point. Boxers often railed against the shortcuts Jonathan took in the area of opsec—operational security. It wasn't beyond the realm of possibility that he'd let his tongue wag more than was prudent.

"It doesn't matter," Gail said, dismissing her own argument. "We're where we are. How we got here matters less than fixing it. We need to find a way for them to get out of there." She started typing. "Let's start with the topo maps."

While Gail typed some more, gaining access to the computer files Jonathan had used to plan the mission, Venice brought the giant wall screen to life. From there, they could monitor each other's screens. Two seconds after the images appeared, Venice's computer rang like an old-fashioned telephone.

Venice's heart jumped, and as her hands flew to enter the right commands, Gail said, "What's that?"

"Bad news," Venice replied. "Always, always bad news."

Boxers drove slowly—on these roads, slowly was about the best you could do—while Jonathan worked his GPS and map. They'd set a general course to the north, just to put distance between them and the bad guys. Outside, the scenery never changed: a wall of green wetness that smelled of rot. They kept the windows down and the air-conditioning off, both to give the engine a break, and to keep their sense of hearing intact.

"I wish we'd had a chance to collect intel," Boxers said. "Maybe those guys had shit in their pockets that would give a clue who they are."

"Woulda, coulda, shoulda," Jonathan said without looking up. "I'm thinking that maybe when we get to the U.S. border, Wolverine will be able to talk us across. Without passports, that could be a problem."

Boxers laughed. "Yeah, well, on the spectrum of our problems right now, let's call that one minor."

Jonathan looked over his shoulder again to check on their PC. Now that the shooting had stopped, he let the kid sit upright in his seat. "Hey, Tristan, did they let you keep your passport?" He wasn't surprised that the answer was no, but it was worth checking, just to be sure.

"Why are they doing this?" Tristan asked. "What did I do to hurt them?"

Boxers smirked to his boss. Between the two of them, Jonathan was by far the more sensitive, and that was a very low bar. Jonathan hated the touchy-feely stuff. Back in his days with the Unit, they had psychologists to take care of that crap.

"You didn't do anything, Tristan," he said. "You can't think of it that way. You were in the wrong place at the wrong time. Sometimes, it's no more complicated than that."

"But we were *targeted*," Tristan said. "They knew exactly who they were coming for. They even had our pictures."

A bell rang in Jonathan's head, and he sat taller in his seat. The maps could wait for a minute. "You mean physical pictures?"

"Yes. Well, not on paper, but they had it on their iPhones."

Jonathan cursed under his breath. Yeah, they should have gathered intel; but it would have been a ridiculous risk. "What did they tell you about why you were being taken?" Jonathan asked.

"Nothing," Tristan said. "They just told us, you know, to stay in our seats and be quiet and stuff. They never said why."

"You didn't ask?"

"Allison did," Tristan said, "but that really pissed them off. They yelled really loud and hit her. Told her to shut up." His voice caught at that last part. "After that, I guess nobody wanted to chance it again."

The SUV hit a pothole that caused them to lurch hard to the left. Jonathan damn near lost control of his computer.

Boxers said, "Sorry about that. I'm lodging a complaint with the Department of Public Roads."

Jonathan kept focus on Tristan. "Did they speak English or Spanish?" he asked.

"Both. They mostly spoke Spanish to each other, but they spoke English to us, even though most of us are pretty fluent."

Jonathan was trying to picture the event in his mind. "So, during your days of captivity, did they forbid talking? Don't speak unless spoken to?"

Tristan shook his head. "It wasn't like that at all. They let us talk among ourselves, but they listened pretty carefully to what we were talking about. One of them was a big fan of pop music. He and Ray talked a lot about that."

Jonathan was sensing the presence of training among the captors. Stockholm Syndrome was a very real factor in hostage situations, and smart hostage takers know how to build rapport with the victims they intend to kill. Done skillfully, that engineered sense of friendship will cause victims to take violent action against their rescuers.

"Four people were missing in the bus back there," Boxers said. "All the adults. What happened to them?"

"Mr. Hall and Mrs. Charlton were killed in the beginning, when the terrorists first stormed the bus. They tried to stop them. The terrorists didn't give a warning or anything. They just came in, shouting. Mr. Hall and Mrs. Charlton stood up—not really interfering, even— and they shot them down without a word. Just bang, bang." Tristan's eyes narrowed. "How did you know how many people were taken? How did you know my name?"

"Homework doesn't stop when you graduate from school," Jonathan said. "People who care about you hired us to rescue you."

"People who care about me? Who's that? What does that even mean?"

"Believe it or not, that's none of your business," Jonathan said. "Tell me about the executions."

"I did. After they killed Mr. Hall and Mrs. Charlton, they just dragged the bodies out of the bus and dumped them on the . . ." The boy's voice caught in his throat and he went quiet. A few seconds later, he cleared his throat. "They dragged them out onto the street and we drove off. The terrorists kept yelling at us to keep our heads down and to stay in our seats. While we drove through the streets, they made us change seats—nobody could sit with who they were sitting with—and then they passed out handcuffs and ankle cuffs, and made us chain ourselves to our seatmates."

Jonathan admired the level of detail in Tristan's storytelling.

"After a day or so, maybe two, that guy who was dead in the aisle made a speech about nobody caring enough to pay for our release, so he unlocked Mrs. Blazak's handcuff and he let her ankles go and then he dragged her out of the bus by her hair. He took her right outside the bus and made her kneel down, and, you know, just put his rifle to her head." His eyes reddened again. "She was a really, really nice lady and they just blew her head off." He grew quiet.

Jonathan gave him a half minute or so to collect himself. "What happened after that?"

"He just left her there. Climbed back into the bus, and within an hour, he was trying to do small talk again. I hated that son of a bitch."

Hate was good, Jonathan thought. As emotions went, that was one that tended to focus the mind.

"That leaves one more, right?" Jonathan asked. "Miss James?"

Tristan pushed filthy tendrils of blond hair out of his eyes. "We'd been held hostage for a couple of days, I think. The kidnappers said something about people not being fast enough. They took her outside and two of them . . ." His voice faltered again.

"Take your time," Jonathan said.

"You have to understand that she was really a nice lady. She was like a thirty-year-old grandmother, you know? She was all about stopping the death of decorum. That's what she called it."

Jonathan just waited through the preamble, confident that the boy would get to the point.

Tristan struggled more with this story than he had with the others. "So, there were two of them, so they took her out just like they did Mrs. Blazak. They made her kneel on the ground, but then they made her give both of them a blowjob. In front of everybody. I tried not to watch, but . . ."

There was no reason for a seventeen-year-old boy to finish that sentence.

Tristan settled himself with a long, deep breath. "And after she'd done them both, they shot her in the face. A third one took videos of the whole thing."

Jonathan inhaled forcefully through his nose and held the breath in for a few seconds. There were levels of cruelty that he just could not comprehend. He got the panicked shooting that happened in the bus after the assault started back there at the drop site. He didn't endorse it, but he understood it as *if I'm dying I'm taking you with me.* But to humiliate someone in the most brutal way like that made no sense to him at all.

If nothing else went right with this mission, at least he could rest comfortably that he'd increased the population in Hell.

"Those are some pretty ugly pictures to have swimming in your head," Jonathan said.

"Tell me about it."

"I am," Jonathan said. "When you get back to the World, people aren't going to want to hear those stories, but you're going to need to tell them. Make sure you find yourself a good shrink."

Tristan seemed anxious to push that topic aside. "So, how long will it be before I'm home?"

"A day or two," Jonathan said. It was a flat-out guess, but he'd have a plan soon, and when that happened—

His earbud popped. "Scorpion, Mother Hen."

"Ten bucks says this isn't good," Boxers grumbled.

Tristan cocked his head. "What are you talking about?"

Jonathan pointed to his chest so that Tristan could see him press his transmit button. "Go ahead," he said.

"I just got an alert from ICIS," she announced. Jonathan knew that she was referring to the Interstate Crime Information System, pronounced EYE-sis, a post-9/11 invention that tracked criminal investigations in real time, in hopes of encouraging better communications between law enforcement agencies. "You know I always put tracers on your aliases and your real names whenever you go out on an op. If you blow your cover, then I want to be the first to know about it."

Boxers grumbled, "Just once in her life, that woman is going to get straight to the point."

"Well, that tracer just paid off. Leon Harris and Richard Lerner have both been accused of murder," she said. Those were Jonathan's and Boxers' aliases, respectively. "It says here that the charges were filed by Mexican authorities as a result of thirteen murders you committed today. They even list the names of the victims. Names I don't recognize—I assume they're the terrorists—and the dead hostages, too."

Boxers said on the air, "That's not possible. The bodies are still warm."

"I'm just reporting what I see, Big Guy," Venice said. "Interpol is involved. The borders are closed to you. The FBI has pledged to do everything in their power to bring you in. You'll need to switch to alternative identities."

Jonathan and Boxers looked at each other, and in unison they said, "Shit."

Jonathan keyed the mike. "That's a problem, Mother Hen," Jonathan said.

"You left them in the captured vehicles, didn't you?" Venice was very good at connecting those kinds of dots.

"That's affirm. We'll need more to make the crossing."

A long silence followed. In his mind, Jonathan could see the concern in her face, the eye creases that always appeared in her flawless chocolate-brown skin when she was worried. Jonathan gave her a lot of cause to worry. "This is really, really bad," she said.

How artfully understated. "Thanks, Mother Hen," he said. "I'll get back to you. Keep us informed as things change, and find me a good forger in Mexico."

"Who's Mother Hen?" Tristan asked. He leaned forward in the backseat so that his head was closer to theirs.

"I need you to be quiet for a few minutes," Jonathan said. To Boxers, he said, "This is a problem."

"Yes, it is," Boxers agreed. "And I have every confidence that you'll devise the perfect plan." He waited a beat. "Have I ever told you how much I enjoy our times together?"

Jonathan looked out his side window at the passing jungle, trying to force the pieces to fit. "Assuming all the names are correct, how did anybody know we were going to kill the guards?" he asked Boxers.

"Because they forced our hand," Big Guy replied. Jonathan guessed that they'd been thinking the same thoughts—not an unusual occurrence after the number of years they'd worked side by side.

"That's right," Jonathan agreed. "By firing that first shot and killing the driver, they guaranteed that the guards would have to die. More to the point, they guaranteed that you and I would be the ones to kill them. You can't pin the title of murderer on somebody without some bodies to point to."

"You mean that wasn't you who shot the driver?" Tristan asked.

"Yes, that's what I mean," Jonathan said, his patience thinning. As a rule, the precious cargo was not a part of strategy sessions.

"Then who?" Tristan pressed. He retreated, though, from whatever flashed behind Jonathan's eyes.

"They haven't even had time to find the bodies," Boxers said. "This whole thing has been a setup."

Jonathan closed a loop in his mind. "What do you bet that the second ambush—the one we didn't walk into—was all about taking us into custody?"

"And how the hell did they know about Leon Harris and Richard Lerner?" Boxers pressed. He gave a bitter laugh. "I almost admire the guy who set it up. I'll be sure to tell him when I blow his brains out."

Jonathan didn't respond to that. He wished sometimes that the Big Guy would be less harsh in the presence of others.

"What about the PC?" Boxers asked, tossing a glance back at Tristan. "We gonna drag him along to a forger? Seems like a lot of extra exposure."

Jonathan winced. Big Guy had a point. The mission was to repatriate the hostage—the one who still lived—with his family. For whatever reason, it appeared that Mexico had declared war on Jonathan's and Boxers' aliases. The shortest distance between right now and repatriation couldn't possibly include a side trip to some forger's outfit.

"Maybe we can find a church somewhere," Jonathan said. "With the ransom money, we can make a hell of a donation. Maybe big enough to handle the repatriation."

But man, oh man, he didn't like the thought of it. When the stakes were this high, delegation to others always felt like a mistake.

"I think you might want to think that through a little more thoroughly," Big Guy said. Clearly, he didn't delegate well, either.

"I'm not getting handed off to anybody," Tristan said. "I'm only hearing a little bit of this stuff, but if I just heard something about handing me over to a church, I'll tell you right now that that's not happening."

"Look, kid—" Boxers said.

"The name's Tristan. T-R-I-S-T-A-N. And from this point on, I'm hanging with you guys—the people who have at least as many guns as the terrorists do. You just need to know that."

Jonathan smiled. He admired attitude from people in general, and hearing it vented against Boxers was doubly entertaining. The kid—Tristan—felt exactly the way Jonathan would have if he'd been in that position.

"There are a lot of decisions that lie between here and there," Jonathan said in an attempt to defuse things.

Where the *hell* had the authorities gotten ahold of their aliases? Add that to the fact that the bad guys had known exactly where the drop-off was going to be made, and it all became very perplexing.

Was it possible that Reverend Jackie Mitchell was somehow in on this? Was there any conceivable reason why she would jam him up? Could that even make sense? No, he decided, it couldn't. Jonathan wasn't so naïve as to think that members of the clergy were beyond heartless schemes to collect money or gather power—the Crusades, anyone?—but the risk to the children, and the deaths of the chaperones was beyond the pale, even for the worst. Even Jonathan's cynicism had its limits.

If not the Crystal Palace, then who? If he hadn't been betrayed by the good guys, then by process of elimination, he'd been betrayed by the bad guys. They were the only other people who knew the details of the ransom exchange. He still couldn't imagine how they'd known his alias, but at least the location part was plausible. And the bad guys would certainly know the names of the hostage takers. Just as they would know the names of the hostages.

"Uh-oh," he said aloud, drawing a look from Boxers.

He keyed his mike again and got Mother Hen's attention. "Do you still have ICIS up?" he asked.

"Affirmative."

"Do me a favor and run the names of our intended PCs."

"What are we looking for?"

"Whatever pops up."

It only took thirty seconds or so. "Oh, my goodness," she said. "I ran your guy Tristan and he comes up as an accomplice to murder. Same victims." A pause. "What's happening here?"

"I'm thinking big-time conspiracy," Boxers said. "Too many moving parts to be the work of some drug lord."

Jonathan agreed, but only to a point. The way this operation was playing out—with lies planted about not just him and Boxers, but about Tristan, too—the police had to be a part of it. If not the police, then the people the police reported to, which would be the Mexican government. By extension, the Mexican government meant the controlling drug lords.

"Is Gunslinger there?" Jonathan asked over the radio.

Gail's voice chirped in his ear. "It's Lady Justice now, remember?"

Of course. She'd specifically rejected the handle Jonathan had assigned to her after that unpleasantness in West Virginia. She'd chosen the new nickname herself, and while Jonathan thought it sounded stupid, he wasn't going to fight that battle.

Jonathan said, "I need you both to start asking the right people the right questions and see how we can undo this nonsense before it spins out of control."

As if it weren't out of control already.

He went on, "In case we can't clear the record in time, we're going to need papers for our PC, too, so the quicker you can find me a reliable craftsman, the better off we're going to be. Advise when you have an answer. Meanwhile, have our Special Friend contact Wolverine and see what he can dig up."

He glanced over his shoulder at the blood-spattered apparition that had once been a healthy, stable young man. Now, he had that faraway look that never meant good things. The kid needed a break, and with a thousand-mile slog lying ahead for them, they all needed rest.

"Set the craftsman for tomorrow," Jonathan said. "For tonight, see if there's not a town somewhere nearby with a church. We can hole up there, gather our wits, get a shower and a change of clothes for the PC."

A pause. "Are you looking at the same map I am?" Venice asked. "Your location defines the middle of nowhere." Another understatement. They were driving through endless jungle, somewhere near where the states of Oaxaca and Guerrero met each other—in an area where the prominent feature was a lack of prominent features. Jonathan had heard that people actually take vacations out here. Amazing.

A couple of minutes passed before Venice contacted him again. "All right, I think I've found a place for you to go to ground tonight. Let me know when you're ready to copy map coordinates."

The easiest way was to enter them into his handheld GPS. "Go ahead," he said.

Venice slowly read off the minutes and seconds of longitude and latitude, enunciating carefully while Jonathan punched in the numbers. When he was done, it took a few seconds for the map to materialize, and when it did, he had to look carefully to see the village that lay camouflaged beneath the canopy of leaves.

Venice explained, "That large building on the far northeast corner of the village is a Catholic church, Santa Margarita. I crossed that with church records and I found there's a priest attached to it, a Father Jaime Perón. Beyond that, I don't know much of anything."

Actually, considering how little time it had taken, that seemed like a lot.

Jonathan checked the stats. "I show twelve-point-one miles as the crow flies, nearly due north, but I don't see any roads. Can you help out there?"

"That's affirmative," Venice said. From the smile in her voice, he suspected that she'd been waiting for him to ask. "Churches need to be built. I found directions for the construction materials. Let me plot the route and upload it to you. Give me ten minutes."

CHAPTER SIX

Jonathan took the opportunity for them all to stretch their legs. Given the weaponry and equipment, the Toyota's front seat got awfully small. It felt good to stand. It had to be over a hundred degrees out here, and the humidity topped the charts. And now that they'd stopped moving, word had traveled to the vast population of biting insects that it was dinnertime. The foliage on either side had a predatory, man-eating look to it. Stories abounded of soldiers who became separated from their units for a minute or two, only to get hopelessly lost when they tried to reconnect. Perhaps not in Mexico, but as far as Jonathan was concerned, all jungles shared the same primary danger: they removed him from his slot at the top of the food chain.

As Jonathan adjusted his vest and weapons to get them to set more comfortably, he kept an eye on Tristan, who walked to the edge of the road to pee. He noted that there wasn't much of a stream.

When the boy returned to the vehicle, Jonathan pulled a water bottle from a side pocket of his ruck and handed it to Tristan. "Here," he said. "It's important to stay hydrated."

Tristan shook his head. "No, I'm fine."

"You're in the jungle," Jonathan said. "I can tell you're dehydrated. You need to drink this. Sip it, don't gulp."

Reluctantly, Tristan accepted the offer and stripped the cap off the bottle. He took a sip. As he lowered the bottle, Jonathan handed him a package of Pop-Tarts, also from his ruck. "Give yourself some calories and carbs, too."

The kid looked like he might turn those down, as well, but then accepted them anyway. "Please tell me what's happening," Tristan said as he ripped open his package. "I know there's something wrong." He sat on the Toyota's back bumper.

Jonathan sighed. There were advantages and disadvantages to honesty when things went bad. For Jonathan, truth was always the easier option. As harsh as the truth may be, at least there wouldn't be feelings of bitterness down the road.

"I'll start with the good news," he said. "You're alive, and my single mission right now is to make sure you stay alive. You can call me Scorpion, and my friend is Big Guy."

"Those are code names," Tristan protested. "They're not real names."

"True enough," Jonathan said. "But that's the way it's going to stay. Our mission is to get you home to your family. I've never once lost a precious cargo."

"Until today," Tristan said. "You lost a lot of them today."

Jonathan bristled, yet fought the urge to equivocate.

He said, "You're right. And I'm sorry about that. I wish I could have done more."

"So, is that what I am?" Tristan asked. "Precious cargo? I'm the 'PC' I hear you talking about on the radio?"

"Exactly."

"You talked about me a lot," Tristan said. Jonathan interpreted the statement as his request to hear details.

"That brings me to the bad news," Jonathan said. While he caught the kid up on the recent revelations from Venice, Boxers continually scanned the surrounding jungle, his hand never leaving the grip of the rifle that he wore slung across his ample belly. Boxers had the kind of gut that looked like fat from a distance, yet would doubtless break your entire arm if you tried to hit it.

When the story was done, Tristan gaped. "So you're telling me that the Mexican government thinks that I killed the people you killed?"

It wasn't exactly the way Jonathan would have phrased it, but he conceded the basic point.

"But why would I do that? I mean, why would they think that I did that?"

Jonathan hesitated. Did he really want to give up that much detail?

Screw it. "You're not thinking of it the right way," he said. "People don't actually believe that you killed anyone. They want other people to *think* that you did. You were framed. All of us were framed."

Tristan squinted against his confusion. "But *why*?"

"Exactly the right question," Jonathan said. "Only I don't have an answer. I don't know that I'll ever have an answer, and for right now, that's less of an issue than getting the hell out of here. Drink some of your water."

The abrupt change of subject took some of the dread out of the air. Tristan took another mouthful.

"So here's what I need from you," Jonathan said. "For this to have some semblance of a happy ending, I'm going to need something really close to blind obedience from you."

The comment drew a skeptical look.

"Bear with me," Jonathan went on. "I pledge two things to you. Number one is to bring you home safely. The second is to tell you the truth. That's what I've been doing here. I know that the truth isn't all that pleasant, but it is what it is. People are looking for us to hurt us, and if we don't get out of this country sooner rather than later, they're going to find us. At this juncture, that's about the worst outcome I can think of. So we're going to have to keep moving."

"A shit sandwich," Tristan said. "That's what my dad used to call bad choices. Nobody wants to eat it, and no amount of mayonnaise or mustard can make it better than what it is. Still, it has to be eaten."

Jonathan laughed. "I like that," he said. He'd heard the analogy before, but hearing it come from a kid this young somehow made it funnier. "Your dad sounds like somebody I'd get along with."

The words seemed to cause pain for Tristan. "Yeah," he said, but he didn't elaborate.

Jonathan didn't press. "A shit sandwich is exactly what we have. I know that it's stressful and that it's unfair, and scary as hell, but you're going to have to suck all that up and get over it. If that sounds harsh—"

"It doesn't sound harsh," Tristan said. "It sounds real. I've always been a better runner than a fighter anyway. What do you need me to do?"

On a day that was marked by countless surprises, the kid's attitude marked yet another one. Jonathan had been prepared for whining and fear and maybe even re-calcitrance. But "What do you need me to do?" had been nowhere on his list of expectations.

"Mostly, I need you to stay adaptable," he said. "Tonight we're going to find a place where you can change clothes and get some rest, and tomorrow we've got a couple of cloak-and-daggery things to take care of, and then hopefully, we'll be on our way."

Tristan's eyes narrowed as he cocked his head. "What does cloak-and-daggery mean?"

Jonathan laughed again. "You'll know it when you see it, I promise," he said. He checked his GPS again to see if Venice had loaded the route yet. Nothing.

"Can I ask a question?" Tristan said.

Jonathan looked at him and waited.

"Shouldn't we think about just contacting the po-lice? I mean, framing people for murder has to be as il-legal here as it is at home. If we talk to the police and tell them what really happened, maybe all of this will go away. If we run we'll just look guiltier, won't we?"

Jonathan's GPS pinged. Literally saved by the bell. He checked the screen, and sure enough, there was the route to Santa Margarita. "This is it," he said. "Mount up." He looked to Boxers. "Big Guy!"

"On it," he said. Even as he strolled back to the car, his eyes never left the woods.

"You a little high-strung?" Jonathan asked.

Boxers gave him a droll look. "Funny how I get that way when people shoot at me."

Once inside with the engine started, Jonathan oriented himself to the map and pointed the way.

Father Dom D'Angelo crossed the parking lot that separated St. Kate's from the Security Solutions offices and headed straight upstairs. Dom was the only civilian on the planet—"civilian" was Jonathan's slightly derogatory term for anyone not a part of the community that included employees and Special Forces operators—who had ready access to the inner sanctum of The Cave, passing unmolested through multiple layers of security.

The inside of The Cave was larger than it appeared from the outside. Occupying the third floor of the firehouse that served as Jonathan's home, the main part of the office space housed twenty or so investigators and support staff. The Cave, on the other hand, housed only three offices and the War Room, though it occupied one-fourth of the total floor space. Opulence was the order of the day in The Cave—the best of everything, from technology to furniture.

Whereas Jonathan's taste ran to clubby leather and dark woods, Venice's was chrome and glass all the way. Dom crossed the thickly carpeted space quickly and made a beeline for the high-tech teak conference area that someone had dubbed the War Room.

Venice and Gail were already at work. Each had taken a position at the massive conference table and was clacking away at their own built-in computer terminal. The enormous screen at the far end showed a map of Mexico. He presumed—correctly, it turned out—that the blinking dot in the far southwest corner of the country marked Jonathan's location.

"What do we know?" he asked.

"Clearly, Digger's been sold out," Gail said. "What I can't figure out is, who would have that level of knowledge? They had *names*, for heaven's sake."

"Could it be the Mexican government?" Venice asked. "If they decided to get into the kidnapping business, they would certainly have the planning resources to pull it off. Plus, if they were using their own people, they would know the names of kidnappers. Getting the hostages' names after they'd been taken would be a cakewalk."

"But they wouldn't have Leon Harris's name," Gail said. "Or Richard Lerner's. I can't imagine why the Mexican government would want to engineer a kidnapping, but even if they did, they couldn't engineer the rescue. How did they get the guys' aliases?"

"You're thinking that Dig was the target from the beginning?" Venice asked.

Gail nodded. "I don't see another way. I think whoever is responsible knew about some guy named Leon Harris, or maybe they knew about someone named Scorpion. With all the cutouts and email diversions it takes to contact our covert side, there's no chance that anyone could link it to Security Solutions. Without Dig's real name, and without a company name, they'd have no dots to connect. Maybe this whole rescue op was just bait to snare the guys"

Dom's next thought arrived whole and fully formed. And it scared the hell out of him. Gail's comment about bait triggered it. "It's the church," he said. "The

Crystal Castle or whatever. That has to be the source of
the betrayal. They found Jon as the rescuer, and then
passed the information along to someone in Mexico.
That has to be it."

Gail shook her head. "There has to be an intermedi-
ate step," she said. "There aren't many who do what we
do, but there are a few. What's the guarantee that the
church would choose Security Solutions for the rescue? Surely, it's not just a random plot to entrap random rescuers."

"I don't think that at all," Dom said. "I've been
chewing around the edges for a while now, ever since I
heard about the three-million-dollar ransom. Where
does a church get that kind of money? I'm sure they
have good reserves, thanks to their television stuff, but
three *million*? That's a lot of money, even before Digger's fee. What does that run, anyway?"

"Six figures," Venice said. Money matters always
embarrassed Jonathan, and as a result, his fee was a
more closely guarded number than nuclear launch
codes.

"Okay, six figures," Dom said. "Another big sum.
Thanks to Dig, St. Kate's is one of the best-endowed
churches in the diocese, but a number like that would
bring us to our knees."

"Maybe the Crystal Palace is *really* rich," Gail suggested. She looked to Venice, who started tickling the
keys right away. "Maybe three million is just a drop in
the bucket to them. The Crystal Palace is a money-
making machine. Have you ever watched one of their
broadcasts?"

Dom smirked. "Um, no."

"Well, I have. Every other verse of the Bible is followed by a plea for money. There's the Building Fund, the Outreach Fund, the Prayer Circles, and on and on and on."

"I wonder what happened to their fund-raising after the good Pastor Mitchell was caught in her dalliances," Venice thought aloud. She turned to her keyboard and started typing.

Over the course of the past year, Jackie Mitchell had spent more time as a punch line than a preacher, following some Internet videos that showed her providing extra-special counseling to a young male member of her flock in one of Scottsdale's finest hotels. Over and over again. The righteously aggrieved Mr. Mitchell—the pastor's husband—had not only left her, but had recently started taking to the airwaves to pronounce her a fraud.

Pastor Mitchell had many defenders among her congregation, of whom more than a few had written op-ed pieces for the newspapers. But as far too many celebrities had learned the hard way, once you earn a slot in Jay Leno's nightly monologue, your future is more or less sealed in poo.

"Uh-oh," Venice said. "Oh, my God, this can't be true."

"What?" Dom and Gail asked together.

Venice scowled and shook her head. "Is this even possible?" She looked at the others and typed some more. "Check the screen," she said. As she spoke, she pushed a button on the master control panel that she alone knew how to operate, and the lights dimmed. Not all the way, but enough to make the screen more prominent. Given the technology of the room, Dom imagined that she could make it snow in here, too, if she'd wanted. Or maybe not.

She tapped a few more keys. The map of Mexico dissolved to a screen full of numbers arranged in neat columns. "These are the bank records for the Crystal Palace."

Dom's jaw dropped. "How did you get those?"

Venice raised an eyebrow. "Do you really want to know?"

"Actually, I don't."

"Me either," Gail said. "When the feds finally figure out what we do, I want to have some shred of plausible deniability."

"According to Google, the Crystal Palace scandal first broke about fourteen months ago, just after they'd committed to a multimillion-dollar building project, and contracted for three more years of television time." She looked to the others. "I guess you know that unlike commercial television, where the networks pay for the programs they broadcast, these religious shows have to pay for their own time."

Dom hadn't realized it because he'd never given it any thought. Now that he did, it made sense.

As Venice went on, she used the cursor as a pointer. "If I'm doing the math right, for the two years previous to that time, they averaged an income of four-point-three million dollars a month, with expenses of just about four-point-three million a month. They were just breaking even. I haven't had time to find out where all that money went, but it's probably not important for our purposes. At least not yet. Now look at this."

She clicked, and the records scrolled at a dizzying speed, stopping on another set of numbers. "Here are the records for the first month after the scandal broke. Expenses stayed at four-point-three million, but revenues dropped to three-point-six million." She clicked again. "The month after that, they brought in two point seven. Fast forward a few more months, and they're getting only eight hundred twenty thousand dollars. The month after that, two-eighty. They're hemorrhaging cash."

Gail made a face. "I don't understand—"

"I'm not done yet," Venice said. She scrolled month by month. "Look here. That trend continued month after month, not a single deposit over three hundred thousand. Until three months ago, when they started making four million again, and then five. Last month it was five-point-nine million dollars."

"Now, give me a minute or two," she said before disappearing into thought while her fingers pounded the keyboard.

Confident that the results would be impressive, Dom waited quietly with Gail while Venice worked her magic.

"Oh, now this is interesting," Venice declared when she was done. A new image appeared on the screen, this one showing two lists of names. "The list on the left shows the various contributors from twenty months ago, back when Crystal Palace was in its heyday. On the right is the list of donors from five months ago, during the darkest of their dark days. You can see there are way, way fewer donors." She stroked the keys, and after only a few seconds, the computer spit out the number 0.992.

"Okay," she explained. "Of those remaining die-hard faithful, ninety-nine-point-two percent of them were on the original list of donors."

"Isn't that to be expected?" Dom asked. "I can't imagine that accusations of statutory rape are going to bring in a lot of new donors."

Venice pointed to the priest as if to indicate that he was her brightest pupil. "You just made my point," she said. "Because look here." More clacking and another screen change. "This is a list of the donors over the past three months, when they were making money again. If we match them against the original faithful, we get . . ."

More tapping and a new number on the screen. "Zero-point-four-six-four. That means that of the one hundred twelve recent donors, only forty-six-point-four percent gave money before the scandal." She looked up. "Put another way, fifty-three-point-six per-cent of the newly inspired donors never gave to the Crystal Palace before."

"You tell us that with such grave emphasis," Gail said. "What exactly are you suggesting?"

Venice looked like she didn't want to speak the thoughts aloud. "I think someone paid the church to allow the kidnappings to happen."

Gail's jaw dropped. "*What?*"

"I've heard Dig say it a thousand times," Venice pressed. "There are no coincidences. How convenient to receive unique donations just before such a huge outlay. That money was given for a *reason*. The timing is what it is for a *reason*. Because of timing alone—the contributions coming right before a major outlay of ransom money—the two have to be connected some-how."

More furious typing. "Here it is. Those sixty new donors represent nearly ninety percent of the donations received, and wouldn't you know it? While the individual amounts are all over the board, those sixty, isolated out and taken together, come to just north of six million dollars—almost exactly twice what the ransom was."

Dom squinted at the numbers. "It's six-point-two," he said. "I think you're stretching."

"You have to correct for random givers," Gail said. "Not all of them are going to be a part of whatever plot this is." She turned to Venice. "What can you get us about those sixty donors? Almost all of them appear to be corporations."

Venice turned back to her friend the keyboard. "Give me a few minutes. Talk quietly among your-selves."

Dom watched, fascinated by the speed of Venice's fingers, and by the variety of expressions on her face as she plowed through whatever databases she was invad-ing. Her big brown eyes cycled among frustration, amazement, surprise, and awe.

Ten minutes later, she was done.

"Sorry that took so long," she said. "Especially since I didn't come up with anything useful. I've got All American Industries, CEO Dennis Hainsley, no record of either beyond individual white pages listings. I've also got a Global Transformations Inc., with an equally invisible CEO named Harold Scolari. Interest-ingly, it appears that Global Transformations is a subsidiary of All American Industries. I've got Tiger Creek Industries, also invisible, and Big Daddy Carpet Cleaning, run by an apparently nonexistent person named—wait for it—Nancy Drew. Every one of these companies has Federal Employee ID numbers, and every one of them pays taxes. All this, despite the fact that no one has ever praised them, blogged about them, or filed a DUNS request. Does this pattern remind you of any companies you know?"

Gail and Dom looked at each other, and then they both got it at the same time. "The Family Defense Foundation," they said in unison.

Venice's eyebrows danced. "Bingo." Jonathan Grave was the king of the cutout corporation. He'd funneled millions of dollars to Resurrection House through the Family Defense Foundation.

Dom decided to test-drive the theory. "Maybe these companies believe in the mission of the church but don't want to be associated with the scandal."

It was obvious that Venice had already considered this, and had rejected it out of hand. "Where were they before the Pastor Mitchell was accused of boffing a child?"

"They saw that the Crystal Palace was being run out of business, and they thought it was a witch hunt." Dom realized that he was taking the role of devil's advocate, but the stakes here were very high.

"I don't buy it, Dom," Gail said. "That feels completely wrong to me. This feels more like government cutouts."

"*Our* government?" Dom said. "And why would they do that?"

"I guess that's what you need to ask Wolverine when you meet with her," Gail replied. "When does that happen?"

"This afternoon at three," he said. "I guess I can float these names past her and see what she comes up with."

"Meanwhile, I'll keep poking around the sources I can find," Venice said. She looked to Gail. "Any and all assistance is appreciated."

"Not me," Gail said. "I'm boarding the first flight I can find to Scottsdale. See if I can't leverage an audience with Reverend Jackie Mitchell."

"Leverage?" Dom asked.

"You like 'persuade' better?" Gail asked with a smile.

"Reading your body language, I'm thinking 'extort.'"

She tasted the word. "I can live with extort," she said. "In fact, I kind of like it."

CHAPTER SEVEN

To call this rutted pathway a road was to overstate the case by half. Steep and unpaved, the dirt-and-grass clearing was barely wide enough for the Toyota, and it was steep enough to make the little engine scream. It was going to be a very long twelve-point-one miles. The jungle pressed in from both sides, and overhead, the canopy was so thick as to render Jonathan's party invisible from the air. No wonder the aerial map was so unhelpful.

"What are those plants with the great big leaves?" Tristan asked from the backseat. "They're every-where."

"I call them the plants with the big leaves," Jonathan said. He'd never been a flora-and-fauna kind of guy. In his experience, terrain and indigenous living things were either tactical tools or they were irrelevant. As far as he knew, the plants with the big leaves weren't a source of food, so their only relevance was their ability to provide cover for people who wanted to do him harm. They unnecessarily lengthened the trip.

At this rate, Jonathan figured it to be at least a sixty-minute trip to the village. Every few hundred yards, the road bulged to the right, providing space to pull over to allow an approaching vehicle to get by, or for a faster vehicle to pass from behind.

It turned out to be a ninety-three-minute trip.

As Boxers drove the SUV up the steep hill into the village of Santa Margarita, people on the narrow street cast curious glances their way. Jonathan guessed that white faces were rare in these parts, and that a collection of three was unheard of. Throw in the cammies and the weapons, and the locals had every right to turn away as they did, pretending not to see. Some turned their backs, some stepped into buildings, but in general, everyone looked everywhere but at them.

"These folks are scared," Jonathan said.

"What's your bet?" Boxers asked. "Are they afraid of us, or are they afraid of getting caught in the act of something?"

"Why are we letting ourselves be seen like this?" Tristan asked.

"Because I don't know how to be invisible," Boxers quipped. To Jonathan: "The kid's got a point. I don't like all this attention. Scared people drop dimes on the people that scare them."

Indeed they do, Jonathan thought.

Though small, the village was colorful, every building painted a different pastel. Jonathan figured that the colors helped to make their drab lives a little easier. Yes, that was jingoism, and no, he wasn't going to apologize for it.

"Drop a dime?" Tristan asked. "You mean call the police or something?"

"That's what I meant," Boxers said, "but that ain't gonna happen." He pointed through the windshield to a squatty building on the left side of the road. "There it is," he said. He turned the wheel and headed in that direction.

"What are we doing?" Tristan asked.

"Not now," Jonathan said. As they pulled to a stop, he unbuckled his seat belt and opened his door while Boxers did the same, in his case grabbing his ruck.

"That's not a church," Tristan said.

"Stay put," Jonathan ordered. "This won't take long."

"What are you doing?"

Jonathan winked. "Stacking the odds in our favor."

Digger and the Big Guy walked with purpose to the front door of the little brick and block building that they knew to be the telephone substation. He noted the concrete roof, which eliminated his biggest fear regarding what lay ahead.

Boxers asked, "Do you have the key?"

"Always." Jonathan pulled a leather pouch containing his lock picks from a pocket in his sleeve. After checking to make sure that the door was indeed locked, he inserted the tension bar with one hand, and the rake with the other. Five seconds later, the door floated open, revealing the electronic guts of a telephone switching station. "Need help?"

Boxers gave him an annoyed look. "I'm offended. Just keep an eye out."

While Jonathan stood at the open door, Boxers entered and walked to the far corner of the twelve-by-twelve single-room structure. The Big Guy pulled two orange thermite grenades out of his ruck. He placed one in a panel box that that looked like a knot of multi-colored spaghetti, and staged the second one atop a larger panel that had to be the building's main electrical supply, closer to the door. Moving back to the first one in the back of the room, he braced the grenade with his left hand, his thumb pressing the safety spoon, and pulled the pin with his right. Because thermite grenades had notoriously short fuses, he stepped back quickly as he let the spoon fly. Three seconds later, the grenade belched out a white-hot, forty-five-hundred-degree ball of fire that consumed the panel and its contents, filling the building with smoke.

He repeated the process on the building's power supply on the way out, and then rejoined Jonathan, closing the door behind him. "I hate those damn things," he mumbled as he headed back to the truck. "They don't even go boom."

"What did you do?" Tristan gasped. "Did you set the building on fire?"

"Not the building," Jonathan said. "Just the contents. The brick won't burn." They were moving again.

"We can't afford the risk of someone making a phone call," Jonathan explained before Tristan could get the question out.

"Aren't the police going to come for the fire?" Tristan asked.

"Who's going to call them?" Jonathan countered. "It's a gamble, but I think it's a safe one."

"You *think* it's safe?"

Jonathan let it go.

A few minutes later, they turned a corner to the left, and the hills flattened out to reveal what appeared to be a much older part of the town. A cluster of worn wooden homes surrounded a circular patch of ground—maybe a half acre—that probably would have been grass-covered if given a chance, but that frequent wear had left a churned mess of clotted mud. Presently, a scrum of children—boys and girls aged, say, seven to twelve—was playing soccer in the space, several displaying remarkable skill at the game.

The church of Santa Margarita dominated the western edge of the circle, backlit by the late-afternoon sun. To Jonathan's eye, the place looked more Methodist than Catholic, its thirty-foot steeple casting a shadow across the soccer field. No larger than twenty by thirty feet, the place had clearly been built with a lot of love. It gleamed with a fresh coat of white paint.

"Those kids are good," Tristan said of the soccer players.

Boxers slowed the vehicle at the edge of the field and craned his neck to survey the area. Jonathan did the same, looking for unusual clusters of people, or physical movement that might indicate an impending ambush.

"What are we waiting for?" Tristan whispered from behind.

Jonathan ignored him. Nothing he saw gave him pause. Adults of varying ages sat in front of their tiny homes, watching the children either from stoops or from lawn chairs. Most seemed engrossed in the game.

Jonathan pulled a digital monocular from a pouch on his vest and brought it to his eye for a closer look. In his peripheral vision, he saw Boxers doing the same thing.

"I don't see any weapons," the Big Guy said.

Nor did Jonathan. "I count eight adults plus the children."

"Agreed," Boxers confirmed. "But there have to be more adults than that, just to account for the children."

"I wish I could see a priest," Jonathan mumbled. He brought the monocular down, turned it off, and slipped it back into its pouch. "Okay, Tristan," he said. "You ready to take a walk?"

CHAPTER EIGHT

Father Dominic D'Angelo had known Jonathan Grave for more years than he cared to calculate—since the day they'd moved into long-condemned yet still-assigned Tyler-A dormitory on the campus of the College of William and Mary. Jonathan's last name had still been Gravenow back then, during their freshman year. They were both jocks and party boys—Jon as a track star and Dom as a middling soccer player—and they'd bonded instantly, remaining roommates through their entire college careers.

It's funny, Dom thought, how similar the eighteen-year-old version of one's self turns out to be to the adult version. Even then, long before the Digger handle had even been thought of, Jonathan had been an angry young man. There was a dark side to his competitiveness, a drive to prove himself. Haunted by demons of which Dom had only recently become aware, Jon had a sense of right and wrong—of justice and injustice—that was cast in shades of black and white. Traditional notions of authority meant little to him. Rules weren't necessarily made to be broken, but they were certainly made to be evaluated for reasonableness and then followed or shunned accordingly.

Perhaps that's the natural outcome of having been raised by a mobster and a murderer. Dom always thought it was interesting that he'd known about Jonathan's father's ties to organized crime long before he'd learned that Jon was heir to hundreds of millions of dollars. While it was important to him that people know he was ashamed of his bloodline, the money seemed to embarrass him. Over time, as Dom earned his doctor of divinity, and then his PhD in psychology, he would come to understand the roots of Jonathan's emotional peccadilloes, and he would grow to understand his friend's worldview that right and wrong were absolutes, affording precious little room for relativity.

Jon had been one of those teenagers who could transform from charming ladies' man to ruthless fighter and back again in the space of a dozen heartbeats. All it took was for a person to victimize someone weaker than he. Dom had seen it happen with trash-talking bullies in bars, and he had seen it in classrooms when a professor bullied a student intellectually. Jonathan got away with it because his motivations were always pure, and because, in the end, he was always right.

To Jonathan, the world was full of petty tyrants. He saw it as his life's mission to protect people from them. Sometimes with his body, occasionally with his career, but always with his intellect.

Dom had never known anyone quite like him. Supremely competent at everything he tried, and possessing a near photographic memory for things that interested him, Jonathan could talk anyone into doing anything. Including, it turned out, joining the Army.

To this day, Dom wasn't sure what he'd been thinking when he'd allowed Jonathan to talk him into enlisting, but reasons notwithstanding, he'd followed his friend from graduation to the recruiting station, and from there on to Officer's Candidate School, from which neither would graduate.

OCS turned out to be a bad billet for a young man who resented authority. After only a few weeks, Jonathan resigned and shifted gears to become an "honest soldier," as he liked to call it, meaning a career as a non-commissioned officer. Dom, on the other hand, finally succumbed to the calling of the Church. He did his requisite three years as a grunt, and upon separation from the service moved on to serve the Lord.

When the Bishop of Arlington contacted Dom to offer him the job as pastor of St. Katherine's Church in Fisherman's Cove, he'd jumped at the chance, marveling at the coincidence that he would be called to the oft-talked-about home of the friend with whom he'd fallen out of touch over the years. For as far back as he could remember, Jonathan had gushed about the bucolic community he'd called home as a child, and having served in some of the more unsavory corners of the Diocese, Dom had welcomed the transfer.

He'd barely unpacked his bags in the rectory at St. Kate's when his phone rang and he answered to find Jonathan on the other end. "Welcome to paradise," he'd said, and then he invited Dom to dinner at his house.

Actually, *house* didn't touch it. Palace barely touched it. Easily the largest structure in town, the

Gravenow mansion sat adjacent to St. Kate's, atop a hill that made it the focus of everything. Grand as it was, there was a coldness to the place that made Dom uneasy. That summer night Jonathan had greeted him at the door barefoot, wearing shorts and a GO ARMY T-shirt. Within the first few words, the years had peeled away, and they were old pals again, reliving stories of wild parties and wild women that would have made the parish flock blush crimson if they'd heard.

When the plates were empty, and the bottle of after-dinner Lagavulin was mostly gone, Jonathan leaned back perilously in his chair and gestured grandly with both arms. "So, Dom," he said, "what do you think of the quaint cottage of my youth?"

Dom laughed. "Tell you the truth, Jon, I knew that you were rich, but until I saw this place, I don't think I understood the, uh, *scope* of your wealth."

"Nine figures and counting," Jonathan said. His words were liquid and slippery, thanks to the scotch, and they bore an air of bitterness. "Couldn't spend it in five lifetimes."

Dom knew from just the delivery that something was coming. He waited for the rest, hoping that if the moment came for him to be profound, his own intoxication wouldn't get in the way.

"You know Ellen left me, right?" Jonathan said.

"I kind of sensed that, yes."

"Couldn't handle the pressure of having a warrior husband. Said I make her worry too much."

"So says everyone who's known you for more than a few hours," Dom replied. "Are you divorced or just separated?"

"Separated." Jonathan got a faraway look. "I think I can get her back, though."

"Is this where you lived? When you were together, I mean?"

Jonathan brought his front chair legs back to the floor. "God, no. We had a place down at Bragg. I still have it. She's got a place in McLean now. A five-thousand-square-foot townhouse that I'm paying for."

"How on earth can you make ends meet?"

The question seemed to startle Jonathan, and then he got the joke. "Yeah, right. Well, Dom, it's never been about the money. You know I don't give a shit about money."

Dom smirked. "Bold talk for someone who's never needed any."

Jonathan turned very serious. "Do you really believe that I wouldn't give all of it back if I could bring back one life that my father took to earn it?"

This was new territory for Dom. He just waited for the rest.

"Why are you looking at me like that?" Jonathan asked.

Dom threw an engineered shrug. "You just tossed out a barely veiled admission that your father is a murderer. Having never heard that before, an empty stare seemed appropriate."

Jonathan's eyes narrowed, and then he laughed. "Okay, I'm not being entirely fair. A lot of the family fortune came from the legitimate side of the business— the scrap business. But my father never had much to do with that. He leaned on honest people for that. In his heart of hearts, my father is a thug and a murderer."

He delivered that last line in a way that made Dom think that he was supposed to draw some larger conclusion from it. "I know there's a reason why you're telling me this," he said, "but it's eluding me."

"I don't want it," Jonathan said. "I don't want any of it. It's all blood money, and I'd rather be a pauper than accept it."

"Be careful there," Dom said. "I've known paupers. I've come very close to being one myself. It's nothing to aspire to."

Jonathan waved the notion off. "I couldn't get rid of it all. Most of the money is so tied up in trusts and paperwork that I'm stuck with it forever."

He said that as if it were a bad thing. Something big was on the way, but Dom had no idea what it was, and he didn't like watching his friend navigate this dark place in his mind.

Jonathan stood. "Follow me," he said. He led the way from the dining room back out into the mansion's central hall. The Oriental carpet runner out here was slightly threadbare, but the padding beneath it felt like walking on water vapor. Every angle out here was delicately carved and ornately adorned. Dom had never seen anything like it.

Jonathan stopped next to the massive stairway and turned, "Fourteen thousand three hundred and eighty-seven square feet," he said. "You could fit seven rectories in here, with room to spare. When I was a kid, we had servants on every level bringing us stuff and sucking up to my father's every whim. With that kind of money came real control. That kind of money bought politicians, policemen, and judges by the bushel." He folded his arms across his chest. "Makes a boy proud, don't you think?"

Again, Dom remained silent, assuming that Jonathan would get to the point sooner or later.

Jonathan reached into his pocket and withdrew a key, which he dangled from his forefinger. He held it in front of Dom's nose. "Take it," he said. "In thirty-three days, this will be yours."

Dom's jaw dropped. "*What* will be mine?"

Jonathan grinned. "All of this. The house, the land, everything."

"What are you talking about? I don't need this. I don't even *want* this."

"Keep following," Jonathan said, and he led the way down the hall to another room on the right. He opened the doors to reveal a twenty-by-twenty-foot library that had been decorated in Early Gentlemen's Club. Thousands of volumes decorated the walls from floor to ceiling, except for the near wall on the left, which was dominated by a massive fireplace surrounded by what looked like a mahogany mantel. Jonathan gestured for Dom to sit in one of the luxurious leather chairs while he opened up a panel in the bookcase to reveal his stash of single malts. He poured generously without asking, and handed a snifter to his friend.

Dom took the glass. "Jon, I have to tell you that all of this is making me uncomfortable."

Jonathan took the chair opposite Dom's. "I confess I exaggerated," he said. "It's not really yours as much as it is the church's." He took a sip and he leaned forward to rest his elbows on his knees. "I sold the whole kit and caboodle to the diocese for one dollar on a couple of conditions."

Dom recoiled in his seat, his jaw agape.

"The first condition is that the space be used to create a school for children of incarcerated parents. I want to call it Resurrection House. There are a number of other contractual issues that we're still hammering out, but the second major condition is that you serve in the role of counselor to the kids who come here."

Dom's scowl deepened as he tried to assemble the conversation in a way that would make the words sound as reasonable as Jonathan apparently thought they were.

"Tell me what you mean by *counselor*," he said. Mostly, the question was a dodge for more time.

"You know, *counselor*. Lead psychologist, main confessor. The kids I want to build the school for are going to be damaged goods. They're going to need help working through all the baggage. I think you're the perfect guy."

"We haven't seen each other in years," Dom reminded him.

"Doesn't change anything. I'm an excellent judge of character. Anybody who could tame me during my college years can perform miracles."

Dom recognized Jonathan's Mr. Charming gambit, but effective as it was, he still wasn't buying. "I'm honored," he said, "that you would make such a marvelous donation in the first place, and that you have such faith in me to help the children. But I'm a priest, Jon. I'm not an entrepreneur. I don't get to accept random job offers."

Jonathan took a pull on the scotch. "I'm not suggesting that you'll be working for me, Dom. You'll still be working for God. For the Church. You'll still be pastor of St. Kate's."

Just like that—with a *thunk* that only Dom could hear—a piece fell into place. "You arranged to have me brought to St. Katherine's."

Jonathan made a noncommittal rocking motion with his hand. "I had a conversation with the bishop, yes. Very reasonable guy. I pitched an idea and he accepted it."

Another piece of the puzzle slid home, and as it did, Dom didn't know whether to feel angry or complimented. "Is my participation one of the 'contractual details' in your donation of the property?"

Jonathan's smile morphed into a look of concern. "You're angry," he said, shocked. "I thought this had you written all over it."

"My God, Jon. I'm not an indentured servant. I don't appreciate being traded for property. Did it occur to you to ask me?"

"I *am* asking you. Well, sort of. You have the right to refuse. I only pushed for you to be first choice, and frankly, the bishop agreed without argument. If you don't want to do it, then that's fine."

Dom ended up accepting, of course, and it was the best thing he'd ever done. Since that day so many years ago, Dom had helped countless dozens of boys and girls deal with the trauma of separation from their families, and, in more than a few cases, with the horrors of reunion with their families. What continued to amaze Dom about that day, even through the filter of time, was how honestly clueless Jonathan had been about the difficulty he'd created. He'd seen a problem and a solution, and he'd married the two, fully confident that he was doing the right thing.

For those who understood the purity of Digger's motives, it was hard to be angry with him. For the rest of the world, it was often hard not to be angry with him.

Today, as Dom rode the Metro's Blue Line from Franconia-Springfield to the Smithsonian Station on the National Mall, he catalogued the various adventures that Jonathan Grave had gotten him into over the years. Looking back, he wouldn't change a thing.

His mission this afternoon was to meet with Wolverine—Jonathan's code name for FBI Director Irene Rivers—to get a handle on the Bureau's version of this situation in Mexico. Historically, Irene had been as staunch an ally to Jonathan and Security Solutions as anyone could hope for. The fact that the FBI was one of the agencies calling for his arrest was beyond concerning. It was downright scary.

Irene had run interference for Jonathan's adventures for years, helping to manufacture plausible deniability, and in at least one case intervening personally with the law enforcement process to keep the heat off Jonathan's extra-legal activities. While her intentions weren't always pure—often as not, she and her Bureau got credit for Jonathan's successes—she'd always been a straight shooter. That she'd ordered his arrest without so much as an inquiring phone call had left them all baffled.

Dom traveled empty-handed as he always did for meetings like this. With nothing committed to paper, there were no records to steal or subpoena. As far as the world would be concerned—and in this case, the world consisted of curious passersby and nosy investigators—this would be a meeting between a woman and her priest. That the woman was the chief law enforcer in the United States wouldn't matter. Official Washington might reject the utterance of God's name, but they still respected individuals' rights to commune with Him through his human emissaries.

He felt himself sweating through his black shirt as he climbed the subway station's broken escalator into sunlight, and finally out into the stifling city air. Back in the day, Washington had been considered a hardship post for foreign diplomats, and it didn't take more than three minutes in the August sunshine to understand why. Ninety-eight humidity-soaked degrees hung on his skin like a wet wool coat.

Like any summer afternoon in the District, the Mall teemed with tourists, moving in swarms toward the various museums that defined that part of the city.

He hadn't walked twenty steps when he saw Irene on the far side of Jefferson Drive, SW, rising from a bench outside the Ripley Center, which sat adjacent to the Smithsonian Castle. Dom thought it an appropriate meeting place, given the nature of their conversation. The Ripley Center was itself a structure out of a spy novel, with an entrance that looked like a large information kiosk. The average tourist would have no idea that the kiosk led to cavernous gallery and teaching spaces underground.

Irene wore a Hillary Clinton pantsuit and sported a wide hat that sheltered her from the sun. Truthfully, it was an unusual look for her. In fact, she looked different in other ways, too, but he couldn't quite put his finger on it. On either side, but separated by fifteen or twenty feet, two members of her security detail stood watch. If Irene was doing her best to remain unnoticed, the guards, with their business suits, high-and-tight haircuts, and curlicue earpieces, weren't helping.

As Irene stood, the security guys moved in closer, and a third one materialized out of the crowd to form a kind of phalanx to escort her away from Dom and toward the black Suburban that doubled for executive limousines in these days of heightened security in Washington.

Dom stopped as he saw her leaving, and checked his watch. He was right on time. Two minutes early, in fact. She'd never stood him up before.

He raised his arm to call after her.

He stopped, though, when he was blindsided by a tourist who pushed him to the ground. Dom caught himself with his hands, but there was a good chance that he'd put a hole in the knee of his trousers.

"Oh, God, Father, I'm so sorry. Are you okay?"

Dom looked up to see what could only be a vacationing computer programmer. Maybe forty years old, he guy wore black-rimmed glasses, a Denver Broncos T-shirt, and cargo shorts.

"I'm so sorry. I just wasn't watching where I was going. Here, let me help you up." He extended a hand.

Dom waved him off as he rolled to a sitting position on the ground. "No, I'm fine. No harm done." Good news: his trousers were still intact.

"Let me help you up, Father D'Angelo," the man said in a barely audible voice.

Dom's head snapped up at the sound of his name. Something changed behind the tourist's eyes. It wasn't frightening, exactly, but there was a look of urgency.

"Okay." Dom grasped the man's hand in a power grip that involved their thumbs, and as he did, he felt something pressed into his palm.

"I'm so sorry, Father," the tourist said aloud. As

Dom found his balance, the tourist dusted him off. When he was very close, he said, "Don't look at the note till I'm gone. Wait fifteen minutes and follow the directions exactly."

Dom just stared.

"You're sure you're okay, right, Father?" the tourist asked, loudly enough to be heard by others. "I really am sorry. Hope it doesn't keep me out of Heaven." With that, the man turned away and headed toward the Freer Gallery.

He never looked back.

CHAPTER NINE

Jonathan climbed out of the Toyota and waited for Tristan to join him. "Stick with me like a shadow," Jonathan said. "Remember . . . do exactly what I say exactly when I say to do it."

Jonathan and Boxers spread out as they exited the vehicle, allowing a distance of fifty feet between them. The separation increased the effectiveness of their surveillance while at the same time making it harder for any hidden bad guys to take them out. At this distance, a bad guy would have to be a great shot twice, and even if he hit the first target, he'd likely die while preparing to shoot the second. This game was as much about intimidation as it was about marksmanship, and the more the bad guys second-guessed themselves, the better it was for the good guys.

The residents of the village were slow to catch on to them. It started with the kids in the game. The goalie on the far end pointed and said something Jonathan couldn't hear, and a kid from the other team booted the ball past him while he was distracted, bisecting the wheelbarrow and the tricycle that served as goal posts.

The scoring team started to celebrate, but then they followed his eyes, and they, too, started to point.

The stoppage of the game drew the attention of the adults, who stood and watched.

Jonathan keyed his mike. "Watch their hands," he said. "If they don't go for weapons, we keep our weapons down."

Boxers tapped his transmitter.

The villagers seemed more curious than frightened, though Jonathan noted that two of the adults held their hands out to their sides and splayed their fingers to show that they posed no danger. For their part, the children just stayed put.

"*Oye,*" one of the older kids yelled to his friends. "*Jugamos!*" *Hey, let's play.*

Like the flip of a switch, the children returned to their game.

"Keep an eye on the adults," Jonathan said into his radio. "I'll watch the church."

Boxers tapped again. Ultimately, the adults would be behind them, which meant that Boxers would have to walk backwards, but there really was no other way.

In thirty seconds, Jonathan was at the church door. He turned to Tristan. "Stay out here with the Big Guy," he said. "Stick close to him."

Jonathan considered knocking, but decided that that was unnecessary. The door swung open to a rush of cool, musty air. The sun shining through the glass on the far wall nearly blinded him. Instinctively, he looked to the left and to the right, just in case there might be a lurker in the shadows.

More a chapel than a church, with neatly aligned

folding chairs taking the place of pews, the sanctuary had the look of a work in progress. Framed pictures along the outer walls depicted the suffering and crucifixion of Jesus, together defining the Stations of the Cross. Up ahead at the altar, the cross upon which a wrought-iron sculpture of the suffering Christ had been precariously mounted appeared to be hand-hewn of six-by-six lumber. It sat in what appeared to be a temporary support that had been nailed to the floor.

"How dare you bring guns into the house of God?" a voice boomed in Spanish from somewhere behind the blinding sunlight.

Also in Spanish, Jonathan answered, "I mean no harm. Please step out where I can see you."

"You know the agreement," the voice said. "No guns inside the sanctuary."

There's an agreement? Jonathan thought. He wondered who it might be with. "Are you Father Perón?"

A few seconds passed before Jonathan heard footsteps approaching. "I do not recognize you," the voice said.

"That's because I've never been here before."

Finally, the voice became a silhouette as its owner emerged from the backlight. He carried something long in his hands, and for an instant, Jonathan's hand flinched toward his weapon. He stopped when he saw that the object was a candle lighter/snuffer that was nearly identical to the ones he'd used as an altar boy.

The silhouette's features emerged as a young man of perhaps thirty. His narrow face looked narrower still under the thick mane of black hair that hung nearly to his shoulders. He wore a red T-shirt and blue shorts with flip-flops.

"No guns in my church," he repeated.

Jonathan extended his hand. "My name is Leon Harris," he said. A lie in church.

The young man looked at Jonathan's hand, and then cast a glance over Jonathan's shoulder, out to the door. "And who is that?"

Jonathan knew without looking that Boxers had taken up a position in the jamb, scanning the yard for any trouble that might arise. "He's a friend of mine. His name is Richard Lerner. Is Father Perón here?" Jonathan opened the door wider to cast more light on the man.

"You are American," the man said. "I can tell by your accent."

Jonathan felt disappointed. He'd thought his Spanish was flawless. "*Sí*," he said.

"*Federales Americanos?*"

"No," Jonathan assured. "I'm not military, and I'm not with the government. I'm just a private citizen in need of help."

The man took a second look at Boxers. "An American private citizen with many guns and a bodyguard."

"If I could speak with Father Perón, I—"

"I am Father Perón," the man said.

Jonathan cocked his head. "Really?" as soon as the word left his throat, he knew that he'd insulted the man, but good Lord, he looked like a college student.

"Loyola University," Perón said in English. "I assure you that I look younger than I feel."

Jonathan felt himself blush. "I meant no offense."

"None was taken. Yet you still have guns in my church. I don't allow that."

This was a tough spot for Jonathan. There's a cliché that covers moments like this that involves the phrase, *when you pry it from my cold dead fingers*. He didn't want it to come to that. "Can we sit for a minute?" he asked. "I think when I tell you what is happening, you'll understand why I'm hesitant to give up my weapons."

Perón put his hands on his hips and considered the request. He nodded with his chin. "We'll talk outside."

The note was written in a woman's hand on a plain piece of white paper:

Dom,
Follow these directions precisely. Walk to the
L'Enfant Plaza Metro. Take the Green Line to
Fort Totten. Transfer to the Red Line and take it
to Union Station. Go to the front of the building
and find the chauffeur waiting for Fr. Carlino.
He works for me and will take care of you. I'll
explain when we meet.

Best,
I

Including the fifteen-minute delay in the beginning, and the long interval between trains at this time of day, it took nearly an hour to make his rendezvous with the chauffeur, who was standard-issue FBI, from the glossy shoes to the gray suit that was cut a bit too large in order to accommodate his gun. The only difference was that this guy was a little older than most. He held an eight-and-a-half-by-eleven-inch piece of white paper with *Fr. Carlino* laser printed in large bold type.

Dom approached cautiously, unsure of the protocol. Should he call himself Father Carlino? How far was he supposed to carry the charade? He decided to walk with confidence and let his collar speak for him.

As it turned out, the guy knew exactly who he was waiting for. When Dom closed to within a few feet, the chauffeur lowered the sign and closed the distance with an outstretched hand. "Hi, Father," he said. "I'm Paul Boersky. I've worked with the director for a long time. Follow me."

Boersky led the way out the front of the station and across two lanes of traffic picking up and delivering passengers. As they closed in on a Lincoln Town Car, the vehicle beeped as it unlocked, and Boersky opened the right rear passenger door for Dom.

The priest stopped short. "We've never met, and this feels suspiciously like a slow-motion kidnapping. Do you have ID?"

Boersky smiled. "Was wondering when you'd get to that." He produced a creds case from his suit coat pocket and flashed his gold badge. "Really, I'm a good guy."

As he slid into the offered seat, Dom tried not to think about how many times Jonathan had used false credentials to get his way.

During the drive through progressively more frightening city streets, Dom fought the urge to ask questions. Given the cloak-and-dagger prelude, he harbored no hope for straight answers anyway.

The trip ended after ten minutes at a place that Dom knew well. "You're kidding," he said. "Here?"

Boersky threw the transmission into park. "No one can ever say that Director Rivers doesn't have style," he said. He looked at Dom through the rearview mirror. "I'll be waiting here to drive you back to the Metro."

St. Matthew's Cathedral was a far cry from St. Peter's in Rome, but it was likewise a far cry from St. Kate's in Fisherman's Cove. Most famous, perhaps, as the site of John F. Kennedy's funeral Mass, St. Matthew's had little of the golden grandeur of its Roman father. It was dwarfed in size not just by Saint Patrick's in New York, but even the Episcopalian Washington National Cathedral just a few miles away in Upper Northwest. Still, Dom's heart beat a little faster as he entered.

Following his final instructions from Paul Boersky, Dom turned left as he entered the nave and headed for Our Lady's Chapel. Again, he spotted Irene's security detail first, chiseled men in dark suits standing just outside the chapel. Once you know what to look for, these guys might as well wear T-shirts that read BODYGUARD. Only in Washington were such teams so commonplace that they were barely noticeable.

Irene sat contemplatively in a pew near the stunning sculpture of the Blessed Mother reaching down toward her children and stared straight ahead, her hands folded in her lap. She still wore her ubiquitous pantsuit, but this one was a green print instead of the monochrome navy blue she'd worn outside the Ripley Center. She wore her strawberry-blond hair pulled back in a tight ponytail.

Dom sat next to her. "Good afternoon," he said. "You changed clothes quickly."

"Hello, Father. I was going to call you if you hadn't called me. And the last me you saw wasn't really me. She's my body double. It's a security thing. Her unofficial, entirely impolitic alternative job title is my bullet catcher. May it never come to that."

Dom didn't know if that was highly likely or virtually impossible. Throughout her career, Irene had had a reputation for getting involved in firefights, and being named director hadn't done anything to change it.

"I'd be lying if I said I wasn't a little unnerved by all this," he said.

"Join the club." Irene moved only her head to look at him. "I have it on good authority that I'm being watched."

"By whom?"

She shrugged. "I have my thoughts, but I was hoping perhaps that you could tell me."

Dom recoiled. "How would I know who's following you?"

"Call it a hunch. My security detail picks up an electronic tracking device, and then a physical shadow on me on the very day that Digger goes on an alleged shooting rampage in Mexico. As you know, our mutual friend would be the first to disavow the validity of coincidence."

"All due respect, you're director of the FBI. Aren't you followed all the time?"

"Not so much as you might expect. And when Scorpion is caught in a crack, all other ancillary events take on special meaning."

"Can't you just arrest the followers?"

Irene laughed. "Not in the United States, you can't. If they don't make a threatening move, they're within their rights to follow anyone they want." She waved her hand, as if swiping an invisible marker board. "Enough about me. Tell me what Digger has gotten himself into."

"It has to stay off the record," Dom cautioned.

"As do all things Digger-related."

Dom related all the details he knew. "Frankly," he concluded, "our biggest shock was when we came to realize that the FBI is gunning for him."

Irene's jaw tightened at the mention of her Bureau; then she smiled, albeit without humor. "We've known each other too long for a shot like that, Dom."

"Are you saying that you're not out to arrest him?'

"Of course we're out to arrest him," Irene said. "Or at least our border field offices are. But that's not because of anything I did. That's because the Mexican police labeled him a mass murderer and reported him to Interpol. I have pull, but I can't keep the country from complying with its international treaties."

Irene steeled herself for something, and when she looked at Dom again, the sadness in her eyes pained him. "Don't you need to put on a stole or something? I want you to hear my confession."

. The question startled him. "Oh, my goodness, Irene," he said. "I had no idea." They'd played the confession ruse so many times that it never occurred to him that she might be seeking absolution for real.

He pulled a leather pouch from his pocket and removed from it a square of purple cloth. When he shook it, the square fell away from itself to form a clerical stole. "Are you sure you wouldn't prefer to do this in a more private place?"

"This place is fine," she said.

"But you're such a public figure. If people eavesdrop—"

She held up a hand. "I'll share a secret with you, Father. This spot—these few pews in this tiny chapel—is one of the most acoustically dead spots in Washington. If someone's not within, say, ten feet of us—and my detail will make sure they're not—they couldn't hear a word we say."

Dom felt his jaw drop. "How can you be so sure?"

There was that tired smile again. "Because I oversaw the project to make it so. We sweep for listening devices twice a day on random schedules." What she saw in Dom's face made her laugh. "This is Washington, Father. It's a spooky town. Truly private meeting space is essential. Even the NSA doesn't know about this spot, and the CIA is the reason we have it in the first place. The Agency has been paying a lot of attention to us recently."

She nodded to the stole in Dom's hands.

He jumped a little, brought back into the moment. "Of course," he said. He kissed the stole and draped it around his shoulders.

Irene crossed herself. "Bless me, Father, for I have sinned. It's been a long, long time since my last confession."

"And what are your sins?"

"Well, that's the thing," she said. "It's not so much about what I've done as what I'm about to do."

Dom felt a pang of paranoia. Was it possible he was in danger?

"Oh, for heaven's sake, Father, I didn't mean it that way."

Tension released from his shoulders.

Irene scowled, looked genuinely hurt. "One day we'll have to discuss how you could even think such a thing. No, the sins I'm about to commit are of the national-security variety."

Something snagged in Dom's gut. "Irene, I can't absolve sins for which you are not repentant."

Her face darkened. "Oh, I'm repentant, Father. I am also appalled and ashamed that it's come to this. In the end, I submit that absolution is your call, but the act of confession is mine, and Father, I need you to listen."

Dom had learned over the years that no two confessions were alike—except for adolescent confessions, of course, which were *entirely* alike—and that when dealing with powerful people, the plea for absolution frequently sounded like a demand. It was the way those egos were wired.

"Very well, then," he said. "I'm all ears."

"I'm going to need more than your ears, Father. I'm going to need your whole person. You remember All American Industries, don't you?"

"One of the big-money contributors to the Crystal Palace Cathedral," Dom said.

"Exactly. Now pay attention because this gets complicated. Based on the information you gave me in your first call, my people did a thorough background check on them."

"So did Venice. She came up with nothing. Such a nothing, in fact, that Gail hypothesized that it was a government cutout."

"Good for her," Irene said. "Because she's exactly right. CIA, in fact. Even we couldn't put meat on the theory until we did complete backgrounds on the members of the board of directors. We hit pay dirt with a guy named Dennis Hainsley. Do you want to take notes?"

Dom shook his head. "I never document confessions. Runs counter to some pretty important vows. Besides, I'll take what you tell me to my grave."

Irene gave a frustrated sigh. "Okay, Father, I'll be blunt. You're going to have to reveal some of this. Lives are at stake. I expect you never to reveal who gave you the information, but I'm going to need you to act on it."

Indeed, no two confessions were alike. "In that case," Dom said, "I've got a good memory. Still no notes."

"Your call," Irene said. "Our computers pinged on Dennis Hainsley. The name showed up on the same kind of list that Digger's name comes up on. A covert list. We had to dig pretty deeply, but ultimately, we tracked it to the Agency."

"CIA." Dom was pretty sure that's what she meant, but given the stakes, it was worth clarifying.

"Exactly. In the 1990s, Dennis Hainsley was the official cover for Trevor Munro, who, until recently, was the CIA station chief in Caracas."

"Venezuela, right?" Geography had never been Dom's long suit.

Irene smiled. "Yes, Father. Caracas, Venezuela."

"All respect, Irene, Dennis Hainsley sounds to me like a pretty common name. Couldn't this be a different one?"

"I'm getting to that. Trevor Munro, aka Dennis Hainsley, has spent most of his career on various Central and South American desks. He goes all the way back to the Contras-Sandinistas mess. Hell, he goes nearly to Noriega's rise in Panama. From the very early days of his career, the drug trade has been front and center on everything he did. Those were the days when America chose which drug lords were successful and which ones suffered, depending upon the degree of cooperation with Uncle Sam's priorities *du jour*. Are you following me so far?"

"I'm not confused," Dom said, "but I'm not connecting any dots yet, either."

"Well, then get ready. One of Munro's primary points of contact for getting leverage against the drug lords was an American named Mitchell Ponder. Ring any bells?"

Bells, no. Brass gongs, yes. Mitchell Ponder had been instrumental in the kidnapping of two children from Resurrection House not too long ago. During the mission to get them back, Jonathan and Boxers killed Ponder and destroyed one of Colombia's most profitable cocaine rings, literally burning up tens of millions of dollars in product and processing equipment.

"Since you're mentioning his name, I'm assuming there's a connection," Dom said. "I mean, between that incident in Colombia and what's happening now."

Irene nodded. "We think there is, yes. I just learned that at the time of Digger's adventures in Colombia, Trevor Munro was on Mitch Ponder's payroll, offering protection to Ponder's operation in return for serious cash."

"How serious?"

"Does it matter? Serious enough to justify retribution."

Dom took some time to process the details. "So the CIA is behind all of this?"

"Not behind it," Irene corrected, "but complicit in it. It turns out that Mitch Ponder was a manufacturer of product, not a distributor. His primary customer was a very bad guy named Felix Hernandez—one of Mexico's big three drug lords. When Digger stopped the music by killing Ponder, Hernandez was the one left without a chair, and he was not happy about it. Beyond the economic loss, he was doubly pissed because he was convinced that Digger's mayhem was an Agency operation. He thought Munro had betrayed him.

"Munro denied it, of course, but an angry drug lord is a very scary animal. Fearing for his life, Munro got himself transferred back to Langley, where, typical of the Agency, they promoted him to bigger and better things. As we speak, he's one retirement away from being named ADD/CIA."

Dom showed confusion.

"Oh, sorry," Irene said. "Associate deputy director of the CIA. Number-three guy. Just south of requiring Senate approval."

"How do you know all of this?"

"I'll get to that. Bottom line, all of this has convinced Hernandez even more that he's being betrayed. And I can't prove any of it. Yet. We have a source inside Hernandez's cartel, though, who's been working with us in return for future asylum. She tells us that Hernandez has been leaning hard on someone inside the U.S. intelligence community. She doesn't know a name, but she knows it has something to do with betrayal and an Agency op gone bad. Hernandez keeps talking about having an important spy's balls . . . um, *sensitive parts* in his hands.

"Now this comes up. A lot of the rest is conjecture, especially the connection to the Crystal Palace, but really, what is the likelihood that a CIA cutout company would give a surprise donation to a troubled church just weeks before that money would be needed to pay off a ransom that happened to be delivered by the very team that caused the original mayhem? That's a coincidence that comes as close to impossible as any I can think of."

There was no arguing the point. "It just seems to be the long way around the barn to get three million in ransom."

Irene made a shooing motion. "I don't think it was about the ransom. I think it was about killing Digger and his team. I think Munro threw him under the bus."

"Then why go through the whole charade of the kidnapping and Mexico? Why not just kill them on the street?"

She smiled. She'd been waiting for this question. "Again, I have to conjecture, but my guess is that Munro doesn't know who he's looking for. That's why the Interpol alert is for Leon Harris and Richard Lerner. Dig and Boxers have used those handles for a long time, but because the covers are buried so deep, the names have never meant anything. Are those the names they used on their Colombia op?"

Dom had no idea.

"Let's assume that they were," Irene continued. "To get them, Munro had to stage a kidnapping and get the Crystal Palace to hire Security Solutions—again, not by name, but by the operators' aliases."

Dom sorted it in his head. The dots all seemed to connect. That it made sense disgusted him. "So the church gets a six-million-dollar donation, and all they have to do is agree to give away three million in ransom."

"It's not a pretty world, is it, Father? For all I know, the three million in ransom might have been earmarked to be returned to the church."

Dom's mood darkened even more. "*Children*, Irene. *Children* have died for this plan. How can that be worth it?"

"From the church's point of view, I don't have an answer for you. On Hernandez's side of the equation, his business is defined by murder. After you've killed dozens, what's a few more?"

Dom put a hand on his forehead, as if taking his own temperature. "I'm trying to figure out how this can help Dig. It's one thing to understand why all of it is happening, but we still have to find a way to bring them back into the country."

Irene's eyes flashed. "I think I might have something for you there. I want to nail Trevor Munro—not just for this kidnapping and murder business, but for selling out his country. To do that, I'm going to need the testimony of our mole in Hernandez's cartel. Her name is Maria Elizondo, and it's time to bring her in. She's earned her asylum—or *will* earn it as soon as she brings Digger back into the country."

Dom gaped again. "How is an informant going to do something that the FBI to whom she reports cannot?"

"Maria's been playing a few games with us," Irene said. "She's been baiting us with knowledge she claims to have about a network of smuggling tunnels into Texas, Arizona, and California that we don't know about. She's been telling us that if we give her asylum, she'll reveal the tunnels."

"I've heard about these," Dom said. "I've seen it on the news."

"You haven't seen these," Irene corrected. "Every time we hear about one, we blow it up or fill it in. These are new. And they're the team's route back into the country without being caught."

"How sure are you that she's telling the truth?"

"I'm rolling the dice. Given the stakes, she's got every reason to be honest. She knows that if we took her bait and it turned out to be a lie, we'd throw her back like an undersized fish."

Dom cocked his head. "Would you?" he asked. "Throw her back, I mean?"

"Right into Hernandez's arms," Irene said. "Betrayal is a tough business, Father, even when you do it for the right reasons." She looked away. "I fear that I am about to become a living example of that."

Dom sensed his cue and he scowled. "Are you telling me that you think our conversation here is a be-trayal?"

"I took an oath, Father, and here I sit violating that oath. I can't think of a finer definition of betrayal, can you?"

Dom felt his face flush. "Forgive me, Irene, but that's bullshit."

Irene recoiled, shocked.

"And I say that in the presence of the Blessed Virgin. Correct me if I'm wrong, but I believe that your oath was to the Constitution. I don't care what's classified and what's sensitive information, and I have no idea what the laws are about such things, but I have dedicated my life to God's law. Legal technicalities and career considerations aside, when we're put in a position to choose between right and wrong, our obligations are clear."

Irene gave him a patronizing smirk. "I wish my world could be as simple as yours," she said.

Dom inhaled sharply through his nose and held it for a second as he considered how far to take this. He put his hand on hers.

"Irene, I have to tell you that I could not care less that you're the director of the FBI. I take no pride in that. I take pride in knowing a fine human being named Irene Rivers. In the years that we've known each other, you've always impressed me with your ability to put what is right ahead of everything else. Principle above practicality. At the end of the day, I believe that that is why you happen to have been promoted to an extraordinarily stressful job.

"You and Digger are cut from the same cloth. He likes to tell people that he's on the side of the angels, and when he does, he always injects a note of sarcasm so that people will know that he's half joking. The fact of it is that he's right. He *is* on the side of the angels. So are you. You risk everything that's dear to you for the single purpose of protecting people who cannot protect themselves. If doing that is somehow a sin, then all I can say is God help us all."

Irene's eyes had turned red and moist, something that Dom had never seen before. "Side of the angels, huh?" She tasted the words. "I like that, Father. Thank you."

"You're welcome. And you can call me Dom."

Another tired smile. "You know, I don't think I'd like that at all, Father. Have you ever just wished that you could unlearn things?" she asked. "Un-see things?"

"I'm a priest, Irene. And a psychologist. I think that every day."

Irene stood, and Dom stood with her. Her security team became suddenly attentive.

"Please be careful, Irene."

Before letting go of his hand, Irene bent and kissed it. "You're very good at what you do," she said. "I still don't know if I can put the pin back in the grenade to get the murder charges turned back. I'll keep trying, but do what you can with what I've given you. If the guys can hook up with Maria Elizondo, and just a few things go right, we should be able to get them home. And then we can mete out some serious justice for Trevor Munro."

CHAPTER TEN

Father Perón led the way to a bench in a garden on the southern side of the church. They sat in the shade of an exotic-looking tree, on a bench that was more appropriate to a picnic table than a place of reflection. Overhead, an arbor boasted dozens of sweet-smelling red blooms.

Jonathan filled the priest in on what had transpired today. As he got to the end of the story, the sounds from the soccer game out front came to a crescendo.

"The bottom line is this," Jonathan concluded. They'd fallen back into Spanish. "I need to seek sanctuary for this young man until I can figure out what is going on."

Perón's eyes narrowed. The sun was a half hour away from being gone now, and in this light, the priest looked somehow even younger than before. "You are all wanted by the police," he said, as if thinking aloud. "Because you claim you are innocent, I am to believe you, and I am to endanger everyone in this village to help you. Is that correct?"

The soccer field erupted in cheers.

"Yes," Jonathan said. "But it's more complicated—"

Father Perón silenced him by raising his hand. "The Catholic Church did away with the notion of sanctuary as canon law nearly thirty years ago."

"That may well be," Jonathan countered, "but given all the help American churches have lent to Mexican refugees—Latin American refugees in general—granting them safe harbor from immigration enforcement, I thought you might take a chance with us." He hoped he was playing a strong hand. While U.S. law had never embraced the tenth-century notion of churches as safe harbors, there was a growing movement among American churches to fight against draconian immigration law.

"And because a few churches in Illinois and Indiana have shown sympathy to men and women whose only crime is to find a job, I should feel obligated to shelter murderers?"

Jonathan sighed as another cheer rose from the soccer field. "We're not murderers, Father."

From the far side of the church—the north side—an adolescent voice yelled a triumphant "Yes!" in English, instantly drawing Jonathan's attention.

Damn kid can't follow even a simple order, he thought.

Jonathan stood. "Come with me, Father," he said. Knowing exactly what he was going to find, he led the priest to the front corner of the church. From there, he could see Tristan mixing it up with the kids on the field. He was shirtless now, and barefoot, playing soccer in a pair of boxer shorts.

Jonathan shot a look to Boxers and got a shrug in return. "What did you want me to do?" the Big Guy asked.

"Where are his clothes?"

"Better half-naked than thoroughly blood-soaked, I suppose. Less of a buzzkill for the other kids."

Jonathan turned back to Father Perón. "Forget about me," he said. "Does that boy look like a murderer to you?"

Perón watched the children play for a few seconds, and then he looked at Jonathan. "You are welcome inside my church," he said. "Your guns are not. You decide."

With that, the young priest turned to his left and walked back through the sanctuary doors into the dark coolness of the church.

Jackie Mitchell's gut seized when her phone rang. This was what her life had become. Her office, once so beautiful with its soothing blues and modern leather and glass furniture, had become her prison—the place she dared not leave. The caller ID read, BLOCKED.

She lifted the receiver. "God bless you."

"Um, Reverend Mitchell?" The male voice on the other end sounded impossibly young.

"This is she." Jackie's sprits rose as she considered the prospect of dealing with something other than the violence she had wrought. "Who's this?"

"My name is David," the young man said. "David Border. I'm your IT manager here at the Crystal Palace."

It took her a second to process "IT" as meaning information technology. "Of course, David," she said. "What can I do for you?"

He cleared his throat. "Well, ma'am, I don't know if this is a problem or not, but Pam Vargas in the Security Department called me a few minutes ago to tell me that someone's been trying to hack into our system."

Jackie closed her eyes. This couldn't possibly be anything but bad news. "What does that mean, exactly?" She was pretty sure she knew, but she'd long ago learned that in times of crisis, it was important to make sure you defined all terms.

David cleared his throat again. "Um, well, it means that someone was trying to get information off our system that they're not entitled to have."

"What kind of information?"

"Well, ma'am, that's the thing. That's the reason why Pam called me. Apparently, since the time of the, you know, *incident*, we've gotten a lot of attacks on our website and on our Good Works Pages, but this one was different. This one targeted contributors."

Jackie's sense of dread blossomed to the size of a malignant basketball. "Any contributors in particular?" she asked, even though she felt certain that she knew the answer.

Again, he cleared his throat. "Well, yes, ma'am. He seems to be focusing on our most recent contributors."

Exactly as she had feared. Just to be certain: "How recent?"

"Call it the past six weeks," David said.

Jackie fought the urge to cry. She concentrated on keeping her voice firm and businesslike. "Can you give me names?"

Another throat thing. She realized now that it was a nervous tic for him. "Yes, ma'am. The biggest push seems to be on All American Industries and Global Transformations. Most of the others, too, but those are the ones under the greatest scrutiny."

"Do we know what they were able to glean from these attacks?"

Now he fell silent.

"David?"

"Well, ma'am, they pretty much got everything we have. I frankly can't imagine how the information could hurt the companies involved, but I thought you needed to know. In fact, the absolute value of the information wouldn't even have prompted me to call you. My concern is the ferocity of the attacks. In fact, there were at least *two* attacks. Almost simultaneously."

Her heart hammering, Jackie kept it together. "Where are they originating?"

"We can't trace that," David said. "And that fact alone means that the hackers are very good at what they do."

Jackie didn't know exactly what it all meant, but it felt distressingly like the end of everything. "As we speak, have the attacks stopped?"

Ahem. "Yes, ma'am, they have."

"Does that mean they gave up?"

He hesitated. "I suppose it could mean that," David said. "But they really hit us hard. The smarter bet is that they got what they were looking for and they left."

It was exactly as Jackie had feared, her worst nightmare. "All right then," she said. "Thank you, David. Is there anything we can do to stop this sort of invasion in the future?"

"I'm not even sure how they broke through the firewall," he said. "When I figure that out, maybe we'll be able to stop it. But I'm telling you, Reverend Mitchell, that these were very sophisticated attacks."

"God bless you for your efforts," Jackie said. "Please keep me informed of your progress."

She laid the receiver back on its cradle, but she kept her hand in place. She had to make another phone call, and it was the last number in the world she wanted to dial. How could things have spun so desperately out of control?

Tears pressed against her eyes, but she willed them away. She'd broken her vows to God, and now this was His will. She would suffer in Hell for all that she'd done, but there were others to think about right now, and they needed to be her concern. She needed to make the call to protect them.

Steeling herself with a giant breath, she picked up the receiver and pressed in the number from memory.

In the end, Jonathan had no choice. He left his arsenal in a pile outside the door, under Boxers' watchful eye. All but his backup piece, a .38 revolver that he kept in a patch pocket on his right calf. Call it his little poker bluff with God.

"I'm back here," the priest called from the darkness as Jonathan reentered. The sound came from a room off to the right-hand side of the altar. Jonathan strolled down the center aisle, between the two rows of chairs, and when he arrived at the foot of the altar, he cast a quick glance over his shoulder to make sure no one was looking, then crossed himself and offered a shallow genuflect.

"You are Catholic," Father Perón said from the shadows. He held a cup and saucer in his hand, stirring it slowly.

Jonathan could smell the coffee from thirty feet away. "More so than I usually behave," he said.

"True of most Catholics from your country. May I offer you some coffee?"

The room off to the side wasn't exactly a vestry, but it appeared to serve in that capacity. Call it a cross between vestry and bar. Built cheaply yet sturdily of what appeared to be local hardwoods, the room had a utilitarian yet homey feel about it. Jonathan just wished that he could turn up the light a little. Tall shelves lined two of the four walls, and when Jonathan noted the contents, he smiled.

Father Perón was not a teetotaler, and his tastes apparently ran toward single malt scotches, forming an instant bond with his parish's latest visitor. Sixteen-year-old Lagavulin was a religious experience unto itself, and there it was on the top shelf of the racked and stacked liquor, just at eye level.

Jonathan settled for the proffered coffee.

"Please have a seat," said Father Perón, gesturing with an open palm to a wooden chair that might have been part of a dining room set in a different world. "Make yourself comfortable, and then tell me the rest."

Jonathan cocked his head.

"Tell me what you are not telling me," he clarified. "You can start with the reasons why my telephone stopped working more or less at the same moment when you arrived."

Jonathan sipped from his cup to stall for time. He valued information above gold or diamonds, and as philanthropic as he was with his financial treasures, he hoarded information like the bitterest of misers.

"Why did your villagers so quickly show their hands as we were approaching? They clearly wanted us to see that they were unarmed."

The priest smiled. "Asking another question is not the same as answering one," he said.

"I'm getting there, I promise."

"But first you must be sure whether the parish priest is trustworthy?"

This guy was good. Jonathan thought about dodging the question but decided on a nod. "Exactly. In my line of work, an abundance of caution is never penalized."

"And what is your line of work, exactly?"

"I rescue people."

Perón's eyes narrowed. "Rescuing must be a dangerous business to require so many guns."

"I rescue people from kidnappers. They tend to be a violent bunch. With all respect, Father, your country has turned kidnapping into something of a profit center."

Something changed in Perón's face. A cross between sadness and anger. "If Americans bought fewer drugs, and sold fewer guns, the world would be a safer place."

"I'm not a politician, Father. I'm a tactician, and I need your help. That child's life depends on it."

The priest held up his hands, as if to fend off an attack. "Don't place that on me," he said. "Whatever trouble you are in is self-inflicted. If that child is hurt, it will be your responsibility, not mine. My *responsi-*

bility is to notify the authorities that you are here, and let them sort it all out. Except I cannot do that because the telephones no longer work. I believe you still owe me an answer on that one."

Jonathan shrugged. "I'm a careful man, Father. And the fact that you tried to make your call tells me that my caution is well-founded. And you still owe me an answer on your willingness to help me reunite a child with his family."

"You're asking me to grant you a favor, despite your threat of violence," Perón said.

"I'm doing exactly that, Father," Jonathan said. "If you turn us in, I believe the authorities will kill us. What damage I have done is merely defensive."

Perón recoiled. "Why would the authorities do such a thing?"

"I don't know."

"Yet you sound so certain."

They'd arrived at the details that Jonathan had wanted to keep off the table. "They've already tried."

"To kill you?"

Jonathan nodded.

It only took a few seconds for the priest to connect the dots. "This must mean that you are talented with the guns you carry."

Jonathan shrugged.

"Who did you shoot?"

"The kidnappers," Jonathan said. "What was supposed to be a simple ransom exchange turned out to be a bloodbath. I believe that this is being organized by people who have the ear and the resources of the local police. Who would have that kind of power?"

Perón shook his head. "I have no way of knowing."

Jonathan smiled. "It gives me hope for the future that a man of your calling would be such a terrible liar. My only desire is to get that young man to safety. You can trust me, Father, just as surely as I must trust you. Now, please help me."

Father Perón took a long time to decide on his next course. After settling himself with a deep breath, he said, "The drug lords own everyone. Those who don't cooperate with them are killed."

"Including the government?" Jonathan asked. "I've heard rumors to that effect, but is that what you think?"

Perón gave a coy smile. "Like you, I am not a politician, merely a parish priest. I am certain that our president could look your president in the eye and tell him earnestly that such is not the case." He leaned forward to rest his elbows on his knees. "But presidents don't always know all the things that their surrogates do. Perhaps they don't want to know. It seems odd to me, however, that in a nation where the government controls other elements of our lives, they are somehow unable to stop these drug lords. Local politicians are terrified to stand up to them and enforce the laws. To do so would quite literally cost them their heads. Beheading is among their primary intimidation tools."

"Do you know names?" Jonathan asked.

Perón's features hardened. "You're playing a very dangerous game, Mr. Harris."

"I'm a pretty dangerous guy, Father."

"To know names merely increases the danger. I can arrange for you to have shelter for the night. After that, you must go."

Jonathan sighed. "Well, you see, Father, that's where it gets really complicated. The level of betrayal to which I've been exposed is extreme. Whatever is happening, my route home is blocked. A name will help me unblock it."

The priest shook his head. "A name will help you find someone to hurt," he corrected. "Once hurt, they will want to retaliate, only you will have moved on, leaving no other targets but my parishioners."

Jonathan let the implication of it all sink in. "I'm sorry if I brought trouble to you."

Perón allowed himself a smirk as he leaned back into his chair and crossed his legs. He sipped his coffee. "There is no 'if' in this equation, Mr. Harris. You have brought the most dangerous kind of trouble. And now you ask me for a favor."

Jonathan slurped his coffee, then shook his head. "No, Father, I'm not asking you for a favor. I'm asking you to show Christian mercy for a teenager who has spent the last week being brutalized. I wish I could have helped him without hurting anyone, but it didn't work out that way."

Father Perón's eyes grew sad as they focused on a place beyond Jonathan's shoulder. "In short, you are asking me to do my job," he said. When his eyes returned to meet Jonathan's gaze, he'd clearly made a decision. "Tell me what you would like me to do."

"Tristan needs to sleep and take a bath," Jonathan said. "He could use a decent meal, as well."

"This church has no kitchen."

"But there are kitchens in your parishioners' homes," Jonathan countered. He pulled out a wad of hundred-dollar bills. "I can pay them for their efforts."

"They won't want your money, sir. My parishioners are good people. If they take in your—Tristan, is it?"

A nod.

"If they take in Tristan, they will do it out of the goodness of their hearts."

Jonathan shook his head. "I insist. The people here have so little. I don't want us to be a burden."

Father Perón smiled. "Unless you feel that we might make a phone call."

Jonathan let the comment hang. It was what it was.

Perón said, "And might I presume that if your money could buy silence, that would be okay?"

Jonathan hiked a shoulder and smiled back. "That would be fine with me, yes."

"You have far more to fear from the people you cannot see than from those you can. Those families out there at the *fútbol* field will do Tristan no harm. Most don't even have phones. But those businesses you passed down the hill do have phones, and while we peasants pay the drug lords, some of those businessmen are paid by them. It is not safe for you here."

"Just a meal, then," Jonathan bargained. "And some supplies. Enough food and water for a few days, and as much gasoline as you can spare."

Father Perón regarded Jonathan for a long time before he spoke. "I'll ask the parishioners to feed you and allow you to bathe. Perhaps some fresh clothes as well. You need to change your appearances, yes?"

"All things considered, I don't think that matters much."

"Perhaps not for you—I could clothe you in a dress and you would still look like a soldier—but Tristan appears to have no clothes."

Jonathan decided not to explain about the blood, and to accept the offer. "I insist on paying," he said.

"As they are part of the church's charity stores, I will gladly accept."

"Excellent," Jonathan said. Then he hesitated.

"There's more?" Perón asked.

"Well, yes, sir, there is," Jonathan said. "That Toyota out there belonged to the terrorists who started all this. Assuming, as I believe we both are, that the original attackers are friends, not foes, of the local officials, I'd rather not spend any more time than necessary driving a vehicle that they'll be looking for."

Perón gave a patient smile. "That was a lot of words, Mr. Harris. Can you state your desire more simply?"

"Sure," Jonathan said. "I want to buy your car."

Father Perón coughed out a laugh. Clearly, it was not what he'd been expecting. "I don't own a car," he said. "The diocese owns the car."

"What kind of car is it?"

"It's not for sale."

Jonathan's eyes flashed. "Let's be honest with each other, shall we? Everything is for sale. Every*one* is for sale. The only variable is price. What kind of car, Father?"

"It's a three-year-old Nissan Pathfinder," Perón said. "And it's not for sale."

"I'll pay you one hundred thousand dollars for it," Jonathan said. "Cash."

Perón's jaw dropped.

"But I need gasoline, too," Jonathan said. "Ten twenty-liter cans. Enough to get me to the American border."

Perón furrowed his brow as he thought through the opportunity that had just been presented to him. "You understand that the monies you pay go to the parish, yes? Not to me personally."

"I would never suspect otherwise," Jonathan said. And since he wasn't spending his own money, he couldn't have cared less. "You should think of this as a unique opportunity."

"Well put," Perón said. "Ours is an impoverished parish with many charitable needs."

"Indeed," Jonathan said. It's not often that you get to watch the process of rationalization in real time. "So, we have a deal?" He extended his hand.

"The gasoline will cost you another hundred thousand dollars," Perón said. "Cash."

At first, Jonathan was stunned. Then he erupted in laughter, throaty and guttural. "Father Perón, I like your style. Go for the gusto, right?" He reemphasized his waiting hand. "Two hundred and twenty five thousand dollars it is."

Perón started to shake hands, but then the hand paused in midair. "Two hundred," he corrected.

Jonathan winked. "Hey. I'm a sucker for a charitable cause."

CHAPTER ELEVEN

Jackie filled Abrams in on the details of the cyber attack, pausing every few sentences to let the raucous boor vent his derisive laughter.

When she was done, Abrams said, "Holy hell, Madre. Your shit pile just keeps getting deeper and deeper, doesn't it?" And then he laughed again. Everything Jackie said was a giant joke to him. "How the hell am I going to keep your ass off the gurney in the lethal injection room if you keep screwing up like this?"

In her mind, she could see his big frame with his gray hair and his bushy mustache. That threatening air about him that permeated everything he did and every word he spoke.

"It's your own fault, you know," Abrams pressed. "I told Mr. Hainsley just this afternoon that it was a mistake for you to overreach. It's not enough for you to be three-million greedy, you needed to be six-million greedy. How many friggin' pink limousines do you need, anyways?"

Never in her adult life had anyone spoken to her as Abrams did, and never before would she have tolerated it. She'd learned, though, that she needed to endure, because Abrams was her connection to the practicalities that governed the dark side of humanity.

And he wasn't done. "I hope that sixteen-year-old was hung like a stallion, lady, and sent you to the moon with orgasms. Otherwise, I can't imagine how all of this was worth it."

"He was seventeen!" she snapped. "And he said he was eighteen. I am not a pedophile." And he had indeed been hung like a stallion, and a more tender, sensitive soul never walked the earth. But no one cared about such details.

"Tomato, to*mah*to," Abrams said. "It's still a stinkin' shit pile."

"Enough, Mr. Abrams," she snapped. "Must you take such pleasure in your work?"

"You can't even call it work if you have fun at it, Madre. But let's talk about what kind of special shovel we can build to make that pile smaller."

The scatological metaphors had long ago grown tiresome. "First tell me what you think it all means," Jackie said.

"I can't say for sure, but there's a good chance it means that somebody is putting the right pieces together. That's bad for you and your board members."

"It's bad for you, too, Mr. Abrams."

"Probably not, actually. You must have figured out by now that my name's not really Abrams. My client isn't really Dennis Hainsley, either. They can trace all that to ground, and they got nothing. What are the chances that somebody called the cops on you?"

Jackie switched to her wireless headset and paced her office as she spoke. When she got to the window, she traced the pleats of the Belgian linen drapes with her finger. "I can't imagine who," she said. "Outside of a very small group, no one even knows that the children were taken." A thought flashed through her mind, triggering a gasp. "Oh, my goodness. When the bodies were found, were the families notified?"

"Negative," Abrams said. "The bodies were found by the right people. Nobody's gonna know anything about them."

She stopped pacing. "You're planning to repatriate the remains, aren't you?"

"Repatriate!" Abrams laughed. "Who the hell uses words like that? What, you walk around with a friggin' dictionary? No, we're not going to *repatriate* the bodies. We're not even gonna return them. We're gonna burn them so no one will ever know they were there."

"But you can't," Jackie declared. "The families!"

"Are you friggin' kidding me? Now you're worried about the families? Holy shit, Madre, you really are a piece of work." Another long laugh.

Jackie Mitchell hated this man. Hated everything he stood for, and hated herself for ever being persuaded to go along. She was tempted to remind him of his promises that no one would be harmed, but she knew that her words would be met with more laughter. She was tired of the laughter. And the thought of those young men and women's bodies being burned, no doubt without even rudimentary Christian services, made her stomach churn. It just got worse and worse.

Abrams regained control. "I gotta tell you, then, if it ain't the cops that are comin' at you, then chances are it's the targets that are on the way. I don't really know who these guys are, but I know people who've crossed them in the past, and frankly, Madre, you'd be better off if it was the cops. Give me a second to think this through."

Again, she could see his face in her mind. He had a tendency to rub his mouth with his fingers when he was steeped in thought.

"Okay, here's what I'm gonna do," Abrams said. "I'm gonna lean on a friend to beef up your security forces there. Give you some real professional talent."

"We have a security force," Jackie said.

"No, you don't. You've got rent-a-cops who hang out in your lobby and look important. The guys I'm sending over actually know what they're doing."

"What are they going to do when they get here?" Jackie asked. "I mean, what will they, you know, *do*?"

A beat passed in silence. "My God, Madre, you really don't get it, do you? You helped us try to kill two very, very dangerous men. Only it didn't work. The fat lady hasn't sung yet, but if we don't stop them, these very dangerous men are gonna declare war. If they've figured out that you're connected to it all—and I'm guessing that if they've followed the trail to the donors, then they've figured it out—your Crystal Palace is gonna be like the modern-day Omaha Beach. Are you following me?"

Again, it was important to make sure that all terms were properly defined. "You're saying that they're going to seek revenge."

"That's one way to put it," Abrams said. "Only last time I saw these guys *seek revenge*, they burned close to a hundred acres and killed a couple dozen people. That's more than your standard revenge, don't you think?"

As her knees went weak, Jackie sat on the edge of

her desk, in the process knocking over three pictures of her standing with as many presidents of the United States. "Oh my good Lord," she said.

"Well, he'd be good to have on your side," Abrams mocked, "but I'm betting He's gonna let you ride this one out without Him. If these folks bring you a war, I think you should have some soldiers to fight back with. That's what I'm gonna send you. They should be there in the morning."

It was all more than Jackie could process. Might there be violence here? In this holy place? Surely not.

"You still there, Madre?"

"Yes, Mr. Abrams, I'm still here."

"Good, 'cause I got one more bit of advice for you: If this shit doesn't get straightened out, it's time to have a rearview mirror installed on your forehead."

The church kept its truck in a makeshift garage—a cross between a barn and a shed—in the far northwest corner of the property. Boxers had moved the rickety Toyota to the yard next to the barn, and Jonathan worked with him to transfer their gear from the Toyota to the Pathfinder. The jerricans of gasoline took up far more room than anything else. Tristan was off with his host family, and while that instilled some element of unease in Jonathan, it was nice to be shed of the kid for a while.

"Okay, Boss," Boxers said, "so now we've got a new vehicle. What are we going to do with it?" He carried two fifty-pound rucksacks as if they were briefcases.

Jonathan laughed. "Here's where the plan gets a little fuzzy."

"You don't have a clue, do you?" Boxers joined him in the laughter.

"We actually have a contact now. In Ciudad Juárez. Her name is Maria Elizondo."

"Where does this name come from?" Big Guy asked.

"Wolverine via Special Friend via Mother Hen."

Boxers laughed louder. "One day, I want to see a transcript of my life. Even I am shocked that all this shit makes sense to me. Who, pray tell, is Maria Elizondo?"

Jonathan filled him in on the details relayed from Irene Rivers.

Boxers threw the rucks onto the backseat, leaving just enough room for their PC's narrow ass. "Does Ms. Elizondo know we're coming?" he asked.

"Probably not. But we bring the offer of asylum if she shows us the way to the secret tunnels she claims to know about."

"Wonderful. So all we have to do is convince her to believe a couple of random gringos. What could possibly go wrong?"

"Suppose I promise to let you shoot someone?" Jonathan quipped. "Will that make you feel better?"

"Don't tease me," Boxers joked back. "What about new IDs?"

Jonathan shrugged. "If this works, we won't need them. And if it doesn't work, we *really* won't need them."

Boxers turned serious as he dumped the last of the duffels onto the floor of the Pathfinder. "We're putting a lot of faith in someone we've never heard of."

"No," Jonathan corrected. "We're putting a lot of faith in Wolverine, who's never let us down." It was a statement of fact, but Boxers' larger point was undeniable. Trust did not come easily to either one of them. After the events of today, it was an especially rare commodity.

"So, all we have to do is cross a thousand miles of jungle and desert," Boxers said. "And after that, we get to the hard part." The center of Mexico was much like the center of Nevada—a lot of hot, sandy rolling nothingness.

"Something like that," Jonathan agreed. Boxers sounded cranky, but Jonathan knew that he loved a good adventure. "It'll be dark in twenty or thirty minutes. We'll give Tristan an hour or two to clean up and grab some food, then we'll head out."

Boxers scowled as he ran numbers through his head. "You know that's thirty or forty hours of driving time, right? Divided by ten hours of darkness each night, that's four days, Dig. That's a lot of time for the bad guys to get their shit together. The last five hundred miles or so will be through the desert. That means we'll be *really* exposed."

Jonathan wasn't hearing anything he didn't already know. "I thought about going to the coast and finding a boat, but once we get close to the U.S. shore, the Coasties will be all over us."

"How's that different from a land crossing? I mean if Maria What's-her-face turns out to be a bust?"

"Uncle Sam doesn't have radar deployed along land. Terra firma leaves us with more options to duck and dodge. And if Maria Elizondo turns out to be a dead end, we'll have to go back to the original plan and find us a forger."

Boxers crossed his arms and leaned back against the

side of the truck, his legs crossed in front of him. "You figuring to drive at night and hunker down during the day?"

"Exactly," Jonathan said. "I think it's foolish to assume that someone in this village isn't going to turn us in. We took out their ability to make a landline call, and I don't think there's a useable cell tower within twenty miles, but there's still shortwave and God knows what else. Father Perón made it abundantly clear that he doesn't think that we're safe here, and that the longer we're around, the more danger we pose to the villagers. I want to be well-gone before any of that happens."

Boxers shrugged. "Maybe we should just plow straight through and take our chances. The less time in country, the better our chances, right?"

"Depends. There are a lot of moving parts to this thing. The closer we get to the border, the more surveillance there is. I'm not sure it's in our best interests to get there before Mother Hen and Lady Justice have had a chance to work out what's really going on here. I know that you won't go to jail without a fight—"

"Got that right."

"—and I know that Wolverine doesn't want us in custody, either. Meanwhile, we've got to assume that there's a shoot-on-sight order out there for us here in Mexico."

"So let's just plow through and take our chances," Boxers said.

It was a fair argument, Jonathan thought. The toughest roads were going to be through the jungle. Once they hit the desert stretches of Chihuahua they'd be able to haul ass. Using night vision, they could haul ass invisibly. "Okay," he said. "I say we drive hard and long to put as much space as possible between us and this place. Under the cover of the jungle, I don't see a problem driving in the daytime. When we get to the desert, we pull out all the stops. That'll give the home team two days to untie the other end of the knot."

Boxers sealed the deal with a nod. "Done," he said. Then: "Who do you think is trying to screw us?"

"According to Mother Hen, Wolverine thinks she knows." He caught Boxers up on all that he had learned through Dom's chat with Irene.

"Unbelievable," the Big Guy said when he was done. "So that asshole Ponder is diddling me from the grave. Man, I knew I should have killed him twice."

CHAPTER TWELVE

As Tristan's hosts led him into their house, the father flipped the light switch on. Tristan was surprised to see that it still worked, but then remembered that Scorpion had killed the telephones, not the power. The mother gestured to a cane-back chair that was pulled up to a four-place wooden table. As far as he could tell, the tiny house consisted only of two rooms—the kitchen, which was just inside the front door, and a dark living room on the far side of an archway.

She nodded to Tristan. "I am Dorotea," she said. "This is my husband Roberto—"

The man nodded, but he did not offer his hand.

"—And this is our daughter Rebecca. She is fifteen."

Fifteen my ass, Tristan didn't say. *She's equipped like she's eighteen.* He tried not to be a perv and stare, but the girl had the kind of chest that was hard to ignore. He found himself becoming aroused by the oscillating breasts beneath her T-shirt, and tried to think of something else. He was in enough trouble already; the last thing he needed was to piss off her already-grumpy father by pitching a tent in his underwear while ogling jailbait.

"My name is Tristan," he said. He sat in the chair, and Rebecca sat opposite him. She smiled. Constantly.

"Father Perón tells us that you are in trouble," Dorotea said. "What kind of trouble would that be?"

"I, um, don't think I'm supposed to talk about that," he said. Fear grabbed a fistful of his guts. Why hadn't anyone prepared him for this question?

"Yet we are supposed to feed you," Roberto said. "This seems unfair, does it not?"

Actually, it did. "I just think I'm not supposed to say anything. If you knew, you'd be in danger."

"Are we not in danger already?" Dorotea used a hand pump to fill two five-gallon cook pots with water, and hefted them onto the stove, which she lit with a wooden match after cranking on the gas.

"Of course we are," Roberto said. "This boy and his friends have placed us in danger."

"His name is Tristan, Papa."

Big tits, a hot smile, and now she was defending him. Tristan prayed that he wouldn't have to stand up and reveal that which was standing up.

"Where are your clothes?" Roberto asked. "And why is there blood on your arms and legs?"

Tristan's stomach seized again. How do you explain blood without triggering something akin to panic? "I, um . . ." It was the best he could do.

Dorotea took stuff from the refrigerator and started preparing dinner. She fired up some other burners on the stove, and the kitchen filled with the rich aroma of spicy food. "Are you a killer, Mr. Tristan?" she asked.

The fist in Tristan's gut tightened more.

"You're being rude," Rebecca said. "Tristan is our guest. Can't you see that he doesn't want to talk about this?"

Roberto pressed on. "Tell me, Tristan. How can it be that in these troubled times, a boy as young as you can look as if he's seen so much violence?"

Tristan cleared his throat. "It's very . . ." He searched for the correct word in Spanish. "Complicated."

Roberto pulled out the chair to Tristan's right and sat down. "I'm sure it is," he said. "What simple solution could there possibly be for such a thing?"

The heat of the man's glare was unbearable.

"Papa, you're frightening him."

Roberto didn't reply, but Tristan guessed that frightening him was very much a part of the plan.

"Tell us what happened to you, Tristan."

Tristan opened his mouth to answer—to say something, probably a lie—but then his voice wouldn't work. Out of nowhere, completely without warning, he found his lip trembling. His vision blurred and the current reality of accommodating hosts was replaced with the old, far more vivid reality of Miss James being raped and murdered. He remembered the look in that soldier's eyes on the bus when he was going to murder him.

Then he remembered how Scorpion's face filled his field of view. He remembered the blue eyes and the calm tone. These men had sacrificed everything to deliver him from certain death.

Tristan was not going to betray all of that just for a meal.

"I can't tell you that," he said.

*   *   *

With the Pathfinder loaded up and ready to go, Jonathan and Boxers sat on the steps of the church where they could see the incoming routes and ate MREs from the supplies in their rucks. They both went Italian—Jonathan with ravioli and Boxers with spaghetti.

Boxers said, "So, what happens when we escort this Maria Elizondo babe across the border and she gets asylum?"

"I don't know," Jonathan confessed. "Special Friend thinks that Wolverine is depending on her testimony to bury the guy who got us into this. A senior spook named Trevor Munro."

"Agency, right?"

"Correct."

"And he's tied to Colombian drug money."

Jonathan hesitated, wanting to capture the nuance of it, as passed along by Venice and Dom. "He's tied to a lot of drug money. Enter Felix Hernandez. Apparently, our time in Colombia cost him a boatload of cash, and he blames Munro and the Agency for it."

Boxers coughed out a laugh. "They *wish*. The Agency could never pull off as cool an op as we did. Not in Central America, anyway. All the good spooks are working the Sandbox now." Sandbox meant the Middle East.

"Perception is reality, Big Guy. So Hernandez is putting pressure on Munro, who, coincidentally, is in line for a big promotion in Langley. This Elizondo lady is Wolverine's key to a case that will take care of all of it."

Boxers' expression darkened. "You're talking courtrooms and lawyers."

"Exactly."

"After all this, I think he deserves worse than that."

"What do you have in mind?" Jonathan asked, as if he didn't already know.

"I think he needs some *special* attention."

Jonathan waved him away. "We're not vigilantes."

Boxers made a puffing sound with his lips. "Easy on the *we* shit, pal. The plan sucks."

"Duly noted," Jonathan said. He could think of no greater waste of time than getting crosswise with Boxers when he was in one of his bloodlusts.

"Suppose Wolverine is wrong." Boxers said. "Suppose all that financing shit is a coincidence? What happens then? We'd have unidentified enemies lurking out there."

"You know what I think about coincidences," Jonathan said. "If we start citing possible enemies, the list gets really long really fast. Frankly, at this moment, the list is operationally irrelevant."

Boxers thought about that for a few seconds. "Oh, I don't know. I think people's efforts to kill me are always relevant."

"Fair enough. But at the end of the day, we still have to get that kid home." He looked at his watch. "Do you think he's had enough time to eat and bathe?"

Boxers laughed. "I dunno. He was pretty rank."

Jonathan decided to give him ten more minutes.

* * *

Dinner was a quiet, unfriendly affair. Tristan knew that they were pissed at his silence, and they rewarded it with an icy silence of their own.

All except for Rebecca, who seemed to be on his side. She said so with her eyes.

The meat was pretty good. He thought it was chicken—okay, he *prayed* it was chicken, forcing himself to ignore all the possible alternatives that people said tasted like chicken—and it came with rice and beans and a vegetable that he'd never tasted before, and hoped that he'd never taste again. He forced himself to eat slowly, in part because he knew how long it had been since his stomach had seen real food and he didn't want to barf it all up in front of his hosts, but mostly because the Gonzalezes ate slowly. Given all that had transpired since he'd last seen kindness, the last thing he wanted to do was insult people by being gluttonous.

But Jesus, the vegetables were just plain awful. Still, he choked them down. Surely, there'd be brownie points awarded somewhere for that.

When the meal was done, Rebecca cleared the dishes, refusing Tristan's offers to help, and Dorotea single-handedly wrestled the big pots of water one at a time over to a small porcelain claw-foot tub that had escaped his notice in the corner of the kitchen and poured them in.

"For you," Dorotea said in Spanish.

Apparently, this was for him to take a bath. A new terror arrived. He was supposed to get naked in front of all these people? At the thought, the tent reappeared in his undershorts. An image flashed through his mind of Rebecca soaping him down, and in that instant, his ability to stand without embarrassment disappeared. Again.

"I promise we will not peek," Dorotea said, apparently reading his thoughts. Her smile told him that she *truly* read his thoughts. "Come, Rebecca."

Yeah, cum, Rebecca.

God, did I really just think that?

Thirty seconds later, he was alone in the kitchen. He considered the option of ignoring the bath, but when sanity overtook him, he realized that he smelled like a team of horses.

Moving hesitantly, he rose from his chair and walked to the tub. Having witnessed the heft of the water, he was shocked to see how two potfuls barely covered the bottom—would barely cover his bottom.

He stripped quickly and lowered himself into the tub, taking comfort in the fact that the lip of the tub extended above his shoulders. The feel of hot water against his flesh brought a level of comfort that shocked him. It was as if someone had injected a shot of civilization into an existence that was only evil and dark. He found the soap in the dish and started the process of washing away the nightmare.

By the time he was done, the water was the color of rust. And cold.

He'd nearly fallen asleep when the door banged open, revealing the enormous hulk of Big Guy filling the frame. "Quit playing with yourself, kid," he said. "It's time to go." Then he left as abruptly as he'd arrived.

In a flash of panic, Tristan looked down at his lap, just to be sure. "I wasn't playing with myself," he said to the empty room.

When he was dried and dressed—the family had left him a new pair of shorts and a T-shirt, just inside the door—he stepped out of the kitchen out into the night.

"Do you feel better?" Dorotea asked.

"He smells better," Roberto said. The comment drew angry glares from both his wife and daughter, but he clearly didn't care. He headed back into the living room.

"I do feel better, yes," Tristan said. "Thank you all for taking me in."

Dorotea grabbed his hands in hers. "Go with God," she said.

Tristan felt his throat thicken. "I hope so," he said.

Rebecca was next. "I hope you don't get killed," she said. She flashed him a shy smile, and then turned away.

As Jonathan watched the good-byes between Tristan and his hosts, and Boxers cranked the engine on the Pathfinder, Father Perón stepped up on Jonathan's right. "You have a difficult trip ahead of you," the priest said. "You know that, right?"

"Father, when you get right down to it, just about everything I do is hard as hell. We'll make it."

"He is very young," Perón said, nodding toward Tristan.

"He's seventeen," Jonathan said. "I've commanded soldiers his age. They always surprise me with their toughness in the end."

"After years of training, no?" Perón countered. "And the training comes only after a stated desire to be a warrior."

Jonathan planted his fists on his hips and gave the priest a hard look. "Father, if you're here to make a point, how about you just get to it?"

"These people who are chasing you," Perón said. "These drug lords. Very, very bad people. Every one of us has suffered at their hands. Every one of my parishioners will be terrified of retribution."

Jonathan said nothing, let the words carry their own weight.

"I hope that you will forgive the betrayal that no doubt lies in your future," Perón said.

Ah, so that was it. "Father, we all make choices. Some are courageous, and some are not. You and your parishioners have shown us only kindness. When this is all over, I'm confident that that's all I will remember."

CHAPTER THIRTEEN

As they climbed into the Pathfinder and closed the doors, Jonathan inventoried their situation. They had plenty of water and gasoline, adequate food, and roughly eight hundred rounds of ammunition between them, counting all the weapons. Throw in the supply of GPCs—general purpose charges, blocks of C-4 with det cord tails that were good for so many things—a couple of claymores and assorted other toys, and they should be able to sustain themselves in an all-out firefight for at least a few minutes.

With the engine started, Boxers fitted a pair of NVGs—night vision goggles—over his eyes, but Jonathan stopped him. "Let's save those for the desert," he said. "Or for an emergency. I don't want to run out of juice. Remember, we don't have any spares."

He could tell that Boxers wanted to argue—ownership of the night was an operator's leading advantage over the bad guys—but the facts were the facts. The Big Guy grudgingly turned on the headlights and headed down the road they'd marked on the GPS.

Boxers announced, "Next stop: The middle of friggin' nowhere."

* * *

Tristan settled into the corner where the seat met the back door, and tried to find a comfortable position among the cargo. The smell of gasoline from the jerricans on deck behind him was slightly nauseating, but he hoped that he'd stop noticing it after a while. He closed his eyes and tried to imagine a better place.

Instead of a better place, though, he thought about home. He wondered if his mom had told the family that he'd been kidnapped. Isolde, his older sister, would certainly be worried, but twelve-year-old Siegfried probably wouldn't understand. What responsible parent would saddle his kids with such ridiculous names? It was his dad's inside joke to the world. A fourth-generation American, his father, Richard Wagner, had thought it would be fun to name the kids after operas written by the nineteenth-century composer of the same name yet different pronunciation.

Tristan had never wanted to come on this stupid trip in the first place. In fact, he'd already arranged a cool job as a ticket taker at the local Cineplex when Pastor Mitchell announced this missionary opportunity. She was always announcing that sort of thing, so Tristan hadn't paid much attention at the time. When they got home from services, though, his mom was way spun up by the opportunity to do the Lord's work for the poor people of Mexico.

"If it's so important," Tristan had argued at the time, "why don't *you* go? I'll stay home and take care of Ziggy." See what happens when you start with a name like Siegfried? It becomes an even stupider name like Ziggy.

His mom hadn't taken well to the backtalk. Once

she finished bitching about his attitude, she dialed in to the need for him to expand the extracurricular chapter of his high school résumé. How else, she asked, could he expect to get into the Ivy League?

He hadn't yet broken it to her that he had no interest in working that hard for a piece of paper when nearly identical pieces of paper could be obtained from Buttscratch University in Bumfuck, Idaho. All things in time.

And that night wasn't the time. Thinking back on it, he wasn't sure he'd ever actually said yes; but he had never said no either, so *voilà*. A living nightmare.

He wondered if Mom's excitement at sending him to Mexico wasn't tied to just getting rid of him for a while. He'd become something of a pain in the ass in the past few years—ever since Dad's cancer—but from where he sat, pains in the ass were in the eyes of the beholder. As Mom got more and more enraptured by God (*Thank you very much for taking my mother away, Pastor Mitchell*), she'd made it her mission to keep Tristan from having any fun.

And come on, let's be honest. Tristan wasn't a druggie and he wasn't a boozer. He'd never even gotten a stern lecture from the principal, for God's sake. Look up "good kid" in the dictionary. You'll find Tristan's picture.

But that wasn't enough. Rachel Wagner—Mom— had taken it upon herself to monitor his email and the books he read. In the case of the latter, a single bad word rendered a book the work of the devil and it was therefore banned from the house. *Hell* was first and foremost a bad word, by the way, not a place of eternal damnation. Oops, *damnation* was a bad word, too. See how ridiculous this shit got?

As for his emails, Mom expected him to *not use it*. No shit. That was her solution. His time would be far better spent reading the Bible and surrounding himself with the wonders of the Lord's love. Tristan didn't even know what that meant.

Isolde, meanwhile, knew a losing battle when she saw it, and decided to stay on the sidelines. *Just do what Mom says.* Helluva battle cry, Sis. And brave, too, being fifteen miles away with her live-in boyfriend.

Tristan had actually tried to live with all the restrictions for a while, but it didn't take long for him to start identifying with Carrie White from the Stephen King book. Having already been born into Ichabod Crane's body, and carrying the name of some German knight, he didn't need any other fictional metaphors in his life, thank you very much.

So he started to push back. Hard. In so doing, he discovered that Mom's parenting weaponry was pretty much limited to guilt speeches and crying jags. As a teenager, you can adapt to those pretty quickly, but parents adapt, too. She started invoking Dad's memory—specifically, how disappointed he must be in his son.

So Tristan adapted again. The secret to success, it turned out, was simply to hide everything and lie like a rug. It works, he figured out, because deep down inside, she didn't want to know the truth. As long as he had the decency to pretend, she would never look past the thin outer crust that his private life had become.

Isolde had moved out by the time the craziness started, so she was totally disengaged, but Tristan worried about Ziggy. He wasn't more than a few years past Santa Claus, so he took a lot of Mom's bullshit as gospel—literally—and it was already beginning to get him beaten up in school. Tristan did what he could to serve as a sanity buffer, but next year he had an appointment with Buttscratch University, and when that train pulled into the station, there was no power on earth that would keep him from climbing aboard.

As the time for this trip had approached, he'd talked himself into believing that maybe it would be a good time. He did, in fact, spend too much time on his computer, whether with surreptitious emails or games—*truly the devil's work*—so he'd suspended disbelief just enough to give it a try.

There were supposed to be more people than this on the trip back then. Bill Georgen was supposed to be here, and so was Bobby Cantrell. Neither were what he'd call good friends, but they were decent enough, and they'd shared a few laughs over the years. A week before the trip, though, both of them dropped out, leaving him alone with two jocks, a diva, and a cheerleader, all of whom seemed far more attached to the party potential than the doing of God's work on Earth.

When Tristan had found out about the change in the cast, he'd considered petitioning his mom for a reprieve, but abandoned the thought before even trying it.

It wasn't a battle worth fighting.

So here he was, the lone survivor, sitting among guns and explosives and gasoline, in the company of people whose primary talent seemed to be killing people. With his eyes closed, he could see the carnage all over again, the white flashes of bone against the crimson background of extruded tissue. If he allowed himself, he could even smell the blood. *Who even knew that blood* had *a smell?*

"You okay back there, kid?" the driver asked. Big Guy.

"Tristan. Not kid. Tristan. And no, not especially. To be really honest, I'm scared shitless."

"Good," Scorpion said.

"Excuse me?"

He turned in his seat to look back at him. "The thickest streams of bullshit flow from terrified people who claim not to be scared."

"Does that mean that you're scared, too?"

Scorpion thought about it before answering. "Scared's not the right word," he said.

"Frightened?" Tristan helped. "Terrified? Paralyzed with fear?"

Scorpion laughed. It was a hearty, happy sound that showed genuine amusement. "None of the above," he said. "Big Guy and I have been doing this stuff for a long time. It's more like that feeling you get before you walk out on stage to give a speech. Anticipation, I guess."

Tristan smiled. "You must give some wild speeches, dude. Seriously, what do you think our chances are?"

"Chances are of what?"

"Getting home."

The humor drained from Scorpion's expression. "Remember that you asked," he said. "And that I promised not to lie to you."

Tristan felt the wash of dread.

"None of this is going to be easy," Scorpion went on. "People want us dead, apparently in a bad way. If they want it badly enough, they'll put bounties out on us, dangling cash for the person who kills us, or at least turns us in."

"Holy shit," Tristan breathed.

"While we've got a thousand miles to travel through some pretty hostile terrain. Then, when we finally get to where we're going, it looks like we're going to have to be smuggled out of the country."

Boxers growled, "Christ, Scorpion. You're depressing *me*."

"Well, those are just the risks, Big Guy. Now, on the positive side—"

"There's a *positive* side?" Tristan interrupted.

"There's always a positive side," Scorpion said. "On the positive side, these are by no means the darkest odds I've ever faced, and I'm still here. Plus, I have a team of colleagues back home who are moving heaven and earth to help us work out the details."

"Mother Hen?" Tristan asked.

"And others," Scorpion confirmed. "You eavesdrop well. You'll make a good intel officer one day."

Tristan assumed that to mean intelligence officer, and if that was a job that involved shit like this, he wasn't interested.

"Plus," Scorpion said, "be honest with yourself. I know you've seen a lot of trauma and you've lost friends, and I don't mean to take anything away from that. You'll have a whole lifetime to grieve. But ask yourself this: Aren't you living pretty intensely right now? I mean, if you take away the fear and the loss and the pain, can you think of any time in your life that has felt like a bigger adventure?"

Chapter Fourteen

Here it was nearly midnight, and when Captain Ernesto Palma of the Mexican Army's *La Justicia*, or military police, should have been home with his mistress, he was instead in Santa Margarita, investigating the immolation of a telephone substation. The miscreants had used thermite, for heaven's sake. They'd made no attempt even to give the impression of a natural fire. His sources here in the village told him of visitors who'd arrived in a vehicle that fit the description of the very vehicle for which he'd been alerted to be on the lookout. By all accounts, the occupants of that vehicle were American military, and the presence of thermite certainly seemed to back that up.

A second source told him of larger cooperation among the villagers. The sort of cooperation that was always disturbing, if only for its ability to spin out of control. Once you allowed peasants to feel powerful, the first casualty was respect for authority. And once people stopped fearing authority, violence was inevitable.

So here he was, in the unlikeliest of places—a tiny country church—having to mete out discipline to the unlikeliest of people. "Father, be reasonable," Palma said. "The questions I ask are simple to answer. It needn't be this difficult."

Father Perón stood naked at the altar, his hands folded across his privates. It was a supplicant posture, an attempt to mine dignity out of a confrontation that would ultimately allow none. Members of the clergy in general—priests in particular—posed special annoyances for Palma during interrogations. They seemed to feel that the costumes they wore and the deference given to them by their followers earned them a kind of immunity. Palma had seen it so many times that he'd come to expect it. There was a time in his life—his adult life, even—when it might have worked; but that was well before the cartels had started running the country. With all that money to be made, there was precious little room in the world for magical deities and superstition.

Nakedness was in itself a form of torture for some people. The sense of helplessness and exposure went beyond bare flesh, and the more power the individual perceived himself to wield, the more devastating the humiliation. With the clergy, the underlying sexuality of nakedness made it an especially useful tool. Sometimes, being stripped naked was all that it took to glean the information he sought. If more effort was required, then the subject's nudity took on a practical efficiency.

"I cannot answer your questions," Perón said. "The sanctity of the confessional—"

"Please spare me," Palma interrupted. He rolled up the sleeves of his uniform to reveal heavily muscled forearms. "This needn't be complicated, Father. In fact, by embracing the inevitable, you can save us all a lot of time, and yourself a lot of discomfort."

"I am not choosing not to tell you," Perón said. "I *cannot*."

Palma paused, pretending to collect his thoughts. Timing was an important element of interrogation, an element that less experienced soldiers often neglected. Moving slowly prolonged the subject's mental agony. Each additional second of discomfort led the subject a step closer to revealing the information that would bring the return of comfort.

"How did that vehicle end up being stored in your barn, Father?"

"Someone stole the truck that the parish owns," Perón said. "I don't know how that other vehicle got there. I didn't even know that the Pathfinder was missing."

Palma sighed deeply. He was going for the sound of a disappointed parent. "Please don't insult me and disgrace yourself with a lie, Father. Don't disappoint the Lord that way."

"I am not lying," Perón insisted.

"Then who stole it?"

"I have no idea," the priest said. "You must believe me."

So, this was the way it was going to be. Ruis nodded to one of his non-commissioned officers, Sergeant Sanchez, who nodded in return and left the sanctuary. He knew exactly what he was supposed to do.

"I'll make a deal with you, Father," Palma said. He paced at the foot of the altar, measuring his words carefully. "I will start believing you when you start telling the truth."

"But I'm telling—"

"I know about the Yankee missionaries," Palma interrupted. "The two men and the boy. I know that you helped them get away."

Perón's veneer cracked. Not much, and not for long, but for long enough for Palma to know that he'd touched the right nerve. "I don't know what you're talking about."

Another sigh. "You surprise me, Father," he said. "And you disappoint me. For the record, I am not insensitive to your predicament. You committed yourself to a lie, and now you feel compelled to defend it. In your job, you must encounter such dilemmas among your parishioners all the time. Now, I'll ask you again. How did that vehicle get into your garage?"

Perón's posture straightened. He stopped covering himself, and he put his fists on his hips. Palma recognized it as the second or maybe third stage of the interrogation process: rebellion. He'd done this enough that he could even have predicted what the priest was going to say.

Perón didn't let him down. "If you already know the answers, Captain, why is it important even to speak with me?"

"One never has *all* the answers, Father. Each new interview brings an additional detail, a tiny nuance." He paused to allow himself a smile. "But mostly, it's the principle, Father. My employer's business runs on respect, and respect is born of fear. Surely you must know this better than most. Your business runs on the fear of Hell."

"My *business*, as you put it, runs on the love of the

Lord." He started to cover himself again, but aborted the effort.

In Palma's mind, that was a gesture of pure defiance.

"And according to your uniform," Perón continued, "your employer is the United Mexican States."

Palma let those words hang in the air, hoping that their absurdity alone would cause Perón to recant. When he didn't, Palma allowed himself a laugh. A loud, boisterous one. As he climbed the three steps up to the altar, Perón resumed his supplicant pose. Palma came in close, to within inches of the priest's face.

"And who does the United Mexican States work for, Father?"

Without hesitation, and with no waver in his voice, Perón said, "The people."

Palma could feel the fear spilling from this man, and as he did, he found his tolerance for these games diminishing. "The people don't know what they want," he said. "The people are sheep. They line up and wait to be told where to go. Like the rest of the world, we all work for the United States of America—but more specifically, for the drug addicts of the United States of America. More immediately, however, we work for the people who supply the drug addicts."

He moved in so close that their noses nearly touched. He could smell the soap that the priest had used. Ivory. "So let's not fool each other, Father," he said. He'd modulated his voice to a barely audible whisper. "Let's not even try. The political government means nothing in this part of the Mexico. Money rules, and the money is controlled by Mr. Felix Hernandez. It's important to him that intermediaries like me are feared, and through that fear are treated with respect. Are you seeing the circularity of all this, Father?"

Something changed behind Perón's eyes. Finally, there was the fear he'd been waiting for. "So, Father, one more time before you leave me no choice, how did that truck end up in your garage?"

Perón's eyes reddened, and tears balanced on his lids. "Our truck was stolen."

Another deep sigh. "Oh, Father, there comes a point where bravery and foolishness become one."

He turned to another of his noncoms. "I want thirty villagers in here in the next ten minutes. I don't care how you get them. I want ten of them to be children."

Eight minutes later, the church was filled with sleep-starved villagers. Palma's men stood behind them with their weapons at a loose port arms. Their stances were threatening, but the directions of their muzzles were not.

"Thank you for coming on such short notice," Palma said. The crowd before him was mostly dressed, but entirely barefoot. Two or three of the men were bare-chested, and five of the women wore nightclothes that would otherwise never have seen public scrutiny. A few of the children appeared to still be asleep, but Palma forgave that. It was the wailing baby that he could not forgive. With a single glance, he granted special dispensation for the baby and her parents to leave.

"We are here for a difficult task," Palma went on. "Your village had visitors tonight. They are known murderers, and wanted by the police. I asked Father Perón for details, and he refused to give them. Now he has to pay the price."

A man stepped forward from the crowd. Palma recognized him as Roberto Gonzalez. "I know who took the truck," he said.

"Many of you know who took the truck," Palma replied, "Father Perón among them. Even I know the truth of who took the truck. But I need to know it from this man."

The parishioners had difficulty looking at their pastor in this condition. They diverted their eyes.

"Bring the cross forward," Palma ordered.

Sanchez and Corporal Martinez walked up onto the altar to the life-size crucifix and pulled the statue of Jesus from its mountings. They brought the cross downstage and poised it next to Father Perón.

"Please don't do this," the priest whispered. He didn't want to beg in front of his congregation, but neither did he want to suffer the agony that lay ahead for him.

Palma watched the crowd. They were appalled, but they were with him. Palma had found it to be a quirk of human nature that the torture of others served two masters. On the one hand, witnessed agony transferred as a negative—a fear-inducing event—to those who watched, even as it provided a sense of relief that the torture was being endured by someone else, and therefore brought a measure of peace.

Watching others suffer bred fear, and fear brought cooperation. People needed to understand that actions had consequences, and if the consequences were brutal beyond proportion, the cooperation was even more guaranteed.

Because today's victim was a priest—and no matter how jaded to violence a soldier became, there was always a special place in the heart for a man of the cloth—Palma decided to drive the nails himself. With the hardwood cross on the floor, they forced Father Perón to lie with his shoulders at the spot where the horizontal members met the vertical members. Sergeant Sanchez literally sat on the priest's chest to hold him in place while Palma stretched one arm as far out to the side as it would go. Planting a knee on Perón's wrist, he pried open the priest's fingers and pounded the four-inch twenty-penny nail through the flesh of his palm, directly below the space between the second and third knuckles.

That was when the priest screamed for the first time—the moment when the nail pierced his flesh and the oak with the same hammer blow. In Palma's mind the scream was one of fear more than it was one of agony. How much could it hurt, after all? Palma had taken care to avoid bone and tendon, and he'd done this enough to be very skilled.

The wood was harder than Palma had anticipated, though. It took seven hard blows with the carpenter hammer to sink it deeply enough to serve its function. At that, he left half an inch of the nail head exposed so that the villagers could later remove it.

As he moved to the other hand—the priest's left— Father Perón started to spew information. "Two men took the truck," he said. "Three Americans."

"You're giving me information that I already know," Perón said around the nail he had poised between his lips like a cigarette about to be smoked. He pulled on the left arm and kneeled on the wrist.

"I know that they're going to Juárez," Perón said.

Palma pried open the fingers, noting that the priest had rough hands, the hands of a man who was used to physical labor. "How are they getting across the border?"

As he placed the point of the nail against flesh, Father Perón started speaking faster. "Please don't," he said.

Palma raised the hammer high over his head.

"I don't know," the priest blurted. "I swear to all things holy that I don't know."

Palma smiled. The hammer remained poised in the air. "I believe you, Father," he said.

"Thank you."

And then he drove the nail through his hand.

CHAPTER FIFTEEN

Venice lay on the white leather sofa in her office, neither awake nor asleep, waiting for something to happen. As the clock closed in on 9 AM, she recognized that it was time for her to be functional again. Her twelve-year-old son, Roman, had already called to ask if he could go to the pool at Resurrection House—the answer was yes—and she'd already taken her tongue-lashing from Mama Alexander for putting work above family. Mama knew that that was not the case, but sometimes she had a hard time controlling herself. It was as if a lecture was born out of the ether, and it was Mama's mission to make sure it got delivered. And who better to deliver it to than her only daughter?

Beyond the doors to The Cave, Venice heard the sounds of arriving employees. Part of her wanted to greet them—nearly half of them worked for her—but she didn't have the energy. She was closing in on thirty hours without meaningful sleep, and no one needed to witness that.

Dom strode into her office without knocking, looking every bit as exhausted and harried as she. He carried a manila folder in his hand. "I've got it," he said.

Despite the overall exhaustion, he seemed completely energized. "The secret isn't in who the hostages are. The secret is in who they aren't."

Exhaustion was playing tricks on Venice. Dom's statement no doubt made sense, but she had no idea what it meant. She waited for it.

The priest dialed it back, settled himself with a breath. He walked across the office and helped himself to one of the guest chairs near her desk. She rose from the sofa and walked over.

"I'm sorry," Dom said. "I'm so tired I don't even know if I'm speaking in complete sentences."

"That makes two of us." Venice sat at her desk and leaned in, signaling her desire to hear what Dom had to say.

Dom met her halfway. "I pretended I was you last night," he said. "I started searching through the historical record, just trying to find some clue as to who was betraying whom and why. Did you know that there were originally supposed to be seven pilgrims on this trip? Two more than the five who showed up?"

Venice shrugged. She hadn't thought much about it, one way or the other.

Dom opened his folder and extracted a sheet of paper that looked like a printed news story. "This is from three months ago," he said. "A news story from the *Phoenix Sun*. It announces the pilgrimage to Mexico, and in so doing lists seven names. We know who five of them are, but there are two more, as well: Bill Georgen and Bobby Cantrell. Those two apparently dropped out."

Venice scowled. "And?"

"I just thought it was strange," Dom explained. He

pulled another news story out of the folder. "Look at this. Two weeks before the trip, another news story, this one from a local weekly, lists the same kids."

"So, they got sick," Venice said. "Or they lost their nerve. How is this an answer?"

"We're following the money, remember? We're trying to decide if there's a payoff among all those contributions."

"Okay," she said. Good lord, she needed coffee.

Dom settled himself again. "I'm not being clear. I'm sorry. I got to wondering how many people in a church organization would have to know if the pastor sold out a missionary trip. I've no way of knowing that, of course, but I have trouble believing that Reverend Mitchell could truly act on her own in something like this. I'd think there'd have to be a presbytery or a board of governors or something. I can't imagine that there wouldn't be *somebody* in a position of authority who would be involved, if only as a second opinion."

Venice shrugged one shoulder and sort of nodded.

Dom smiled as he handed over the next sheet of paper. "Here's a list of the Board of Governors for the Crystal Palace Cathedral." He waited for Venice to absorb it. Then he helped: "In alphabetical order, you've got Gordon Cantrell, Bobby's father, and Eric Georgen, Bill's father. As coincidences go, how do you like those?"

Venice's eyes grew huge. "They were part of the plot," Venice said.

Dom smiled. "I believe so."

"But why?" Venice asked. "Why would anyone endanger children like this?"

"I've been thinking about that," Dom said. "Maybe in their minds, they *weren't* endangering the children."

"With all respect, Father, they were *kidnapped*."

Dom had obviously thought this out. "Maybe the kidnapping was just part of a show. Maybe they thought that no one would get hurt."

She got it. "Except Jonathan," Venice said.

"Right. Plays to the notion that he was really the target of this thing from the very beginning."

Venice sat back in her chair and tried to take it all in. If Dom was correct—and his theory felt right—the board of directors for one of the most famous churches in the country was funding an effort to have Jonathan and Boxers killed. Digger had the personality and the work history that collected many enemies, but how was it possible for anyone to get this angry at him? And how was it possible that mere money would be enough incentive for Reverend Mitchell to so vastly betray her trust?

"I know what you're thinking," Dom said. "It's not that big a jump from humiliating yourself with an under-age boy to endangering people for money."

Venice was stunned that he'd so closely read her mind. She pressed her hands flat against her temples. "Think about what you're saying, Dom. Think about the depth of the conspiracy."

"I have," he said. "That's why I haven't slept. Beyond the depth of the conspiracy, I think about the breadth of influence. How many people in the world are powerful enough—or wealthy enough—to invest millions of dollars in a charity for the sole purpose of committing this kind of a crime?"

"We don't know that that happened," Venice corrected. "That's the theory, but there's real danger in ignoring other possibilities."

Dom nodded unconvincingly. "Fine. I suppose. But I haven't seen anything yet to convince me—or even make me think seriously—about an alternative scenario. And whoever is that powerful and that wealthy also, according to Wolverine, has the power to influence law enforcement agencies in two countries."

It was almost too much. "You start saying this stuff too loud," Venice said, "and you start sounding like those wackos who've been abducted by aliens."

"We need to talk to the Georgens and the Cantrells," Dom said.

"And ask them what?"

"Get them to tell what they know."

Venice laughed. "Would you tell what you knew if you were them?"

Dom smirked. "Maybe I would if the motivation was strong enough."

"What are you suggesting?"

"I don't know exactly," he confessed. "But these are essentially religious people. They know right from wrong. I'm guessing that they got to this place in their lives via a route that they'd do anything to overturn. Between my psychologist's hat and my priest hat, what do you bet that I can make that happen?"

"I don't think Digger's going to go along with it," Venice said. "Let's let Gail talk to them while she's in Scottsdale."

Dom shook his head. "She's going to play cop with them. That will lock them down. Scare them."

Venice tickled the keys and used Jonathan's GPS

signal to find him on the map, and then fiddled with the imagery from SkysEye to zoom in to see if she could get a peek at their vehicle. She was surprised at how short a distance they had traveled since the last time she checked up on them. It looked like only fifty or sixty miles.

"Father Dom, you know I love you, right? So I say this with all the respect I can muster. Your business isn't about going face-to-face with killers."

He stood. "I'll call you from Scottsdale."

Her eyes snapped up from the screen to see him striding toward the door. "Oh, come on, Dom. Let's at least talk about this."

He waved without looking as he walked through the door.

Venice slammed her desk with the heel of her hand. Digger bred this kind of impulsiveness in his friends and associates, and it drove her crazy.

When the satellite image refreshed, Digger's truck and his team showed up as a hot spot among the blur of tree cover, absent any detail to even indicate that the heat was coming from a vehicle.

Now that she'd found them, she pulled the image back some to reveal more details of their surrounding location. Accessing publicly available geographic data, she was able to superimpose contour lines that revealed them to be on the edge of a steep slope that fell away to the west, their left. That probably explained the slow going.

When the image refreshed again, something had changed. Venice squinted at the screen for a better look, and then it was obvious.

"Oh, no," she said aloud, reaching for the satellite phone. "Oh no, oh no, oh no . . ."

Gail Bonneville had taken the earliest flight out of Washington Dulles and was able to be at the front door of Reverend Jackie Mitchell's Crystal Palace Cathedral when it opened at nine o'clock. Because it was the middle of the week, she didn't have to deal with the flood of parishioners that she would have faced on a Saturday or Sunday, but tourists still flooded in by the busload to *ooh* and *ah* over the ultra-modern icon of Protestant devotion.

The place was huge—easily fifty thousand square feet—constructed of towering glass walls held in place by technology that she didn't begin to understand. The sanctuary—the part you saw on television—was just the very tall first floor of a white skyscraper.

Unlike so many other places she'd seen in real life after coming to know them via television, the Crystal Palace Cathedral was actually larger than she'd expected it to be. Nowhere near the scale of St. Peter's Basilica in Rome—nor as robustly reverential—the Crystal Palace was closer to Gail's vision of Hell than her vision of Heaven.

Entering the giant front doors along with the first wave of tourists, she paused in the massive lobby— really, that was the best name she could call it—and looked around for a place to start. The overall feel of the cavernous front area was more office building than place of worship. Accordingly, she made her way to the security desk, where two uniformed contractors seemed thoroughly engaged in a passionate discussion about the Houston Astros, who, according to the larger of the two, had no business calling themselves a professional baseball franchise.

Try being a Chicago fan, Gail thought. Even after so many consecutive years without any professional sports team that couldn't be vanquished by a marginally talented college squad, the bitterness never faded.

"Excuse me," Gail said. "Where might I find Reverend Jackie Mitchell?"

The smaller of the two regarded Gail with undisguised annoyance. "Who are you?"

"I'm Tess McLain," Gail said, stating her alias of the day aloud for the first time. She pulled out a badge next—the very one she'd used when she'd been sheriff of Samson, Indiana. "But most people call me Sheriff."

The badge had the desired effect, rocking the guards back just enough to give her the psychological edge. "You were about to tell me how to find Reverend Mitchell," she prompted.

The small guard—she could see now that his tag read VOLPE—turned to his buddy, Corbin, who puffed up a bit when he asked, "Do you have an appointment?"

Gail made a show of pulling the badge back closer to her face and looking at it before pivoting it around for the guards to see again. "You see this, right? It's a badge."

"But this isn't your jurisdiction," Volpe said. He seemed proud that he'd read a comic book that mentioned laws. And, you know, stuff.

"Exactly," Gail said. This was all one big bluff that

ran opposed to every oath she'd ever sworn, but
Jonathan's life was at risk. She had no idea what *exactly* would mean in this context, but it sounded good.

Corbin reached for the phone. "I should call up
there first."

"Actually, no," Gail said. She found herself falling
back into her former role all too easily, and this guy
was beginning to piss her off. "You should call up there
after you tell me where Reverend Mitchell's office is."

It was Volpe's turn. "Well, Sheriff, Reverend Mitchell has a full schedule. You pretty much need an appointment to see her."

"Are you her secretaries?" Gail asked.

They recoiled in unison. "No, ma'am."

"So that means that you're not the keepers of her
schedule, right?"

Corbin said, "No, ma'am, we're not. Harriett Burke
is Reverend Mitchell's assistant. She'd have best access
to the pastor's schedule."

"And where might I find Ms. Burke?"

"The pastoral offices are on the fourteenth floor,
but—"

Gail smiled and walked off toward the elevators,
tossing a casual "thank you" over her left shoulder. She
noted that Officer Volpe was reaching for the phone,
and wondered what the next layer of security in a place
like this might actually be.

"Excuse me, Sheriff, but you can't just go there."

Gail didn't slow. Call it the Badge Effect. What were
they going to do? Tackle her? She imagined that there
must be additional security up on the "pastoral floor"—
and what peculiar breed of hubris must there be to even

have such a thing?—but she was confident that she could deal with them

This was the effect that Jonathan Grave had on people, Gail thought. There was a thrill to breaking rules. His was an intoxicating view of the world: a place where justice is held hostage to personal ambition, and where the powerful are neutered by the simple act of individuals exercising their rights.

Once Gail arrived at the elevator lobby, she pressed the up button and waited.

Corbin strutted toward her. "Ma'am. Sheriff. I can't let you go up there."

Gail looked at him and smiled. "I understand that. I apologize for putting you in a difficult position."

"No problem," the guard said, and he started to lead the way back toward the security desk.

Only, Gail didn't follow.

"Ma'am?"

"Yes?"

"I said I can't let you go up there."

The elevator arrived. "I know," Gail said. She stepped inside. "And I apologized for putting you in a difficult position."

As the elevator doors started to close, the guard thrust his hand out to stop them, and the doors rebounded. Gail locked eyes with the guard, daring him to make the next move.

"I'm a law enforcement officer," Gail said after the door rebounded for the third time. "How much harm can I cause?"

CHAPTER SIXTEEN

In calculating the travel time, Jonathan had woefully overestimated the quality of the roads through this part of the world. Mud holes, nonexistent pavement, tight switchbacks, and steep drops made thirty miles an hour feel like speeding. And the heat. Good God, the heat. During the ten hours they'd been at it, they'd encountered maybe a dozen other vehicles, split more or less evenly between those that came at them and those that were anxious to pass from behind.

For Jonathan, who'd never been a great fan of high places—parachute jumps notwithstanding—the sunlight made the trip more harrowing than it had been during the night. It's one thing to know intellectually that the road dropped away, but something else entirely to see how far away the landing spot would be.

"How are you holding out, Big Guy?" he asked.

"I can do this all day," he said. "We're gonna need to stop again to fill up on gas soon."

"How much longer?"

"The computer in the dash tells me sixty miles, but the way this engine's screaming, I don't know that I trust the computer."

"Well, this isn't the place," Jonathan said. "Next time the road flattens out or widens up, we'll take care of it."

A chirping sound drew his attention to the Pathfinder's center console. The satellite phone. "Oh, this can't be good," he said. He pressed the connect button. "Hello."

He knew it would be Venice even before she said a word. She was literally the only person not in the Pathfinder who had the number. "Scorpion, we have a problem. SkysEye shows a military vehicle approaching you from the opposite direction."

Jonathan sat up straighter in his seat, and motioned for Boxers to stop the truck. "What kind of military vehicle?"

Boxers made a growling sound. "This just friggin' gets better and better."

"I can tell you that it's green, it's bigger than you, and that it's a vehicle," Venice reported. "Sorry, Scorpion, but that's the best I can do. It just happened to be passing through a clearing when SkysEye took its picture."

"Stand by," Jonathan said. He caught Boxers up on the details. "I'm open to suggestions," he said.

"I got nothin'," the Big Guy said. "I sure as hell can't turn around here. I lay myself at the altar of your superb leadership." That was Big Guy speak for *Tell me what you want to do.*

Jonathan surveyed the surroundings, hoping that the terrain itself might give him some ideas. On his left, the heavy underbrush was unrelenting, and on his right, the roadway fell off into a valley of rolling green that would have been beautiful if featured in a *National*

Geographic photo spread, but was in fact an ugly problem that put them at a tactical disadvantage. Anytime you find yourself in a position where your only escape routes involve the same ones your enemies are using to attack, you can pretty much anticipate a really bad day.

He keyed his mike. "How far away are they?"

"Call it a half mile," she said. "But they're headed downhill. I give you three minutes."

Shit.

"What's going on?" Tristan asked from the backseat. His voice sounded thick with sleep.

"Park it, Big Guy," Jonathan said. "Tristan, out. Now."

"What are we doing?" Tristan squeaked.

"Yeah, what are we doing?" Boxers matched the tone perfectly.

Jonathan reached to the pouch on his vest behind his right shoulder and turned on his radio. "I'm switching to radio, Mother Hen," he said, and then he closed the sat phone and slipped it into a different pouch. To Tristan, he said, "There's another vehicle approaching, and I don't want to be trapped in here."

"Who is it?"

"Just get out and stay with me," Jonathan said. "Big Guy, slide me my ruck when we get out, and keep the ransom bag with you."

"What's *happening*?"

"We're taking cover." Jonathan shouldered his door open and opened Tristan's door from the outside. "Walk or be carried," he said. "Decide."

Tristan's first effort to hurry out of the backseat was thwarted by his still-buckled seat belt. His second effort did the trick.

In Jonathan's ear, Venice said, "Scorpion, the picture just refreshed. They're on top of you. Thirty seconds, max."

Boxers slid Jonathan's rucksack across the hood of the car to Jonathan, and then headed south to the steep side of the roadway. Jonathan led Tristan north, past the front of the vehicle.

Venice said, "The picture hasn't recycled yet." The most annoying quirk of the SkysEye Network was its four-minute refresh rate.

Jonathan heard the sound of an approaching vehicle. They all heard it.

Tristan's breathing changed to a huffing sound that Jonathan recognized as a precursor to panic.

"Move," Jonathan commanded, "but don't panic. We have some time." It was a lie, but sometimes you just have to stay smooth to keep hysteria from taking root. He tossed a look over his shoulder to see Boxers disappearing into the weeds. If things went to shit, they'd be set to kill the bad guys in a cross fire.

He and Tristan were barely ten feet off the road. "Down," Jonathan commanded at a whisper.

Tristan dropped as if his legs had disappeared.

Jonathan eased himself down more slowly, keeping his eyes on the road. To his left, Boxers had made himself completely invisible.

Jonathan stooped to his haunches, where his knees hovered above Tristan's shoulders.

"No matter what happens, I want you to stay flat," he said. "Understand?"

"Who are they?" Tristan whined. His face was hidden in the crook of his elbow.

"Trouble," Jonathan said. "Let's hope that's all it is. I'm moving away from you. If there's shooting, I don't want you to be in the way. Don't go anywhere, and try not to move."

That brought a panicked look from the boy.

"I'll stay close," Jonathan promised. He didn't wait for an answer.

Jonathan let his carbine fall against its sling and drew his MP7 from its holster on his left thigh and extended the collapsible butt stock. The M27 was a great weapon at longer ranges, but its sixteen-inch barrel could get unwieldy in close quarters. With a barrel length of only seven inches, the MP7 was a cross between an assault rifle and a bad-ass pistol. It fired its wicked little 4.6-millimeter bullets at a rate of 950 rounds per minute with a muzzle velocity of over two thousand three hundred feet per second, and the bullets themselves were essentially steel penetrators that rendered even advanced body armor useless. For CQB—close-quarters battle—the MP7 had all but replaced the Mossberg twelve-gauge that had long been Jonathan's good friend.

He moved at a crouch through the tangled undergrowth, putting more distance between him and both Tristan and Boxers. That was the plan, anyway. Ten paces and as many seconds later, the jungle revealed a Mexican Army Sandcat winding its way down the hill, its engine screaming in too low a gear. Jonathan had never seen one of these vehicles up close, but he'd read about them. It looked like a cross between a Humvee and a Jeep, but with an outer skin that jutted at odd angles, giving it a stealthy appearance. He remembered reading that the Sandcat might or might not be armored. It looked to be designed for eight people, but probably could hold up to twelve in a pinch.

Jonathan craned his neck to check on Tristan, and was pleased to see no trace of him.

Out on the road, the Sandcat slowed as it approached Jonathan's parked Pathfinder. When they were still thirty feet away, it stopped and held its position. For a good twenty seconds, no one moved. A bug in the back of Jonathan's brain calculated what would be left of him if this turned out to be some kind of rolling car bomb. It wasn't pretty.

It also wasn't logical, so he pushed it aside. Even if it turned out to be true, he'd never know it.

When the doors opened simultaneously, and the vehicle disgorged six soldiers, Jonathan pressed the MP7's butt stock more tightly into his shoulder.

They wore green jungle camouflage uniforms, and carried assault rifles that Jonathan recognized by their bizarre shape as FX05s, the standard-issue rifle for the Mexican military. Ugly as sin, the weapons were more or less unique to Mexico, and fired a 5.56-millimeter NATO round that was identical to those fired by Jonathan's slung M27.

"The Pathfinder's blocking my view," Boxers whispered into Jonathan's earpiece. "Are we in trouble?"

"Too soon to tell," Jonathan whispered back, though these guys were evidently expecting trouble. Flashes of green on the epaulettes told him that they were members of *La Justicia*—the Mexican military police. He also noted that none of them bore the markings of a commissioned officer. He wasn't sure what that meant, exactly, but he found it interesting that a truckload of noncoms happened to be on this stretch of road.

The soldiers took defensive positions on their respective sides of the Sandcat, their weapons trained on the woods, waiting to shoot. Jonathan offered up a silent prayer that Tristan wouldn't choose this moment to sneeze.

"Are you sure this is the right vehicle?" one of the soldier asked his comrades in Spanish.

"One hundred percent sure," another one answered. "It belongs to the church. This is the fugitives' vehicle."

Jonathan's heart skipped. Father Perón had gotten that one right, though the betrayal had come faster than Jonathan had anticipated.

So, were these guys real cops on a real manhunt, or were they more terrorists on a murder mission? Jonathan figured he'd know soon enough.

One of the soldiers approached the Pathfinder while the rest of his team covered him. Jonathan kept the red dot of his sight on a spot just in front of the point man's left ear as the man reached out and touched the hood. "The engine is warm. They must have heard us coming."

"That means they're still here," said the soldier who'd been riding shotgun. Jonathan figured him to be the leader. The words made them all shrink by two inches as they crouched a little deeper and pressed their weapons more tightly into their shoulders. The posture spoke of fear.

"They could be watching us," one of the other soldiers said. He started sweeping the woods with his rifle, desperate for something to shoot at.

"Raul!" the commander barked. "Settle down. If you see them, shoot them."

Something flipped in Jonathan's stomach. "Did I just hear what I think I heard?" Boxers whispered in his earbud.

Jonathan tapped his chest. Just once, which meant yes. There was in fact a kill-on-sight order out for them. Not "arrest on sight," or "detain on sight." Shoot on sight meant that a death warrant had been written on them.

"I still can't see anything," Boxers whispered, "but say the word, and I can step out into position. I'll take whatever's on the left."

The bad guys were too close for Jonathan to risk answering. Was the shoot-on-sight thing just bold talk, or was it truly the order that had been issued? He needed to be sure before he took action. Once he opened fire on military personnel, he'd set events in motion from which there'd be no recovery. He decided to wait them out a little longer.

While the rest of the soldiers covered him, the point man approached the Pathfinder, his weapon at the ready and trained at the windows. Each step took him closer to Tristan's hiding place.

Jonathan kept the soldier squarely in his sights every step along the way.

Jonathan tapped his transmit button once, paused, and then twice again. That meant *Stand by*. In his mind, he could see Boxers grinning.

The presumed commander ordered, "Search the jungle." As he spoke, he started walking directly toward Jonathan.

Scorpion didn't care about the approaching commander. At least not yet; he was still twenty feet away. Jonathan was way more concerned about the point man, who couldn't be more than five feet from Tristan's hiding place.

The soldiers scanned their sectors of the compass with a professionalism that Jonathan hadn't anticipated. As they swept their weapons from left to right, they showed admirable muzzle discipline, never endangering the soldier next to them. That was good news for their own safety, but not good news for Jonathan's.

"I've got good sight pictures on two," Boxers whispered.

Jonathan tapped another *Stand by*. He wanted to see how this would play out. Chances were good that Tristan would be discovered, and when that happened, Jonathan wanted—

"Shit!" the point man yelled in Spanish. "You! Stand up! I found one!"

Jonathan slipped his finger into the trigger guard and prepared to fire. The soldier's posture spoke more of fear than intent, however, so Jonathan gave him the benefit of the doubt.

"Stand up, stand up, stand up! Put your hands up!" The others cut their respective searches short—exactly the wrong thing to do—and turned to confront the threat that their colleague had discovered. That put six guns all trained on Tristan.

Jonathan knew that Boxers must be borderline apoplectic. He understood Spanish at least as well as

Jonathan did—in fact the Big Guy was something of a genius with languages—so he knew exactly what was happening. All of their tactical training told them that this was the time to take the bad guys out—while they were out in the open and exposed—but Jonathan wanted to give them a little more rope. If they were truly going to shoot on sight, then Tristan would already be dead. He wanted to see what their plan really was.

He keyed his mike and dared to whisper, "Hold your fire." He held his aim on the no-reflex zone of the lead soldier's brain. If Jonathan pulled the trigger, his bullet would unplug his central nervous system in a microsecond. There'd be no twitch of a trigger finger.

Tristan rose from the spot where he'd been hiding, his hands held high over his head. "Please don't shoot me," he said, first in English, and then he said it again in Spanish.

"Jesus, Scorpion," Boxers whispered. "Now's the time."

Jonathan let the comment hang in the air.

The point man leveled his rifle at Tristan's face. "Step out here," he said. The soldier motioned for Tristan to step out into the roadway.

The boy was only one notch away from panic. His eyes darted from left to right, looking for reinforcements as he stepped free of the undergrowth and into the clearing of the road cut.

"What's your name?" the solider asked in Spanish.

"Tristan Wagner," he answered. His eyes never touched his questioner. Instead, they were all about finding Jonathan and Boxers.

"Why are you hiding here?" the soldier asked.

Tristan hesitated. Clearly, he wasn't sure how to answer or what to do. "I was kidnapped by terrorists," he said. "My friends and I."

"Your friends?" the soldier said. "Where are these friends now?"

"Dead," Tristan said.

The leader stepped forward, moving away from Jonathan's location and closer to the boy's. "You killed them," he said.

Jonathan shifted his aim from the point man to the leader, whose back was now turned to him. He settled the sight on the base of his skull, right where the spinal cord joined the brain.

"I didn't kill anybody," Tristan said. "The terrorists killed them."

"Are you one of the Yankee missionaries?" the leader asked.

An invisible hand pulled Jonathan's spine.

Tristan hesitated. He was close to breaking. "I-I don't know what you're talking about."

"You're American," the leader said.

"Yes, sir."

"And you are here from Scottsdale, Arizona."

This time, Tristan's hesitation was the loudest confession Jonathan had ever heard.

"I thought so," the leader said. He raised his pistol.

Jonathan squeezed his trigger, and the MP7 roared. His first two bullets shredded the leader's head, and his second two did the same for the point man. Ahead and to his left, Boxers' rifle discharged what sounded to be a half-mag of 7.62-millimeter bullets. Three more dropped, and Jonathan took out a guy who just looked confused.

The gunfight lasted less than a second and a half. When it was done, Jonathan and Boxers had fired twenty-five rounds between them, and all six soldiers were dead, their bodies dropped like so many sacks of manure.

CHAPTER SEVENTEEN

One day, Gail would learn that people's names rarely matched the pictures those names evoked in her mind. She'd expected Harriett Burke to be a mousy sixty-something in a print dress and gray hair pulled back in a bun. She'd smile sweetly and say God-loving things.

Instead, she was a sturdy thirty-something with shoulders that were broader than most men's. Smart money said her résumé included time on a roller derby team. Where the sweet smile should have been, there was instead a set jaw and firmly pressed lips. Clearly, her buddy Volpe from downstairs had called upstairs.

As the elevator doors opened on the opulent four-teenth floor, she was right there, doing her best to block the path down the hallway. "Reverend Mitchell doesn't have time to meet with you," she said.

Gail stepped into the elevator lobby. "And I don't have the inclination to put you in handcuffs," she said, and she skirted the human roadblock.

Tried to, anyway. Harriett grabbed Gail's sleeve. "You may not go in there."

Gail drew her badge as if it were a gun and pointed it at Harriett's forehead. "This is your moment to make careful choices," she said, startling herself by the ease with which she slid back into her old role.

"Do you have a warrant?" Harriett said. The badge and the speed with which it appeared had startled her.

"I'll get one for your arrest if you don't let go of my sleeve."

Harriett pulled her had away as if it had touched a hot stove. "Sorry," she said.

"Good for you. Where will I find Reverend Mitchell?"

"I'm sorry, Officer . . ."

"It's sheriff. Sheriff McLain."

"Sheriff McLain, Dr. Mitchell left very specific orders not to be disturbed today."

"I'm guessing she didn't anticipate my visit when she said that."

"I could get fired."

Now they were squarely in territory where Gail had stopped caring. "If she fired you for this, then you probably should consider working somewhere else."

The elevator dinged, and Volpe joined them. Harriett looked genuinely relieved until the guard rested his hand on the revolver he wore on his hip.

Gail hated rent-a-cops. She pulled back her suit jacket to reveal the grip of her Glock. "I've got one, too," she said. "And I'll bet you a million dollars that I'm better with mine than you are with yours."

Volpe lifted his hand from his weapon and ostentatiously splayed his fingers. "I wasn't threatening you," he said. His voice cracked a little.

"That's exactly what you were doing," Gail countered. "And I guarantee that I am threatening you. Will I find Dr. Mitchell's office down this hallway?"

Volpe looked to Harriett, who said, "Yes. I'll take you there."

Something clicked in Gail's head. That was a big change of heart in a very short time. Was Harriett looking for a reason to be alone with Gail? If so, was that good news or bad news? The most dangerous threats are the ones you don't anticipate.

"She's not going to be happy," Volpe said.

Gail was about to say that she'd be a lot happier than these two would be if she arrested them, but she caught a look from Harriett that made her swallow the words. Besides, she didn't have the power to arrest anyone.

"I've got this, Paul," Harriett said. "You can go back downstairs."

Volpe didn't like it. "You sure?"

"You almost started a gunfight," Harriett said. "Nobody needs this to escalate. It's between Sheriff McLain and Dr. Mitchell now. I'm stepping out of the middle."

Volpe actually looked to Gail for support—an effort that lasted only a second.

"It's not a security issue, Paul," Harriett said, sealing the deal. "Let me do my job. You go back downstairs and do yours."

That final comment felt to Gail like a throw-down, leading her to believe that these two had a past.

No one said anything for about ten seconds as the situation evolved into an uncomfortable standoff. Harriett wouldn't even give Volpe the tiny victory of walking away from him. Instead, she waited while he rang for the elevator and disappeared behind the closing doors. At least the car came quickly.

When they were alone in the lobby, Harriett turned to Gail. "Okay, what's going on around here?" Her tone was more plea than demand. "Why is everyone so crazy?"

Gail's stomach flipped, but she covered it. "What do you mean?"

"You're a cop," Harriett said. "And you're here. Please don't play games. I'm scared."

Jonathan Grave often said that life was one big poker game. Now, Gail had to play her hand carefully. "I'm here to help, Ms. Burke. But you must understand that my business is with Reverend Mitchell. I'm happy to listen to you and answer the questions I'm able to, but I can only be but so forthcoming."

That sounded really good, she thought.

"Something terrible has happened in Dr. Mitchell's life," Harriett said. "I don't know what it is, but it's affecting everything. She looks terrible. She's stopped taking any visitors. She's positively gray."

"Perhaps it's the sex scandal," Gail offered. Cops were all about advocating for the devil.

"No. That was an embarrassment and a distraction. I was here for that. That was never as big a deal as the media made it out to be."

Gail scowled. She was a minister who had sex with a seventeen-year-old boy. How was it possible to make a big *enough* deal about that?

"Please don't judge," Harriett said.

So much for Gail's poker face.

"You don't begin to understand the pressures that Reverend Mitchell is under."

"I'm not here about any of that," Gail said. Just speaking of this stuff made her feel like she needed a shower.

"I understand," Harriett said. "This new thing. I have no idea what it's about but I know it's bad. It's tearing her apart."

Gail's cell phone rang. She fished it out of her jacket and looked at the number. Fisherman's Cove. "Excuse me," she said to Harriett. She turned away and pressed the connect button. "Hello?"

"Are you alone?" It was Venice, and there was urgency in her tone.

"No."

"Oh." Disappointment. "If you can extricate yourself from Jackie Mitchell, we have better leads for you to follow."

"That's not possible," Gail spoke harshly, as if confronting a subordinate. She hoped that Venice would be able to read between the lines.

"Quickly, then," Venice said. She relayed the news about the Georgens and the Cantrells. "We were thinking that it might be better to build from the bottom up instead of starting at the top."

"I've got it," Gail said. She clicked off, staying in character even as her mind raced for the best way to go. Fact was, she was already here. While a direct confrontation with the head of the snake would likely result in a fusillade of denials, it was sometimes helpful for an adversary to know that you knew they were up to no good.

On the other hand, you only got one shot at a first drink from the well. If Jackie Mitchell outmaneuvered Gail and got the upper hand, Mitchell could get the first shot at the Georgens and Cantrells, causing them to clam up forever.

Gail decided to play the hand she'd been dealt. "Sorry about that," she said, turning back to Harriett. "What do you suspect the problem with Dr. Mitchell might be?"

"I have no idea."

"Now who's playing games?" Gail accused. "You engineered this opportunity to be alone with me. People who 'have no idea' don't do that."

Harriett took three steps over to the little sofa that sat along the wall opposite the elevator doors and sat down heavily. "I only screen the phone calls, you know? I don't listen to them."

Gail sensed that she was supposed to know what Harriett was talking about. "Except sometimes," she helped.

Harriett tried to look wounded, but in reality looked like she'd been caught in the act.

"You brought it up, Ms. Burke," Gail said.

Harriett inhaled deeply to prepare herself. "I've only done it a couple of times. When I thought that Dr. Mitchell might get taken advantage of. You can tell from the tone in some people's voices. She can be so trusting sometimes. Naïve, even. That's actually how she got involved with that boy. He swore to her that he was eighteen."

"Again, I don't care about that," Gail said. "What did you hear on the phone calls?"

"There were a couple. It started with this creepy guy named Abrams. He had a thick New England accent, and just gave me the creeps. He had a scariness about him."

Gail's heart skipped. She'd dealt with a similar malevolent presence in the past. That name wasn't Abrams, though.

"Do you know him?" Harriett asked.

Great intuition, Gail thought. "I don't think I know anyone by that name."

Harriett didn't look like she bought the answer a hundred percent, but she didn't pursue it. "Well, Abrams would call on behalf of Mr. Hainsley, a major contributor to the Crystal Palace. He would talk to Dr. Mitchell and arrange off-site meetings."

"Where?"

"All over Scottsdale. Always in a public place."

"How many meetings?"

"A lot. Ten or twelve, I'd guess."

"And who is Mr. Abrams?"

"I have no idea. Dr. Mitchell never mentioned him, and since I wasn't supposed to be listening, I couldn't bring it up." She dropped her voice by half. "Thing is, Dr. Mitchell always said yes to the meetings."

"That's significant?"

"Sheriff McLain, Dr. Mitchell runs an empire, okay? You have no idea how many moving parts there are, how hard she works. If she didn't say no to people—frequently—she'd never have time for anything. It would all fall apart."

Gail waited for the rest.

"She didn't just say yes, okay? She dropped everything, like right now, to jump through hoops for him. She'd be gone for a couple of hours, and when she got back, it was like she'd sold a part of her soul. Whatever it was, it was eating her alive. I hated seeing that. She deserves better."

"You must have some idea of what's going on," Gail said.

Harriett started to say something, but checked herself. She geared up again, and again stopped. This time, the silence prevailed.

"Does it have something to do with the kidnappings in Mexico?" Gail fired the question like a weapon.

"You know?" Harriett gasped.

Gail stayed in character. "This would be the perfect time to tell me everything you know, Harriett. If anything happens to those children, your window for negotiation will slam shut with startling speed."

Harriett's look of shock morphed into a look of horror. "You think I had something to do with that?"

"If you didn't, I think you know who did. You at least know who would know. Under the law, that's called being an accessory. You go to jail for that. This is your one and only chance to set it right."

"Those children were taken by drug lords," Harriett said. "How can you think even for a minute that—"

"The timing, Harriett," Gail interrupted. "Think. When did the phone calls start?" This was pure bluff. "And when did Dr. Mitchell's mood start turning dark?"

Harriett closed the loop quickly. She covered her mouth with her hand as the truth dawned on her. "Oh, my God. How can that be?"

"That's what I'm here to find out."

"I don't know anything, Sheriff. You have to believe that."

Gail offered a soothing smile. "I believe that you don't think you know anything. I also believe that you've heard significant and important information. You just don't realize it."

"I really haven't." Panic was beginning to set in.

"You really *have*. You just haven't thought it all the way through. For example, when Mr. Abrams called and asked to speak with Reverend Mitchell, what did he tell you?"

Harriett shrugged. "Nothing, really."

Gail scowled. "He just said, 'Hi, I want to speak to Jackie Mitchell' and you said okay?"

Harriett made a face. "Of course not. He said he was calling on behalf of Mr. Hainsley."

Gail sighed heavily. "Work with me here. You're the assistant to a very powerful woman. No one gets past you without a compelling reason. What was Abrams's compelling reason?"

"He said it was personal," Harriett said. "When I pressed him for more, he wouldn't give it. He said, 'When you tell her it's Mr. Abrams calling, I guarantee that she'll take the call.' Turns out he was right. I told Dr. Mitchell what he said, and she took the call."

Gail's bullshit alarm started to buzz in her head. "You're telling me that you didn't do any research on Mr. Abrams, even though these meetings had such a negative impact on your boss?"

Harriett blushed. "I checked a little."

"And what did you find?"

"Nothing, actually."

Gail waited for more.

"Okay, I heard him mention All American Industries as a company name. They're very big donors to the cathedral. When I searched our database, though, I didn't find his name."

Gail recognized the company from Venice's list. "They're new donors, aren't they?" she asked.

There was that shocked look again. "How do you know this?"

"Knowing things is how I make my living," Gail said.

The elevator dinged, drawing Gail's attention, and halting their conversation. It always happened this way. Just when you think you have control of a conversation somebody interrupts and—

It all registered in the space of a heartbeat.

She saw a shotgun. A man in a suit held it at port arms, poised across his chest to make room for it among all the other men and firearms in the elevator car.

The man with the shotgun made eye contact with Gail when the doors were still only six inches apart, and he brought the weapon to bear, aiming through the expanding opening.

She moved without thinking, grabbing a fistful of Harriett's blouse and diving sideways onto the floor, pulling Harriett down with her. They were still in the air when the shotgun fired. Above and behind, Gail more sensed than saw the cushions of the sofa erupt in a cloud of fabric and foam rubber.

Harriett screamed, but Gail had no idea if she'd been hit, or was only frightened. She didn't care. She didn't have time to care.

By the time Gail rolled to her stomach, her Glock was already drawn and ready. That first shot had established the rules of engagement. The guys in the elevator were here to murder her, and that gave her license to shoot to kill anyone who showed his face.

They seemed to realize it, too, because no one stepped out. There was a lot of shouting, a lot of commotion, but no one showed himself. When the doors cycled closed, someone stuck the barrel of a weapon out just far enough to cycle it again.

Their diddling gave Gail the opportunity to move, and she decided to capitalize on it. "Are you hurt?" she asked Harriett.

"What's happening?"

"Are you *hurt*?"

"I-I don't think so."

Rising to a knee, Gail one-handed her Glock, aiming it at the cycling doors, and with the other, she smacked Harriett on the shoulder and pointed to the exit door to her right. "Go to the stairs," she ordered. Access to the emergency exit wouldn't require them to pass in front of the elevator.

"But what—"

The guy with the shotgun—Gail saw now that it was a Winchester pump—pivoted out of the elevator car with the weapon to his shoulder, ready to shoot.

Gail nailed him high in the forehead. He fell dead in a spray of bone and brain matter without touching his trigger.

Harriett screamed again. "Oh, God—"

"The stairs!" Gail shouted it this time, vaguely worried that she'd given too much information to the bad guys. Then again, given the options from the fourteenth floor, the emergency exit wasn't all that hard to anticipate. It sounded as if the guys inside the elevator were beginning to panic. It didn't help that the dead guy's foot was keeping the door from closing.

Harriett scrambled along the floor, her face and belly barely above the carpet, and her extremities moving as if she were trying to gain footing on ice.

As always happened to Gail in high-stress encounters, time seemed to slow and she became aware of every detail of her surroundings. She held her aim at the elevator, covering Harriett's escape. These guys had been caught off guard by the fact that Gail was right there when they opened the door, and that had thrown them off their plan. But ten seconds had passed since then, and one of their own had been killed. They weren't going to stay under cover for long. And when they showed themselves, they were going to be pissed.

When Harriett finally found her feet, she bolted out the emergency exit, slamming the door open hard enough for it to rebound off the concrete block wall of the stairwell.

As Gail had expected, the attackers interpreted the noise as their cue that it was safe to move.

One took a half step out the door, but the muzzle of his pistol wasn't pointed at Gail, so she fired two quick rounds into the stainless-steel frame, just to drive him back inside, and then it was time for her to go, too.

Never breaking her aim, she backed quickly toward the door, found the latch with her left hand, and slipped through, into the escape well. Harriett's footsteps three floors below made a strange flap-clack sound as she tried to run in her girlie sandals.

Gail searched for something with which to block the door shut, but a glance told her that it was fruitless. She started down the stairs quickly but carefully, never turning her back on the door from the fourteenth floor. This was when she would be most vulnerable, and she wasn't about to give them a fleeing target to shoot.

Why weren't they following? She was a nearly stationary target. If these attackers had a mind in their head, they would—

Then she got it.

"Harriett!" she yelled. "Stop!"

CHAPTER EIGHTEEN

"**W**hat the hell was that?" Tristan shouted. Fresh blood spatter dotted his face. He stepped over the headless body and stormed toward Jonathan. "You're supposed to protect me! He was going to kill me! You used me as bait!"

Jonathan dropped the partially spent mag out of the grip of his MP7 and exchanged it with a fresh one from a pouch on his vest. He made a point of not engaging the enraged teenager. He pressed his transmit button. "Mother Hen, scene is secure. Six visitors sleeping."

"I copy six sleeping," she confirmed. Her voice telegraphed her stress.

"How could you do that?" Tristan railed. "What kind of coward hides in the bushes with an arsenal of weapons while the unarmed kid damn near gets killed?"

"I'd go easy on the C-word, there, kid," Boxers growled from the other side.

"Fuck you!" Tristan yelled, whirling to face the Big Guy. Think Chihuahua versus mastiff.

Boxers recoiled, his face a combination of surprise and amusement. Not many people talked to him that way. Fewer still remembered it afterward.

"What, you think this is *funny*?" Tristan asked. "This is fun for you? A new game to see how close we can come to getting the precious cargo killed? Is this what you do for grins? Jesus, do you know how many people you've killed in the past two days?"

"Which is it?" Jonathan asked. He kept his tone soft and reasonable.

"What?"

"I said, which is it?"

"Which is what? What are you talking about?"

Boxers was already at work collecting intel from the pockets of the deceased, stripping them of identification, notebooks, and anything else he could find and stuffing them into his rucksack for later evaluation. When that was done, he'd move on to the Sandcat and strip it, as well.

Jonathan continued, "Well, on the one hand, you're pissed that we didn't shoot sooner, and on the other, you're pissed that we've killed too many. I don't think you can have that one both ways."

"You know what I mean," Tristan said. "That guy was *this close* to blowing my brains out."

"Yet your brains are still tucked in and his are hanging out his forehead." Jonathan holstered the MP7 and made his first real eye contact with Tristan during this exchange. "I did not use you as bait. I left you alone so that if shooting started, the bullets aimed at me would in fact stay away from you. Sometimes Lady Luck gets in the way. You happened to be right where that point man walked."

"But you waited—"

"—until exactly the moment when I had no choice but to shoot." Jonathan completed Tristan's sentence for him. "As for the numbers killed, trust me. I'd be thrilled if all I had to do in my job was to ask for the peaceful return of hostages and then get them. It so rarely happens that way."

The sound of radio chatter drew Jonathan's attention to the Sandcat. Someone was asking for a situation report.

"Big Guy!" Jonathan yelled.

"I heard."

"Let's drag these bodies off the road and get the hell out of here."

"What's happening?" Tristan asked.

Jonathan grabbed a corpse by his shirt collar and started dragging it back toward the vehicle he'd arrived in. "These guys are from the Mexican Military Police," he explained, a little embarrassed by the strain in his voice caused by the physical effort. "They knew the terrorists who kidnapped you by name, and they were out here specifically looking for the vehicle that we took from the church. In my book, that ties them to the terrorists who took you and your friends."

Tristan stepped over to help, grabbing the guy's pant legs and lifting.

"Thank you," Jonathan said. He was liking this kid. He even liked the flashes of anger. They meant he was working his way out of the poor-me funk and could actually become a helpful player in his own rescue. When Jonathan hefted the body onto the floor of the backseat and went back to grab another, Tristan went with him.

"Anyway," Jonathan continued. "These guys clearly called in the fact that they had found the vehicle, and they'd clearly been given orders to kill us on-site when they found us. Now, their commanders are calling them back, asking how things went. The smart money says that when there's no answer, somebody's going to come looking for them."

"Plus, what would happen if somebody else just happened to drive past on this road?" Tristan offered.

"Now you're getting it," Jonathan said. They lifted a second body and carried him to the Sandcat as well.

"I just don't understand why all of this is happening."

"At this point, none of us do," Jonathan said. "Right now, we're at that a stage that we used to call 'adapt and evade.' "

"Used to? So you were in the Army or something?"

Jonathan answered with his eyebrows. It never paid to get into details about the past.

Clearing the road of the bodies didn't take long at all. Clearing it of the blood would be a job for Mother Nature. Jonathan didn't worry about that. (They called it a rain forest for a reason.) By the time he and Tristan had finished with their third corpse, Boxers was already done and in the process of rummaging through the front seat of the Sandcat.

"Hey, Scorpion," Big Guy called. "You'll want to see this."

Tristan followed. He was becoming a shadow.

"Whatcha got?" Jonathan asked.

Boxers handed him a sheaf of papers. Printouts of pictures. Each of the kids from the school bus, plus airport security pictures of both Jonathan and Boxers. As Jonathan paged through them, he cast a glance toward Tristan. The sadness had returned to his eyes, but he managed it.

"Well, they definitely knew who they were looking for," Jonathan mused aloud.

"I don't like this at all," Boxers said.

"Why?" Tristan asked. "Aren't the police supposed to be looking for us? I mean we were kidnapped."

"The police weren't supposed to know that," Jonathan explained. "That's why Big Guy and I were here in the first place. Keeping the police in the dark was a specific element of the ransom demand. Our job was to drop off the ransom and take you home. Now, it turns out that the police were involved from the beginning."

"Not just the police," Boxers corrected. "The military police."

"The chaperones aren't here," Tristan said.

Jonathan cocked his head. "Excuse me?"

"The chaperones," Tristan said. "Their pictures aren't here. All of us kids, but none of the chaperones."

"I thought they were all killed," Boxers said.

"They were," Jonathan said, catching Tristan's drift. "But how did the police know that?"

The question stopped Boxers dead. After a beat, he snorted out a laugh. "Yep, it just gets better and better."

Five minutes later, they were ready to go. With the bodies and the vehicle stripped of weapons, ammo, and any conceivable intel, Jonathan and Boxers made sure that the corpses were all tucked inside. Boxers restarted the engine, turned the wheel just so, and then used a stout stick to lean on the gas.

The Sandcat lurched forward, then slowed to a steady roll downhill. For a second or two, it looked as if it might hit the Pathfinder, but then, in the final few feet, it veered as it should, and rolled off the edge of the road. It crashed through the underbrush, tearing up ferns and bushes. Gaining momentum on the hill, it grazed a tree, then flipped onto its side, beginning a roll that ultimately took it over the edge and down a hundred feet or more into the rocky gorge below.

When it was gone, Jonathan high-fived Boxers and then they turned to see Tristan staring at them, dumbfounded. "You know, they had families," he said. "I don't think there's anything to celebrate."

"How about the fact that that's not us?" Boxers said.

Jonathan put a hand on the Big Guy's arm. "Not now," he said, and he led the way back to the Pathfinder.

As they started moving again, Boxers pointed out his mirror at the column of black smoke that was beginning to fill the sky from the spot where the Sandcat had crashed. "Yes, siree," he said. "Better and better."

Either Harriett hadn't heard, or she'd chosen to ignore Gail's warning. Either way, she was dashing toward her own death.

"Harriett!" She yelled it louder this time.

The clacking stopped.

"Come back up! They'll be waiting for us in the lobby."

"Waiting for *us*? They're here for you."

Gail moved faster down the stairs. Even though she was confident that they would not be followed, she kept her eyes and her weapon trained up the stairs. "They shot at you, too," she corrected. "Do you know who they are?"

"I don't know who *you* are," Harriett countered. "You sure aren't any cop."

Gail stopped at the thirteenth-floor landing. She had to get out of this death trap of a stairwell. "I'm not going to argue with you," she said. "If you want to have a chance at seeing tomorrow, you need to come with me."

"Where are you going?"

"Not out the door to the lobby. Now, Harriett. Decide."

From up here, Gail could just see the top of her head down on the eleventh-floor landing. Harriett's hands were to her mouth, a posture of stress and indecision. This was taking way too much time, but Gail couldn't just leave her. If it hadn't been for Gail, Ms. Roller Derby wouldn't be in this mess to begin with.

The clacking started again, and Gail was thrilled to see that Harriett was coming back up.

"Faster!" Gail hissed, and she headed down to meet her at the twelfth-floor landing. "What's in here?" she asked, reaching for the door handle.

"Storage, I think," Harriett said. "Used to be offices, but they moved everybody out."

Gail pulled the door open carefully, revealing a large unlit space that looked like it used to be a cubicle farm, but was now home to a maze of boxes and assorted junk. On the far side, a building width away, she saw what she hoped to see: another emergency exit, with a reasonably clear aisle leading to it. As she closed the door behind her, it all went black.

"I can find the light," Harriett said.

"I don't want the light," Gail said. "Why are there no windows?"

"The office doors are closed. Only the executive of-fices have windows."

Then Gail got it. The lights would stay out. This cu-bicle farm was the center ring of a square. The bad guys had all the advantage now as it was. If darkness could give Gail a tiny edge somehow, she was all for it. "What do you know about the security systems here?"

"Why are those people after you?" Harriett's mind seemed stuck on stuff that just didn't matter.

"Focus, Harriett. The security systems."

"I have no idea. You saw the guards."

"Do you know where the cameras are?"

"Everywhere, I guess."

Useless.

Gail reached out into the darkness. "I'm going to grab your hand," she said, "and I'm going to put it on my belt. I want you to hang on and keep up." Once linked, she started moving down the center aisle, plac-ing her feet in spots where she saw in her memory were not occupied by junk. After twelve steps—a number chosen because she knew that her full strides while walking equaled about twenty-six inches (see what routine exercise does for you?), and correcting for the smaller steps in the darkness, she figured that twelve steps gained her about twenty feet of distance.

From there, she pivoted what she estimated to be ninety degrees to her left, and she started walking more carefully, cautious of bumping into something.

"I want you to listen to me carefully, Harriett," she said. "If the lights suddenly come on, or if the door opens, I want you to drop to the floor right away. And I mean drop where you stand."

"Why?"

"Sweetie, you just need to stop asking questions for a little while. But the answer is so you don't get shot. The bad guys won't hesitate to fire, and I need a clear lane of vision to fire back. How's that?"

"I wish I didn't ask."

"I get that a lot from people at times like these."

"You mean you get a lot of times like these?"

If only you knew, she didn't say. In fact, she didn't say anything.

Gail holstered her weapon and walked with her arms outstretched before her with her forearms crossed. That way, if they ran into an unseen vertical obstacle that was thin—say, a pillar or an open door—there was zero chance that the obstacle would smack her in the face. She moved with frustrating caution, fully conscious of the fact that a stack of tipped-over stuff would be a clear indication for the bad guys of where she'd gone.

The destination was an office. She didn't care which one; she just wanted a place where she could make the most important phone call of her life.

Harriett turned out to be more adept at following than Gail had expected. She stayed with her every step, never going faster, never dragging her down, and, most important, never falling, which is more difficult in a dark environment than most people think.

Finally, Gail's hands found a wall. From there, she started moving to the right. In theory, sooner or later they'd encounter a doorknob, and that's where she'd declare that they'd found a place to stop.

It turned out that the doorknob was only a few steps away.

Gail drew her weapon again—not because it made

any sense that someone might be on the other side, but because she wanted to have a weapon in her hand.

As she pushed the door open, the splash of sunlight was startling.

"Quickly now," she said. She pivoted her hips to sort of sling Harriett into the office, and then she followed behind quickly.

"Why are we here?" Harriett asked. "What are we going to do from here?"

"We're going to call the cavalry," Gail said. She pulled her cell phone out of her pocket and hit the speed dial. When the other party picked up on the second ring she said, "Mother Hen, this is Gunslinger. I need help."

CHAPTER NINETEEN

Venice's mind raced as she listened to Gail over the open phone line, leaning on Venice to engineer a way out of the predicament. As she pulled her keyboard out from under the edge of her desk, Venice slipped her headset into her ear and hit the button to redirect the sound.

"It's not that easy to pull up security plans," she said as her fingers flew across the keyboard. With advance notice, she could research sites and steal passwords. With a little planning she could be brilliant with this sort of thing. Doing it on the fly was second to impossible. "It could take some time."

"I don't have time," Gail said. "They have to know that we ducked into one of the floors. If they have enough cameras in place, they may even know exactly where we are."

Venice's stomach clamped. Gail had stated it exactly: when a commercial facility had any security at all, they tended to have a lot of it. It was an either/or kind of thing. The bad guys probably knew exactly where she was hiding. Even if Venice could pull up the access she needed, it was likely too late to be of much help. With advance notice, she could have recorded empty hallways and played them on the security screens in real time, but even that would have been difficult.

"I just don't know what kind of help I can be." She searched for some way to gain access into a system that she'd never researched.

"Then take a few notes," Gail said. "Dennis Hainsley is the key player here. Remember—" Venice heard chatter in the background as Gail turned away from the phone. "All American Industries. One of the big last-minute donors. He's very important to Reverend Mitchell. Harriett Burke says that his meetings had a big negative impact on Dr. Mitchell's mood."

Venice clicked to a different screen and typed the information formlessly, as stream-of-consciousness words.

Then she clicked back to the business of getting Gail and her new friend out of harm's way. She started with the easy stuff, cross-referencing Crystal Palace with security companies, but that produced nothing. Then she found the Scottsdale building permits office. Most jurisdictions required that building plans be submitted to the public record. If she could find those, and the schematics for the Crystal Palace, then she should be able to find a way out for them.

The problem was the lack of time. Even with the highest of high-speed connections, it took time for—

"Shit," Gail said. Her voice dropped to a whisper. "They're on the floor. The lights just came on."

"Keep the phone live," Venice said. "Whatever happens, don't hang up." She glanced across her desk to make sure the recorder was running, and the green light assured her that it was. She looked to her key-board, but realized that with the clock run down to nothing, she had no options available that would help.

The sound in her ear rustled as Gail put the phone down. That's what Venice assumed she was doing, any-way.

"I want you to lie flat on the floor," Gail whispered. "If I tell you to do something, do it. But if I don't you just stay put till it's all over."

"Are they here?" another voice asked. Venice as-sumed that to be Harriett.

"Shh."

Then things went silent. Venice froze at her key-board, hands poised over the keys as she leaned closer to the screen, as if by doing so she could get her ear-piece closer to the action. She closed her eyes, trying to turn the sounds into images, but the electrical con-nection combined with the fuzziness of the cellular service made it almost impossible to discern nuance.

A minute passed, maybe two. Twice, she heard Har-riett ask something, but both times, Gail responded with a long, soothing *shhh*.

More silence.

Then a crashing sound, loud and tinny through the phone line.

"Here!" a man's voice yelled, but a gunshot cut it off.

Then there were a lot of gunshots. One weapon was louder than the others, and it hammered long and hard in three-round bursts.

Gail was shouting something, but over the cacoph-ony, Venice couldn't make out words. Men shouted, too, and in the background, a woman screamed. It was the sound of panic.

The maelstrom continued for fifteen or twenty seconds before it finally ended in a silence that lasted for a few seconds, then erupted again for a few shots and then fell silent again.

Venice sat riveted in her chair, her eyes closed, trying to see through her ears what was going on.

"Are they down?" a man's voice asked.

Venice's eyes filled with tears.

"What is this?" the voice asked, and then there was a shuffling sound again in Venice's ear. "Hello?" a male voice said into the phone. "Anybody here?"

Venice wanted to hang up, to run away, but she didn't. If the phones hadn't been encrypted, this would be the time to break the connection, before the bad guys could trace it back. As it was, the phones and their signals were untraceable, and it therefore posed no harm for Venice to remain on the line.

"Who are you?" she asked. She winced at the tremor in her voice.

"That's a stupid question," a man said. "If you've been listening, then you know I'm the guy who just killed your friends. Have a nice day."

The line went dead.

CHAPTER TWENTY

By the time Captain Ernesto Palma arrived at the site of the massacre, all but one of the bodies had been pulled back up to the road. They were twisted and horribly burned, but he was able to recognize a couple of the faces. The stench in the morning heat nearly overwhelmed him. The others on the scene—a couple of local police officers plus the three soldiers he'd brought with him—stood silently, clearly waiting to see how he would react. Their silence somehow amplified the noise of the flies.

Despite the damage done by the fire, they'd obviously been shot. Each in the head, for sure, but in at least one case, he saw blood on a soldier's shirt that indicated a back wound as well.

"It appears they were executed," said Cayo Almanza, the police corporal who commanded the local authorities.

"Does it?" Palma asked.

"I believe so. Clearly they were shot in the backs of their heads."

The erupted foreheads told him that much. "Execution is a loaded word, Corporal."

"How else to explain it? They appear to have been shot and then shoved into the vehicle to cover up the murder."

Palma knew that the corporal was wrong about the execution, yet he decided to let the misperception lie unchallenged. "As you say," he said. It was a sentence he'd found to be useful over the years to leave people in a kind of limbo, wondering whether he'd just agreed or disagreed with what they'd said. Palma enjoyed keeping people on edge. Nervous people were easier to work with.

"I believe that this was the work of the American missionaries," Almanza said.

On that, the corporal was almost certainly correct, but again Palma said nothing.

"The alternative would be that it is the work of the cartels." For whatever reason, it seemed important to Almanza that he impress Palma. The idiot had no way of knowing that the work of the cartel and the work of the missionaries were one and the same. Even the missionaries didn't know that.

While no one but their families would mourn the loss of the soldiers who had been killed in the past two days, the rising body count could begin to project weakness, and the perception of weakness could unnecessarily complicate everyone's lives.

"Who found the bodies?" Palma asked.

"A businessman on his way over to Santo Miguel. His name is Emilio Madrigal. He was driving—"

"Is he still here?" Palma had no interest in hearing what had been told to someone else. He wanted to hear the details firsthand.

"Of course, Captain." Almanza pointed back toward

the road. "I knew that you would want to speak with him." He started to lead the way, but Palma wasn't quite ready.

"Sergeant Nazario?"

A young, handsome, and impossibly fit young man took a step closer. "Yes, Captain?"

"I believe that your comrades have been gawked at quite enough. There are disaster pouches in the back of the truck. See to it that the bodies are treated with respect."

"Yes, sir." Nazario turned to the remaining soldiers and set them to work.

Palma watched them for a few seconds, and then started for the road, grateful to have a reason to turn away from the carnage. Corporal Almanza led the way out of the jungle and across the road toward a rotund middle-aged man whose posture and pallid skin color spoke of profound illness or crippling fear. Under the circumstances, Palma favored the latter. The man sat on the ground near the edge of the jungle on the opposite side with his legs crossed, and his arms outstretched behind him to allow for his substantial girth.

"Mr. Madrigal!" Almanza called as they approached. "On your feet."

That was easier said than done. Madrigal rolled to his side and then onto his knees in order to find his feet. By the time he'd arisen, Palma was only a few feet away. He offered his hand. "I am Captain Palma."

"Emilio Madrigal." His handshake was wet.

"Tell me," Palma said.

Madrigal spoke quickly, as if anxious to free himself from the memory. "I was on my way to Santo Miguel. I am a manufacturer's representative for auto parts, and I was on my way to pay a service call to several of the car dealers up there. When I turned that curve over there, I saw the smoke billowing up over the rise, so I stopped and looked. I saw the path that the vehicle had cut through the bushes, and then as I got closer to the edge, I saw that a car was on fire, and I thought I saw that people had been thrown clear of it."

"Did you go down to check out the scene?" Almanza asked.

Palma gave him a harsh look. "Leave us, Corporal," Palma said.

The policeman looked stunned.

Palma glared, waiting for Almanza to comply with his order. When he'd slunk away, Palma returned his attention to Madrigal. "You were saying?"

"Well, I was shocked. Not able to help—I am not a man who climbs steep slopes, if you know what I mean—I went back to my truck and I called the police."

Palma studied the man. "I heard a report that you then drove away. Is that correct?"

His posture spoke of fear. "I won't lie to you, Captain. I was very frightened. I saw buzzards starting to circle overhead. My heart is not as strong as it once was. Once I'd made the phone call to alert the police, I wanted to get away from here. Then within a few minutes, my dispatcher called and told me to come back here to wait for the police."

Palma had a proven record of correctly judging people's character during interrogations. Emilio Madrigal impressed him as a hard worker who had stumbled into a frightening scene.

"Did you give someone from the police your name and contact information?" Palma asked.

Madrigal nodded enthusiastically. He seemed to sense that he was about to be released. "Yes, sir. Three times, in fact."

"Are you planning to travel in the next week or so?"

"Only within my territory for work. Driving range."

Palma saw no reason to make him stay any longer. "Thank you for your cooperation, Mr. Madrigal. You may go."

The man looked like he might cry. "Thank you, Captain. Thank you very much."

Palma started to return to the bodies when a new thought occurred to him. "Mr. Madrigal!" he called.

Madrigal turned.

"If you need to speak to me about this further, please give me a call." He pulled a business card from his wallet and a pen from the pocket of his uniform blouse. He circled a number on the card. "This is my cell phone," he said.

Madrigal took the card, but hesitantly. "Did I forget to tell you something, Captain?"

Palma offered a cold smile. "I hope not," he said. "But only you can answer that question honestly." He meant his words to be chilling, and it was obvious they'd had the desired effect.

"Certainly," Madrigal said. He hesitated, looked back, and then returned to his red pickup truck.

As soon as Madrigal walked away, Almanza reappeared to fill the vacuum. He seemed at once excited and disappointed. "Alas, Captain, perhaps I was wrong." He displayed a shell casing in his open palm. "The reports said that the missionaries were using five-five-six and seven-six-two millimeter ammunition. This casing is much smaller. In fact, I've never seen so small a bullet."

Palma's stomach twisted as he took the casing from the corporal and examined it more closely. This was the 4.6-millimeter ammunition that was the new favorite of the American Special Forces. What did that mean? What it *could* mean was that he—as well as Felix Hernandez—had been lied to. They'd both received specific assurances that the American government would not interfere.

"An interesting piece of evidence," Palma said. "But it does not rule out the American missionaries."

"So you believe they have many weapons?"

Palma nodded to the section of the jungle where the bodies were being cared for by Sergeant Nazario. "They have at least six rifles and six sidearms that they did not have before this incident happened."

Almanza let that sink in silently. Something changed behind his eyes as it seemed to dawn on him for the first time that Palma knew more than he was sharing. "Do you know where these men came from?" he asked.

"They worked for me, Corporal. Of course I know."

"I need to know as well," Almanza said. "I need to know anything that will help in the investigation."

Palma pursed his lips and made himself taller. "Actually, Corporal, you need to know what I decide to share with you. Nothing more."

Almanza's face reddened. "It is my job, not yours, to investigate crimes. I understand that these murdered men were in the Army—"

"You think too much of yourself, Corporal Almanza,"

Palma interrupted. "Or perhaps you believe that I think too much of you. We both know that your job is to *pretend* to enforce laws, much as I *pretend* to serve our commander in chief. In reality, we all serve Felix Hernandez."

The corporal's face darkened still more. "That is not so!"

"It *is* so. I know it is so because you are still alive. Such cannot be said of so many men with badges who chose to fight the inevitable. You live to pretend, and you pretend so that you can live. We can say this out loud because there are no reporters here. The president himself pretends because he, too, has children and parents and siblings. He knows that one day he will no longer be president, and when he no longer has his security detail, he does not wish to be spirited off in the night to have his joints crushed and his private parts shredded."

As Almanza listened, he lurched his head from side to side, worried that his men might hear.

"Do you think they are different, Corporal?" Palma went on. "Do you believe that anyone on any police force in Mexico wishes to see their families killed? These games of pretend in which we engage are the worst kept secrets in the whole country. We do it to allow the population to believe that the government is in control, but in their quiet moments, I'm sure that every citizen understands the reality."

"I do not appreciate being lectured to like a schoolboy," Almanza said.

"I'm sure that no one would. That's why I'm urging you not to be as naïve as a schoolboy." Palma said this in a way that he hoped would not sound patronizing. It made no sense to anger the man. "I will ask you this as a favor, then. Would you please be so kind as to allow me to conduct this investigation, and to stay out of my way while I do it?"

"What will I tell my superiors?"

Palma placed a hand on the corporal's shoulder. "Tell them that you are acting at the request of Captain Ernesto Palma, and that Captain Ernesto Palma is working very closely with Felix Hernandez." He gave Almanza a few seconds to absorb the full meaning of his words. "Once your superiors hear that, I think they will understand. Don't you?"

Once the bodies of his men were properly bagged, Palma left them in the custody of Corporal Almanza, with very specific instructions to have them delivered to military authorities who would manage the details of notifying families. On the one hand, it felt like a waste of precious time to go through all the ceremonial rigmarole, but on the other, he understood the importance of such things to his men. Soldiers made many sacrifices in service to their country. Often, the only true respect they ever saw was that which came in death. Palma did not consider himself to be a sentimental man, but even he could understand the need for dignity.

Besides, so much time had already elapsed that an extra forty-five minutes would likely make no difference. Now that it was done, he and his soldiers were driving north. He didn't yet know what the Americans' plan was, but logic dictated that it included return to their country, and the only way to get there was to head north. By his estimation, the Americans had at most a five-hour head start.

Palma had alerted his forces along the coast to keep an eye on the marinas and the ports, but his instincts told him that the Americans would stay to the interior. That's what he would do if he were in their position. Traveling by land left near infinite options for evasion. Once on the water, they would be exposed to too many interdiction assets, not the least of which would be the ones designed to keep them out of their own country, now that they were the subject of an international warrant.

Sergeant Nazario drove their Sandcat, and Palma could tell from his posture alone that the man was uncomfortable. "Tell me what's on your mind, Sergeant," Palma said.

The driver's ears reddened. He hesitated.

"You may speak freely," Palma said.

The sergeant settled himself with a deep breath. "Sir, the men are concerned about the killings." He spoke softly, despite the noise from the engine, which would drown out any possibility of being heard by the soldiers in the back.

"I'm concerned about them, too," Palma said.

"That's not what I mean. Nothing has gone right in this mission. It has the feel of being cursed."

Palma shot his driver a disgusted look. "Are you believing in ghosts and goblins now, Sergeant?"

Nazario laughed without humor. "Not me, sir. But some of the boys. Not ghosts and goblins perhaps, but you have to agree that the corpses are stacking up."

Indeed they were. And Palma knew how susceptible

soldiers could be to superstitious nonsense. The mere suggestion of a curse could make perceptions of bad luck become self-fulfilling.

"The killing of those soldiers was a terrible thing," Palma said. "But the kidnappers? Their deaths speak of good luck, not bad."

"I understand, sir. And I agree with you. But even the ambush went bad."

"They have only themselves to blame for that. I'm still considering a posthumous court-martial for Private Prado."

"He misunderstood his orders," Nazario said. "If you're going to court-martial anyone, court-martial me. I'm the one who didn't make myself clear."

Palma smiled. He admired non-commissioned officers who defended their troops. It spoke of integrity and inspired respect from subordinates. "Don't think I'm not considering that, as well," he said.

Nazario knew better, yet he shifted uneasily in his seat. "I have another question, sir, but it is certainly out of line."

Palma waited for it.

"It's about the ambush," he said. "How did we know that the mercenaries would be there? How did we know where their vehicles would be?"

Palma stared straight ahead as he tried to form an answer. According to Felix, the CIA had been feeding them satellite tracking information, and as outlandish as it sounded, Palma believed it to be true. To invoke the CIA, however, would only make the troops more uncomfortable. He chose to say nothing.

After a moment of silence, Nazario got the message. "Yes, sir," he said. "I'm sorry, sir."

CHAPTER TWENTY-ONE

Dom D'Angelo nearly ran as he crossed the lawn from the St. Katherine's rectory to the sidewalk that would lead down the hill to the converted firehouse. Going to Scottsdale would wait. Everything would wait. If what Venice told him was true, the world had been knocked off its axis.

"Director Rivers's office," a voice answered. Even calls on Irene Rivers's secure personal line were screened.

"This is Father D'Angelo," Dom said. "I need to speak to Irene, please. It's urgent." He imagined that he was one of a very small handful of people who asked for the director by her first name. By doing so, he hoped that the gatekeeper would be less apt to ask questions.

Dom slowed his pace as he waited to be connected. He'd nearly made it to the firehouse when the line clicked.

"Hello, Father," Irene answered. "Look, unless it's really important, I am swamped with—"

"Venice says that Gail is dead."

"Oh, my God."

"She was shot in the Crystal Palace Cathedral about

twenty minutes ago. We need to get police there, but we can't call without revealing why she was there."

"The Crystal Palace is in Scottsdale, isn't it? Is Venice sure?"

"She sounded sure on the phone. I don't know how she knows. I'm on my way to her now. But if it's true—if Gail has been shot, irrespective of whether or not she's dead—time is of the essence. I thought you could pull a few strings to get the police out there."

He could almost hear the FBI director's brain whirring. She had to have a thousand questions—he had at least that many—but she also had to know that they could wait. "I'll do it," she said. Then she hung up.

He assumed she would reestablish contact if she got anything.

Pulling open the street-level door to the office, Dom tore up the stairs two and three at a time, startling Rick Hare, the armed security officer who stood guard outside the door to Security Solutions.

"Father Dom," he said. "Are you all right?"

Dom didn't pause to acknowledge him. Instead, he swiped his key card and punched in the entry code with the forefingers of both hands.

Rick grabbed the priest's biceps. "Father, I know you're a friend of Mr. G's, but I can't let you in if you're this agitated. What's going on?"

Dom paused. Despite his early years in the Army, cloak and dagger was not his business. Secrecy, however, *was* his business, and Venice had been clear about not sharing the news. He steeled himself with a breath. "Mr. Hare, you're going to have to make a decision. I'm going in there. If you feel the need to shoot me, then may your soul be spared."

Clearly, it was not what the guard had been expecting, and the look in his face nearly made Dom laugh. He used the awkward silence as an invitation to enter the office suite.

A second armed security guard, this one named Charlie Keeling, stood at the entrance to The Cave, and judging from the way he touched his ear, Rick had just told him about the nutjob priest who was on his way in. Rather than trying to stop him, though, Charlie used his own card to buzz him in.

"Thank you, Mr. Keeling," Dom said as he passed.

"Rick said it was important, Father." That was it; no further inquiry. If ever there was a place of business where need-to-know was the mantra, Security Solutions was it.

Venice sat on the far side of her desk, tears streaming down her face as her fingers flew across the keyboard. Dom had been telling himself that maybe he'd heard her wrong, but now that he saw her face, he knew that the worst fears were true.

Venice made no notice of him until he appeared in her doorway, and when she made eye contact, she melted entirely. She rose from her chair and hurried around the desk, her arms out and her wrists drooping, ready for a hug. As soon as Dom folded her in his arms, she started to sob.

"It's my fault," she cried. "She asked me for help and I couldn't give it to her." Her words were barely audible through the choking sobs.

Dom held her tightly as she pressed her face into his black shirt and let the emotion pour out. He felt the wetness in the fabric, and he just let her go. He stroked her hair and patted it. As he did, he tried to wrap his mind around the enormity of it.

Gail has been killed.

Articulating the words, even in his head, made it sound impossible. Gail was too *alive* to be dead. His head reeled with questions, but until Venice regained control, they would remain unasked.

It took her five full minutes to calm herself to the point where she could speak, and even then, her voice quavered. Her eyes burned red.

"Oh, Dom, what's Digger going to do? After he lost Ellen, Gail was all he—" Her voice caught and she abandoned the thought.

She pushed away from Dom and stomped her foot once against the floor. "No," she commanded, though Dom wasn't sure if she was speaking to herself or to him. "We are not doing this. We are not getting emotional. Not now. There's plenty of time for that later." She turned her back and headed to her computer.

Dom followed. "You're absolutely sure that she's dead?"

"I heard it happen," she said. "On the phone." She made a show of pounding the computer keys.

"You heard her *die*? How do you know she's dead?"

"I heard the shots, and I talked to the killer." Her tone could not have changed more dramatically. Now it was as if this were a simple business matter. She swiped angrily at the remaining tears in her eyes, and typed some more.

Dom reached over her shoulder and thumbed the power button on her monitor.

"Dammit, Father!"

"Dammit, Venice!"

The exchange hung in the air.

"Please talk to me," Dom said. "I've already got Wolverine involved. She's finding a reason to send police to the cathedral to look around."

Venice looked stunned that she hadn't thought of that herself. "That's good," she said.

"Wolverine is going to want to know details," Dom went on. "You're going to have to share them."

Venice had always been intimidated by Irene Rivers. Dom knew how little she liked to speak to her.

Venice steadied herself with a breath, then spun in her chair to face Dom. "She called me from an office inside the cathedral. I think she said it was on the twelfth floor. She was there to meet with Jackie Mitchell, and somehow or other, she ended up coming under fire. She called me to see if I could pull up drawings to get them out of there." Her lip startled trembling again. "I just didn't have time. They found her when I was still looking. That's when I heard them kill her."

"I still don't know what that means," Dom said. "I don't know what you mean when you say you heard them kill her. You mean you heard them shoot at her?"

Venice nodded. "There was a *lot* of shooting. Shooting and yelling. And then it just stopped. A man picked up her phone and said that he'd just killed her."

"So, you don't *know* that she's dead. There's no certainty."

Venice looked confused. Maybe a little angry at being questioned.

Dom explained, "Suppose she just dropped her phone in the fight? Suppose she was on the run and it just dropped out of her pocket? Just because some guy—a bad guy, no less—*says* that she's dead, that doesn't necessarily mean that she is."

Venice thought about it and seemed to allow herself a tiny glimmer of hope. She turned back to her screen and powered it up again

Dom's cell phone rang. Wolverine. He snapped it open. "Please tell me you have good news." He pressed the speaker button. "Venice's on the line, too."

"The news is neither good nor bad," Irene said. "The chief of police down there is an acquaintance of mine. He sent a unit to the Crystal Palace. They spoke with the security team on the main floor, and they said they knew nothing of a shooting."

"Did they check the place out?" Dom asked.

"They didn't feel it was necessary," Irene said. "Under the circumstances, with the extremely limited information we have to offer, I can't say as I blame them."

"Are they at least going to keep the police cars on the property for a while?" Venice asked.

"I can't imagine that they would," Irene replied. "Venice, I need you to catch me up with the details."

It only took a couple of minutes.

When the explanation was finished, Irene said, "I don't suppose you recorded this conversation, did you?"

Venice's face turned into a giant O. "Oh, my God," she said. She pushed her chair across the mat to her credenza, where the push of a button produced a postage stamp–size memory card. "I did record it." She placed the card in her computer and clicked a few buttons. The whole horrible scene played out all over again, from the initial contact through the shooting and finally the ominous voice at the end.

Halfway through, Dom felt himself turning pale and he leaned forward, his elbows resting on his knees. When it was over, he understood Venice's feeling of helplessness.

Silence hung in the air until Irene broke it with, "I'm sorry, guys, but that really doesn't sound good for Gail."

"There's always hope," Dom said. He looked to Venice, but didn't get the support he was hoping for.

"If you say so, Father," Irene said. "Matters of faith are much more your bailiwick than mine. I want to know whose voice that is at the end. Venice, can you send me a digital copy of that? I'll try to get it voice printed and see what we can find."

Dom shared a smile with Venice as she clicked send on the file she had already been copying. She was already a step ahead. "On its way," she said.

"I want to pull out that shouting on the recording, too," Irene said. "Maybe we can isolate something in the noise that will be helpful to us."

"I really appreciate this, Wolverine," Dom said. "I know you've got a lot going on. It means a lot—"

"You people mean a lot to me too, Father," she interrupted. "I'll be back to you if I get anything useful out of any of this."

With that, the line went dead.

"I can't put my finger on why," Venice said as she turned her attention back to her computer. "But I really don't like that woman."

"She's pulled Dig's backside out of a lot of fires," Dom said.

"She's set a few of them first," Venice replied.

Jonathan and Irene had a history that even Dom didn't fully understand, but he knew that there was at least as much angst between them as there was trust.

Dom scowled as he watched Venice become lost in whatever she was typing into her machine. "What are you doing?" he asked. "You look like you've discovered something important."

Venice shook her head, but she didn't move her eyes from the screen. "I should've thought about the shouting," she said. "Pisses me off that Irene got to that one first. I even have the same software they do."

Dom smiled. "I'm guessing that if you were Catholic, I'd have heard a confession after you got your hands on it?"

"That's why it's good to be Baptist, Father. Everything we do is a sin. We don't draw hard lines on things like borrowing without permission."

Dom laughed at the euphemism. He imagined that Saint Peter would have his hands full when the Security Solutions team finally passed on and had to be sorted out. Was stealing still a sin when the stolen materials were put to good use—even if it meant breaking the law? He imagined that God was growing weary of them all.

His attention was drawn to a series of horizontal lines that had appeared on Venice's computer screen. The lines fattened and thinned on the screen, not unlike the lines painted by oscilloscopes and electrocardiograms.

"Noise is the accumulation of many sounds," Venice explained. "Even in the noisiest party, you can pick out the words of the person you want to hear, right? You might have to concentrate and watch their mouth for visual cues, but you'll still be able to get the gist of what they're saying. To do that, though, you make yourself oblivious to the rest of the noise in the room."

She paused in her explanation, clearly seeking an indication of understanding. "I'm with you," Dom said.

"Good. If you were to listen to a recording of that same party, it would be difficult if not impossible to consistently pick out any one voice because the recorder is a piece of electronic equipment that gives equal value to every sound—from the individual voices to the hum of the air-conditioning. That all becomes noise."

Venice liked to show off a little when she was about to slam-dunk a computer. Dom settled in for the rest.

"For years, governments and individuals have been trying to figure out a way to eavesdrop that would allow the listener to weight the importance of different sources of sound. The FBI took the lead for domestic listening, and the National Security Agency got the nod for international eavesdropping. Obviously, the NSA program is more sophisticated, if only because they've got more PhDs per square inch than anywhere else on the planet."

"And you got your hands on the NSA version," Dom said, connecting the dots.

Venice gave a demure smile. "Well, it's not the very latest," she said. "But it's better than what the FBI can use."

"Pesky warrants and such?" Dom asked.

"Exactly. The Constitution really gets in the way of prying into people's business."

Dom got the irony.

"Okay, here," Venice said, pointing. "The program has analyzed the digital recording—it has to be digital for it to work—and separated out what it believes are separate sources of sound. Once separated, it breaks it into separate channels and then scrubs it. The scrubbing process takes a lot of the character out of the voices, but the words should be understandable."

She tapped the lines on the screen. "This one is obviously the sound of the gunshots," she said. "You can tell from the peaks in the noise."

Dom nodded because he knew it was the best thing. In reality, they all looked the same to him.

"I think this one is Gail," she said. She typed something on her keyboard, clicked her mouse twice, and the lines on the screen turned into sounds from her speakers.

Tristan hated guns. It wasn't a political thing, although when he turned eighteen and got to cast a vote that counted, he was going to do his best to outlaw the damn things throughout the world. They were ugly and heavy, and they stank. Literally, they smelled bad, an odd combination of oil and must.

The Big Guy—honestly, speaking of stupid names, that one reset the bar—seemed less than happy to be giving Tristan his firearms class. He'd handed Tristan one of the weird-looking Mexican rifles, along with one of the box things that hung from the underside to hold the bullets, but without any actual bullets. Fifteen or twenty feet away, Scorpion seemed thoroughly engaged in a telephone conversation.

"Okay, kid, listen up," Big Guy said. Then he caught himself. "Sorry. I meant to say Tristan. T-R-I-S-T-A-N." He smiled, Tristan's first indication that the man had a non-abusive side to his sense of humor. They'd stopped in the middle of the jungle and pulled the Pathfinder into a thicket of foliage that camouflaged it, though not to the point of invisibility. They'd already refilled the gas tank, and now, as far as he could tell, they were killing time.

Big Guy continued, "The first and most important lesson about firearms is this—the little round hole in the front points only at the enemy. Never at your own face, never at your feet, never at your friend, and, by God, never at me. Any questions so far?"

Big Guy held one of the bigger guns—an M16, Tristan thought, but that was only because he'd seen the movie *Platoon*—and in his hands, the rifle looked more like a big pistol, and apparently weighed nothing. Tristan's gun, on the other hand, weighed more than he'd anticipated. He had no questions yet because he hadn't really learned anything yet.

Big Guy held up the bullet holder thing. "This is the magazine," he said. "If we get into a shootout, your survival may well depend on how quickly you're able to switch these things out."

"Whoa," Tristan interrupted. "I'm not shooting at anybody."

The Big Guy's eyes flashed anger, and then they flashed patronizing tolerance. "Just humor me, okay?" he said. "My boss wants me to teach you this shit."

When he actually waited for a response, Tristan gave a shrug that meant, *Okay*.

For the next twenty minutes, Big Guy showed him

how to aim the rifle by pressing it into his shoulder, and then how to change the magazines without looking. While shooting, you just raised your trigger finger to stroke the little button, and the magazine fell away. Then, apparently, you could just grab another magazine and slap it into the old one's place without looking. Big Guy made it look like the easiest thing in the world, but Tristan had a hard time getting the hang of it.

"Why do I need to learn this?" Tristan asked. "I'm not a killer. I couldn't shoot another human being."

"I hear that a lot from people who haven't been shot yet," Big Guy said. "Again, just humor me."

From there, Big Guy showed him how to shove as many bullets as possible into the magazine. For his gun, three of the magazines took thirty bullets, but two of them took only fifteen. On full-auto, all of those magazines combined would give him eight seconds of total firepower.

"Fire one shot at a time," Big Guy said. "One bullet per trigger pull. Even though these are machine guns, and they're capable of putting hundreds of rounds downrange, I want you to think of your rifle as a single-shot weapon. Questions?"

"Yeah," Tristan said. "Who will we be shooting at?"

"I have no idea," Big Guy said. "But I can tell you this—if you're shooting at them, it will be because they shot at you first. Once you cross that line, a lot of the rest won't matter. The priority will be to conserve ammunition. Between the various weapons, I figure we have between twenty-five hundred and three thousand rounds. That sounds like a lot, but you'd be surprised at how fast that gets used up."

"Are you going to actually teach me how to shoot this gun?" Tristan asked.

The Big Guy looked confused. "I already told you about the safety," he said. "You take that off, and then you point the little round hole toward the bad guy and you pull the trigger. For you, though, the lesson is to keep the friggin' safety on."

Venice had guessed right, but Dom found the changes in the voice to be unsettling. It was as if the machine had taken Gail's voice apart and stripped away the humanity. The other sounds in the room— everything from the gunshots to the other voices— were completely unintelligible. They reminded Dom of someone moaning into a galvanized tube. The overall effect was beyond unnerving.

They listened to Gail's conversation with Venice, and they heard the long, soothing *shh* that she'd uttered to Harriett. Then the real bedlam started. Above the muffled cacophony, Gail's altered voice yelled, "The guard named Volpe from downstairs! Another white male, six feet, mid-thirties, slender! Black male—"

And that was it. Her voice was cut off, even as the rest of the noise continued to pound in the background.

"She described her attackers," Venice said. Her expression showed that she was somewhere between impressed and amazed.

"More than that," Dom said. "She named one of them. Somebody named Volpe. A Crystal Palace security guard. Are the other descriptions enough to be useful? A young slender white male and a black male?

Between the two, she described half the world and three quarters of Scottsdale." Even as he spoke the words, he had trouble wrapping his head around such a non-emotional discussion of harm against Gail.

Tears returned to Venice's eyes and she started typing again, perhaps just to mask the emotion. "No coincidences," she said. "That means that Volpe and some guy named Hainsley both have something in common with somebody named Abrams."

As Dom watched her do her best to be brave and professional, his already-massive admiration for her grew even larger. She'd known Digger from the day she was born, grown up in the same house as the daughter of his family's housekeeper. She'd endured his Army years, been there for his marriage and divorce, and had been a friend through the ordeal of his ex-wife's violent death. Now she was working hard to save Digger's life, even as she knew that the second love of his life had likely been killed.

"I don't think you should tell Dig about Gail," Dom said.

She looked up.

"You know, when he calls in."

"I can't lie to him," she said. "I won't lie to him. I owe him that much."

Dom sighed. "Truth isn't a fine line," he said. "It's a sleeve. It's entirely possible to vary from the line while staying within the sleeve."

Venice scowled as she looked at him, then cocked her head. "Are you sure you're a priest?"

*   *   *

"I need another way out of here, Mother Hen," Jonathan said into the satellite phone. "We've been made here. We've gone to ground to hold out for the remaining part of the day, but the going is way too slow. If we're going to have any chance at all, we need to compress the time in country. Can you find me an airplane?"

A pause. "Your original exfil aircraft is out of play, right?"

"That's affirmative," Jonathan said. "These guys know too much about our plans. We have to assume that they knew about Gutierrez's plane."

Another pause. Longer, this time. "I'll see what I can do."

"Hey," Jonathan said. "You sound strange. Is everything all right?"

She snapped, "Do you want me to find you an airplane, or do you want to chat?"

"Here's the deal," Scorpion said, interrupting the shooting lesson. "We're veering from our plan."

"Thank God," Boxers said.

"You don't know what the new plan is yet," Jonathan said.

"I don't have to. It has to be better than the one we've got."

Jonathan beckoned them closer to him and offered them a patch of mulchy jungle floor. He pulled his GPS out of its pouch and turned it on. "I had Mother Hen do some additional research for me." He handed the device to Boxers. "Look here. This satellite shot is about an hour old." He brought up an aerial map of a lot of jungle, and then zoomed in until the picture looked like it had been taken from maybe a hundred feet up. "What does that look like to you?"

Boxers smiled broadly. "About the ugliest damn airplane I ever saw." The make and model weren't discernable from this angle, but it looked like a Cessna Skylane, a high-wing single engine plane that was typical of hacienda owners who needed to get from place to place while avoiding the miserable roads.

"Now you're talkin', Boss," Big Guy said. "All this ground-hugging has been getting on my nerves." He moved his head closer to the screen and squinted to see the detail. "That runway looks short, but I guess if he got it in there, I can get it out." He raised his head and looked to the sky, clearly running numbers in his head, "Gas could be an issue," he said. "Even with a full tank and if nothing goes wrong, it'll be tight."

"What does tight mean?" Tristan asked.

Boxers gave him one of the patented annoyed looks. "It means running out of gas and falling out of the sky."

The look of shock on the kid's face made both Boxers and Jonathan laugh.

"Don't worry, Tristan," Jonathan assured. "Neither one of us is suicidal." To Boxers: "How tight?"

"Like running-on-vapors tight."

Jonathan noted the startled reaction from Tristan.

Tristan noticed Jonathan noticing. "Hey," he said. "You promised honesty. I get it." He looked to Boxers. "Does this mean I don't have to learn to shoot?"

Boxers opened his mouth to answer, then deferred to his boss.

"Think of it as a life skill." Jonathan said. "And if things come apart later, we'll be able to use another trigger finger." He let the words settle. "Besides, we have time to waste. We might as well spend it productively."

Boxers cocked his head. "Why do we have time to waste?"

"Because we're going to borrow the plane in the dark," Jonathan said.

"We're never getting out of here alive, are we?" Tristan asked.

"Of course we are," Jonathan said. "Not a doubt in my mind."

"Bullshit," Tristan said. "You can't be sure of that."

Jonathan and Boxers exchanged glances. "Sure we can," the Big Guy said. "I've turned down opportunities to die in way better places than this shit hole."

Scorpion improved on it. "We're getting out of here because that's the only option that Big Guy and I will accept."

Tristan rolled his eyes.

Jonathan sighed. "Look, I know that that sounds like empty talk, but I'm going to share a lesson with you. I've seen more tough days than most people, and I can tell you that commitment is everything. If you're willing to accept failure as an option, then failure is the only possible outcome."

The kid still wasn't buying.

"Okay," Jonathan said. "What's your sport in high school?"

Tristan laughed. "Sport? I'm on the debate team."

Jonathan beamed. "I was on the debate team, too. Have you ever gotten yourself fired up enough to win a debate that you had no right winning because the other team was way better than you?"

Tristan scowled. "Sure, I guess so."

"Of course you have," Jonathan said. "It happens that way with everyone, and it happens that way with everything. If you project success, you cannot fail."

"But the police are following us," Tristan said. "They're as good with guns as we are."

Boxers laughed. "Um, no they're not."

"No one says there has to be shooting," Scorpion said. "And even if it comes to that, no one says that everyone has to shoot. If you can't bring yourself to pull the trigger, then you can reload spent mags. It's all about being a team."

As Tristan listened, something stirred in his chest. From anyone else, this would have seemed like streaming bullshit, but Tristan could tell that Scorpion was spouting what he believed to be undeniable fact. And that fact alone made it impressive.

"We need you to be a solid member of the team, Tristan."

CHAPTER TWENTY-TWO

Trevor Munro tired of waiting for an adequate break in oncoming traffic. His Porsche 911 Carrera had a big enough engine to cut it short and still survive. He gunned it and pulled into the undersized parking lot of the diminutive Vienna Branch of the Fairfax County Public Library, cutting across two lanes of oncoming traffic and eliciting a symphony of blaring horns.

With no parking slots available, he just idled in the lot, waiting for Jerry Sjogren to make his stealthy entrance. It didn't take long. The big Bostonian emerged through the double glass front doors just like any other patron, strolled to the passenger side, and pulled the door open. He stared at the space for a few seconds before he began the process of folding his enormous frame into the low-slung seats.

"Holy shit, Trev," he said as he pulled his legs inside and struggled to get the door closed. "I already climbed out of a womb once. Is your dick really so small that you need to drive a car like this?"

Munro gunned the engine mostly for the noise of it, and circled around the parking lot to head back out on

Maple Avenue, heading north. "You called this meeting, Sjogren," he said.

"And you ought to be saying a prayer of thanks that I did," Sjogren said. "You got yourself what we New Englanders call a wicked problem."

Trevor forced himself to keep his eyes on the road. If he didn't encourage these kinds of games, maybe they would stop, and the oaf would simply get to the point. Meanwhile, the Porsche's horsepower would remain wasted as he surged from traffic light to traffic light, flanked by one strip mall after another.

"I got a buddy in the U.S. attorney's office who keeps me in the loop on important stuff. He tells me that they're on the edge of bringing in your butt buddy, Felix Hernandez. I don't know how you do that from another country, but he's never given me bad four-one-one."

Munro waited for the rest.

"C'mon, Trev, humor me. I got so little in my life. This is where you're supposed to say, 'How does this affect me?' "

And thus the game perpetuated. "Gee, Mr. Sjogren, how does this affect you?"

Sjogren erupted in laughter. "Not *me—you*. How does this affect *you*. I was doing, like a direct quote for you. And remember that my name is Abrams for this op." Sjogren craned his neck to see Munro's face, and then slapped him on the arm. "C'mon, Trev. Engage with me. We're havin' fun here."

"*You're* having fun," Munro said. He knew he was rising to the bait, but he wanted this meeting to end. "You're having it at my expense, and I desperately want you to get on with it."

"Priggish little shit, aren't you?" Sjogren mocked. "All right, fine. If they nail him, I figure that you'll be the first one he throws under the bus. That's what I'd do if I was him. Then I'd pull your skinny ass out and throw it under again. I've checked you out, Trev. You got no friends anywhere. That's hard to do. Shit, I'm an asshole, and even I have friends." He paused for a reaction.

"No freakin' fun at all," Sjogren said. "Now ask me what they've got on Hernandez."

Munro looked across the console. He hoped that his contempt for the man was plainly evident. "Really?" he said.

"Do you want to know or don't you?"

A deep sigh. "Okay, Mr. Abrams, what do they have on Hernandez?"

"An informant." He fired the answer like a weapon, and it hit its mark. "There's somebody inside his organization that's funneling information back to the U.S. attorney's office. The FBI's doin' a little happy dance over it."

Munro felt his face going pale, and he let off the accelerator a bit. This could be the nightmare of nightmares. Hernandez knew way too much about everything. The drug lord had thoroughly insulated himself from the Mexican authorities, but there were still elements within the Mexican government that wanted democracy to return. Those elements had been working with the American State Department for years trying to find a workable leverage point. And, of course, wherever State goes, the Justice Department isn't very far behind. It would be just like those agencies to negotiate leniency for a Mexican in favor of the hard line against a career patriot like Munro.

"You don't look so good, Trev," Sjogren said. "You maybe need to pull over or something? I'd hate to test the air bags on your midlife crisis car."

"Go to hell, Sjogren."

"It's Abrams."

"Fuck you."

Sjogren laughed again, a hearty thing that shook his whole frame. "There you go, Trev! That's what I've been mining for all this time. I really can get you to cuss! I'm proud of you."

Munro couldn't even process the mockery. This was beyond a crisis. This was a disaster of incalculable proportions. "We have to stop it," he said.

"Yeah, well, good luck with that. What do you have in mind?"

Munro's mind swam in options. "How much would it cost for you to kill him?"

Sjogren's jaw dropped. "Who, Felix Hernandez? You don't have that much money. They don't *print* that much money. He's got more security around him than the freakin' president of the United States."

Munro felt the panic building in his gut. He tried to press it down, but this was too big to suppress. "But he has to be stopped. If what you say is true—"

"Back up a second," Sjogren said. "You're not hearing what I'm telling you. He's got an informant in his inner circle. My guy at the AG's office thinks it's a woman, but he wasn't sure of that. You just need to tell Hernandez that he's got a spy, and then Hernandez needs to clean his own house. Without the informant, the government's got no case. No case, no arrest. No arrest, you get to retire alive."

There, finally, was the glimmer of hope. He didn't know why he hadn't thought of it himself. "You need to get me a name."

"You say that like it's easy. If I coulda got you a name, I'd have done it."

"How much?" Munro asked.

"How much what?"

Returning anger started diluting his fear. "Don't be obtuse," he said. "How much will a name cost me?"

Sjogren put a hand over his chest, as if to fend off a heart attack. "You offend me, Trev. You make it like I do this only for the money."

Munro shot a look that triggered another laugh. "How much?"

"Ten thousand."

"*Dollars*?" Munro croaked. "I don't have that kind of money."

Sjogren made a show of stroking the lush leather interior of the Porsche. "This is really a nice car, Trev. The whole poverty thing doesn't resonate well with you."

Typical talk from a lout like Sjogren. "But ten thousand dollars? That's outrageous."

"Hey, you asked me, okay? You want the name, you pay the money. You don't, you don't. I don't give much of a shit either way."

Munro ran the options through his head and determined within seconds that he didn't have any. "First the name, and then the payment," he said. "I'm not going to pay that kind of money on a roll of the dice."

"Fine by me. I figure you know the penalty for stiffing me, so what the hell?" He slapped Munro on the shoulder again. "See, Trev? We got us a trusting working relationship now. When you foul things up, I'm always there to help you clean up the mess."

Munro felt his face flush. Just once, he wanted to hear Sjogren—or Abrams, or whatever the hell he wanted to call himself—face up to his own mistakes. That's what bothered Munro the most in his dealings with the Bostonian: he managed to remain self-righteously smug, even as he shared at least half the blame.

"When can you get it to me?" Munro asked. "The name, I mean."

"I don't know that I can. I don't know that my guy even has it. Even within the AG's office, people tend to be pretty tight-lipped. Or so I'm told."

"You need to hurry," Munro pressed.

"I can just make something up, if you want," Sjogren said. "That's what you get when you hurry. I'll do what I can, and then we'll see what we end up with."

Munro executed a treacherous U-turn in the middle of a block, throwing Sjogren against his door, and pressing him there with centrifugal force.

"Who the hell taught you to drive?" Sjogren bitched. "Don't they have police officers in this burg?"

"I want it by tonight," Munro said.

"And I want a date with a supermodel. Wanting it don't make it so, you know? Even when you're a big-friggin'-shot with the CIA. I'll do what I can. Keep your cell phone handy."

Munro recognized the closing line of their last meeting being turned against him, but pretended he didn't. They drove back to the library in silence, only this time, Munro avoided the tough left turn entirely and instead pulled into a parking lot across the street.

"I'll let you out here," Munro said.

Sjogren pulled the latch and pushed the door open. It was a comical thing to watch him unfold himself and find his feet.

"Hey, Mr. Abrams," Munro said as the door was about to close.

Sjogren bent at the waist and peered back into the vehicle.

"This source you have. Why does he give you this information? What's his angle?"

Sjogren's smile betrayed the fact that he'd been waiting for the question. "That's the coolest part of all," he said. "In Washington, D.C., everybody's got secrets to share. All you gotta do is tell them that you're an investigative reporter. I even have fake business cards, just in case, but not one of these self-righteous bozos has ever asked for one."

Munro scoffed and shook his head. What was the world coming to?

"And before you get all high-horsey on me," Sjogren said, "you spooky guys at the Funny Farm are the worst of the lot."

With that, he slammed the door and walked away.

So, now they were marching. And sweating. They'd become a part of the jungle, bait not just to the gajillion insects that had already feasted on every square inch of Tristan's exposed skin, but now to sharp-toothed mammals as well, now that the afternoon was dying and darkness lay only three or four hours ahead.

Yeah, good times. And for the record, flip-flops made shitty hiking shoes.

Until, say, five hours ago, Tristan would have sworn on a stack of Bibles that he'd already reached the bottom of his life experience. Hah!

This was the stuff of nightmares. All the killing, all the blood. He wondered if he'd ever be able to close his eyes and not have those images invade his brain.

Would it ever be possible to be happy again? Would he ever be able to think about Allison and Ray and Mrs. Charlton and the others and see them in his mind the way they used to look, or would those memories forever be dominated by shattered bone and extruding brain tissue?

What was it that Scorpion had said to him before? That he'd served in war with soldiers who were younger than Tristan. He wondered now if those were all the ones who came back mentally crippled from the experience. If you can never find happiness, then what's left for your life other than anger, depression, and suicide?

You're catastrophizing. The thought startled him. He hadn't heard his dad's voice in his head for a very long time. *Catastrophizing* had been Dad's favorite word for describing Tristan's tendency to view a problem purely in negative terms and then spin it into a negative prediction for the future. Even Dad would have to cut him a little bit of a break on this one.

Even the ever-optimistic, ever-cheerful Dad, whose pancreatic cancer had taken him out within three weeks of his initial diagnosis. That had been one time, in fact, when Tristan had decided to take the positive route, if only because the negative was so depressing.

All things considered, calling Tristan's life a catastrophe sounded more like a statement of fact than a projection of gloom.

Since it was too dangerous to use the Pathfinder anymore, they'd formed a three-person parade, with Scorpion in front and Big Guy in the rear. Big Guy had modified one of the dead guys' bulletproof vests so that it would fit Tristan, so now, despite the zillion-degree heat, he was wearing a thirty-pound sweat machine that was crammed with magazines for the rifle that he'd practiced so diligently to load and unload.

He also carried a rifle they'd taken from one of the dead Mexicans, slung as the commandos' rifles were slung, hanging across his chest. He kept his hand on the grip because that was where it felt most comfortable (and, he thought, looked most cool). Consequently, he endured a reminder every few minutes from Big Guy to make sure that the safety was still on. That seemed to be a real sore spot for him.

Tristan tried not to notice the bloodstains on the vest. At least it was black, and Scorpion had done his best to wash them off. If you didn't look too hard, you couldn't even see them.

When they'd first started out, this hike was announced to be about twelve miles in duration. Tristan wasn't sure it was possible to drink enough water to keep up with the sweat that poured out of him. In the oppressive humidity, none of it evaporated, either. He didn't get how Scorpion and Big Guy could do this with the long sleeves and long pants and the backpacks. Then again, their legs probably weren't bloodied from thorns and bug bites. Everything's a trade-off, he supposed.

The exhaustion and dehydration and the insects were to be expected, he thought, as unpleasant as they were. What really surprised him was how badly the jungle stank. Take the worst combination of gym socks, skid-marked underwear, and mold and blow the resulting smell through a hot, mildewed towel, and you'd come close.

Scorpion led them with purpose, rarely stopping to readjust to his map. Tristan figured that the box in his hand was a GPS of some sort, but it was way more exotic looking than anything he'd ever seen in a store.

Tristan picked up his pace to catch up with the leader, doing his best not to make a lot of noise.

"You'd be wise not to sneak up on people," Scorpion said without looking. When he turned around for eye contact, he was smiling. "Come on up and walk with me." He moved to the side to open up a gap between him and the foliage on his left.

Tristan stepped up.

"How are you holding up?" Scorpion asked.

"I wish I didn't have to wear all of this crap," he said. "It's heavy and hot."

"It'll also stop a bullet," Scorpion said. "Keep it on. How are you doing otherwise?"

"I'm scared," Tristan said. He worried that they were the wrong words, but they were the only ones that came to mind.

"Good for you," Scorpion said. "Give yourself an A in humanity."

Tristan didn't get it. How did someone endure this

kind of pressure and drama yet remain so calm? He actually wanted to ask that as a question, but he didn't know how to phrase it without sounding like a toad.

"You should feel proud of yourself," Scorpion said. "I've rescued a lot of people over the years, and not all of them held up as well as you have."

Tristan said, "Thanks," but it sounded hollow, even to his own ears. What else was there to say?

"Tell me about home," Scorpion said. "I know you're on the debate team, but tell me something else I should know about you."

Inexplicably, Tristan found himself blushing. "That's it," he said. "I'm boring. I'm a geek. I'm the anti-you."

Scorpion laughed. "The anti-me? What does that mean?"

Under different circumstances, the laughter might have been offensive, but in this case, Tristan kind of liked it. He'd planted the joke, after all. "Look at you," he said. "Now look at me. Any questions?"

Scorpion laughed again. Then he seemed to notice that he was laughing alone, and he turned serious. "Look," he said. "I'm not going to bullshit you with a bunch of esteem-building nonsense, okay? I bet you have enough of that in your life. I'm really sorry about all your friends. I wish I could have done something for them."

Tristan looked away. He felt emotion pressing behind his eyes, and he didn't need anybody to see that.

"You know that there are bad folks in the world," Scorpion went on. "You probably always knew that, but now you *really* know. Your best revenge is to come out on the other end of this alive."

"I can live with that," Tristan said. He didn't mean it as a pun, but once he heard it, and the chuckle that it elicited, he allowed himself a smile.

"I bet you can," Scorpion said.

A minute or two passed in silence as they trudged on. Tristan pulled at his vest, trying to get it to sit comfortably.

"How do you do this all the time?" Tristan asked. "How do you handle the stress?"

Scorpion answered without dropping a beat. "Scotch," he said. "But not just any scotch. Good scotch. You're too young for it, but when you get older, remember the name Lagavulin. Doesn't get any better than that."

Tristan smiled because he knew he was supposed to, but it had been a real question. Disinclined to ask it a second time, he stared ahead.

"I don't know if I can make you understand," Scorpion said. "I tried to touch on it before. It's not about stress for me. It's about success. No matter how bad things look sometimes, there's always a happy solution to be found somewhere. You just have to stay with it until you find it."

"But suppose you don't?"

"You always do. That's the reality. If you're willing to commit everything to finding the answer—and I mean *everything*, up to and including your life—then the answer will be found, even if it costs everything you were willing to risk."

Tristan scowled, not sure that he'd actually heard the words. "You mean, even if you die."

Scorpion nodded. "That's exactly what I mean. I'm

the first to admit that I've got a weird squint on the world, but the way I see it, the business of living is all about the *living*. Too many people devote their lives to not dying, even though none of us gets out of this experience alive. To me, that's just squandering limited days on the planet."

The words clanged Tristan's bullshit bell. He wanted to ask how Scorpion could get so used to killing people, but he didn't know how to phrase it so it wouldn't sound like an accusation.

After a pause, Scorpion said, "Now, can I ask you a question?"

Tristan shrugged. "Sure."

"Why did Bill Georgen and Bobby Cantrell back out of this trip at the last minute?"

The specificity of the question startled him. "How do you know about Bill and Bobby?"

"You don't do what I do without a lot of research," Scorpion said.

"I don't know," Tristan said. "But it happened pretty quickly. I didn't know they weren't coming until just before we left. Lucky bastards."

"From what you could tell, were they looking forward to the trip?"

Something tugged at the back of Tristan's brain. "Why are you asking this?"

"For exactly the reason you think I am," Scorpion said.

"You think they had something to do with this?"

"Not them, necessarily. But maybe their parents."

Tristan knew that the very thought of such a thing should offend him. So, why didn't it?

When it became obvious that Scorpion was actually waiting for an answer, Tristan hedged, "I can't say for certain. We weren't exactly close."

"What did the chaperones tell you about them not coming?"

Tristan shrugged. "Nothing, really. Just that they wouldn't be."

"Surely someone must have asked."

"I guess I did, but Mrs. Charlton just said there was a change in plans. She seemed kind of pissed about it, actually. Something about having to change the numbers on a bunch of reservations. It didn't seem all the important to me, but Mrs. Charlton is kind of a control freak. I mean, *was*." Man, oh man, he was going to need some serious shrink time when all this was over.

Tristan changed the subject. "So, am I right that the plan is to steal an airplane and sneak back into the United States?"

"Um, no. Not exactly. There's no way for us to just fly across the border. The United States doesn't like airborne invasions. Especially these days. We have to pick up a passenger first, and then she's going to smuggle us across the border."

The pieces didn't fit in his head. "Aren't we still wanted for murder? What happens when we get back?"

Scorpion did a bobblehead thing with his neck. "That's where it gets complicated," he said. "This passenger we're picking up has information that will clear your name. Actually, she'll have information that will bring all these bastards to justice."

"What about your name?" Tristan asked.

"Excuse me?"

"You said that this lady will clear *my* name. What about yours?"

"Mine, too," he said, but there was a sparkle that spoke of an inside joke.

"How long?" Tristan asked. "You know, before we're there? It'll be dark soon"

"We want it to be dark," Scorpion said. "I'd say we're about three miles out."

"Isn't it easier to fly an airplane in the daytime?"

"It is," Scorpion said. "But it's much easier to borrow them at night. Some people get nervous when you borrow their stuff without asking."

"That's because the rest of the world calls it stealing," Tristan said.

Scorpion made a puffing sound. "We're not going to *keep* it. We're just going to use it for a few hours."

Tristan shook his head. "I'm pretty sure the law—"

"Tristan."

Tristan blushed. "Oh. You knew that."

"Yeah, pretty much."

Tristan wanted to ask one more time if Scorpion thought everything would be all right, but he already knew what that answer would be.

"What's the first thing you're going to do when you get back home?" Scorpion asked.

"Seek counseling."

"No, that might be the second thing. What's the *first* thing?"

He had no idea. "It's like I haven't allowed myself to think about that. Maybe for fear of jinxing it."

"Oh, you've got to think about home," Scorpion said. "That's where all the good stuff is. That's where the reason to fight resides. No matter how intense the here and now is, you never want to lose sight of the goal. I can't tell you the number of times the image of home has inspired me to take a step I didn't think I was capable of taking."

"Where is your home?" Tristan asked.

Scorpion waved the question away. "The where isn't important. That it's waiting for me is all that matters."

"Are you married?"

Scorpion stared straight ahead. "For me, the first thing will be a shower. A long, hot shower. Long enough to drain the water heater."

Great dodge, Tristan didn't say. "The scotch won't be first? The Laga-whatever?"

"Lagavulin," Scorpion said, donning a pensive expression. "Good point. I might actually bring a wee dram into the shower with me."

Tristan cocked his head and couldn't help but smile. This man—this *Scorpion*—was such a contradiction. He'd seen him be so brutal, so ruthless, yet here he was chatting like a friendly neighbor. In the wash of the casual conversation, the weapons and the bloodstains somehow mattered less.

This guy projected such confidence and so little fear that Tristan found it impossible not to be inspired by him. He wondered if this was what the real face of bravery looked like. It wasn't about the swagger and tough talk that passed for manliness in the halls of his high school. The real thing was about understatement and the projection of calm in spite of whatever heart palpitations were hammering in your chest.

You don't get people to follow you by telling them what to do. You do it by being forthright and friendly.

"Yeah," Tristan said at length, "I think a shower will be first."

CHAPTER TWENTY-THREE

Trevor Munro lived an immaculate life. Where so many others in his profession had surrendered to the temptations of women and alcohol and overeating, his was a life of discipline. It was a point of pride.

He'd written more than once in his diary that precise men lead precise lives, and precision translated to cleanliness and restraint. People could sense these traits in him. That was how he earned their trust. And once earned, that trust was never broken. Not by him. And if it was broken by others, then he made sure that they paid a heavy price for their betrayal.

This business with Felix Hernandez was particularly troubling for him because Felix was convinced that Munro had betrayed him. That of course meant that Hernandez would be after his blood, but that was far less of a concern than the affront to Munro's reputation. The record needed to be corrected.

As he entered the mudroom through the garage door, he punched in the code to disarm the alarm, and then armed it again as soon as the door was closed. The light switch on his left illuminated a pathway into the kitchen. His was a world of white on black. The overhead lights sparkled against the polished white Silestone of the countertops, which blended perfectly with the white walls and the white cabinetry. Together, they provided stunning contrast against the gleaming black appliances and the black-stained walnut floors that he buffed to a high gloss every Sunday.

He crossed through the kitchen to his den, which doubled as a home office on the occasions when he just couldn't bring himself to make the drive from Reston to Langley, and laid his briefcase on the floor at the edge of his desk.

The curtains and blinds were closed throughout the house, as they would remain until this terrible business in Mexico was resolved. Munro had received no specific intel that Hernandez had dispatched hit squads to the United States, but the man certainly had the resources to do so, and the temperament to make it happen. For the next few days, his would be the life of an undercover operator, reminding him of his early years with the Clandestine Service. He would stay away from windows, avoid prolonged exposure out in the open, and drive different routes to work, traveling at unpredictable hours.

The point wasn't to be bulletproof, but rather to make it as difficult as possible for the bad guys to execute whatever plan they might have. Evasion, then, combined with the protection that Sjogren's people provided, should give him an edge until this mess stabilized.

Should. Far from a guarantee, but perhaps that's the way things should be. He was in charge of an operation that hadn't gone well, and now pipers needed to be paid.

As Munro reentered the kitchen, he turned on the broiler on the wall oven and then walked to the refrigerator to retrieve the filet mignon that he had set in there this morning to allow it to defrost. As he lifted it, he knew from touch alone that the six-ounce filet was ready to cook. It was exactly six ounces, too—306 calories—specially cut and packaged by the butcher at the Whole Foods up the street. Throw in a cup of corn at 183 calories, and he had a healthy meal that wouldn't add an ounce to the reading on the scale. He hadn't exceeded his budget of 1,750 calories a single time in the past ten years.

Discipline and precision.

He'd just removed the steak from its plastic wrapping when his BlackBerry buzzed on his hip—a phone call, number blocked. He answered it. "Mr. Abrams. Do you have a name for me, or are you just calling to pester?"

"As much friggin' fun as it is to pull your chain, Trev, I'm looking forward to the moment when I don't have to chat you up at all anymore."

"At last," Munro said. "We have found common ground. Do you have a name or not?"

"Nope, no name," Sjogren said. "But I do have a plan."

Munro's heart skipped a beat. Finally, some progress.

Sjogren continued, "My guy at the AG's office says that they're smuggling the snitch out of Mexico in the next day or two."

"Through where?"

"He doesn't know specifically, but somewhere in Ciudad Juárez."

Munro's bubble of hope burst. "That's hardly help-ful," he said. He pulled a package of corn from the freezer, then pulled a measuring cup from the cabinet over the stove.

"I think it's more helpful than you recognize," Sjo-gren countered. "The only reason my guy knows what he knows is because the FBI is pulling strings from a really high level to grease the skids for this thing. What he told me was that the snitch isn't coming alone. Specifically, she's coming in with three fugitives. Does that ring any bells for you?"

Munro sighed. Everything with this man was such a tug-of-war. Why couldn't he just—

"Did you say *three* fugitives?"

"There you go, Trev," Sjogren said with a laugh. "Now you're catching on. Care to guess what the names of the fugitives are?"

Hope bloomed again. Much larger than before. "Don't toy with me, Mr. Abrams."

"I got a Tristan Wagner, a Leon Harris, and a Rich-ard Lerner."

Munro coughed out a laugh before he could stop it. "I don't understand how you can know the names of the fugitives and not know the names of the informer," he said. "We need to know them all if we're going to stop them."

"No, we don't," Sjogren argued. "All we need to do is find your commando buddies and follow them. They'll take us to the snitch. Then all we have to do is take them all out."

"You say that as if it's a simple thing to do. Have you any idea where Harris and his friends are?"

"Actually, I do. They had a bit of a firefight. They won, of course. But they couldn't have gotten very far because the Mexican Army is out in force, looking for them. They even know what vehicle to look for. I've already talked with the Army commander down there, and he's ordering his troops to sight and follow."

"We can't let them get through," Munro said. The true ramifications of this new discovery hit him in a rush, eliciting an audible gasp. "My God, this means they know everything. We know they've connected the dots to the cathedral, and because they're hooking up with this informer, that means they've connected it back to the drugs and Hernandez."

"That's the way I see it," Sjogren said. "But there's light at the end of that tunnel, too, if you look hard enough for it. Apparently, they need this guy's testimony to make any kind of case. Otherwise, they'd be all over Hernandez, and after that, they'd be all over you."

"You need to get a name," Munro pressed. "We cannot wait for Harris to hook up with the informer. We need to take the informer out first."

"I don't think anybody disagrees with you, Sport, but weren't you listening? We don't know who the hell she is. Your butt buddy's got himself a hell of an operation down there. I imagine it could be any one of hundreds of people. It's not like they're salt-of-the-earth types like me and you."

Munro pulled the phone away from his ear and let it dangle by his side for a few seconds while he collected his thoughts. Part of having a disciplined mind was the ability to control the flow of information. This situa-

tion was at the proverbial tipping point, equally capable of going well for him or turning into a complete
catastrophe. Progress one way or the other would be
entirely dependent on the decisions he made in the next
few minutes.

And then the decisions to be made after those. And
after those. On and on for God only knew how long it
would take. Munro needed to embrace this as a siege,
not a—

As a bell rang in his head, Munro brought the phone
back to his ear.

"—did you go? For God's sake, Trev—"

"I'm here," Munro said. "I had to put you down so I
could think. Tell me where this shootout was. The one
the Harris and his team won."

"A few hours north of the exchange site," Sjogren
said. "North and east. I don't have a name of the town.
Hell, I don't even know if there is a town. That's still
pretty remote country."

"So they were still in the jungles?"

"Oh, hell yeah."

"And who was killed in the shootout?"

"What, you want names?"

Munro rolled his eyes. "Heaven forbid," he said.
"We all know that names are beyond you."

"Hey, screw you, Trev."

"Of course I don't need names. I don't know these
people. But who were they? Bystanders? Local cops?
Army?"

"Oh, they were definitely Army. Why does that
matter?"

This is what happened when you're forced to deal

with people of inferior intellect. You had to explain *everything*. "It matters because Harris knows he's being looked for. He knows that the Army is involved, and he may very well know that they will recognize his vehicle."

"How would he know that?"

"I would assume, were I he, that the group who spotted them would have called it in on the radio. Isn't that in fact how your Army friends know the identity of the vehicle?"

Sjogren's response was more guttural than verbal. Having some of his shit fed back to him apparently disagreed with him.

"I'll take that as a yes," Munro pressed. "So, if they think that they're being looked for, don't you think they may take some countermeasures? Perhaps they've changed vehicles by now. Isn't that what you would do?"

"Yeah, I suppose I might."

"So here's the bottom line, Sjogren. You don't have a clue what you're looking for out there. You can't follow what you can't see, and without following, there's no stopping these people. You need to get a name."

"I don't *have* a name, Trev." Sjogren's voice vibrated with frustration. Munro had clearly struck a nerve. "It's not like I'm holding out on you. I don't *have* it."

"I don't hire you for what *you* know," Munro fired back. "I hire you for the information that your *contacts* know. Sounds to me like it's time to put some more pressure on your own butt buddy in the U.S. attorney's office."

"He doesn't know, either. If he did, he'd tell me."

Munro closed his eyes as he fought to control his

temper. "Don't concentrate on what he *does* know. Concentrate on what he *can* know. Everything's possible when the stakes are high enough."

All the derision was gone from the Bostonian. In fact for the very first time in Munro's memory, Jerry Sjogren may have just been rendered speechless.

"Hey, Jerry?" Munro said.

"Abrams."

"Right. You know that part I said about anything being possible when the stakes are high enough? You might want to take that one personally."

He pushed the disconnect button. As he turned back to the business of fixing dinner, he felt a sense of calm, as if he might have taken the first step toward victory.

Maria Elizondo stuffed three hundred thousand American dollars—all hundred-dollar bills, banded in five-thousand-dollar stacks—into a Tyvek envelope, sealed it, and placed the package on a shelf in the massive safe that sat next to her desk. That brought the daily total to three million five hundred forty-two thousand dollars. She made the appropriate notations in the ledger book, and then placed that into the safe as well. She pushed the door closed, turned the bolt, and then spun the lock.

It was time to go home. Her office, such as it was, occupied one hundred square feet of tile-floored grandeur in the far southeast corner of the main building of the compound known as Hacienda del Sol—a ridiculously pretentious name, she thought, for a hideous concrete bunker of a house surrounded by fifteen-foot-high walls in one of the more squalid sectors of Ciudad Juárez, which itself was one of the most squalid cities on earth. Yet another expression of narcissism from a man whose opinion of himself could not possibly be overstated.

Maria shed the sweater that she always wore to counter the chill of the air-conditioning and hung it over the back of her chair, where it would be waiting for her in the morning. She had to hurry now, before another delivery of cash was dropped through the louvered steel slot in the reinforced concrete wall.

She grew so tired of the overbright yellow light that shined from behind the wire-reinforced recessed light fixtures in the ceiling that some days she swore that she felt ill from the lack of sunshine and unfiltered air. After days like today—ten hours without a break—she thought she might go mad if she had to face this one more time.

Face it she would, though, because Felix Hernandez trusted her, and only a fool denied Felix what he desired.

With all surfaces cleared, and all drawers and cabinets locked, she picked up the telephone receiver from its hook on the wall next to the entrance and waited while the call completed itself. The person on the other end of the line answered it merely by picking it up. Protocol prohibited him from saying anything until he was spoken to.

Maria said, "Purple, sapphire, salmon, moon."

The guard on the other end said, "Apple, rose, seawater, penguin."

The random words were chosen anew every morning, and they needed to be recited in precisely the correct order for either Maria or her security counterpart on the other side to unlock their side of the door. This was part of Felix's paranoia that his enemies might somehow gain control of the compound, and by so doing merely wait patiently until it was time for the occupant of the vault to go home, and when the door opened therefore have access to his money.

He called it *double redundancy*, which in Maria's mind was itself singly redundant.

With the pass codes properly delivered, she spun the knob of the cipher lock on her side of the door and disengaged the bolts. A few seconds later, she heard the second set slide out from the wall. She pushed while the guard pulled, and as the door moved outward, she wondered if the blast of frigid air felt as refreshing to the guards as the enveloping warmth felt to her.

Per their protocol, all six guards in the adjoining room had their rifles to their shoulders, aiming outward in an arc, waiting to shoot anyone who might attempt to rush the vault during the short time that it was open. Once outside the vault, she let the guard push the door closed, and then she waited for him to spin his lock before spinning her own. Neither knew the other's combination.

"The lock is set," the guard said, and the others lowered their rifles.

Maria said nothing to these men. No pleasantries, minimal eye contact. They were not her friends, and she was not theirs. If Felix so much as suspected relations among them, all of their lives would be endangered. In his paranoid world, people who liked each other were more likely to conspire against him, and any conspiracy could only be about stealing his money.

Or, of course, about taking his life. In truth, there were far more people in the world who wanted him dead than cared about his money. Maria, in fact, numbered herself among them.

Exiting the Banking Room, as it was called, Maria stopped in the doorway to the next room and held her hands out to her sides to be frisked. Though she wore tight-fitting jeans and a T-shirt, the pat-down was necessary, if only to give these teenage guards an excuse to touch her body. She knew that they lusted after her, and she didn't mind it a bit. Let them have their dreams. These days, there was so little to dream for.

After clearing that last search and grope, she was free to go.

Or at least she thought she was. As she passed into the center hall, an all-too-familiar voice called, "Maria! I need you!"

Her shoulders sagged, but only for an instant. Felix expected his women to appreciate his advances. Standing tall and donning a smile, she turned and entered the ornate study that served as Felix Hernandez's office—at least in this house. Hacienda del Sol was only one of four homes where he divided his time in random rotation.

"Hello, Felix," she said. As she approached, he rose from behind his desk and met her halfway for a kiss. It was a lip-only kiss, and he did not smell of alcohol, so she relaxed a little. When he was in this mood, he rarely wanted to root and paw at her as he did when he was drunk.

"You seem surprised to see me," Felix said.

"I *am* surprised to see you. I didn't expect to see you for several days."

He led the way to a pair of love seats that flanked a coffee table in front of his desk. He gestured for Maria to sit, and then sat next to her. He was a handsome man by any reasonable standard, with strong Latin features, jet-black hair, and a dazzling smile that melted every female heart. Maria had always thought that his eyes looked empty, as if made of glass.

"One way to remain unpredictable," he said, "is to occasionally double back on your own tracks."

"You need to be careful," she said. She sold it with a gentle squeeze of his arm, a gesture designed to reassure him that she truly cared.

"That's the second time that's been said to me in just the last hour," he said with a wry smile.

Maria scowled. "Really? Who else?"

"An associate of mine," Hernandez said. "His name doesn't matter."

"What does he say you need to be careful about?"

His eyes grew even emptier as they peered into her. "My associate—who knows many things and is rarely wrong—says that I have been betrayed."

The words chilled Maria's blood far more effectively than the air-conditioning had. She willed herself to maintain eye contact, yet again touching his arm. "I don't understand."

"He tells me that someone very close to me has been talking to American agents, plotting to do me harm."

The chill turned to ice. How could he possibly know? She'd been so very careful. "You mean to *kill* you?"

He cocked his head and stared deeper. Maria felt as if he were trying to set her on fire from within.

"I don't understand, Felix," she said. "Please don't take this the wrong way, but the fact that people are trying to kill you is hardly news."

The glare continued for a few seconds, and then he smiled. "Indeed," he said. "But the threat is not to kill me. The threat is to have me imprisoned for the rest of my life." Finally, he looked away. "But even that is not what troubles me. This associate was very specific. The informant is very close to me, and probably a woman. That means that someone to whom I have been extraordinarily generous is planning to repay me with the worst kind of betrayal."

Maria's mind raced. What was her best play now? Clearly, he suspected her—he'd *have* to suspect her—so would it be most convincing to pretend to be totally clueless, or should she become defensive?

"Surely you don't suspect *me*," she said before she even knew that she'd chosen a course.

"Should I?"

Her strategy materialized out of nowhere. She bolted to her feet and stormed to the door, furious.

On cue, Hernandez shot out his hand to grab her wrist. "Where do you think you're going?"

Maria whirled on him and slapped his face. "How dare you!" she said. Tears clouded her vision.

Hernandez shot to his feet, too, his face red with rage.

"Go ahead!" Maria dared. "Go ahead and beat me. Have me shot. If you think so little of me—if you think for even a second that I could betray you—by all means shoot me yourself." She pulled her arm from his hand. "Bastard."

Her heart hammered at an impossible rate as she headed again for the door.

"Stop!" he commanded.

When she turned this time, he hadn't moved. He still stood in front of the love seat, his face slack with surprise.

"Don't tell me what to do," Maria said, pointing her finger at him. "I am not like your other mistresses. Yes, I know you have them. They pretend to care for you because they fear you. I *love* you, Felix. I would lay down my life for you. How dare you suspect me of such a despicable thing?"

He moved toward her. "Where are you going?" His voice was softer now.

"Home," she said.

He reached for her hands with both of his, but stopped when she recoiled. "I'm sorry," he said. "I didn't mean to hurt you. I was being . . . *stupid*. Please stay. Please stay the night."

"I am going *home*," Maria said again. "Unless, of course, you want to have your guards drag me back here so that you can rape me."

The thought seemed to horrify him. "Maria. I would never—"

"And neither would I," she said. "Never in a million years would I betray you."

"Stay, then."

She shook her head emphatically. "No, not tonight. I couldn't tonight. I need to be alone tonight."

Hernandez seemed to be at a loss for words, as if he hadn't found himself in this position before.

"Will you be back tomorrow?" His voice sounded oddly childlike now.

This was a new expression. There was tenderness there somewhere.

She might actually feel something after she drove a stake through the monster's heart.

CHAPTER TWENTY-FOUR

Two hours ago, when Ernesto Palma had taken the phone call from Felix Hernandez, he'd thought for certain that the point of the call would be to upbraid him for having lost track of his prey. Palma had spent so much time over the years dealing with the peasants and riffraff that defined the population of drug thugs that he continued to be surprised by the savvy and resourcefulness of Harris and Lerner.

It only made sense, of course, that they would disappear after their altercation with the patrol in the jungle. Once they'd been made, they had to go into hiding. That was the bad news. The flip side of that—the good news—was that hiding and getting away were mutually exclusive endeavors. Sooner or later, they would have to make a move, and when they did, Palma would be ready for them. The longer they took, in fact, the more soldiers and police Palma could have out on the streets to intercept them.

He'd talked himself into believing that his prey's disappearance was actually a good thing because it allowed him to marshal more resources to catch them.

But that had turned out to be a fantasy.

Four hours ago, one of his patrols had found the Pathfinder stashed off the road. It had been stripped of all valuable gear, and there was no evidence of what direction they might have gone when they left.

Had they hijacked a car? Had they taken off on foot? That latter option seemed least likely if they were in fact trying to head north—a lot of inhospitable desert lay between here and there—but maybe they'd reached some kind of a hybrid solution, in which they hiked far enough to steal a different car.

For that matter, they had three million American dollars with them. They could buy any car they wanted. They could buy dozens of any car they wanted.

This was the report that Palma had been prepared to give to Felix Hernandez when the phone rang, but as it turned out, he never had to. In fact, Hernandez never even asked him about how the search was going. He didn't say much of anything. He opened with, "My plane will be waiting for you at Hacienda Luna. Be on it in a half hour."

Palma ran the distance in his head. "I don't think that's possible, Mr. Hernandez."

"Make it possible, Captain Palma. Your targets will be leaving from Ciudad Juárez."

"Ciudad *Juárez*? That's twelve hundred kilometers. How are they getting there?"

"I don't know," Hernandez replied. "But when they get here, I want you here waiting for them. You cannot let them leave."

Palma didn't like it. "With all respect, Mr. Hernandez, we have them on the run here. They've left their vehicle and now they're having to improvise on the run. Literally on the run. They are on foot, as far as we know."

"Which means that they could be in a boat, as far as you know. Do yourself a favor and don't leave my pilot waiting."

With that, Hernandez clicked off.

Thus, Palma found himself racing down roads that were never intended for speed, bouncing off the door and roof of the Sandcat as Sergeant Nazario did everything he could to keep it on the road.

As he'd expected, thirty minutes had proven to be undoable, but forty-five looked to be possible.

"We are going to hurry to Ciudad Juárez," Nazario said. "We are leaving all our leads behind us. And then what happens when we arrive there?"

"We await orders," Palma said.

In the lingering daylight, Maria stormed from the compound, every stride covering half again the distance that it normally would. The guards she passed looked startled—some even shifted their hands on their weapons—but none made a threatening move on her.

The fact that her heart did not explode in her chest was testament to the fact that she'd taken good care of herself all these years. She left the house through the front doors and never slowed as she approached the wall. Sensing her ire, the guards moved quickly to open the heavy gates to let her pass without slowing.

Maria felt proud of herself for pulling this off, even as she managed the swell of terror in her gut that her confidence had been betrayed. Her FBI contact had sworn on all things holy that her identity would be protected. Without that assurance, she never would have offered up all the information she had these past two years.

Veronica Costanza had always seemed like a straight shooter to her. They'd first met at a coffee shop while standing in line. Both of them favored cold coffee drinks to hot ones, and that had led to a lighthearted discussion of caffeinated drinks. Looking back on it, Maria realized that the chance meeting had been engineered from the beginning, but that knowledge didn't tarnish the reality that she liked and trusted Veronica.

Even now that Maria knew that she'd been betrayed, she couldn't wrap her head around the notion that Veronica might have done it. Still, what was done was done. Now she had to cope. While Felix might have been taken off guard by her bluff back at the hacienda, his intelligence network would continue to push for details that would ultimately lead them to her. If not tonight or tomorrow, then next week or next month.

As she climbed into her Toyota Celica and turned the key, her mind raced to find the way out of this. There had to be a way. There was *always* a way.

As she drove down the streets of Ciudad Juárez, she checked her mirrors frequently, fully expecting to find a machine-gun-bearing technical closing in on her from behind. Such had been the fate of countless others whom Felix had suspected of betrayal. Yet none appeared.

Could it be that her performance had truly been that convincing? Could it be that he actually believed that she loved him? Maybe so. Why else would he have confided so much in her?

Still, his perceptions were at best a ruse. Soon he would learn the truth, and when he did, Maria's life would be measured in units of agony.

She could never go back, that much was clear. But how was she supposed to make her way out of the country? What were her options? She'd never discussed these things with Veronica. The plan had always been to endure—to wait until the FBI said that it was safe for her to enter the United States. Even as she heard the words the first time they'd been spoken, she'd realized their true meaning to be, *after she had provided adequate information to the United States,* but that was okay. No favors in the world came free.

She didn't understand what had changed. Only three days ago, she'd met with Veronica, begging her to bring her in, but as of then, the FBI wasn't quite finished with her. Maria had even offered up new intelligence on the location of smuggling tunnels, yet Veronica had remained unmoved.

What could possibly have reordered the world to such a large degree? If Felix's intelligence was right— and Felix's intel was *always* right—Veronica would have no choice but to get her out of the country. Surely, she wouldn't let Maria just die at Felix's hand.

Unless there was a second informant. Was that even possible?

Of course it was possible. There was no level of betrayal that was impossible within the American intelligence community. But was it *reasonable*?

Why not? If Veronica Costanza had engineered an

excuse to meet with Maria, could she not have created the same opportunity for all of Felix's mistresses? Could she not have created it for dozens of people who worked for him?

As she pulled onto the main road leaving the compound, Maria shook these thoughts out of her mind. They were silly. Veronica would have told her if there were additional agents within Felix's compound. To deny that kind of information would be to impose that much more danger on her, and Veronica wouldn't have done that.

The fact remained that Maria and Maria alone had lost both parents and a brother to Felix's brutality, and she alone had worked for five years to infiltrate his network for the express purpose of bringing him down.

She *had* to be the one that Felix had been talking about in his rant. She *had* to be. She didn't know that she could live with the knowledge that it was otherwise. When he ultimately faced his punishment, she *needed* for her hands to be on the chain of evidence and testimony that put him away. In a perfect world, they would be on the apparatus that executed him in prison, but Veronica had prepared her for the fact that execution was unlikely.

She'd prepared her, in fact, for the likelihood that Felix would testify his way to a criminal charge that was barely a criminal charge. Instead, he would give up the American coconspirators who underwrote his criminal activities in return for little or no jail time. That, Veronica had warned her, was the state of panic that existed within the administration in Washington. They were willing to let murderers go free in return for information that would allow them to imprison disloyal bureaucrats.

Maria was a creature of habit. She followed the same route to and from the office every day. For starters, she felt entirely safe doing so—Felix's enemies knew the faces and names of all of his mistresses, and there was no quicker route to the morgue than to lay a hand on one of them—but also, Maria needed to look for a sign from Veronica that she wanted to meet.

As she drove past the post box at the corner of Chelsea Street and Frutas Avenue, her heart fell. If they were to meet outside the pharmacy in the 2700 block of Santa Anna Boulevard, there would be a chalk mark on the paint—an X if the meeting was to happen tonight, and a heart if it was to happen tomorrow night. The box was in fact the flat green that it normally was.

She drove toward the Church of St. Michael the Archangel, hoping to see a bicycle chain on the wrought-iron fence out front. A silver chain would have had them meet in lobby of the Omniplex Theater for the nine o'clock show tonight, a black one for the same show tomorrow. Maria cursed under her breath as she saw no chain at all.

How could this be? If her cover had been blown this badly, surely Veronica would know about it. And if she knew about it, surely she would want to arrange a meeting.

A chill crawled up her spine as she considered the alternative: that the FBI was unaware that they had their own informant in their midst. That could be a disaster.

Maria resolved that when she got back to her house,

she would post on Facebook that her tooth was hurting today. That was the signal for Veronica to make contact as soon as possible.

While she would never reenter Felix Hernandez's world, she could pretend to be sick tomorrow as the details worked themselves out. Her absence would undoubtedly raise Felix's suspicions, but there again Maria's histrionics at the hacienda might serve her well. If she failed to show up, maybe Felix would merely assume that she was angry.

Maria lived in the Campestre neighborhood, once a lovely place where as a child she never would have dreamed she could afford to live. Now, the drug violence had driven most of the decent people away. Many had just abandoned their homes and their businesses, leaving the streets to the warriors. More than a few of the side streets had been completely blocked off with stacks of boulders in an effort to dissuade kidnappers and extortionists from gaining access to their enclaves.

Her heart raced as she pulled to the curb in front of her house. She slapped the transmission into neutral, set the brake, and hurried out of her seat. She made no effort to lock the car because locked doors just made the thieves break windows. Let them explore her ashtrays and the center console. If they found a few pesos, let them have them. Anything to take the edge off those poor wretches' misery.

Please, God, she prayed silently, *deliver me from this place soon. Please make it end.*

Even in the diminishing light, the heat remained oppressive as she scurried across her yard toward the front door. On Felix's suggestion, she'd long ago taken out all the shrubbery from around the single-story structure, in theory eliminating places for attackers to lie in wait.

But dusk brought shadows—nature's own hiding places.

As was her habit, she had her keys out for the entire walk, the longest of them—the one for the padlock on the security gate—extending between her fisted fingers. In the past few years, attacks against women—once unthinkable in Latin cultures—had skyrocketed. Thousands of rapes and murders, most unsolved because they were never investigated. The police knew who the offenders were, but to investigate would be to confirm those suspicions, thus prompting an arrest that would cost the police officer and his extended family their lives.

With her key deployed, an attacking rapist would have to sacrifice an eye to earn his prize. And after the first eye, his second one, and then whatever else she could destroy until the attack resolved itself one way or the other.

The wrought-iron gates over the door and the matching ones over her bulletproof windows had been Felix's idea, as well. In fact, he'd had his own people install them. That was how much he cared for her. And while they gave her some sense of peace while inside, it always felt like too many locks while she was trying to get in.

Tonight, as her paranoia spiked beyond desperation, Maria's hands trembled and made the operation of the keyway that much more difficult. Finally, with the massive padlock freed from its hasp, she pulled the hundred-pound gate away from the solid core door. Two more keys turned two more dead bolts, and then she could finally see into her home. She pulled the gate closed next, and slipped the padlock into a hasp on the inside that was protected from bolt cutters by a heavy steel plate.

With the door closed and those bolts thrown again, Maria allowed herself to relax just a little. With her hands pressed against the door, she leaned forward and touched her forehead to the cool wood. With her eyes closed, she tried to imagine what the future could be like for her if the FBI would only come to her aid. And how short it would be if they did not.

She'd given them so much. She'd fulfilled her promises, every one. Yet they always wanted one more. Maybe now—

Her head jerked up and her eyes shot open as she whirled to confront the darkness of the house.

"Who's there?" she shouted.

"What do you think, Big Guy?" Jonathan whispered. "Is it airworthy?"

The three of them crouched in the undergrowth just on the edge of the makeshift runway. Ahead about fifty yards and to the left, a high-wing Cessna sat bathed in dim white light under a pole barn. It looked as if it was lighted by a single incandescent lightbulb. The rest of the area shone silver in the light of a nearly full moon.

"Does airworthiness really matter at this point?" Boxers asked. "One way or another, that's what we're flying out on, right?"

"Way to make the PC feel confident," Tristan said.

"Don't worry about it, kid," Boxers said. "I'll be able to get it off the ground."

"Yeah, but will you be able to land it?"

Boxers smiled. "Takeoffs may be optional—"

"—but landings are mandatory," Jonathan finished.

With his night vision in place, Jonathan could see the look of concern in Tristan's face, and he slapped his knee. "We're kidding, Tristan. We'll be fine." Say it with enough conviction and maybe it will come true.

"How do you want to handle it?" Boxers asked.

"You're the pilot," Jonathan said.

Boxers brought a night vision monocular to his eye and scanned the area more closely. "Well, I see a gas pump," he said. "That's a bit of good news. I'm not sure that a thorough preflight makes a lot of sense at this point, but we'll want to make sure we have gas."

"How long will take to fill it up?" Jonathan asked.

"Kinda depends on how empty the tank is and how fast the pump pumps." Boxers' tone said that he thought it was a stupid question.

For good reason, Jonathan thought. "Okay, here's what we'll do," he said. "We'll stay in the weeds until we're even with the aircraft, and then we'll move in."

"Do you want me to stay here?" Tristan asked.

"No," Jonathan said. "I want you to stick to me like a shadow. You should be able to see well enough in the moonlight."

"Is your safety on?" Boxers asked. Jonathan heard the teasing in his voice, but Tristan evidently did not.

"Yes!" the kid hissed. "I've got the freaking safety on. I've never taken it off."

"Just checkin'," the Big Guy said.

Jonathan led them forward more quietly now. Clearly, they were in somebody's yard, and the last thing he needed now was a blown cover. Whatever complication the bright moon threw at them was com-

pensated for by the white light in the pole barn. The
light was bright enough, in fact, that Jonathan pulled
his NVGs out of the way to surveil the scene unas-
sisted. The area beneath the pole barn looked like any
other mechanics' workshop. Chests of tools served as a
surrogate wall on the far side—the western side—and
there appeared to be a waste oil drum in the far southwest corner. The gas pump looked like something for a
1980s gas station, but with a long hose to accommodate the fill spout on the upper surface of the wing.

Jonathan's stomach fell when he saw that the engine
cowling was open. He pressed his mike button. This
close, he was less likely to be overheard whispering
loudly enough to be picked up by his ear mike than he
was whispering loudly enough to be heard through the
air. "Looks like they're in the middle of a repair."

"Movement," Boxers said.

As the announcement registered in Jonathan's brain,
the Big Guy brought his weapon to his shoulder.
Jonathan followed the line of sight and saw a twentysomething young man wandering through the night
back toward the pole barn from the direction of the
outhouse on the far side. He wore the uniform of kids
the world over: T-shirt, shorts, and flip-flops.

"I can take him," Boxers whispered.

"Negative."

The Big Guy's rifle didn't move as he turned his
head to look at the boss. "Negative?" he said through
the air. "Really?"

Left to his own devices, Boxers would cut a much
wider path of destruction than Jonathan. You don't kill
an unarmed mechanic just because you need his airplane.

"What are we going to do, then?" Boxers asked.

"We're going to negotiate."

The Big Guy's shoulders sagged. "Ah, shit. Talk is how little wars get big."

Tristan asked, "Suppose he has a gun or something?"

"Yeah," Boxers said. "Or something."

Jonathan thought it through for a few seconds just to make sure his plan wasn't stupid, and then he said, "Keep an eye out, and keep your sights on the mechanic. If a weapon appears in his hand, take him out."

Tristan raised his own rifle to his shoulder.

"Put that down," Boxers said. "And check the safety."

"You stay with the Big Guy," Jonathan instructed. "If there's any shooting, hide behind him. He's thicker than any tree."

Boxers flipped him off.

Jonathan stood to his full height and started walking. He kept his NVGs on his head, but tilted up out of the way, and he kept his strides long and even. In a few seconds, the mechanic was going to see him coming, and if Jonathan kept his bearing just so, the kid would know that any aggressive move would be fatal. Those were the kinds of revelations that kept kids like him alive. He also took care to stay out of Boxers' firing lane. It made no sense to have someone cover you from behind if you put yourself in the way of the covering fire.

The mechanic had a stepladder in his hand, and as he crossed under the propeller, Jonathan thought for sure that he'd looked right at him. Then he saw the earbud cords hanging down the sides of the kid's face, and he got it. Apparently the music or podcast or whatever he was listening to was far more relevant to his world

than the armed man who approached from the shadows.

The mechanic placed the ladder on the ground near
the nose of the aircraft on the starboard side—the near
side—and then climbed four steps to see into the open
cowling.

As Jonathan got closer, he swung a wide arc to the
kid's left, approaching him from the side. As he closed
to within ten feet, he became worried that the kid
would be so startled when he finally saw Jonathan that
he'd fall off the ladder and hurt himself.

"Excuse me," Jonathan said.

Boxers' voice said in his ear, "Tell me you're joking.
'Excuse me'?"

Jonathan chuckled. As tactical approaches went,
this was definitely one of a kind. More loudly this time:
"Excuse me!"

Still nothing.

"Okay, fine," Jonathan said. He walked up to the
ladder and touched the mechanic's leg with a gloved
hand.

The kid jumped as if he'd been hit with fifty kilo-
volts, dropping something into the engine—it sounded
like a wrench—and overbalancing the ladder. As the
ladder and the mechanic tumbled directly toward him,
Jonathan reached out and caught the kid under his
arms, breaking his fall before he could hit the ground.

"God *damn* it," the kid said in English. Then he saw
Jonathan's cammies and the weapons, and he switched
to Spanish. "Who are you?" He got his feet under him
and adjusted his skewed clothing.

Jonathan stayed with English. "Are you American?"

The kid's eyes grew wide as they took in everything.

The rifle, the sidearm, the holstered MP7, the sheathed KA-BAR knife. "Holy shit."

"Focus, son," Jonathan said. "What's your name?"

"Oscar," he said. "Who the hell are you?"

"I'm hoping I'm a friend," Jonathan said.

"Dude, with that many guns, I'll be your friggin' brother."

Jonathan touched the transmit button on his chest. "Okay, come on in."

For a second or two, Oscar looked confused. Then he winced. "Aw shit, there's a bunch of you? Look, man, I just work here. I don't know anything."

Jonathan thought that was an odd reaction. "In my experience," he said, "people who say they don't know anything in fact know quite a lot. They at least know enough to lead with the fact that they don't know anything."

Oscar's features folded into confusion. "Dude, I bet that actually made sense to you. What are you, FBI? CI—holy shit, you brought Sasquatch." He pointed over Jonathan's shoulder to his approaching colleagues.

He leaned in closer to Oscar and affected a conspiratorial tone. "I really wouldn't make fun of him. He's cranky on a good day. Today, he's hungry and tired. I already stopped him from shooting you."

The kid recoiled a step, and then glanced back at Boxers. "Um. Thanks?"

Jonathan winked. "Don't mention it. Does your airplane work?"

"Huh?" The world clearly was not yet making sense to Oscar. "Oh, the plane. *This* plane?"

"Have you got another one?"

"Sure, it works. I don't know how to fly it, though, so if you're thinking I can—"

Boxers and Tristan arrived.

"What the hell kind of army are you?" Oscar said. He seemed particularly amused by the skinny soldier in the shorts and flip-flops.

"Do you want me to show you?" Boxers menaced.

Some color drained from Oscar's face. "Actually, no." He looked back to Jonathan. "But like I said, I can't fly you anywhere."

"I don't need you to fly me," Jonathan said. "I just want to buy the plane from you."

Oscar's scowl deepened and he looked from face to face. "What, is this some kind of a setup?"

"Will three hundred thousand dollars cover it?" Jonathan asked.

"Bullshit. You don't have three hundred thousand dollars."

Jonathan raised his eyebrows and waited.

"You have three *hundred* thousand dollars." Oscar laughed and pushed his fingers into his hair. "Where does anybody get three *hundred* thousand dollars?" He seemed to like saying the number aloud.

"I don't see how that matters," Jonathan said. "I have it, and it's yours for the airplane."

"But it's not even my plane."

"So much the better," Jonathan said. "That makes it all cash. You don't even have a bank note to pay off."

Oscar's mind started whirling at a thousand miles per hour. You could see it in his face as he tried to decipher the deal that lay before him. "How do I sell you something that I don't own?" he asked.

Jonathan wondered if the kid was in denial, or if he

truly was this dense. "Maybe sale is the wrong word under the circumstances," he said. "How about three hundred thousand dollars to let me borrow the plane? For an indefinite period."

"You mean steal it," Oscar countered.

Jonathan made a face. "If I paid for it, I couldn't be stealing it, right?"

The comment seemed only to deepen Oscar's confusion.

"I'm taking your airplane," Jonathan said, cutting to the chase. "I can pay you for it, in which case I expect a certain level of silence." He adjusted his hand on the grip of his M27. "Or, I can assume the worst and just take it away."

Oscar took a few seconds to process it. "I'm hearing that you can kill me and take the plane, or that you can pay me and take the plane."

"Not exactly as I would have put it, but close enough."

"How is that even a choice?"

"My point exactly."

The kid stuck out his hand. "Deal," he said.

They shook. "Excellent," Jonathan said.

With the engine reassembled, they buttoned up the cowling and pumped in as much gas as the Cessna's tanks could take.

"This is five hours of fuel," Oscar said. "Plus a fifty-minute reserve. I wouldn't depend on the reserve for more than a half hour though. Just to be on the safe side."

Jonathan looked to Boxers for an assessment. Would it be enough?

The Big Guy shrugged. "It is what it is," he said.

"How far do you need to go?" Oscar asked. As soon as the words were launched, he held up his hands, as if in surrender. "Sorry. None of my business."

"Ultimately, it's Buenos Aires," Boxers lied.

Jonathan shot him a glare, hoping to sell the deception.

"There's no way," Oscar said.

Boxers replied, "We have a refueling stop along the way."

"How about you shut up?" Jonathan said.

For his part, Tristan remained conspicuously silent, for which Jonathan sent up a silent prayer of thanks.

"I'm not going to tell anyone," Oscar said. "I swear." He opened his backpack one more time just to make sure that his windfall was still there. The pouch that used to hold his lunch was now stuffed with sixty bundles of banded hundred-dollar bills.

Jonathan thought of it as ransom money well spent.

"Now comes the hard part," Oscar said.

Jonathan cocked his head, waited for it.

Oscar took a deep breath. "Yeah," he said. "Thing is, I like Mexico. Okay, actually, I hate Mexico, but my girlfriend is like the Mexican Chamber of Commerce. She loves it here. I could never convince her to leave."

Jonathan sensed where this was going, but he had to be sure. "So, how is this a problem?" he asked.

"With that kind of money you could buy any girlfriend you wanted," Boxers offered. Ever the romantic.

"My boss—the one who owns this plane—is not a nice man. In fact, he's the opposite of a nice man. He's also my girlfriend's father. When he finds out that his plane is missing, he's going to be pissed. I mean seriously pissed."

"Just tell him that someone stole it," Boxers said.

"Well, that's the thing," Oscar said. "I'm not just the mechanic. I'm also the security guard. It's my job to make sure that no one steals the plane."

The words hung in the air for a few seconds, and then Jonathan and Boxers burst out laughing together. Oscar clearly was offended.

"Sorry, Oscar," Jonathan said. "But maybe you need to think of another line of work. How did a nice American boy end up in this shit hole anyway?"

Oscar shrugged. "I already told you. A girl. I used to work at a little regional airport in the middle of nowhere—Manassas, Virginia—as a staff mechanic. Even worked on jets—Lears and Gulfstreams, mostly. Anyway, I met this Mexican girl and I fell hard. She was going to school then. When she went home, she told me that her father owned an airplane, and that he would match my salary if I came to work for him. I figured it was a no-brainer. Money goes a hell of a lot farther out here, you know?"

Boxers scowled in disbelief. "What could you possibly want to buy?"

"Well, there's that."

"He's in love, Big Guy," Jonathan said. "Give him a break."

Oscar continued as if uninterrupted. "Throw in the fact that her father is a friggin' gangster and you see my dilemma."

"Three hundred grand buys a lot of choices," Boxers pressed.

"Yeah, well, I need to live long enough to exercise them."

Jonathan planted his fists on his hips. "You seem to have a plan," he said.

Oscar took a huge breath this time, and he closed his eyes, as if dreading his own words. "I want you to hit me and tie me up."

Boxers took a step forward. "Okay," he said.

Oscar jumped and retreated as if he'd touched something hot. "No! Jesus, not you. I said hit me, not kill me." He pointed to Jonathan. "You," he said.

"Yeah," Boxers teased. "He only wants a little girlie tap. Give him the best you've got."

Jonathan ignored him. "So, what's the longer plan?" he asked Oscar. "Is the story that a stranger sneaked up on you in the middle of the night, coldcocked you, and stole the plane?"

"Right. He'll still fire me, but I figure that's okay." Oscar smiled. "He won't know that I got a really good severance package."

His smile turned to a frown. "If you don't mind, though, I'd like to limit the amount of money I have to dedicate to medical care. I think—"

Jonathan fired a savage punch with the heel of his hand, connecting at the point in front of Oscar's left ear where his jaw met the rest of his head.

The kid was out cold even before his knees buckled.

Tristan yelped, "Holy shit!"

Boxers grinned like a proud father.

"It's easier if you don't talk about it first," Jonathan said.

CHAPTER TWENTY-FIVE

Maria Elizondo's hands tore at the lock, trying to get it open so that she could escape with her life. She'd never dreamed that the security system that had been installed to keep madmen out could actually trap her inside with one.

"Oh, please," she begged to God. "Oh, please, oh please."

Between the sound of her own cries and the pounding of blood in her ears, she heard nothing at all. Her only reality was terror. The certainty of her death.

When the hand came down on her shoulder, then, she screamed and whirled around for her last fight.

Her attacker was shorter than she'd expected. And lighter.

And female.

"Maria, stop!" the woman insisted. Her tone and her gestures told Maria that she'd been saying those words over and over, but Maria had not been hearing them

"It's me," the woman said. "It's Veronica. You're all right. I'm not here to hurt you."

Realization—and reason—came slowly. How was this possible? "How did you get in here?" Maria asked.

Veronica placed her hands on both of Maria's shoulders. It was a gesture designed to calm her. "That's not important," she said.

Are you insane? "Do not tell me that it is not important," Maria yelled. "You are in my home!"

"I am here to help you," Veronica said. She wore her dark hair long, and tied with what looked like a decorative rubber band in the back.

"You are in my *home!*" Maria insisted. Whatever else was happening, whatever power the Federal Bureau of Investigation might have, this was an important point. Despite the stakes and the danger—despite the fact that Veronica was the very person Maria had been hoping to see—she needed to acknowledge that this was Maria's *home*. It was a private place, and Veronica had no right being here.

"Your escape tunnel works both ways," Veronica said.

Maria's jaw dropped. "*What* escape tunnel? I don't have an escape tunnel."

Veronica looked confused. "Are you serious?"

"What escape tunnel?" Maria asked again.

"That panel in your bathroom. Under the sink. Did you really not know that it was there?"

Maria felt a sense of dread washing over her. "Where does it lead?"

"To a storm sewer behind your house. How could you not know it was there?"

Maria pushed past Veronica into the living room. "Felix," she said. Now it was all so obvious. She dropped onto the sofa. "He put in the security for me. The locks, the walls, everything."

Veronica sat next to her. This sofa, like everything else in her house, had been purchased with her own money, and it had been cleaned and maintained by her own hands. It was a point of great pride that she had refused every offer from Felix to furnish the place and staff it with a housekeeper. It was one thing to sleep with the man she hoped one day to kill, but it was something else entirely to have things of his nearby when she was alone.

Veronica asked, "Why put in a tunnel and not tell you?"

Maria looked at her, waiting for her to get in on her own. "It wasn't about me getting out," Maria said, finally. "It was about him getting in." She brought her hand to her head, as if taking her own temperature. "You need to get me out, Veronica. Felix knows—"

Veronica's face lost some of its color as she raised her hand and gently placed two fingers over Maria's lips for silence.

Veronica sifted through the accumulated papers and magazines on the coffee table, searching for something.

"What are you looking for?"

"The remote control for your television."

"Why?"

"I want to watch it," Veronica said, but her face said, *Give me the damn remote control.*

Maria reached behind a throw pillow. She found the remote and handed it over.

Veronica thumbed the television to life, and then cranked up the volume.

Maria brought her hands to her ears. "What are you—"

Veronica held up a hand to silence her, and then sat on the sofa, pulling Maria down with her. "If they have access to your home," she said softly, "you have to assume that they've installed listening devices."

That sense of indignant horror returned, hitting her like a punch to the stomach. "This is my *home*," Maria said again.

"Not for long," Veronica said. "Tell me what Felix knows."

"Everything, I think. He knows that someone close to him is feeding information to the Americans. He hasn't traced it to me yet, but I know he suspects. He all but accused me today."

"If he thought you had betrayed him, you wouldn't be here right now," Veronica said.

"I took the offensive," Maria explained. "I got angry at him that he could even think such a thing, and I stormed out. He didn't stop me because he was too startled. I can't go back."

"You won't have to," Veronica said. "You're getting out tonight."

Maria stood. "I'm ready."

Veronica pulled her back down. "Not now. Later tonight. In a few hours."

"I can't wait a few hours. You said that Felix is listening. I never listen to the television this loud. That alone will tell him that something is wrong. Besides, he already heard you—"

"No," Veronica said, cutting her off. "I doubt that anyone listens in real time. If Felix is recording you, he's recording many others, too. It's not possible to listen to so many all at once. You should have enough time."

"I *should*? Suppose I don't?"

"I'm sorry, Maria, but that's the best we can do."

"Why do we have to wait? What will be different in a few hours?" It was so easy for American spies to tell others to be patient when the endangered lives weren't their own.

Veronica took a few seconds to frame her answer. She put her hand on Maria's. "Tell me that you were not bluffing about the smuggling tunnels," she said.

The sudden change in subject startled her. "I don't understand."

"The smuggling tunnels," Veronica said again. "The ones that you have been holding out as an incentive for me to get you out of Mexico. Are they real?"

"Of course they're real."

"Then tell me where they are."

This wasn't right. Something in Veronica's eyes gave away a bad intent. The rules had been the same from the very beginning: Maria would reveal the location of the tunnels *after* she had crossed the border into the United States. It was her only bargaining chip, and she dared not squander it.

"There are many of them," Maria said, stalling for time.

"How many?"

"Veronica, this is inappropriate. First you tell me that I cannot leave the country, and then you tell me that I have to wait a few more hours. Now you want the one piece of information that I will not give you. You know our rules."

"Your cover's been blown," Veronica said flatly.

"This is a new day, and it comes with new rules. Unless you tell me where they are, we will not be able to protect you as you use them."

Her words launched a chill. "What do you mean, *as I use them*?"

As Veronica shared the details of the plan, Maria felt her life caving in on her. She was to wait for strangers to arrive, and then those strangers would get her out of the country. It all seemed unnecessarily complicated.

"I don't understand," Maria said after Veronica was finished. "Why can't you just drive me across the border? For that matter, why can't you just drive these other people across the border, too?"

Veronica gave her a long look before responding, "That's very complicated."

"That's not an answer."

"You're right, it's not." Veronica seemed to be struggling with what she could and could not say. "Let me put it to you this way," she said. "What is happening here tonight is not officially sanctioned by the United States. In fact, if you are caught in the process, you will be on your own. At best, if you are caught by the police or the Army, you will be arrested. Obviously, if you are caught by Felix Hernandez's men, you will be killed. For political reasons, I cannot provide you with any assistance until you are on the other side of the border."

Maria's head swam. "For political reasons? What does that even mean?"

"That's the complicated part. These people you'll be with are being hunted by the Mexican government as murderers. I'm told by my supervisors that they are innocent—that they are the victims of a conspiracy devised by Hernandez—but what is important to Hernandez is also important to the police. It is equally complicated on my side of the border, where the return of these people you'll be meeting, and your testimony against Hernandez, will bring very bad news to some very powerful people."

Maria listened intently, hoping that these details would start to make sense. Then, when they did, she wished that they didn't. "So, when you say we'll be on our own, what you really mean is that we'll have no allies. None at all."

Veronica's face turned grim. "Exactly. Until you get to the other side. If you give me the address where the tunnel ends on the American side of the border, I can be there waiting for you. I can take you into protective custody and then we can sort it all out."

This was impossible. The whole idea was impossible. Each of these tunnels was over a mile long, and they were more than mere passageways for the transfer of drugs from one side of the border to the other. They were guarded, and they contained stockpiles of materials. Maria had never visited them personally, but she'd heard from others that processing operations were performed inside some of the tunnels.

"No," Maria said. "I won't do it. This is suicide. I will take my chances with Felix."

Veronica's entire demeanor changed as her posture hardened. "You *will* do this, Maria. You *must* do this."

"But you're asking the impossible."

"Everything is possible. These men who are coming will protect you. I'm told that they are very good at what they do. They will get you safely to the other side."

"The murderers, you mean?" Maria laughed bitterly. "If my testimony is so important, then you drive me out of the country with dignity."

Veronica leaned in close. "Understand this, Maria," she said. "As much as I have come to like you over the years, and as important as your testimony is to our case against Felix Hernandez, these people you'll be helping across the border are far more important to my boss. I don't even know why, but that really doesn't matter."

Maria laughed again. This woman was bluffing. Ever since the beginning, the story had always been the same: Felix Hernandez was one of the most sought-after criminals in the United States. He'd killed federal agents, after all. There was no way—

"Lose that grin, Maria," Veronica ordered. "I would prefer that you do this out of the love of the family members you've lost at Felix's hand. I would prefer that you do it because it is the right thing to do. But if those motivations are not enough, understand that if you don't do this, I will personally deliver your name to Felix Hernandez. You need to decide if it's better to risk death by helping others, or face the certainty of death in one of Felix's torture chambers."

Maria felt suddenly nauseous. This woman next to her had always been so gentle, so accommodating. Could this monster with the blazing eyes be the same person? "You couldn't do that to me," she said.

"I could, and I will," Veronica replied. "I've read reports that Felix can keep his enemies alive and in agony for weeks. They pray for death in the first moments, and the screaming never stops. Imagine how he would treat a woman who he thought was in love with him."

Maria's eyes burned as her heart pounded. "I hate you," she choked.

"That's fine," Veronica said. "I need that address."

The speed and power of the punch were unlike anything Tristan had ever seen. His burst of profanity had erupted out of nowhere. It was just so . . . startling.

Tristan marveled yet again at the dichotomy that was Scorpion. After that savage punch to the head, Scorpion moved quickly to catch the unconscious mechanic before he could hit the ground.

"He'll be all right," Scorpion said. "His jaw will be sore, and it'll swell, but that's what he wanted."

"How do you know you didn't break it?" Tristan asked.

"Because I didn't feel it break. You can tell."

After Scorpion laid Oscar on the ground, the Big Guy rolled the kid over onto his stomach, pulled his hands behind his back, and bound his wrists together with one of those ratcheting plastic ties you see cops using to arrest protesters.

Tristan just stood and watched as his rescuers moved on to the rest of their jobs. The Big Guy messed with the control surfaces of the airplane while Scorpion loaded stuff into the back of the plane. Their bulky backpacks went in first, followed by the other two rifles they'd taken from the dead Mexican soldiers.

The two of them moved with a precision that seemed to be practiced, though it wasn't possible that they'd stolen a lot of airplanes together. Or maybe they had. Given the way the last few days had gone, absolutely nothing was out of the question anymore.

It was almost as if the two men thought each other's thoughts. Tristan envied that kind of friendship.

Oscar stirred. Then he moaned miserably. Tristan went to him and kneeled by his side. "You okay?" He spoke at a whisper, but he had no idea why.

Oscar groaned, "Ungh. What did he hit me with?"

"His hand," Tristan said. He tried to keep the admiration out of his voice. "Really, his hand. Not even his fist. You'll be okay, though. Scorpion said your jaw didn't break."

Oscar moaned again, and his shoulders twitched as he tried to move his hands. "Handcuffs are a nice touch," he said. "They'll help sell the story."

"What about your backpack with the money?" Tristan asked. "Do you want me to hide that somewhere for you?"

Oscar shook his head and winced. "Shit, it's like my brain is bruised," he said. "No, leave the backpack where it is. I always have it with me. If it was missing, they'd be suspicious."

A shadow fell over them, and Tristan knew without looking that it was Scorpion. "Hey, kid," he said. "Howya feeling?"

"Like you tried to kill me and missed," Oscar said.

"Yeah, well, your face looks like hell," Scorpion said. "In a half hour, I doubt that you'll be able to see out of your left eye. Don't worry about it when it happens. It's just the swelling. I don't think I broke anything, so if you can handle the headache, you shouldn't need any medical time at all."

It seemed like the appropriate time for Oscar to say thank you, but Tristan understood that that would have been weird.

"You ready to go?" Scorpion asked Tristan.

"Sure," he said. As if any other answer was possible.

"All right, then," Scorpion said. "Mount up."

Tristan rose from his haunches and waited for a few seconds for Scorpion to come with him.

"You go ahead," Scorpion said. "Give me a minute with Oscar."

Tristan felt himself blush. He didn't like being dismissed like that. What did Oscar do to deserve alone time? He realized that it was foolish to think such things. He should be champing at the bit just to get the hell out of here. It shouldn't matter to him who Scorpion talked to or what he said when he did. Still, what made Oscar special?

He approached the airplane from the front, but stopped when he saw the Big Guy's arm waving at him through the open cockpit window, motioning for him to go around the back side to get to the door that was on the opposite side—the right-hand side—of the airplane.

Readjusting the body armor for the thousandth time, Tristan followed directions. He'd only gone a few steps when the engine started to turn, and the propeller caught, launching a hurricane of dust and grass back at Tristan.

The inside of the airplane looked like the backseat of an old car that had been packed for a long vacation.

Tristan's seat was too small with all the shit they made him wear. He had difficulty getting his seat belt fastened. Up front, the Big Guy made the pilot seat and the controls look like they'd been designed for a child.

"Put your seat belt on," the Big Guy instructed.

"Already done," Tristan said. "How long a trip is this going to be?"

"A little over five hours. Call it five and a half. More, if the winds don't cooperate."

Tristan scowled as he remembered a previous conversation. "And how much fuel do we have?"

"Barely enough."

Tristan considered letting it go, but in the end, he couldn't. "Doesn't that mean we're going to run out?"

"That's a possibility."

"It's a *probability*, isn't it?"

The Big Guy caught Tristan's eyes in the mirror. "The boss says we only tell the truth, so are you sure you want to hear it?"

No, he thought. "Yes," he said.

"I give us a forty percent chance," Big Guy said.

"Of landing or crashing?"

He responded with just a look.

"Oh," Tristan said. "Shit."

"Cheer up," Big Guy said. "It ain't worth doing if it ain't exciting. And relax. It's not like we have a better option." He reached onto his lap and lifted his night vision goggles onto his head, with the eyepieces tilted up out of the way.

Off to the right, Scorpion arrived at the door and climbed in, closing it behind him. With only one door for everyone to climb in and out of, it took some maneuvering for him to make his way to the right front seat. All the weapons didn't make it any easier. Once he'd settled, it took him maybe two seconds to read the mood in the plane. "What's wrong?" he asked.

"The kid asked about the fuel situation," Big Guy said. "So, I told him the truth."

Tristan thought he saw the boss's jaw twitch, but it was gone in an instant.

"Oh," Scorpion said. "Okay. Let's go, then."

The Big Guy reached forward with his right hand. The engine noise built to a crescendo, and they started to roll. "Thank you for flying Rescue Airways," the pilot yelled over the noise. The runway, such as it was, was made of grass, and the plane bounced like an old stagecoach as it gained speed. Bright lights from the wings illuminated their path as they sped toward the line of trees that blocked the far end of the runway.

"Our cruising altitude this evening—if we ever get this piece of shit off the ground—will be about thirty feet, at a cruising speed of one hundred eighty knots."

The wall of trees approached at an alarming rate, and as the plane moved faster, it didn't seem to be getting any lighter. Without thinking, Tristan pressed himself deeper into his seat. Up front, he could see Scorpion doing the same thing.

It's hard to judge distances at night, but on the approximate scale of close to very close, Tristan had them pegged at a distance of *holy shit* when the wheels finally lifted off the turf and they gained altitude.

As they closed to within *holy freaking shit* the trees still had more altitude than they did.

Just inches short of *holy freaking shit, we're all*

going to die, the plane finally found whatever it was that planes found to give them real altitude, and they were airborne.

For the better part of a minute, no one said anything.

The Big Guy broke the silence. "Okay," he said. "That was exciting. Now, sit back and enjoy the flight."

CHAPTER TWENTY-SIX

Sometimes, Dom D'Angelo wondered what the bishop would think if he knew the real details of how he sometimes tended to his flock. This was one of those times. As he climbed down the stairs of the private Gulfstream jet that had delivered him to Phoenix's Sky Harbor International Airport, he wondered how many of his seminary classmates had even seen the inside of such an aircraft.

It was nearly eleven o'clock when he stepped down onto the tarmac and into the car that was waiting for him. If he'd waited for a commercial flight, the earliest he could have arrived in Phoenix would have been tomorrow morning, and the nature of his business couldn't wait that long.

His FBI seatmate in the back of the nondescript Ford said little, allowing him to absorb the details of the file he'd been given. He'd get only one shot at this, so he needed to get it right. He told himself that God would understand the lies that he would have to tell to put the plan in action, and that the deception was for the greater good.

If God didn't understand, well, Dom would have to take that up with Him later.

"We're getting close," the agent asked. "Do you have any questions?"

"I don't think so," Dom said. "I just hope that I don't screw it up."

"If you play it like we discussed, things should go just fine," the agent said. "But if things go terribly wrong, we'll be close by."

Dom gave a tired smile. If things went *terribly* wrong, close wouldn't be close enough.

The Georgens' house looked like so many other houses in Scottsdale. Where there should have been bushes, there were cacti instead; where there should have been grass, there was white gravel. Even with the sun gone, the air was oppressively hot—103 degrees, according to the thermometer in the dash of the car that delivered him. That should be a noontime temperature, not a nighttime one.

Judging from the number and brightness of the security lights, the Georgens were a paranoid lot. Once Dom stepped from the street to the walkway that led to their front door, every corner of the single-story Spanish-style ranch erupted in the light of double floods. The suddenness of it startled the crap out of him.

"Are you okay?" Venice asked in his left ear, startling him.

"I'm fine," he said. Apparently, he'd yelled out, though he didn't remember doing so. "Security lights."

"You'll do fine, Father," she said. "But you need to relax. I can hear your breathing. I've got tape rolling here in case you need it, and I've got the panic number preprogrammed into the phone. If anything starts to sound wrong, I'll call in the cavalry."

"I understand," he said.

"And you need to quit talking to me. It'll look like you're talking to yourself. Worse, it'll get people thinking that you're wearing a wire."

Which, of course, was exactly what he was doing. He had two of them, actually. One was disguised as a pen in his pocket, and the other was the audio feed that Venice was running via the bud in his ear.

Venice was right, though. He needed to get control of his fear if he was going to pull off this ruse. The plan was to make an end run around the Constitution of the United States by performing a warrantless search. It would be illegal for the FBI to record the conversation that he was about to have, but in Arizona, it was legal for private citizens to surreptitiously record conversations so long as one of the parties knew that it was happening. A thus-legally obtained recording of damning evidence, once turned over to the FBI, then becomes actionable. Dom supposed that this sort of manipulation occurred all the time, but deception had never been his long suit.

And the outright lies that lay in his immediate future made his mouth go dry.

He forced himself not to slow as he approached the front door and rang the bell. Following the instructions he'd been given, Dom stepped back from the door to allow himself to be seen, Roman collar and all.

Lights came on inside, and he saw movement beyond the beveled glass that doubled for a center panel as the occupants moved cautiously toward the door.

Visitors at this hour were unnerving for anyone. For that visitor to be a priest had to add an even more drastic spin.

The bevels bent all the images looking in, and he could imagine it did the same for someone looking out. A man's face appeared in the glass, a hand cupped to the side of his right eye. Dom recognized it as belonging to Eric Georgen, Bill Georgen's father.

"It's a priest," the man said. He turned two dead bolts and pulled the door open a crack. He wore a blue terry cloth bathrobe, and perhaps nothing else.

"I'm sorry to be calling so late at night," Dom said. He kept his hands in front of him, fingers lightly interlaced, as if in casual prayer. "Are you Mr. Georgen?"

The man's confusion morphed to a scowl. "Who are you?"

"I am Father Daniel LaFrada," Dom said, invoking the name of a seminary friend who had passed away a few months ago. "I need to speak with you if you have a few moments."

"I'm not Catholic," Georgen said.

"It's about your son, sir," Dom said. "Bill."

A woman materialized out of nowhere to join the man. This was Tammy Georgen, Bill's mother, and she wore a bathrobe over a nightgown. "Is Billy all right?" she asked. Judging from her perfectly coiffed big hair, she hadn't yet lain her head on a pillow. "Is he hurt?"

The question meant that the boy wasn't home, and that brought a sense of relief. "We need to talk," Dom said.

"Is he hurt?" Georgen asked, building on his wife's budding panic.

Dom kept his face noncommittal. "May I come in, please?"

Husband and wife searched each other for an objection, and then stepped aside to let him in. The house wasn't large, but it was well-appointed. Lots of polished hardwoods, granite, and original oil paintings. Dom led the way to what he supposed they called their family room, where a beamed cathedral ceiling towered over a leather conversation group that was designed to give maximum viewing efficiency for the enormous flat-screen television that was mounted over the wood-burning fireplace.

"Please answer our question, Father," Georgen said, pulling up the rear of the small parade that landed on opposite ends of the curved sofa.

"For now, the answer is yes. Bill is fine."

"What do you mean, *for now*?" Tammy was wrapped tighter than a watch spring.

Dom took his time, both for dramatic effect and to gather his thoughts. "The way it was put to me, Mrs. Georgen, was, *What goes around, comes around.*"

Tammy recoiled while Georgen blanched. "What does that mean?" Tammy asked. She looked to her husband. "Eric?"

"I have no idea what he's talking about," Georgen said, but everything about his demeanor screamed that he was lying.

Dom turned to Tammy. "Have you seen or spoken to Rachel Wagner recently?"

"Tristan's mom? No, why? What does she have to do with Billy?"

Georgen squirmed.

"Tristan and Bill were supposed to go on a missionary trip together, weren't they?"

"No," Tammy said. "Well, yes and then no. Eric decided that Mexico was too dangerous a place to go right now. You know, with the drug violence and all. We told the church that he wouldn't be going. I don't understand what any of this has to do with you."

Dom shifted his gaze to the husband. "How about you, Eric? Do you see any connection here?" Agent Boersky had made it abundantly clear that the words needed to come directly from Georgen in order for them to be useful in court.

"Of course not. I don't know what you're talking about."

Tammy saw it, too. "Eric, what's going on here?"

"The Wagners know, Eric," Dom lied. "They know the details, and they've vowed to make it right."

Tammy reached for her husband's hand, but he flinched and pulled it away. "What's Father talking about?"

Georgen shot to his feet and towered over Dom. "Get out of my house," he said.

"I don't think I will," Dom replied. "The name Abrams mean anything to you, Mr. Georgen?"

Even more color drained from the man's face.

"You know that they're all dead, don't you?" Dom said.

"Who's dead?" Tammy said. "Oh, my God, Father, what is going on?"

Georgen sat heavily onto the sofa. "That's not possible. They swore."

Tammy brought both hands to her mouth as realization dawned that something truly awful was unfolding in front of her. Her eyes filled with tears. "Oh, my God, Eric, what have you done?"

"I haven't done anything," he snapped.

"Tell Tammy the real reason why you pulled Bill off of that trip to Mexico."

"Eric, what is he talking about?"

A fine line separates self-righteous anger from all-out panic, and Dom could tell that Eric was toeing the line. If this was going to get violent, now would be the time.

Tammy rose from her seat and walked to her husband. "Eric, is Billy in danger?"

Georgen looked like a trapped animal, his eyes wild and red as they darted from one corner of the room to another, either looking for an answer or a weapon.

Dom rose to join them. "You can get in front of this," he said. "If you go to the police before the police come to you, I think the Wagners will feel a sense of justice. Confession goes a long way toward counter-acting betrayal."

"Eric, tell me." Tammy said. "Look at me and tell me."

Georgen pushed her gently away and started to pace, nervously adjusting the belt on his robe. "I just want you to know that I told Reverend Jackie that this was a bad idea. I thought it was desperate. She countered that these are desperate times. And Abrams *guaranteed* that the missionaries would be safe."

Tammy reflexively reached out for Dom's arm. He covered her grasp with his other hand.

"What went wrong?" he asked Dom.

"First tell Tammy," Dom said. "You owe her that much." He walked her to the sofa and sat her next to her husband.

Eric started with a huge breath. "This man named Abrams approached us with a plan."

"Approached whom?" Dom interrupted. He needed specifics.

"Reverend Mitchell, I think. I showed up for a board of directors meeting and he was there. Toward the end of the meeting, she asked all but the executive committee to leave the room, and then Abrams made his pitch. We were to allow the missionaries to be taken captive, and when the ransom demand came in, we were to walk through a series of very specific steps to arrange for a particular person to rescue them."

"Oh, my God," Tammy gasped.

"It sounds worse that it was," Georgen said. "Honey, you know how strapped the church has been for cash since . . . well, since the incident. This man—this Abrams—gave us the money for the ransom, with more to spare—millions of dollars—to keep us afloat."

"You're talking about *endangering children*," Tammy said. Dom sensed that if he hadn't been sitting on the other side of her, she'd have pulled away from Georgen.

"No," Georgen insisted. "We're talking about the charade of kidnapping. We were told that no one would get hurt."

"Think of how terrifying that would have been," Tammy said. Giving in to the urge to separate from him, she stood.

"It would be an adventure," Georgen countered. "They'd be held for a couple of days, and then they'd be let go. No one was going to get hurt." He pointed to Dom. "I don't know what you're talking about when you say they're dead. I haven't heard that."

"There has to be an easier way to raise money," Dom said, parrying the question.

Georgen rose to his feet, and Dom followed him. He wasn't going to give him a height advantage. "It's not like we dreamed this up out of the blue," he insisted. "Abrams came to *us* with this. And with the details he knew, I actually thought that he was working for the government."

"That's ridiculous!" Tammy shouted. "Why would the government want to kidnap missionaries?"

"It wasn't about the missionaries!" Georgen said. "It was never about them. That's why we ultimately agreed. This was about arresting some enemies of the state or some such thing. They didn't go into a lot of detail, but it was all an elaborate trap for the rescuers."

He reached out for Tammy and grasped her shoulders. "Honey, you have to believe that we were told that there was zero chance that anybody would get hurt."

"They're *dead*, Eric! Didn't you hear Father?"

Georgen shot a panicked look to Dom. "What happened?"

"Either someone lied, or communications broke down."

"But why haven't we heard?"

"The same reason why none of the families even know that their loved ones were taken captive," Dom said. He felt his poker face slipping away. "Because this whole thing was designed to thrust all of the danger onto the innocents."

"Jesus, Father, do you believe for a moment that I would deliberately endanger children and church volunteers?"

"I believe that you're a coward," Dom said. "And I believe that you had enough shadow of doubt that you pulled your own son off of the trip while you allowed other people's sons and daughters to be slaughtered."

"How dare you speak to me that way?" Georgen boomed.

Tammy was the first to hear the bullshit bell ringing in the back of her brain. "Why are you here, Father?"

"Are you even a priest at all?" Georgen asked. He took a threatening step forward.

Dom stopped him by pointing a finger at a spot above the other man's nose. If it had been a gun, it would have been a sure kill shot. "Is that really where you want to draw the line for moral indignation?" Dom asked. "Enjoy your eternity in Hell."

As he walked back thorough the foyer and out into the night, he heard the Georgens going at it. This would be the fight of fights. And boy, was there a surprise coming their way in a few minutes.

He'd just turned the corner at the end of the walk when he saw Agent Boersky and his driver striding toward him. "Your assistant called from Virginia," he said. "She told us that you got everything."

Dom pulled the recorder from his pocket and handed it over. "She's nobody's assistant," he said, "and you'd do well not to be caught calling her that."

"Give me a heads-up on what I'm going to hear on this," Boersky said.

"He confessed to arranging the payoff, and he confessed to the fraud."

"What about the government connection?"

Dom shook his head. "Nothing solid. He alluded to it, but I don't think he knows those details."

"But we got enough to give us cause to dig deeper?"

"That's your call, not mine," Dom said. "Right now, I just want to go and take a long shower."

"Thank you, Father," Boersky said.

"Let's not do this again anytime soon," Dom replied. "Do I have a ride back to the airport over there?" He pointed in the direction of Boersky's vehicle.

"Yes, sir. Just wander that way. Agent Palmer is looking for you."

Dom tossed off a little wave. Under the circumstances, he wasn't sure if there was a right thing to say.

"Um, Father?" Boersky's demeanor had darkened. "You need to give my boss a call. I believe you call her Wolverine?"

Dom's insides tumbled. "Tonight?"

"She said right away."

With an ever-growing sense of dread, Dom pulled his cell phone from his pocket and dialed the number from memory. He was about to hit Send when the phone buzzed in his hand. The caller ID showed that it Venice calling from the office.

He answered, "Hello?"

"Oh, Dom," she said. She sounded near tears. "I don't know what Digger is going to do."

"What happened?" He asked the question even though he knew the answer.

"I just got a hit on ICIS. The Phoenix police found a woman's body an hour ago in a Dumpster behind a bar. Evidence shows that she'd been shot several times. No identification, but the general description matches Gail."

Dom stopped walking and sat on the curb.

Venice continued, "The body had been wrapped in plastic bags, but a homeless woman looking through the Dumpster for food found it and called it in." Venice snuffled. "Oh, my God, Dom, it's just so horrible."

Dom closed his eyes and pinched the bridge of his nose. This was beyond horrible, beyond it on a scale that he didn't know how to measure.

In that instant, Dom realized what he had to do. A woman had been murdered and her body disposed of as garbage. Even if it wasn't Gail, she deserved better than that. She deserved better than to be left alone on a cold gurney in the morgue.

"Father Dom, are you there?"

"I'm going to her," he said. "Can you get me the address for the morgue?"

Silence. Then Venice said, "I don't think that's a good idea. This is an active homicide investigation. If you get involved, the questions are—"

"She was our friend, Venice. That's really all that matters. Can you give me the address or do I have to look it up on the Internet?"

Consciousness came slowly to Trevor Munro. The phone call came in the deepest phase of his REM sleep.

This particular ringtone—"Ride of the Valkyries"—belonged exclusively to one person.

With the lights still off and his eyes still closed, he slid the phone open and brought it to his head.

"Yes," he said.

"Jesus, Trev," the big voice boomed. "Where the hell—"

"Call me back in three minutes," Munro said. He clicked off.

These were delicate times. He wanted to be one hundred percent sure that he was awake and fully functional, if only as a hedge against saying something stupid. He kicked off the covers, padded to the bathroom to urinate, and then soaked a washcloth with cold water and scrubbed his face with it. Just to be sure that he was completely lucid, he recited the alphabet aloud—backwards.

He'd timed it all perfectly. He was back at his bedside table exactly two minutes and forty-five seconds after he'd hung up. Sjogren was not quite as punctual. It took him three and a half minutes to call back. The time on the clock read 2:37.

"Okay, speak to me," he answered when the Valkyries started singing again.

"Jesus, Trev," Sjogren said through the thick Boston brogue. "This is my third call to you. What the hell have you been doin'?"

"It's called sleep," Munro said. "Among life's most important activities."

"I guess you get to do that if you're the one paying the bills. Me, I work around the clock."

"For what you get paid, that's the least I would expect," Munro said. "The fact of your call must mean that you have a name for me."

"I do," Sjogren said. "And let me tell you, it took some doing to get it, too."

Munro waited for it.

"It's a babe," Sjogren said. "A chick named Maria Elizondo."

Munro jotted the name onto the pad he kept on his night stand. The name rang a distant bell, though he didn't know why.

"And listen to me, Trev," Sjogren went on. "I deeply don't give a shit what happens to you, but I warn you to be prepared for a really bad reaction to this. Elizondo is this loon's main squeeze. He thinks they're in love."

"I'll be damned," Munro said. He remembered now that he'd actually met this treasonous bitch. During one of his meetings with Hernandez, she'd been in the car.

"How certain are you of the identity?" Munro asked. He didn't care all that much, but passing this news along was tantamount to issuing a death warrant. It seemed reasonable to want to be sure.

"I can't speak to that personally," Sjogren said. "But my guy in Justice says it's a sure thing."

"And what's your level of confidence in him?"

Sjogren laughed. "What the hell do you want from me, Trev? You hire me for my sources, and I give you what I've got. You want two-hundred-percent certainty, you need to hire somebody else."

Munro forgave the attitude because the underlying message was spot-on. "Maria Elizondo," he said, repeating the name aloud to make sure he had it right.

"That's it," Sjogren said. "Now it's my turn to go to sleep."

CHAPTER TWENTY-SEVEN

Jonathan hated flying. Airplanes were orders of magnitude better than boats, but given all the years of parachute jumps, fast-roping, and landings-cum-crashes in bullet-riddled aircraft, he worried that he'd made God grow weary of pulling his ass out of trouble.

Now he was in a single-engine airplane that had been officially out of gas for the last ten minutes, flying fifty feet above the rooftops in the dark, hoping that they'd be able to trick the laws of physics one more time. Jonathan forced himself not to dwell on the depressing details, and instead scoured his map of Ciudad Juarez for a suitable place to land the Cessna.

Airfields were out because they would be guarded, which left them with the option of landing on a field somewhere, or maybe on a highway. Either of those scenarios would alert the authorities, but at least Jonathan and his team would have a head start and some tactical flexibility. Problem was, they'd already crossed into Ciudad Juarez, and the urban landscape provided precious few fields. Exactly zero, in fact, by Jonathan's reckoning.

It had become clear quite some time ago that a soft landing was not in their future—perhaps it had never been—and to prepare, they'd secured all their weapons, and tied down as many potential projectiles as possible.

"How flexible is the fifteen hundred feet of landing space?" he asked Boxers. Jonathan tried to keep his voice low so as not to spin Tristan up. The kid had good ears though, and issued a dreadful groan.

"Depends on how much of the airplane you want to be left when we're done," Boxers said. "Nose-first, we don't need any space at all."

Tristan said, "Oh, shit," and Boxers laughed.

"That's not as helpful as you might think, Big Guy," Jonathan said. It was a quirk of Boxers' personality that his lighthearted banter ran inversely proportional to the seriousness of the moment.

"Okay, serious answer," Boxers said. "If I can slow it to nearly stall speed and we don't care about breaking some stuff underneath, then five, six hundred feet should do." The engine coughed. "It'd be good to decide quickly, though."

A solution materialized in Jonathan's head. He triangulated between where they were and where they wanted to be. "Does this beast have five miles left in her?" he asked.

"She's got what she's got," Boxers said. "Give me a strategy."

Jonathan glanced at the compass on the control panel and verified that they were traveling north. "Okay, the north–south streets are pretty narrow, but the east–west streets are wide. This Elizondo chick lives about five miles northeast of our current position. She lives on Calle de Oro, one of the wider streets."

Boxers grinned beneath his night vision array. "You telling me you want to park in the driveway?"

"At the curb, actually."

The engine coughed again.

"Sure," Boxers said. "Why the hell not? We've done crazier shit than that." He banked the plane slightly to the right. "I'm gonna have trouble reading street signs from up here, though."

Below them, the city was mostly bathed in darkness, save for the rows of streetlights.

"You can line up with any of these. We're still fifteen, sixteen blocks south, but better to get lined up than be forced to crash into buildings."

"I thought we were going to be able to land the airplane," Tristan said from the back.

"I already told you," Boxers quipped. "Landings are mandatory. They're just not all created equal."

"Make sure your seat belt is tight," Jonathan said. "And when I tell you, press yourself as far back into the seat as possible. Let the ratchet in your shoulder strap go as tight as possible."

"Should I take the vest off?"

"Negative," Jonathan said. "If we hit really hard, that vest will distribute the impact from the belt. Might save your collarbone." He had no idea if that was really true, but it sounded right. "And lock your jaw tight. It'll keep you from biting through your tongue."

Boxers being Boxers, he flew a few blocks farther north before finishing the turn and lining up with an east–west boulevard. According to Jonathan's GPS, they'd lined up with Calle Norte Americano. That put Maria Elizondo's house four blocks north and three quarters of a mile east of their current location. Every additional second in the air brought them that much closer.

The engine noise pitched down dramatically, startling Jonathan.

"That's me," Boxers said, defusing the concern. "I want to get this baby slowed down." When he lowered the wing flaps, the aircraft slowed even more. To Jonathan, it felt like a walking pace, but he knew that they had no choice. At this low altitude, when the engine died, they would fall like a rock, with virtually no opportunity to react. There'd be nothing they could do about the speed of the fall, but the lower their forward speed when it happened, the more survivable the crash would be.

Now that they were close, Jonathan realized the limitations of his GPS map. While the map images were pristine, the real street was dotted with vehicles, and the occasional trash can, and all manner of urban stuff that you'd never encounter on an airfield. Any kind of obstruction was a huge hazard, but there was something else that posed special hazards.

"Those are power lines, aren't they?" he asked, noting the strings of wire that connected the poles.

"Yup."

"Can you avoid them?"

"I'm gonna try."

As they chugged along as nearly stall speed, Boxers brought the aircraft lower and lower. On either side, the occasional building was actually taller than they were high, and this was not a city of skyscrapers. Up ahead, a car pulled onto the boulevard from a side street, and then careened onto the sidewalk when the driver saw the looming aircraft.

"That guy just got religion," Boxers said through a smile.

Again, Jonathan chose to concentrate on his map. "We're closing to within a half mile."

As if on cue, the Cessna's engine died. No cough this time, no warning at all. Just a sudden silence where there'd been the steady drone of the engine and the rush of the propeller.

The Cessna became a brick with wings, falling with all the grace of an anvil.

"Brace!" Boxers yelled. He pulled back hard on the yoke, but there just wasn't enough speed for the control surfaces to do their job.

Jonathan pressed himself into his seat, locked his jaw, and waited for it. They hit flat and they hit hard. A jolt of pain as old back injuries reawakened, and Jonathan smelled blood in his sinuses. His belts held, though, and the aircraft stayed upright, even as the landing gear bent and broke beneath them. He more sensed than felt the wheel pylon on the starboard side penetrate the underside of the fuselage and jut through like a giant spike. The fact that he was realizing these things meant that he hadn't been skewered. He didn't hear a scream of agony, so he had to assume that Tristan was okay as well.

He'd know soon enough, one way or the other.

Within seconds, a gray-white cloud filled the interior, but Jonathan's initial burst of fear dimmed in seconds when he recognized the smell of steam, not smoke.

Then they were still. Total elapsed time from engine failure to dead stop: probably less than five seconds.

They listed to the right, but there was no flicker of fire. Chalk up one advantage to running out of fuel.

"Tristan!" Jonathan yelled. "Are you okay?" He turned in his seat to see the kid's wide eyes.

"Holy shit," he said.

"Are you hurt?"

"I don't know."

It was a fair enough answer. It'd take a minute to take inventory.

"I'm fine, too," Boxers said. "Thanks for asking."

"You don't get hurt," Jonathan said. "You make dents." As he spoke, he thumbed the release on his seat belt and shrugged free. "Gather your weapons and let's get the hell out of here."

"Hey, Boss," Boxers said, pointing out the front windscreen. "We're attracting locals."

Of course they were. A plane crashes in the street in the middle of the night, people are going to be curious. Jonathan assessed the threat as low—these people were running to help, not to do harm—but among them, someone was calling the police, and that wouldn't help them a bit.

"What's your status, Tristan?" Jonathan said. "Hurt or unhurt?"

"Bruised," he said. "But I don't think I'm bleeding, and I don't think anything's broken."

"Then grab your shit and get that door open."

"There's a big post sticking up through the floor," Tristan said.

"That's the landing gear. Go around it."

As he spoke, Jonathan clipped his M27 to its sling, checked his left thigh to make sure that the MP7 was where it belonged, and his right hip to say hello to his

Colt. To his left, Boxers had already reassembled his arsenal and was waiting for Jonathan to move out of the way so that he could get out.

A face appeared in the window. It was a local, mid-thirties, shirtless and in undershorts, clearly fresh from bed. He was motioning for others to gather around. Someone pulled open the door.

"Scorpion?" Tristan asked. "What do I do? They're not going to like all the guns."

In fact, the guns would scare the crap out of them, Jonathan thought. "Let me go first," he said. He rolled to his left, and climbed around the landing gear pylon.

The Good Samaritan at the door saw only the weapons, and he backed away.

"We're not here to hurt you," Jonathan said in Spanish. "Thank you for your help, but everybody's okay." As he heard his words, he wondered if he'd ever in his life said anything more ridiculous.

"*Son Americanos,*" the man said. *You're Americans.* Then he turned to the rest of the gathering crowd—maybe fifteen people now—and yelled in Spanish, "They are American soldiers!"

Jonathan didn't know if that would be interpreted as good news or bad, but he didn't have time to worry about it. They needed to get moving.

Jonathan climbed out the door into the night and assumed the kind of softly threatening stance that soldiers and cops used to great benefit around the world: feet planted at shoulder width, his rifle slung across his chest with both hands in place, but with the muzzle pointed at nothing, and his finger out of the trigger guard.

"We're not here to cause you any trouble," he said.

"American soldiers!" someone yelled.

He still couldn't read the crowd.

Tristan emerged from the door, his own rifle clipped to his sling, but the muzzle was pointed toward the crowd.

"Get your hands off your weapon," Jonathan snapped. "Just let it hang."

From behind them both, Boxers growled, "And keep the damn safety on."

While Jonathan scanned the crowd for threats that didn't seem to be materializing, Boxers reached back into the ruined plane and recovered the rucks. He donned one of them, and then took his boss's place on guard while Jonathan shrugged into his.

"We're sorry for waking you," Jonathan said as he'd started moving away from the wreckage and down the street. To Tristan, he said softly, "You stay between us."

Boxers said, "And keep—"

"*Really?*" Tristan snapped.

The Big Guy rumbled out a chuckle.

Jonathan led the way east, moving cautiously but with purpose toward the thickening crowd. He kept his weapon in that same noncommittal posture, taking care to make eye contact with every person he saw. The trick was to let them know you were watching but not linger long enough to pose a threat. He knew without looking that Boxers was with him, step for step, though moving backward instead of forward.

The crowd fell quiet as the team advanced, its curiosity about the crash no doubt trumped by their sense of impending danger. Just loudly enough to be heard, Jonathan said, "Tristan, I want your hand on my rucksack. I want physical contact, and don't let go unless I tell you."

He felt a pull on his shoulder straps. "I'm there," Tristan said. "This is a lot of people."

"They're not threatening us, so we don't threaten them," Jonathan replied. "Just keep moving and avoid eye contact."

You could see the confusion and the unasked questions even in the wash of the yellow streetlights. Every person wanted to know what was going on, yet the presence of the team's body armor and weapons rendered them all silent. In the distance, Jonathan heard the first siren.

"This is about to get interesting, Boss," Boxers said. "Any chance we can pick up the pace a little?"

It was a difficult balance. They could walk a little faster, but if they started to run, they could ignite a panic. The people ahead of them would fear that they were running toward them, and the people behind would assume that they were running away from the authorities. Even in a shithole like Ciudad Juárez, people were jingoistic enough to resent lawbreaking by foreigners.

On the other hand, the sirens were drawing nearer, and their arrival would be sure to ignite a shit storm.

Ahead of them, the crowd that had formed a wall of curiosity separated as Jonathan approached, and allowed them to pass through unmolested. They kept their distance, but not by the margins that Jonathan would have thought. It was almost as if they wanted to see the faces of these foreign invaders.

"Thank you," Jonathan said to one of the gawkers as

he stepped out of the way. He made sure to smile, and the gawker smiled back.

In a few more steps, ninety percent of the crowd was behind them.

"Okay," Jonathan said. "Tristan, let go of my ruck. It's time to run."

Ernesto Palma hadn't anticipated so many people awaiting his arrival at the small military airfield on the outskirts of Ciudad Juarez. There must have been thirty soldiers there, all in uniform, and all from *La Justicia*. Palma had long suspected that his commanders were likewise on Hernandez's payroll, but the fact that this many soldiers had been mobilized removed all doubt. He wondered if the president himself had been informed, if only to begin preparing his denials if things went badly.

Hernandez's Learjet had made tremendously good time, covering the distance in just under two hours. Palma had no idea how much a jet like that cost, but it was a lot of money. The fact that Hernandez even had one gave context to what all he was trying to protect.

As he climbed down the stairway from the jet, the lack of military bearing among the gathered soldiers bothered him. He waited at the bottom of the stairs for Sergeants Nazario and Sanchez. He pulled them aside.

"I want you to relieve the soldiers' current unit non-commissioned officers of their commands, and assemble the troops for formation in twenty minutes," Palma said. "Any questions on that?"

Nazario said, "No, sir. No questions at all." He

snapped a regulation salute, spun on his heel, and headed off to do his job.

Of all the tasks faced by soldiers every day, none was as demoralizing or soul-stealing as idle time. Vigorous firefights raised morale, while awaiting orders merely built a sense of dread.

Palma believed that the solution lay in vigorous training in military things, even if the training was nothing more than standing formation and marching. Such basic military drills also gave Palma some idea of the mettle and competence of these troops who were newly under his command. The task that lay ahead for them fell outside the normal bounds of military activity, so he needed to know that these men could be flexible under fire, and that they would perform their duties without question.

That was a tall order, given the fact that Palma had no idea when his prey would come into range. He was utterly shocked, then, when his phone rang so soon.

"Palma," he said, bringing the phone to his ear.

"It's that bitch Maria Elizondo," Hernandez growled.

Palma recognized the name, but it took a few seconds to process the significance.

"She betrayed me, Ernesto. I gave her everything, and she *betrayed* me."

Palma waited for more. When it didn't come, he said, "What would you like me to do?"

Hernandez gave him the address.

Palma wrote it into the notebook he pulled from his shirt pocket. "I presume you want me to kill her?"

"Absolutely not," Hernandez said. "You are not to hurt her, merely take her into custody. Bring her to me. I'll take care of the rest."

Palma closed his eyes against an image of the last traitor on whom Hernandez had taken his revenge. He remembered his disgust as the man's flayed skin hung from his waist like bloody drapes, the muscle and nerves of his upper body fully exposed and relentlessly tormented. By Hernandez's account at the time, that traitor was on his third day in the hacienda's torture chamber.

"And what about the Yankees?" Palma asked.

"What about them?"

"If your intelligence is right, they will be coming to join her. I believe we should surround the house and wait until—"

"No," Hernandez said. "Get her and bring her to me now."

The line went dead.

CHAPTER TWENTY-EIGHT

Tristan wasn't much of a runner, even on a paved track wearing a T-shirt and shorts. Loaded down with the flopping and rattling gear that felt like it doubled his weight, every step hurt. How these old guys did it so easily was beyond him. The fact that Scorpion could do it didn't surprise him so much, he supposed, because he had that wiry athletic look about him that suggested he jogged a lot just to keep in shape, but that the Big Guy could jog with so little effort was pretty incredible.

And as shitty as flip-flops were for hiking in the jungle, they truly sucked when running for your life.

"Keep it up, Kid," Big Guy urged from behind. "Forward motion is what's keeping us alive now."

Tristan didn't have the spare breath to offer up an answer. He just forced himself to keep up with Scorpion.

God, would it ever stop? He didn't know how long they'd been at this, but he'd run far past the stage of *Tough it out, you can do this*, and was now in the stage where every additional step was a forceful command from his brain.

They'd been running a kind of a zigzag pattern, a block or two east followed by a left turn that would take them a block or two north, followed by a right-hand turn and another block or two east. He'd long ago lost track of how many such turns they'd made, and he'd now stopped even paying attention to his surroundings. They just ran. He found himself focusing on the distance between his toes and the heels of Scorpion's boots. If the distance opened up, which was happening more and more now, then he'd throw another log onto the fire and push himself a little harder.

Hey, if living wasn't a strong enough motivation to give a little more, then what was?

His lungs screamed, and sweat poured into his eyes from the soaked tendrils of his hair.

He'd heard athletes on television talk about some transitional phase where running triggers endorphins or whatever and then running is like the greatest high there is.

What utter bullshit.

If there was anything good about this much discomfort, it was the fact that it displaced a lot of fear. Through the thrumming of the blood in his ears, he could still hear a growing chorus of sirens, but they didn't seem to be getting any closer.

After ambushes, shoot-outs, and now a plane crash, maybe it was safe to assume that the worst was already behind them.

The instant Captain Palma heard over the radio that a plane had crashed, he knew that it was Harris and

Lerner. The reports spoke of three armed soldiers who had all survived, and were moving east.

That put them on a direct path into the trap he had set for them. This time, they would not escape alive. He'd ordered his men to shoot at first sight.

He'd also decided to ignore his orders from Felix Hernandez. The man was acting out of anger, not out of reason, and decisions made as such were always the wrong ones. He'd be able to extract his revenge against Maria Elizondo in his own time, but Palma was not going to ruin his tactical advantage to serve a personal vendetta.

Or, more truthfully, maybe his own personal vendetta had taken precedence over that of Hernandez. Harris, Lerner, and the Wagner boy had caused too much trouble in his life these past two days to be allowed to escape yet again. Whatever their real identities—and Palma suspected strongly that they were American Special Forces—these soldiers were very good, and luck seemed to be running on their side.

By staking out Maria Elizondo's house, Palma had set up the perfect ambush. He'd chosen the one spot on earth where his prey had to go. He felt like a cat watching a mousetrap.

While the police and the rest of the local Army forces closed in on the crash site and scoured the streets for these three who had been so evasive, he needed only wait until they came to him.

Rising from his own place of concealment behind a parked car directly across the wide street from Maria's house, he surveyed the concealment of his troops. Even knowing where they were, he could see no sign of them. The streets were empty this time of night, as they should be, and despite the reasonably bright glow of the streetlights, he could see no shadows, no sign of an errant foot sticking out from behind a vehicle or a wall.

The street looked perfectly normal. He'd even stashed their Sandcats two blocks away so that his prey would not be spooked by their presence.

While he recognized that radio reports were never completely reliable, by all accounts, Harris and his team were unhurt. If they moved quickly, they could easily reach Elizondo's house in the next ten or fifteen minutes.

If Palma's men did their jobs correctly, the invaders should all be dead in the next eleven or sixteen minutes.

He lowered himself behind his concealment and waited once more.

The kid's stamina surprised Jonathan. He'd been able to keep up for most of the run. Now that Tristan was struggling hard to keep up, Jonathan was even more impressed with his heart. The kid was working his ass off, and he wasn't complaining about it.

Jonathan's GPS showed them to be less than a quarter mile away now—just a few blocks, actually—and if their intel was correct, the Elizondo chick would be waiting for them when they arrived. From there, it would be a ride to wherever the hell these tunnels were, and then they'd be back in nearly friendly territory. If their covers were still intact, Jonathan and Boxers would be absorbed back into obscurity while Leon Harris and Richard Lerner disappeared forever. Those aliases had had a good run. It was time to shelve them anyway.

Tristan's future would be up to whatever Gail and Wolverine turned up. Under the circumstances, he didn't think the charges against the kid could have any legs in the United States. As long as the idiot in the White House didn't force some crazy extradition controversy, everything should work out fine.

Good God it was hot. Unreasonably hot, given the time of day. If he didn't follow his own advice and hydrate soon, he was going to start cramping up.

Their current trajectory through these residential neighborhoods was going to bring them up behind the Elizondo residence. According to the maps, the street that ran behind her place was narrower and therefore presumably darker and less populated.

As Jonathan jogged north past yet another cross street, preparing to turn east again at the next corner, his earbud popped and Boxers' voice said, "Whoa, Boss, hold up."

Jonathan stopped, and Tristan collided with him. If Jonathan hadn't grabbed him by the vest, the kid would have fallen to the ground.

"Jesus!" Tristan spat, a little too loud. "What'd you—"

"Quiet," Jonathan said, looking not at Tristan, but at Boxers, who had taken a knee behind the fender of a parked sedan, his weapon up to his shoulder and trained on a spot down the perpendicular street. Never letting go of Tristan's vest, Jonathan pivoted him toward a parked car, and pushed him down. "Sit and stay," he said. He knew the tone would bother the kid, but he didn't care.

As he bent low and closed the twenty feet that separated him from Boxers, Jonathan keyed his mike and whispered, "Whatcha got?" He approached with his M27 up and ready to shoot. He matched Boxers' line of fire, but he had no idea what the target was.

Boxers waited till Jonathan was squatted at his shoulder. "Sandcat," he said, pointing with the muzzle of his rifle.

For a second or two, Jonathan didn't see it, but then there it was, parallel parked among other vehicles on the residential street.

"I've come to dislike Mexican Army vehicles," Boxers said.

It was hard not to. And seeing one this close to where they were going rang a thousand warning bells in his head. Assuming that the Mexicans treated their Sandcats the same way that Uncle Sam treated his Humvees, these were not take-home vehicles.

That meant that someone had stashed it here to keep it out of sight. Since the Sandcat was a troop transport vehicle, Jonathan had to assume that the transported troops had been deployed somewhere nearby.

And while it was entirely possible that the Mexicans were deployed on a mission that had nothing to do with him, he was going to go with the smart money and assume that he and his team were the targets.

Jonathan turned to where he'd left Tristan, and motioned for him to join them. Following the example that Jonathan had set, the kid approached bent low at the waist, and squatted in close to Jonathan and Boxers.

"What are we doing?" Tristan whispered.

"You're staying quiet," Boxers said.

Jonathan softened the message by holding a finger to his lips in a silent *shh*.

Jonathan keyed his mike. "Mother Hen, Scorpion. You there?"

"I heard Big Guy," she said. "What's wrong?"

He told her about the vehicle. "I have to assume that we've got OPFOR deployed around our target building. What does SkysEye show you?" He knew that she'd recognize the shorthand for opposition force.

"We had a tasking problem," she said. "So we're just now getting images. Want to be patched in?"

"Negative," Jonathan said. "Can't afford the light wash." While the SkysEye system and Venice's bag of toys allowed her to download imagery to be shared in real time on Jonathan's PDA or even a laptop, here at night in the middle of the street, the glow would be too obvious and could easily give away their position.

While they waited to hear back from Venice, Jonathan pulled a digital night vision monocular from its pouch on his ruck. While Boxers continued to hold his aim on the street, Jonathan rose above their cover and scanned the area for risks. Just beyond the wash of the streetlight that illuminated the Sandcat that Boxers had discovered, he saw another one parked along the curb.

"I've got another vehicle," he whispered. "Shit, and a third." This one was parked across the road from the second one, on their side of the street.

"See any guards?" Boxers asked. "If I were their commander, I'd have left at least one guy to keep an eye on the trucks."

In a neighborhood like this, it made even more sense.

His earbud popped. "Scorpion, Mother Hen. I've got bad news."

Of course you do, Jonathan thought.

"SkysEye's thermal imagery shows a number of people clustered around the target property. They all seem to be huddled behind some kind of shelter. Vehicles, mostly."

"Shit," Boxers spat.

Tristan went on alert. "What?"

"A small setback," Jonathan told him. Into his radio he said, "Okay, download the photo to my PDA. I'll find a way to look at it."

Jonathan shifted his monocular away from the Sandcats, where he was certain there were guards, even if he couldn't see them, and surveyed the surrounding buildings. In this part of the city, so many residences had been abandoned in place that it was hard to tell the ones that were occupied from the ones that were empty.

The houses here weren't row houses in the strict sense of the term because they didn't physically touch, but they were so close together that the difference was academic. Most were in various stages of rot, but a few showed visible signs of prosperity in the form of flower boxes in the windows or a wreath on the door. Scanning the closest structures on his side of the street, Jonathan focused in on the third property down, where the frayed drapes on the house were open yet the lights were off. That struck him as an odd combination. If people lived in the house, and if they were home, wouldn't they make a point of closing the drapes—especially in a neighborhood as dangerous as this one?

If only because it was convenient, Jonathan locked on to that as an undeniable truth. He tapped Boxers on the shoulder and brought his lips to within an inch of his ear. "We need to get under cover," he whispered. "I want to target the third house down on the left. It looks empty to me."

Boxers said, "Aim my weapon and I'm yours."

That was Boxers' way of saying, *Let's go.*

Jonathan turned to Tristan. "How're you doing?"

"I'm okay. I think." His eyes were wide, but his focus seemed sharp.

"I can't explain all the details," Jonathan said, "but we need to seek some shelter for a few minutes. We're targeting the third house up there on the left. I don't need you to do anything but stay close. Are you cool with that?" He asked the question as if there truly was a choice.

Tristan nodded. "I'm good."

Jonathan flashed him a smile. "You're my shadow, remember?" He stuffed the monocular back into its pouch.

"I remember," Tristan said. He looked at Boxers. "And my safety is on."

Boxers smiled, too. "I figured as much."

"Hand on my ruck," Jonathan said to Tristan. When he felt the tug, Jonathan snapped his night vision back into place and started moving.

The first two houses were obviously occupied, one of them playing the television or radio loudly enough to be heard out here on the street. That was good news. It covered the sound of their movement.

They advanced to the base of the short stairway that led to the front door of the abandoned house. Jonathan keyed his mike. "I vote we enter from the black side," he said.

Boxers made a sweeping motion with his arm that said, *After you.*

While the Big Guy took a knee at the front corner of the house, his weapon to his shoulder, Jonathan made his way down the side of the house toward the back, taking care not to brush the side of the structure next door—they really were that close. About halfway down, he encountered a window that had been broken out. The bottom sill lay at chest height, an easy climb inside.

Jonathan hated anything that was easy. He didn't trust anything that was easy.

Even with night vision in place, it was hard to see any detail of the interior, so he raised his M27 and twisted the lens ring on his muzzle light to ignite the infrared flashlight. With night vision in place, the infrared beam operated just like a visible light beam, except it was, well, invisible. Through Jonathan's lenses, he might as well have been peering through a green-tinted window at midday.

From this angle, furniture and fixtures blocked a thorough view of every corner, but he saw no signs of recent occupancy. In fact, there appeared to be a huge water leak in the middle of the front parlor. Given that there was a second floor above the first, Jonathan considered that kind of uncorrected damage to be a good sign of abandonment.

"Do you need a boost or can you climb?" Jonathan asked.

"I think I can climb," Tristan said.

That was the right answer. "Okay, stay there for a second."

Jonathan shrugged free of Tristan's grasp, planted his gloved hands on the gritty ledge, and hefted himself up. He didn't feel any broken glass or nails or any other nasty stuff that could hurt Tristan when it was his turn. When his waist was clear, and he pulled himself inside, he drew himself to a knee, brought his rifle to his shoulder, and waited.

When no one shot at him or jumped out at him, he allowed himself to rise to a crouch, and then to a standing position. He keyed his mike. "I'm in," he said. "I'm going to sweep the building."

"Roger," Boxers said. "I've got eyes on the PC."

Some might argue that it was overkill to search the entire house for other people—they only needed shelter for a few minutes, after all—but a hidden bad guy had the power to ruin Jonathan's day in enough ways that it was worth the time it took to make sure there was no one else in the building.

It took him all of three minutes. Once he got past the two front rooms on the first floor, the rest of the house had virtually no furniture, and therefore no place for bad guys to hide. He checked every closet, and saved the basement for last. He chuckled in spite of himself. He wondered if anyone entirely escaped their childhood fear of basements. Still, despite the creepiness, the cellar harbored no terrors.

As he climbed the steps back to the first floor, he radioed, "The house is clear."

"The sidewalk isn't," Boxers replied. "I found our sentries. There are at least two, and it looks like they kill time crashed in the front seat of the vehicles. Lazy bastards."

That news was bad, but it wasn't devastating. It wasn't even unexpected. Jonathan asked, "Are they an immediate problem?"

"Negative," Boxers said. "So long as we're quiet."

Back on the first floor now, Jonathan walked casually back to the window where he'd made his entrance and announced to Tristan, "No bad guys."

"I figured that from the absence of shooting," the kid replied. "Am I supposed to join you in there?"

That had been Jonathan's original plan, but now it didn't make a lot of sense. "No, just stay put," he said. "I'll do this and we'll get going."

Jonathan moved away from the window, back toward the house's tattered kitchen, and nestled himself behind some cabinets and a bar to fire up his PDA and open the attachment Venice had sent him.

He keyed his mike. "Okay, Mother Hen," he said. "You have the controls. Give me a tour."

Squinting to see the tiny screen, Jonathan opened the encrypted link and watched the satellite image move to Venice's commentary.

"Here's where you are," she said. The image zoomed from a few hundred feet up to maybe thirty feet above the ground. On the screen, he saw himself and his team squatted at the corner. It was creepy to watch yourself in the past.

Then the image lifted to a hundred feet and tracked due north, passing over rooftops and abandoned streets. After three blocks, the image tracked eastward and then stopped on a building that Jonathan recognized as the target house. "As the crow flies, this distance is about a quarter mile," Venice said. "A little less."

Jonathan squinted harder. He couldn't see any people, but he knew that Venice would get to it. She had her own pace for these things, and she was not to be hurried.

"You'll note that there aren't any people," Venice said. "Now watch when I put in the infrared filter."

The picture blinked, and there they were: a dozen or more human-shaped heat sources crouched behind vehicles and corners of nearby structures. While their weapons did not show up well, the ghosts of rifles were visible, and the postures of the forms holding them sold it.

"I count fourteen people," Venice said, "but there could be more. Actually, there are more. Seventeen, counting the soldiers Big Guy spotted." Clearly, she'd been monitoring the radio traffic.

They'd set up a textbook ambush—not that it was a particularly difficult one to engineer. "They've got the front pretty well covered," Jonathan said. "Show me the black side."

The image moved again, and when it settled down, he saw an aerial view of a standard alleyway that could have been in any city in America: tiny backyards that appeared to be enclosed by stockade fences, backing up to other backyards with stockade fences. The space in between was barely big enough to accommodate a sedan, let alone the trash trucks that no doubt cruised the space once or twice a week.

The infrared imagery revealed two more people

hunkered down back there. "There are numbers eighteen and nineteen," Jonathan said. "This isn't going to be easy."

"Are they ever?" Boxers asked over the radio.

When the odds were this badly stacked, their only chance for success lay in speed and overwhelming violence, and the configuration of the OPFOR confounded both of those factors. Taking out the guys in the alley would be a simple matter of expending about three dollars' worth of ammunition, but doing so would alert the troops out front, and ignite the kind of firefight that was especially difficult to win. Throw in the fact that these guys were real soldiers—as opposed to the thugs and posers that Jonathan so often encountered in his job—and the odds diminished even more.

There had to be a way, though, because there was always a way.

"Can you pull up engineering drawings for the house?" he asked. He had no idea what he was looking for, but if you didn't look, you couldn't find anything.

"Stand by," Venice said.

"Holy shit," Jonathan said off the air. He was in Mexico, for God's sake. How could she possibly—

"Hey, Scorpion, I've got good news. I just got a call from Wolverine. The house has a tunnel."

CHAPTER TWENTY-NINE

Veronica Costanza left the way she had come, through the panel in the bathroom, and from there to wherever the tunnel led. A sewer. How appropriate. If Maria had a brain in her head, she'd have used the escape route herself by now. This waiting was killing her. It had been hours, and the phone Veronica had left behind hadn't rung.

Was it possible that this was an elaborate setup? Had Maria's safety been traded by the FBI for some larger prize? She'd heard of such things happening before. The Americans were famous for turning their backs on one friend in favor of a newer, more important friend. Just ask the citizens of Vietnam, Iraq, and Afghanistan about that. Americans' priorities changed with the wind. Perhaps Maria's usefulness had been expended, and now they needed to give her over to Felix to gain some larger prize.

Maria told herself that these were foolish thoughts—the paranoia of the moment—yet they continued to nag at her. Was it so different from what Veronica promised would be her fate if she failed to wait for the Americans whose lives were so important? Yet wait she did, even as soldiers surrounded her house.

She never looked out a window—in fact, she made a point of staying away from the windows lest she present too enticing a target, bullet-proof glass notwithstanding—but she knew they were out there, and she knew that they were planning to hurt her.

But she would not go quietly. Or peaceably. Her six-shot revolver would see to that. Weighing over a kilogram once it was loaded, her Taurus .44 Magnum was designed to kill attacking bears. She imagined it would stop Felix and his men. It would stop five of them, anyway. The sixth bullet would be for herself.

She knew the horrors that awaited her if Felix ever got his hands on her. She wouldn't give him the satisfaction.

So she continued to wait in the dark, both literally and figuratively. She'd turned off the lights so as not to throw shadows across the windows, and at the same time to be able to better see shadows that were thrown from outside. She sat in a fat padded chair in the only windowless corner in her house. The front door stood to her left, the kitchen and its back door to her right. Through the kitchen and into the bedroom lay the route to her survival—perhaps the route to the soldiers' invasion.

And she waited. If the soldiers charged, it would end in seconds. If she fled, the end would be delayed—perhaps for moments, perhaps forever—but at least the end would come on her terms. That was worth something, wasn't it?

You will *do this, Maria. You* must *do this. These people are more important to my boss than you are.*

As Veronica's word replayed through Maria's mind, she remembered the glare of the agent's eyes. The coldness of them. All of those meetings they'd had exchanging information, all those friendly chats, she realized now had never been about friendship. They'd never been about good triumphing over evil. In the FBI agent's mind, it had only been about a job. It had been about getting a conviction against Felix Hernandez. Maria was important only so long as she was useful.

And she didn't doubt for a moment that Veronica Costanza and her FBI would hunt her down and see that she was killed if she did not do exactly as she had been told.

And so Maria waited for the American fugitives who were more important than she.

"You were a fool to be a patriot," she said aloud. If there were listening devices, so be it. Let there be a record of her final thoughts.

Saying those words aloud, though, made her cringe. This had never been about patriotism. It had never been about justice or about returning her beloved Mexico to the way it used to be. From the very first days, it had been about revenge.

Maria closed her eyes and forced herself to recall the images that she had spent so many years pushing away. She made herself look once again at her big brother Jaime, and the gaping wound in his throat, cut all the way back to the bones in his neck. She remembered the dullness of his once-bright brown eyes, lifeless under their drooping, half-open lids. She remembered the brightness of his blood-soaked T-shirt. He was only sixteen when Felix's men murdered him and left the body on the hood of her father's car, a piece of paper

stuffed into his mouth, scrawled with the word, *ladrón*—
thief. Skinny and awkward, he'd been seeking respect
when he began running money for the drug lords. One
day, he took enough pesos for himself to buy a sandwich and a Coke.

For that, they took his life.

For weeks afterward, men stalked Maria on her way
to and from school. They wanted her to know that they
were watching, and that she would live or die at their
whim. They wanted her to know that they were above
the law—better still, that they *were* the law—and that
murder was but one of the enforcement tools at their
disposal. That was twelve years ago. She was only ten
years old, but like everyone else in her neighborhood,
both her virginity and her life were as fragile as the de-
sires of the men who paid allegiance to Felix Hernandez.

After Jaime's murder, Maria's parents had moved
her away. Her father was an engineer by training and
education, but to be an engineer one had to live in the
city, and where there were cities there were drugs. So
they moved to the country, where her father dedicated
himself to farming, yet nothing grew at his hand.
When her mother died of a heart attack two years later,
the pressure and the stress became too much for Papa.
Maria was only sixteen when he hanged himself in the
barn. His note apologized for his weakness. Apologized for leaving her alone in the world.

Terrified of a life on the street, Maria turned to the
convent, but her anger burned too deeply. Even as she
prepared to take her vows to God, she found herself
vowing to seek revenge on Felix Hernandez, who had

killed not only her brother, but by extension her mother and father, as well. He'd murdered her entire family, and she was going to hurt him.

Maria had heard her entire life how beautiful she was, and sometimes she could even see the beauty herself in the mirror. With no money and no education, and with a future as a nun shut down by her heart, she turned her beauty into a weapon.

Everyone knew that Felix Hernandez liked his mistresses young and beautiful. Though well into his forties himself, he was never seen in the company of a woman older than twenty-five, and occasionally his tastes ran to those in their early teens.

Getting close to him had been surprisingly simple. With short enough skirts and enough cleavage showing, it was just a matter of being seen.

Felix liked coffee, and he liked to take it in the same café every morning. To launch their relationship, Maria made sure to be there at the same time he was. She made eye contact and looked away, and that was all it took. Felix sent a henchman to her table.

"That man over there is Felix Hernandez," the henchman said. "He would like you to join him at his table."

Maria made a show of looking over there and then said with as much disinterest as she could muster, "I know who he is. Tell him that only a coward sends a surrogate to ask such a thing. If he wants me to join him, he may ask me himself."

The henchman looked horrified.

"Are you *afraid* to repeat my words?" Maria pressed. "If so, send Mr. Hernandez over, and I will be happy to tell him myself." It was risky to say such a thing, but her mother had told her that to be of value, something—some*one*—must be difficult to obtain. Maria wasn't interested in a one-night stand. She wasn't interested in being one of many mistresses. Her plan from the beginning was to win her way into Felix's inner circle where she could do as much damage as she possibly could. In order for the plan to work, he needed to feel that it was his idea.

The henchman didn't appreciate the affront to his masculinity. "I will tell him," he said. "It is your life to lose." He returned to Felix's table, and Maria forced herself to return her eyes to the newspaper from which she hadn't read a word.

She heard laughter from Felix's table, and then about a minute later, a shadow fell across her paper. Its owner said, "Excuse me."

Maria looked up to see Felix Hernandez looking down at her, his arms folded across his chest. "May I sit down?" he asked.

Maria folded her paper to make room and gestured to the chair opposite hers. "Please," she said.

Felix pulled the chair out and sat, his forearms resting on the table. He leaned in close. "My friend tells me that you know who I am," he said, "yet you are unimpressed."

"If that is what he told you, then your friend is a coward." She had never been in such close proximity to a murderer before. She'd expected the eyes of a beast, of a predator, but instead saw amused softness.

Felix smiled. "So, *coward* is your word of the day, is it? First you use it in reference to me, and now you use it in reference to my friend."

Maria gave a coy smile. "So he told you," she said. "And you are here. You have proven me wrong twice."

He laughed and sat back in his chair. He crossed his legs and folded his arms again. Maria would later come to recognize this as his most thoughtful pose. "You are a beautiful woman," he said. "And though I might not impress you, I assure you that you impress me. What is your name?"

"Maria Elizondo," she said. The name was pure fiction, adopted in case Felix actually remembered any of the names of the children he'd murdered.

"A beautiful name," he said. Then he stood. He bowed slightly from the waist and said, "Maria Elizondo, would you please do me the distinct honor of joining me at my table for coffee?" There was no hint of threat in his tone. In fact, he seemed genuinely charmed.

Maria stood and—

She jumped as the phone in her hand rang. Snapped back to the reality of the present, she wondered if she'd perhaps fallen asleep. It rang again. The incoming number was blocked from her caller ID. Maria slid the phone open and brought it to her ear. "*Hola.*"

A woman's angst-filled voice said, "Oh, dear God, please tell me that you speak English."

"Who is this?" Maria asked in English.

"Are you Maria Elizondo?"

"Who are *you*?"

"Let's please not play this game," the voice said. "I need you to go first."

Maria hesitated, assessing the degree of threat this call might pose. Finally, she said, "Yes, this is Maria Elizondo."

"Good. You can call me Mother Hen."

"Excuse me?"

"Yeah, I know it's a stupid name, but it is what it is. I got this number from your FBI contact."

"And that is supposed to make me trust you?" Maria scoffed.

"Actually, I don't care. All I know is that your time in Mexico is about to come to an end, and that you're going to escort my boss and a couple of others out of there." She paused as if awaiting a response, but when Maria didn't offer one, Mother Hen went on, "There's been a complication."

Maria's heart fell. This was when they would tell her that she was on her own.

"You're surrounded by a lot of soldiers, and that's going to make it very difficult to get you out of there."

"How many people are with your friend?" Maria asked.

"They're three in all, but one of them is just a boy."

"Two people, then?" Maria pressed her hand to her forehead. "So, we are finished," she said.

"Heavens no, you're not finished," Mother Hen said.

"But with only two—"

"They're a very special two," Mother Hen said. "We have a plan. But for it to work, you have to listen very carefully."

Normally, it was Boxers' job to set explosives. In fact, blowing stuff up ranked among his favorite things to do. Tonight, though, the task fell to Jonathan because he was smaller and he could move faster and more quietly. In fact, he'd been able to run the first two blocks out in the open, albeit in the shadows, but now that he was so close to his prey, he had to slow down and be extra careful.

At an intersection three blocks west of the target house, he stopped completely, dropped to a knee, and flipped down his night vision goggles. Given the high levels of ambient light from the streetlamps, the NVGs were only moderately useful, but he'd take whatever advantage he could get. The nearest Mexican soldier should be only twenty or twenty-five yards away now. Jonathan pressed against the side of a pickup truck, and took time to survey his surroundings. For a long time—probably a minute—he saw no sign of the soldier he expected, and that concerned him. People who weren't where they were supposed to be were by definition someplace where he wasn't expecting them. He hated surprises.

Then he saw the guy. He was crouched behind another vehicle, and from the way he stretched, Jonathan figured that his leg had cramped up on him. *Relax, kid,* Jonathan thought. *You'll be moving soon.*

Having left his ruck back with Boxers and Tristan, it was easy for Jonathan to lie on the ground next to the truck and prepare his charges. He'd stuffed his pockets with six GPCs—general purpose charges—which were wads of C-4 explosives with tails of detonating cord. Each packed a hell of a wallop, and in all the years he'd been using them, he'd never once experienced a failure. He pulled two from the thigh pocket of his trousers and pressed them into the wheel well of the pickup. He'd previously attached the electronic detonator and set the timer for seven minutes, a random number that he thought was sure to give him enough time to get back to the others before the show started.

He gave the explosives a light tug to make sure that they would hold, and pressed the button to start the countdown.

It wasn't until he started to rise that he heard the footsteps approaching.

Shit.

"Hey, you!" someone called in Spanish. Jonathan knew without looking that it had to be the soldier. "What are you doing?"

Jonathan didn't move. On the ground, on his side, his back facing the approaching soldier, Jonathan was a scary curiosity—maybe an enemy, maybe a passed-out drunk. The soldier wouldn't shoot until he was sure one way or the other. That bought time. Now Jonathan had to figure out what to do with it.

Still on his side, he unclipped his rifle from its sling so that he'd have more mobility when he stood, and then he reached across with his right hand, unsnapped the strap that secured his KA-BAR knife to the scabbard on his left shoulder, and drew it. Gunshots at this moment would ruin everything.

"You there," the soldier said. "Stand up."

Jonathan didn't move. The voice still sounded too far away. Much closer, though, and Jonathan's clothing would give him away. Footsteps approached. Then they scraped to a halt and Jonathan heard the clatter of the guy's weapon as he shouldered it.

It was time.

Jonathan spun from his side to his back, and as he did, he slashed the gleaming edge of his knife across the tendons behind the soldier's knee. He dropped before his mind could register the pain, and as he fell, Jonathan sat up, pushed the soldier's rifle to the side and slashed the knife across his wrist, severing the tendons that controlled his fingers. Without fingers, you can't pull a trigger.

Jonathan's final slash opened a gaping smile in the soldier's throat. Amid a fountain of blood, the soldier toppled to his side, dead.

"Sorry, kid," Jonathan said softly. Like soldiers everywhere, the youngest always died first. Inexperience bred hesitation—the deadliest of all weaknesses on a battlefield. In close-quarters battle, victory was won in the blink of time when questions formed in the other guy's mind. In a fight with Jonathan, the odds were never evenly stacked. Even after so many years, though, he never got used to the killing.

To become inured to that kind of violence would be to surrender your humanity.

The clock ticked. In six and a half minutes there was going to be a crater where he was standing, and between now and then he had two more bombs to set.

Big Guy was a scary, scary man. He reminded Tristan of one of the predatory animals you see on cable television. As Tristan sat on the ground, his knees up and his back against the house where Scorpion had checked his email, he could see the intensity of the Big Guy's glare even in the dark. He seemed perfectly at rest balanced on one knee. His rifle wasn't at his shoulder, but it might as well have been. He held it as if it weighed nothing, his hands loose on the grip and the barrel.

There was a stillness about the Big Guy that seemed unnatural, or maybe supernatural. Only his head and eyes moved, and they moved constantly. Every time Tristan stirred, those eyes darted to him, and his spine melted. The man oozed lethality the way others oozed sweat on a hot day.

If Tristan understood the plan he'd overheard, Scorpion was planting bombs around the neighborhood to distract the people who were trying to kill them. There'd be a total of three explosions, each of them drawing the bad guys—that's what Scorpion actually called them, bad guys—in different and wrong directions.

In the confusion, they would steal one of those army trucks—a Sandcat—to pick up somebody named Maria, and then yada, yada, yada, they'd be back safe in the United States.

Less clear to him was that middle part, the yada, yada, yada. They must have worked that part out when he wasn't listening. It had something to do with tunnels. Tristan didn't know how to break it to them, but he had a real problem with claustrophobia. He didn't do tight places at all. It'd been all he could do to keep from going bat-shit crazy when he was shackled to Allison in the bus.

Jesus, how long ago was that? Was it only yesterday? Was that even possible?

And how long had it been since he'd slept? Not the occasional dozing he'd been able to pull off at various times, but *real* sleep? Surely longer than a week.

Just thinking about sleep made his eyelids heavy. He felt exhausted at a level that he'd never experienced. It was as if energy were held into your body by a spigot, and someone had twisted his all the way open. So tired that it hurt. As he closed his eyes, he wondered if he'd get in trouble for falling asleep at his post.

As he listened to the sounds of the night and the rhythm of his own breathing, Tristan's mind took him back home. He saw Mom praying in the dark and Ziggy trying his best just to be noticed. He wondered what she'd said when they told her he'd been kidnapped. When you already prayed ten hours a day, was it possible to find room for more?

After they'd grown so far apart, would this nightmare bring them closer together? Even a little bit?

Even as the question formed in his mind, he knew that the answer would be no. Like everything else, this would be written off as God's will, another check mark on His shit list that included Dad's cancer and Tristan's problems in physics class. If you pray hard enough, you never have to confront anything difficult. You never worry about living or dying, winning or losing. All you have to do is pray for strength.

A knot formed in his stomach as he imagined his homecoming. He'd have to explain to everyone how he'd lived while the others all died. Amid all those parents mourning the loss of their children, there would be no room for him to celebrate the fact that he'd survived. Everything he'd experienced these past twenty-four hours, from the shoot-outs to the plane crash to whatever lay ahead, would have to go unspoken. No one would ever be able to understand the intensity of the life that he'd lived since Scorpion and the Big Guy had pulled him from the bus.

He'd never be able to confess that in the midst of all the terror and the bloodshed, there was real *excitement*.

For this slice of time—and only for this slice of time, unique to his years on the planet—nothing had been predictable. Mere seconds separated boredom from mortal danger. No one would ever understand how even though the odds of survival were slim—well, they were what they were—he never thought about dying. He was too busy living.

Too busy killing.

When this chapter in his life closed, what could possibly replace it? Surely there had to be something.

Whatever it was, it wasn't in Scottsdale, and it for sure wasn't in his house. If what Scorpion suspected proved to be correct, the Crystal Palace would collapse, and as it did, it would take Mom with it. That place was her life. Without it, Tristan didn't think she'd have anywhere else to turn.

And when she turned to him, he wouldn't be there. He refused to walk that route. She was his past; something else entirely was his future. He didn't know yet what that was—how can anyone know the future?—but he knew it wasn't listening to a bitter old woman complain about the grave-like existence she'd carved for herself.

When she turned to Ziggy, though, Tristan would try to help. Again, he didn't know how, but the kid deserved better than that, even if he didn't know it.

A cold sense of hopelessness washed over Tristan as he thought these things, and he snapped his eyes open to return to the fears of the present. Those were the important ones to face, anyway.

And if they screwed things up, the future wouldn't matter, would it?

CHAPTER THIRTY

Maria Elizondo couldn't breathe. The stress of the darkness, the tightness of the space, and the sheer burden of the unknown had conspired to pull all the oxygen out of the air.

Intuitively, she knew that was impossible, but as she sat crouched in this tiniest of tiny spaces, reason and logic seemed far away. The tunnel smelled of dirt, smelled like a grave. And how appropriate. This would be the night when she lived or died. Either a future lay ahead for her, or it did not.

And it all depended on strangers. American strangers.

Maria prayed. She prayed for strength and courage and for God to forgive the unrelenting anger that had consumed her all these years. She prayed that He would understand not having heard from her in so long, and that He would see that in her heart she was a good person. If, in fact, this was to be the night when she and Saint Peter made personal acquaintance, she prayed that this would be the first day of a blissful eternity, not a tormented one.

According to Veronica, verified by the strange woman, Mother Hen, this tunnel would dump Maria in a storm sewer that ran under the alley behind her house. From there, she would need to find the ladder to a manhole, beyond which freedom lay. As a random thought, she offered up a separate prayer to thank God for not making it rain tonight. In this climate, the ground was so hard and impenetrable that even an inch of rain turned storm sewers into raging rivers.

As she inched down the incline on her rear end, Maria ran the instructions from Mother Hen through her mind. There would be three explosions, and she was not to emerge from the manhole until after the third. She was to stay close to the manhole and await the arrival of a military vehicle. It would flash its lights twice. She was then to approach the vehicle and get in. There would be three American men in the vehicle, one much younger than the others. The older two were soldiers of a sort, and they would protect her as she led them to the tunnels that terminated inside the United States.

"The FBI will be waiting for you on the other side," Mother Hen explained. "They will take you into protective custody. They wanted me to stress to you that protective custody is not a form of arrest. It is for your own protection, to keep you from being harmed by Felix Hernandez's friends. You'll remain in custody for as long as it takes to convict Hernandez of his crimes."

"Will I be in a jail cell?"

"You will be in a safe house," Mother Hen said. "It's a house like any other, but with guards and security systems."

The news had distressed her. When she thought about her upcoming time in the United States—the nation she'd heard so much about since the day she was born—she'd never thought in terms of security teams and restricted movement. It made sense, she knew, but it was yet another reminder that none of the kindness or cooperation she would see in the future had anything to do with Maria the person. It would all be about Maria the witness.

The end would be the same, yes: a future as an American citizen. It shouldn't matter how the dream was achieved, so why did it make her sad to be treated as the witness she'd volunteered to be?

Maria sensed in the darkness that the pitch of the incline was becoming more severe, and she found herself pressing hard with her hands and feet against the walls. She'd brought a tiny flashlight with her, one that she'd pulled from her keychain, but she dared not use it. She didn't want to risk the possibility, however unlikely, of alerting a passing pedestrian or soldier to her presence by startling them with a flash of white light from beneath their feet.

As the dirt became damp, she realized that she must be getting closer to the sewer. Closer to danger.

Closer to freedom.

How in the world had Felix been able to dig this tunnel without her knowing it? His teams must have done it only during the day when she was at work. And what was the purpose? Was he merely preserving his option for a midnight liaison at a time of his choice?

Then she got it. It was the most obvious thing in the world when you thought about it. This was his planned escape route if his enemies arrived while he was visiting her, which he never did because when they were together, it was always at his hacienda. Such was not the case with his other mistresses, however. They were never trusted to be in the house, so he visited them in theirs, on occasion dismissing the mistresses' husbands from their own beds.

Could it be that each of them have tunnels built beneath their houses?

Of course it could. For something to exist, Felix needed only wish that it be so, and it would appear.

The tunnel walls disappeared without notice. One instant her feet were pressed up against the earthen sides, and the next they were splayed wide, and she was falling. She didn't even have time to dig her fingers deeper into the walls before she was airborne for just a millisecond, and then she landed hard and with a splash against the smooth concrete of the storm sewer.

She landed on her back and slid, her face slipping below the surface of the water before her hands and feet found a purchase and she was able to rise to her knees. Thoroughly drenched, she fought the urge to cough as her hand shot to the waistband of her pants, where she found the .44 Magnum still tucked where it was supposed to be.

She kept her right hand on the pistol grip as she extended her left hand over her head to see how close the ceiling was. When she felt nothing, she dared to stand, ever so slowly, and she was shocked to find that she could rise to her feet and stand to her full height.

That's when she realized that she was casting a dim shadow, despite the pitch darkness. Only it wasn't pitch dark right here. There was no detail to be seen, but when she waved her hand in front of her face, she could definitely see a silhouette.

To her right, she could see the silhouette of a ladder.

When she looked up, she saw two pinholes of gray

light peering down at her like ghostly cat's eyes through the manhole cover.

She'd found her way out. Now all she had to do was wait.

It all took longer than Jonathan had anticipated. Planting of the second charge had been complicated by the presence of occupied buildings. The last thing he wanted was to blast some kid out of his crib. By the time he'd found a suitable vehicle to booby-trap, he'd already lost an extra ninety seconds off the timing of the first charge.

Thus, when he planted the third bomb, he could allow only forty-five seconds on the fuse.

He pressed the button to activate the countdown and then he ran like a bunny rabbit across the street and down one block to join the rest of his team. With his NVGs in place, there were no obstacles that he couldn't see, and as he closed the distance, he saw Boxers with his rifle up and ready to shoot anyone who might threaten Jonathan's retreat.

Jonathan slowed and backpedaled and dropped to his knees as he joined the others.

"Jesus, Boss, if I knew you were going to stroll, I'd've come along."

"Stuff it and take cover," Jonathan said, pressing the NVGs out of the way. "The first one's going to be close and it's going to be soon." As he spoke, he cupped the nape of Tristan's neck and pulled him forward and down to the grass. With the PC pressed into the dirt, Jonathan lay down on top of him.

"Oh, shit," Tristan grunted. "What are you doing?"

"Sorry, kid, it's just part of the job."

"But you're—"

The camera strobe of the detonation silenced him, and an instant later, the ground shook as if struck with a massive bass drum mallet.

Boxers laughed. "Well, shit, Scorpion. At least you gave us a show worth waiting for."

They all held their positions on the ground for the better part of ten seconds to allow whatever debris was launched to land wherever it was going.

When there was no impact, he rose from on top of Tristan and helped the kid rise to his knees.

"Well, the overture's over," Jonathan said. "Time for the first act." He stood, and pulled Tristan with him. "Ready to run again?"

Palma just happened to be looking right at the detonation when it happened. His first instinct on seeing the pulse of light was that it was a muzzle flash, but in the instant that it took him to flinch, he saw the eruption of debris, and he knew that it was a bomb. The chatter of automatic weapons fire followed almost immediately, followed by panicked reports from the guards at the Sandcats that they were under attack.

Within seconds, the police channels came alive with reports of the explosions and the gunfire.

To his left, Sergeant Nazario said, "Captain, sir, we have to go and help them."

Did this make sense? Palma asked himself. Why would they choose to fight so far away when their true target was right here? Could this be a diversion?

"Help us!" cried a Sandcat crew member.

Palma pounded the hood of the car that shielded him. Somehow, they'd found out about the trap. Were they adapting, or were they merely being stupid?

"Sir, please," Nazario said. "Let me go reinforce them."

In his heart, Palma knew it was a mistake, just as splitting your forces is always a mistake. These terrorists had fooled him before, and he sensed that they were doing it again.

But men under his command needed help.

"Very well," he said, finally. "Take second and third squads to reinforce the Sandcats. You are in charge. I want a full report. They're panicking out there."

Nazario threw off a quick salute and brought his portable radio to his lips.

The Sandcat crews started shooting even before Jonathan and his team were there to engage them. The first blast, triggered at the end of the block where they'd parked their vehicles, had incited blind panic, and they were firing randomly at the source of the explosion.

"I feel sorry for the poor schmucks who live on the other end of the block," Boxers quipped over the radio. Bullets flew until they hit something. That meant hundreds of rounds were chewing up the properties downrange.

A minute thirty in, the plan was working perfectly.

Stealth no longer mattered. Jonathan and his team sprinted full out two blocks east, and then turned south for a block. When they turned west onto the street where the war was happening, the Mexicans were so outflanked that they actually had their backs turned to them.

It shouldn't be this easy. There were six in total.

Jonathan and Boxers fired in unison, and two seconds later, the Sandcats were theirs.

Jonathan held his aim for a few seconds to verify that there was no movement, and then he turned to Tristan. "Almost home," he said. "Let's go."

Something had changed behind the kid's eyes. Jonathan didn't know what it was, and he didn't particularly care, but he got the distinct impression that he'd somehow crossed a line. For a second, he thought that maybe Tristan was going to pull back, but it only took a slight tug on his vest to bring him along.

Tristan's mind screamed, *They just murdered those men. Shot them in the back. They never had a chance.*

"Fair fights are for dead fools, Tristan," Scorpion said, somehow reading his thoughts. As he spoke, he hooked his foot under the belly of one of the dead men and rolled him to his back. The soldier's cheek had erupted into a hideous blooming rose.

"Forget everything you've heard about honor in war," Scorpion went on. "The winners are the guys who are still alive when the shooting stops." As if by rote, he took the soldier's rifle away and then moved on to the next corpse. "You've got to exploit every weakness."

Scorpion made a point of establishing eye contact. "No matter how you cut it, it's an ugly business."

The engine on the closest Sandcat turned and caught. Tristan jumped at the sound and whirled to see the Big Guy in the front seat, smiling broadly and giving a thumbs-up through the window. He said something, but the words were lost in the crisp *thump* of another explosion.

Scorpion checked his watch and gave a quick, satisfied nod. "Mount up," he said.

With the second explosion, Palma knew that his worst fears had been realized. The timing had been brilliant. If his mental calculations were correct, Nazario and his men would have been very near the blast.

The debris had barely stopped falling when the screaming erupted on the radio. At first, all he heard was noise, irrational unintelligible yelling that overpowered the radio mike.

"Calm down, soldier," Palma said, but he knew they'd stepped on his transmission.

He was about to try again when he heard the worst of the worst: "Sergeant Nazario is dead!"

Maria felt the first explosion more than she heard it. She assumed it was the first explosion. More a pulse than a boom, it launched waves through the knee-deep water that rolled to her waist and slapped against the concrete walls.

Stuff fell from the ceiling, too, though in the darkness she didn't know what it was. It fell in chunks and it filled the air with dust that smelled like mold. Without light, and without knowledge of the truth, her mind screamed that the falling objects were spiders. And crickets. All the insects that most terrified her.

In that flash of fear, the possibility of capture or torture or death mattered less than battling the insects. Maria's hands moved in spasms to brush whatever they were from her shoulders and hair.

Her *hair*! In her mind, her head was infested now, crawling with bugs. With pregnant bugs, determined to lay their eggs on her scalp.

It was all preposterous, of course—the ridiculous ramblings of a frightened little girl who'd never fully overcome her fear of the dark.

She told herself that none of it was true—*insisted* that none of it was true—but it did little to settle her racing heart and trembling hands.

This will be over soon, she told herself. What was it that Mother Hen had said? Three explosions in the space of five minutes, and she was to wait until—

There was nothing subtle about the next detonation.

It must have been much closer, because a pressure wave rolled like an earthquake through the storm sewer. She felt the walls move as the wave swept past her, and a tsunami of water smacked her like a liquid wall. It broke over her head and knocked her to the floor, where she tumbled under the assault of secondary and tertiary waves.

After a somersault, Maria came up sputtering and coughing, desperate to recover the air that had been pushed from her lungs. As she struggled to breathe, she also tried to find stability for her feet in the slippery muck that lined the concrete floor of the sewer.

By pressing her hands against the walls and digging in with her knees, she was finally able to stabilize herself. She tried to stand, but when she was barely above a squat, her head hit the top of the tunnel and a new wave of panic swept over her. She'd been washed to a new part of the sewer, but she'd been turned and jostled so much that she no longer could tell left from right, upstream from downstream.

She was stranded now on hands and knees, and the water was chin-high. If it started to rain, she would drown.

This new terror eclipsed any horrors of the past. She was blind and she was trapped and she was going to drown. If her remains were ever found at all, they would be tangled among weeds and bushes along the banks of the river, downstream from the outfall of this terrible place.

"Stop it!" she commanded herself aloud.

Nothing was done until it was done. She needed clear thought, not panicked ramblings. The cliché said that panic killed people, and now she knew what the cliché meant. If you're panicking, you're not thinking, and if you're not thinking, you're just giving yourself up to death.

She smelled smoke. The stench of burning rubber. It wasn't very strong, but it was definitely there. How was it possible to set a sewer on fire?

She needed to find the dim light from the manhole cover. If she could—

Light! Of course! Her flashlight!

Holding herself out of the water by planting her left hand in the slimy muck, she explored her pants pocket with her right. Miraculously, the pistol was still there—as if she had any use for it right now. When her fingers found the outline of the three-inch tube that could only be the flashlight, she nearly cried.

"Please, please, please work," she moaned.

The company that sold these things marketed them as waterproof, but how factual was their claim? She didn't even know if the batteries worked anymore. More than that, she wasn't sure she'd even turned it on before.

The fabric of her pants fought her efforts to remove the light, and once it was clear, she nearly dropped it. In the slipperiness of her grip, the light squirted out of her grasp, but somehow, through instinct and divine intervention, she didn't lose it in the black water.

Somehow, Maria knew to twist it. She laughed aloud when the blinding white light appeared.

When she pointed the beam to her right, it revealed nothing but an endless tube of concrete that extended eight or ten meters before curving curved sharply to the right. Intuitively, she knew that that was the wrong way.

She pivoted the other way, where her beam revealed a wall of smoke rolling toward her. It was probably just an optical illusion, but the leading edge of the cloud appeared light in color, followed behind by a much darker, thicker cloud. It started to sting her eyes, but she wondered if that would be the case if she was still blind. Could it be that mere awareness brought discomfort?

But there was something else, something in the water, a ripple of movement that raced toward her, as if chased by the cloud.

Maria understood what it was when the first wave of rats swarmed around her.

She screamed.

CHAPTER THIRTY-ONE

Even two blocks away, the explosion was huge, launching a roiling ball of orange fire that momentarily turned night to day. As the original burst of light faded—not nearly as quickly as it had erupted—a dimmer glow remained, the beginnings of secondary fires.

Boxers gave a wild look as Jonathan dumped his ruck on the floor of the Sandcat's shotgun seat and climbed in after it. "Think you used enough dynamite there, Butch?" Big Guy quipped, stealing a line from *Butch Cassidy and the Sundance Kid*. "Jesus, what did you blow up?" If the second charge had been the first—the closest—it might have killed them all.

"I knew that one was for effect, so I daisy-chained three GPCs on the gas tank."

Boxers laughed. "Holy shit."

Jonathan ignored him and turned in his seat to make sure that Tristan was aboard and secured. When the doors were all closed, he said, "Go," and they were moving.

Jonathan tried not to look at the conflagration he'd ignited. The thought of the lives that he had just ruined sickened him. Even if everyone got out of their homes safely, their possessions—lifetimes of memories—would all be destroyed. And the destruction was all his responsibility. If only there'd been another way.

The first blast had been designed to draw the OPFOR closer, and the second blast had been all about killing as many of them as possible. Because such things were an inexact science, it made sense to use more explosives and to capitalize on the accelerant effect of the gasoline.

If there'd been a propane tanker parked at the curb, he'd have set the bomb on that.

He needed to tweak every advantage he could find to make sure that his PC would rest his head on his own pillow again. Everything else was secondary to that.

If theory evolved into fact, the explosion would have culled the OPFOR herd significantly, and demoralized the hell out of them. That last part was important. A force that can't focus on an objective can't fight effectively.

These Mexican soldiers and the local emergency response agency would all be reeling from the explosive attacks when Jonathan and his team rolled in to take Maria Elizondo to safety. With any luck, he would pluck their new PC without incident, and they'd skip back to America unmolested.

Right. And then pigs would fly.

Hundreds of rats—thousands of them—raced toward Maria, churning the water, presenting as a malignant gray blanket across the surface. They hit her head-on, then flowed around her as if she weren't there.

Poised as she was on her hands and knees, her face inches above the surface of the water, the rats swam through her arms and scampered over her shoulders and down her neck.

Fleeing the advancing and thickening cloud of smoke, they seemed entirely unmoved by her screams.

For long seconds, Maria just kneeled there, allowing herself to be overtaken by the smoke and the fear and the vermin. She felt paralyzed. In her worst nightmares, she had never considered this kind of horror. Part of her reasoned that if she turned off the light, the fear would go away—or at least lessen.

No, she thought with a shiver. *This is not how I am going to die.* But if she locked down, dying was the only possible outcome for her.

Maria had to settle herself down and think the problem through.

The explosion had to have come from upstream of the flow of vermin and smoke. She had a direction to travel. She told herself to ignore everything but the goal. Rats were just more of God's creatures trying to survive just as she was. They had no interest in her.

She forced herself to ignore the smoke that gouged at her eyes and tore at her throat. As long as she felt the pain, at least she knew that she was still alive.

With the light clasped in her teeth like a metal cigar, she crawled upstream through her terror, her face wet and slimy with tears and snot and fetid water. The ladder had to be here somewhere, and with the ladder would come options.

At least she'd be able to—

Stand! In the gathering and thickening smoke, she'd nearly missed the ladder, but there it was, along with the vestibule that allowed her to get her feet under her and rise to her full height. The sudden change startled the rats, and two of them clung to her as she rose above the water, their little rat nails digging into the fabric of her shirt at her shoulders, one on each side.

She swiped at them in hacking, spasmodic movements that sent them tumbling back into the disgusting flow of their fleeing cousins. Spitting out the flashlight, she grabbed the metal rungs of the ladder and started to climb.

Maria decided to ignore Mother Hen's instructions. When she'd issued them, she couldn't possibly have known about these complications. If this was the result of the first two explosions, then God only knew—

The third blast sounded like it might have been directly overhead. The opaque smoke over her head flashed orange with it, and the rungs of the ladder pulsed violently enough to throw her off if she hadn't been holding on so tightly. Below her, the water surged, but she didn't care. Her future lay above.

She climbed the ladder blindly, and with each rung, the atmosphere became less breathable.

When her head hit hard metal, she knew that freedom had arrived. Locking the heels of her shoes against one ladder rung, and gripping the top rung tightly in her left hand, she leaned away for added leverage and used her right hand to push upward with all her strength.

The metal disk moved more easily than she'd anticipated. Maybe it was the adrenaline, or maybe manhole covers just weren't that heavy. Either way, it slid to the side. When the opening was big enough for her head and shoulders to pass, she climbed the rest of the way into the night. In her mind, as she rose through the plume of smoke that gushed from the opening in the street, she looked like a ghost emerging from the mist.

With her waist clear, she bent until she was flat with the street and she dragged her legs out. Soaked to the skin and disgusted by what she'd endured, she shivered in the hot night air. Soon it would be over.

Maria crouched on the ground, looking first to the left and then to the right for signs of danger. She nearly jumped out of her skin when two men approached her from behind with weapons trained on her.

These must be her rescuers, she thought, but why were they pointing guns?

"You must be Maria Elizondo," one of them said. "Felix Hernandez is anxious to chat with you."

In his heart, Palma had known that a third explosion was coming. It only made sense. The first blast was designed to draw his people in. The second was designed to kill those responders—a well-calculated move as it turned out. If he had been planning these diversions—and he knew now that that's what they were—he would have planted a third bomb to invoke utter confusion.

He hadn't expected it to be so close, however—only fifty meters away. That his adversary could get so close without being detected was at once impressive and frightening. Palma had put a man very near that location to watch the oncoming street. He couldn't remember the soldier's name, but that probably didn't matter. The fact that the charge had been planted in the first place probably meant that he was dead. And if he wasn't killed before, then the blast had most certainly taken care of it.

Palma's radio broke squelch. "Captain, we have Maria Elizondo," a voice said.

He smiled. A diversion was only as effective as its ability to divert attention. Once he'd figured out what his adversary's plan had been, Palma had told his remaining forces to hold fast in their current positions.

And now his decision had paid off. With the world around him on fire, he brought his radio to his lip. "Bring her to me," he said.

Jonathan had read about the Sandcat—in the U.S., they were called tactical protector vehicles, or TPVs—but he'd never seen the interior of one. Built on a Ford F-550 chassis, the dashboard looked just like any other pickup truck. And if it weren't for the five-point restraint system, the seats would have looked familiar, too.

But that's where the similarity stopped. The doors felt heavy enough to be armored, but not quite heavy enough to be armored well. Not knowing the Mexican government's specs for such things, the element of doubt translated to a lack of confidence that the doors or windows could stop anything heavier than a slingshot.

Thanks to night vision, Jonathan could make out the details of the interior, as well, and was surprised to see fold-down web benches instead of seats. They attached to the side bulkheads, and to Jonathan's eye could accommodate two people each with body armor, and three each without. He assumed that the black knobs that dotted the bulkheads on all sides were gun ports that provided for a fairly effective field of fire.

The article he'd read about the TPVs had showed a picture of a gun turret with a mounted M60 machine gun. Here, in the spot where that turret would be mounted, was a rooftop emergency exit, instead.

Boxers drove with the lights off and NVGs in place. It looked as if the Sandcat was equipped with a FLIR system—forward-looking infrared—but it was tough enough driving with night vision. Why complicate it with the challenge of driving from a television screen?

Apparently, the third bomb had spread a lot of fire, evidence of a full gas tank on the vehicle where it had been set. As Boxers piloted the Sandcat toward the con-flagration—there wasn't room to turn the beast around in the narrow streets—Jonathan watched flames climb higher than the rooftops. As they turned the corner to head north before going east again, he got a glimpse of the carnage he'd created. Bodies littered the street, some of them clearly dead, and some of them writhing in pain. One of the living guys' clothes were still smoking.

A Mexican soldier—a sergeant, judging from his uniform insignia—spotted the Sandcat and ran toward it, his arms waving for it to stop and help.

"Want me to run him down?" Boxers asked.

"No," Jonathan said. "Not unless he gets in the way or he looks like he's going to take a shot. Just keep going."

Boxers did in fact gun the engine and lurch toward the sergeant, but it was a move designed to make the guy jump back, thereby saving him.

If anyone else had been behind the wheel, Jonathan would have told the driver to slow down, but Boxers was very good at this sort of thing. Jonathan figured they were doing thirty, thirty-five miles an hour when Boxers cut the right-hand turn onto the street that ran behind Maria's house. He cut it short, too, galumphing over the curb and taking out a bicycle that someone had foolishly left in a yard.

Tristan yelled from the back as the impact launched him out of his bench and nearly into the ceiling before he landed in a heap on the armored floor. "Hey!"

"Hang on, kid!" Boxers said through a laugh. The humor evaporated as quickly as it had arrived as he caught a glimpse of what lay ahead. "I think we're in trouble, Boss," he said.

Jonathan saw it, too. A pair of soldiers had a woman in custody, each with a hand on a different biceps while the one on the right spoke into a radio.

"Turn on the headlights," Jonathan commanded, flipping his NVGs out of the way. "And keep going forward."

Boxers shot him a confused look, but he complied without a word.

The guards looked startled as the headlights caught them. The one on the left shielded his eyes right away, but the one on the right had to put his radio down first.

"Go in like we belong," Jonathan said. "I want them to think we're the cavalry." As he spoke, he unclipped his M27 from its sling and drew the MP7 from its holster on his left thigh.

"Your plan is just to go out shooting?" Boxers asked. His tone made it clear that he did not approve.

"She's our ticket out of town," Jonathan said. "I don't see—"

Maria Elizondo moved with startling speed. While her captors stared at the approaching vehicle, she made a wild flapping motion with both arms, breaking free from their grasp. She took a step back.

Jonathan saw that as his cue and he shouldered open his door.

The soldiers were still reacting when petite Maria produced a massive pistol from somewhere. She drew and fired in the same motion. The guy on the right fell.

The recoil was a problem for her, though. Before she could regain control, the soldier on the left had found his own weapon. He was bringing it to bear when Jonathan snap-shot a bullet from his MP7 into the guy's right ear.

Startled, Maria brought her revolver around and took a shot at Jonathan.

He read her body language in time to spin around and duck behind the panel of his open door. The bullet punched through four inches from his ear.

So much for the vehicle being armored.

Maria hadn't meant to fire at the truck. It was a reflex, a body twitch reacting to the sound of a gunshot. She saw a man drop as she pulled the trigger, and now she expected to be shot herself.

For an instant, she considered running away, but the urge evaporated from her brain seconds after it formed.

She had to make it clear that she'd meant them no harm.

* * *

"She dropped her weapon," Boxers said. "She's got her hands up."

Jonathan felt relieved. He didn't think that her gunplay had been an act of aggression. It would have sucked to have to kill her.

"Put your hands in the air!" Jonathan called from behind the door. He raised up high enough to see through the closed window and saw that she was doing as she was told.

Satisfied, he let the MP7 hang at his side as he stepped out into the open. "What's your name?" he asked.

"Are you the Americans here to take me to the United States?"

"That depends on what your name is," Jonathan said. He was nearly certain, but they'd had no visual ID for her, so even shadows of doubt had to be taken seriously.

"My name is Maria Elizondo," she said.

"And who do you work for?"

"Felix Hernandez."

"What is the name of your FBI contact?"

"Veronica Costanza."

Jonathan felt his shoulders sag with relief. He motioned for her to come to the Sandcat. "Come on," he said. "Let's go."

"Can I take my pistol?" she asked.

"Are you going to shoot at me again?" He made sure to ask that one with a smile.

"I didn't mean to," Maria said. Obviously, she couldn't see the smile.

Jonathan pointed to the .44 with his chin. "Sure, go ahead. Quickly."

"Don't be crazy, Scorpion," Boxers said from the driver's seat.

Jonathan ignored him. Maria wasted no time. She bent at the waist, picked up the weapon off the street, and jogged over to him. When she closed to within a few feet, Jonathan extended his hand and smiled again. "You can call me Scorpion," he said.

He opened the back door for her. "The driver is Big Guy, and that young man is Tristan."

Jonathan offered a hand to help her up the big step, but she didn't need it.

He closed the back door, holstered his MP7, and climbed back into the shotgun seat.

"Let's go to America," he said.

Boxers gunned the engine.

She was beautiful.

As incongruous and stupid and juvenile as it seemed, that was Tristan's first thought. Maria Elizondo was the most beautiful woman he'd ever seen. He'd only caught a glimpse of her in dim yellow streetlamp light that made it through the windows. Her huge brown eyes glinted in the light, and as she sat on the bench opposite him, he could make out every contour of her body through the soaked clothing that clung to her skin.

Clung to her breasts. Her breasts that had no bra. The suspension on this truck left a lot to be desired, and every bump caused the breasts to bounce.

Christ, he was getting hard. How much of a pervert do you have to be to get a hard-on when people are shooting at you?

"Hello," she said in English. From her smile, he sensed that she'd read his mind.

Tristan's ears turned hot. "Hi," he said. "I'm Tristan. I'm the one who actually has a real name."

"Maria," she said.

"Tell me where we're going, Maria," Jonathan called from the front seat.

She rose from her bench and duck-walked to where she could look between the two front seats to see out the windshield.

God, her ass looked great, too.

CHAPTER THIRTY-TWO

Palma keyed the radio mike again. "I said, bring her to me," he said. "Do you copy?"

They, too, were dead. It was a conclusion drawn purely from speculation, but given the way everything else was going, that was the only answer.

And why not? Clearly, the plan for their escape would bring Harris and Lerner to the alley where his soldiers had been waiting. It was just a matter of timing.

He spat a curse and kicked the door of the car that had become his command post. He flashed on how furious Felix was going to be when he found out that Palma had not only ignored his order to grab the girl right away, but that as a result she had gotten away.

And make no mistake, she had gotten away. The ruses and diversions had all worked perfectly for them. They could be anywhere now, and they could be driving anything—

Wait.

The Sandcats! In his mind, he plotted the locations of the explosions as a function of the vehicle locations, and it made sense. But how could the Americans have known they were there? Did Palma have an informer among his men?

That didn't matter.

At least he now knew what they were looking for. As he radioed for a helicopter, he dialed his phone with his other hand.

"Do you know the warehouse district off of Hermanos Escobar?" Maria asked.

"I don't know anything about your city," Boxers said. "Start with compass points."

"North and east of here," Maria said. She gave Jonathan the address from memory. "It is very close to the American border."

"It's a freaking tunnel," Boxers said. "I *hope* to hell it's close to the border."

Jonathan entered the address into his GPS system. He also made sure that Venice got the address and the coordinates back in Fisherman's Cove. When he got the results, he shot Boxers a look. "Fourteen-point-three kilometers."

"That's like nine miles!" Tristan exclaimed from the back.

Boxers' foot grew heavier on the accelerator. "I think I read somewhere that these TPVs have a top speed of seventy-five miles an hour," he said. "What say we test that?"

The cityscape sped by faster.

Thank God for the early hour, Jonathan thought. Boxers drove as if Ciudad Juarez were an open racetrack. Traffic lights didn't matter. Stoplights didn't matter.

"Getting there doesn't matter unless we get there alive," Jonathan said. He knew better than to make an overt suggestion that the Big Guy slow down. When he was this close to the barn, any criticism was likely to result in even faster speeds.

"This thing's got lights and siren if you want to use them," Boxers replied.

Jonathan had already considered and rejected that. While it might help clear the way at individual intersections, he didn't like giving such vivid audible and visual clues to a city full of emergency responders who would relish the chance to hurt the people who had done so much damage tonight.

"Didn't think so," Boxers said.

Jonathan undid his five-point restraint and rolled out of his seat into the back. "Tristan!" he yelled over the engine noise.

The kid jumped.

"Come up here. Take my seat."

"What are you doing?" Boxers asked.

"If only one of us survives a wreck, it needs to be the PC," Jonathan said. "Tristan! Now!"

Tristan half walked, half crawled the distance to the front.

"Sit in that seat," Jonathan instructed. He helped the kid climb over the center console.

Tristan continued to have trouble maneuvering all his equipment in such a small space.

"Is that safety on?" Boxers asked as Tristan's butt made contact with the seat.

"Yes! Jesus, yes. I haven't touched the friggin' safety." He pushed Jonathan's hands away from the belts. "I can do that. I'm not a kid in a car seat."

The TPV hit a pothole, and Jonathan literally hit the overhead. He landed on his side.

"Sorry, Boss," Boxers said in a tone that spoke far more amusement than apology.

Jonathan flipped him off, eliciting a laugh. At least Tristan was still secure.

He looked to Maria, who somehow had remained on the bench. Maybe if you grow up in this shit-hole town you get used to the road conditions and don't get bounced around. "You okay?" he asked.

She smiled and nodded.

Even with all the speed in the open spaces, corners and the occasional obstacle still made it slow going.

"We just passed the halfway mark," Boxers announced.

Jonathan looked at his watch. Twelve minutes to go a little over four miles. If he'd read the map properly, the second half of the trip would be on wider, straighter roads. Maybe they might just make it after all.

The thought had barely formed in his mind when he heard the chatter of automatic-weapons fire and the distinctive *tink, tink* of bullets hitting their vehicle.

"We've picked up a tail, Boss," Boxers said, checking his driver's side mirror.

Jonathan reached across the open space of the backseat, cupped his hand at the nape of Maria's neck, and pushed her to the floor. "Get down!" he commanded. "Tristan, undo those belts and hunker down on the floor in front of your seat."

Another burst of gunfire didn't produce any hits that Jonathan could see or hear.

"What is it?" Jonathan asked Boxers. The view through the back windows was too blocked with a mesh of expanded metal brush cages for them to see any useful detail.

Boxers' foot got heavier on the gas and he checked his mirror again. "Wow, it's been a long time since I've seen a technical," he said. He started driving zigzags, S-turns that took the Sandcat from curb line to curb line, with the intent of providing a tougher target.

Jonathan had no idea what the derivation of the term was, but technicals were the preferred vehicles of Third World terrorists everywhere. Consisting of a pickup truck with a mounted machine gun of some sort—usually a thirty-cal M60, but he'd seen a few with a fifty-cal Ma Deuce—they were frighteningly efficient killing machines. In Jonathan's experience, though, marksmanship was an issue.

With the next burst, three rounds punched through the back of the Sandcat. One went on to spider the windshield.

"You want to take care of him for me, Boss?" Boxers asked. His tone had no more edge to it than if he'd asked for the salt to be passed at the dinner table.

"Let me have your Four Seventeen," Jonathan said.

Boxers lifted his rifle from where he'd stashed it next to his right leg and handed it back to Jonathan. Slightly larger and heavier than Jonathan's M27, Boxers' Hechler and Koch Model 417 looked nearly identical, but fired a bigger 7.62-millimeter bullet that had way more penetrating power than the M27's 5.56-millimeter round.

"Here's a couple of spare mags, too," Big Guy said, handing back two thirty-round magazines.

"What are you going to do?" Tristan asked from his perch on the floor. His eyes were huge.

"I'm going to finish what they started," Jonathan said.

He squat-walked to the back bulkhead, to the door in the center. The gun port was tempting, but he dismissed it. Gun ports were for terrified armored car guards who cared less about hitting a target than about putting out a large volume of fire to put people's heads down. That offended Jonathan's sense of professionalism. Suppressing fire had its place, but this was not it. When he pulled the trigger, he wanted to hit what he was shooting at.

As he reached for the handle of the personnel door in the center of the back panel, the technical released another burst of gunfire—a longer one this time—and four more bullets slammed through the bulkhead. The gunner was finding his aim.

Nearly as tall as the crew cab was high, the door was designed for rapid deployment of troops, so when Jonathan pulled the latch and swung the door out, he opened up an enticing vertical trench for the technical's gunner.

The technical's driver, however, read the lethality of the situation for what it was and backed off the accelerator. As the pickup truck fell away, Jonathan heard the gunner yelling for the driver not to be a coward.

Jonathan dropped to his belly on the Sandcat's floor and assumed a classic prone shooter's position.

"Slow down, Big Guy!" he commanded.

Boxers hit the brakes harder than he'd expected, and while the distance between the vehicles closed, the technical hit its brakes hard, too. As the gunner opened up again, his rounds went wild.

Jonathan's didn't. He centered the red dot of the

417's gun sight on the technical's grille, on the driver's side and he unleashed a long burst that shredded the pickup's engine, and then probably went on to shred the driver.

The technical veered sharply to the right—its left—then hit a curb and flipped. While it was hard to see details this far away, there was no mistaking the silhouette of the gunner cartwheeling through the air and skidding into the street.

"All right, Scorpion!" Boxers whooped. "Nice shooting!"

Actually, it wasn't. Anybody who couldn't hit a target that big as it raced straight toward him deserved to be on the other end of the gun. The fact that it had happened at all spelled very bad news.

It meant that the bad guys had connected the dots and knew exactly where they were.

Armed with a compass point and the direction of travel, Hernandez would be able to figure out that that they were headed to the tunnel in the industrial park.

"Maria," Jonathan said, louder than he'd intended, and causing her to jump. "Where's the next nearest tunnel to the U.S.?"

"I already told you. The warehouse—"

"No, you said that one's the closest. Your boss has to know that's where we're going now. Where's the *next* closest?"

"Much farther," she said. "Fifteen, maybe twenty kilometers east of the tunnel off Hermanos Escobar."

"Scorpion, we're only about three klicks out now. With the world chasing us, I don't want to do another twenty on the open road."

"They'll have roadblocks," Jonathan said.

"And we've got a big-ass battering ram. Besides, they haven't had time to set up a good ambush. By the time they do, we'll have already blown past them."

Boxers was spinning himself up for some measure of unearned optimism. There'd been plenty of time. The question was whether or not the bad guys had utilized it efficiently.

It didn't matter. The one thing Boxers was right about was the fact that there was no turning back. With their cover blown, and wrapped in such an identifiable vehicle, a twenty-kilometer open-road sprint would be suicide.

"Have you ever been to these tunnels, Maria?" Jonathan asked. "Any of them?"

"I have been to one—the one we're going to now— but I have not been inside."

"Do you know how to *get* inside?" If ever he'd asked a question to which there was only one right answer, this was the one.

"Yes," she said.

Relief.

"The entrance is really just a hole in the floor with a ladder."

"Is that the only entrance to the tunnel? One way in and one way out?"

"I don't know. I never asked."

"There have to be vents," Boxers said. "Tunnel that long would have to have some form of forced ventilation."

The complexity of the engineering challenge was stunning—made all the more so by the fact that it had presumably all been done by amateurs.

"Why don't we just charge the border crossing?" Tristan asked. "We're close to that aren't we?"

"Can't risk it," Jonathan said. "We've got to get past the Mexican Border Patrol before we get to the American Border Patrol. Even if we made it to the U.S., they'd just hand us back to the Mexicans."

"If they all didn't just shoot us first," Boxers said. "Those guys get jumpy when they're approached by speeding vehicles."

Jonathan's earbud popped. "Scorpion, Mother Hen. SkysEye shows a barricade across the road not too far from you."

Jonathan saw it just as she said the words. It looked like six or seven emergency vehicles across the road, painting the night with red and blue flashing lights.

"The turn into the park is just beyond them," Maria said. "Half a kilometer."

Boxers slowed, but not much. "Tell me what you want to do, Boss."

"Ram 'em," Jonathan said. He moved to the escape hatch in the roof—the spot where he so wished he had a gun turret—and threw it open. "I'll keep their heads down. Tristan."

The kid's head jerked up.

"Climb on back here. Hurry."

The kid pulled himself off of the floor and back across the center console to squat next to Maria.

"There's gonna be a bump, and then there are going to be a lot of people behind us shooting at us."

"I know," he said. "My safety is on."

"Well, take it off, then," Boxers barked.

"When they fire on us, put it on full-auto and open

up through the back door," Jonathan instructed. "Maria, grab a weapon and help."

Maria didn't hesitate even a second. She snatched up one of the rifles they'd taken from the soldiers who'd tried to arrest her and moved to the back door, shoulder to shoulder with Tristan.

"Slow down, Big Guy," Jonathan said. "Get us as close as you can. Let them think we might be surrendering. When I start shooting, gun it and get us the hell out of here."

"Roger that," Boxers said. "Just make sure to leave me enough space to get a good run at the fenders."

The Sandcat slowed to nearly a crawl as they got to within fifty meters of the checkpoint. Jonathan's plan was simple: He was going to do exactly the opposite of what he'd done against the technical. When he started shooting, it wouldn't be about acquiring a specific target and killing it. Instead, it would be about scaring the shit out of all the targets at once so that they'd dive for cover and still have their heads down when Boxers blasted through the barricade.

As they approached, Jonathan kept his head inside the Sandcat, fearing that even the hint of a gun turret might spook the bad guys early and make them start shooting. Up ahead, the soldiers seemed confused. Jonathan guessed there were maybe fifteen of them in total. Some had taken shooting stances, and others were standing with their weapons at port arms.

"I want to do this soon," Boxers said. "I'm running out of runway."

Jonathan steadied himself under the open escape hatch, steeled himself with a deep breath, and then stood to his full height. As soon as his shoulders were clear of the hatch, he brought the 417 to his shoulder and opened up on the roadblock. On full-auto, he raked their positions from left to right, and then back again. He emptied a mag in less than two seconds, and by then Boxers had found the gas, and they were moving fast. For such a heavy vehicle the Sandcat had a lot of acceleration.

Jonathan fingered the release button to drop the spent mag, and then he slapped a fresh one in its place and resumed hosing bad guys.

"Here we go!" Boxers yelled. "Hang on."

Jonathan figured they had to be doing fifty when they made contact. The Mexicans had parked two environmentally friendly, fuel-efficient little toy cop cars nose-to-nose in the middle of the road, no doubt thinking that they'd created a roadblock. Boxers nailed them both simultaneously, just forward of their respective front wheels, and they spun out of the way as if they were made of balsa wood—or, more appropriately, as if pounds of metal had given way to tons of steel.

This stuff was all about the proper application of mass and momentum, and nobody on the planet did it more expertly than Boxers.

Tristan had been expecting something more dramatic than a *thump*. They'd just rammed two cars, for God's sake, but it was less of an impact than the potholes. It knocked him on his ass, but that was about it.

Now, the open back door framed the image of a world that was shooting back at them. As the line of soldiers and vehicles fell away, he watched some of them stand up and open fire. Above and behind, Scorpion's gun continued to pound, and Tristan saw puffs of glass and flying metal as his bullets tore into the soldiers' vehicles and equipment.

A spray of blood announced the disintegration of a soldier's head.

To his left, Maria kneeled squarely in the center of the opening and opened up on the line of cars and people. She fired a long string of bullets, just holding the trigger down until the magazine was empty. As spent shell casings streamed from her ejection port, they showered over him. He didn't know they'd be that hot.

Tristan didn't aim so much as he pointed and pulled the trigger. When his weapon went dry, he dropped out the magazine and reached for more on his vest, just like he'd done a thousand times when they were in hiding, but his hands hadn't been trembling back then. And nobody was—

Something hit him hard in the chest, driving the air from his lungs and causing him to sit down hard on his butt.

"Tristan is shot!" Maria yelled.

"Shoot back!" Boxers hollered.

Holy shit, I've been shot!

He fell backward, and there was Maria, looking down at him and saying something that he couldn't hear. He was too busy trying to take a breath.

Then Scorpion's face arrived. He looked angry. "Where are you shot?" he yelled.

Why is he mad at me?

"I saw it hit his chest," Maria said.

The anger turned to relief. Maybe amusement.

Scorpion lifted Tristan by the collar of his vest and stuffed his hand down the gap. A lightning bolt of pain launched through Tristan, from neck to groin. He yelled.

"I thought your color looked too good," Scorpion said. "That vest just paid for itself, young man." He ruffled Tristan's hair, just the way his dad used to.

Keeping his grip on the collar of the vest, Scorpion pulled him up to a sitting position. "Cracked a rib in the worst case," he said. "You'll be fine."

Scorpion turned to Maria. "Come on up front. Help us navigate out of here."

Maria lingered for just a second or two. She touched his cheek and smiled. It was a look he didn't know how to interpret. Surely, it didn't mean what he wanted it to.

"What?" Tristan asked.

"You remind me of someone I once loved very much. I'm glad you are not hurt." She turned and moved to the front with the others.

What the hell had she been telling him? Could it really be that—

The world erupted in blinding white light.

Big Guy yelled, "Holy shit!" Their vehicle swerved violently and hit something hard. This time, whatever they'd hit won the battle.

Chapter Thirty-three

As soon as Palma told him the story of Maria's rescue, and the bombings, Felix realized that they would attempt to use his tunnels as a means to get out of the country. The question was which one?

He had a vast array of smuggling tunnels—at least eight of them currently in operation—that circulated literally tons of drugs into the United States every year. The Americans were such morons. While they distracted themselves with debates over whether or not to built a multibillion-dollar fence along the border, Felix and a few of his competitors owned the subterranean real estate—just as surely as they owned American Border Patrol agents and the owner of the properties on the other side where the tunnels rose back to the surface.

Every now and then, Felix would tip off the El Paso police and the local news media so that they could discover one of his less productive tunnels and make a show for the American public about the hard work they were doing to stop the flow of drugs into their country. Each new discovery would boost a bureaucrat's career. In their gratitude, they would only look but so hard for the next tunnel.

As a new generation of politicians and civil servants came to power in America—many of them current or reformed consumers of the products Felix created—it became progressively easier to smuggle drugs into the United States. As long as he handed the Americans enough victories in their drug war to allow the politicians to preen, and he cooperated with the Central Intelligence Agency to provide protection for their clandestine launch platforms and listening bases throughout Central America, they stayed out of his way, going so far as to falsify reports to their handlers back in Langley. For that last part—the falsified reports—Felix paid several chiefs of station up to twice their legitimate salaries in thank-you gifts.

Of them all, Trevor Munro had been the most demanding—and, in the end, the most ungrateful.

Until yesterday, Felix had never believed Munro's claims that he'd had no knowledge of the Colombian incursion that had killed Mitchell Ponder and cost him so much. Who but the American military, after all, could have pulled off that kind of operation with such precision? Now that they'd lured the same operators into Mexico, their ingenuity and capacity for violence made Munro's denials more credible.

But the American commandoes were still but a few against many, and soon they would be dead. Palma's guess that they would choose the nearest tunnel had turned out to be correct. And now, according to his last report, they were surrounded.

Soon, they would be dead, and this long, annoying distraction would finally be over.

Even better, if Felix's intelligence gatherers were correct, Munro would soon be the associate deputy director of the CIA, with access to all of that agency's assets. He'd be in a position where one word from Felix could bring him down, with a future measured in prison time.

This blooming reality was far greater than any fantasy Hernandez had ever dared to dream.

One million candlepower.

For the last twenty years, that had been the standard wattage for helicopter searchlights. Jonathan figured that was the minimum wattage of the beam that lit them up, and he could tell from the way that Boxers ripped at his NVGs that the blast of light had damn near blinded him. When he swerved, he ran head-on into three steel-and-concrete bollards that stood sentry outside a warehouse building.

"God *damn* it!" Boxers yelled. The plume of steam from under the hood told them that the Sandcat was dead.

As the chopper continued to circle overhead, the floodlight remained fixed on the ruined vehicle, a beacon to the horde of pissed-off soldiers who would soon be racing after them.

"Big Guy, you all right?"

"I *so* want to kill somebody right now!" Cursing, he undid his harness and shouldered his door open. He grabbed his ruck and shouted, "Where's my weapon?"

Jonathan handed it to him, and without pausing even a beat, Boxers rolled out of the Sandcat, pressed the weapon to his shoulder and fired two quick rounds into the artificial sun that had lit them up.

The chin light flared and went black. You just don't get to see marksmanship like that very often.

Palma saw the shooter step out of the vehicle and drop to his knee, and as the enormous man took aim, he thought for sure that his bullet was somehow going to go straight between his eyes. In the wash of the light, the muzzle flash registered more as smoke than light. The world went dark, and Palma could not have been more impressed.

"Set us down!" he commanded.

Instead, the pilot pulled pitch and they rose higher.

"Down there!" Palma yelled. "Our prey is down there!"

The gunfire had frazzled the pilot. He was not trained in combat tactics. His job was to track traffic and deliver VIPs to their venues of choice. Getting shot at was not part of the deal.

"Everybody out!" Jonathan commanded. "Everybody bring weapons." God knew they had a big enough selection. Jonathan shrugged back into his ruck, and by the time he stood to his full height outside the vehicle, the others had gathered in a semicircle.

"Where are we going, Maria?"

She seemed startled by the realization that they were depending on her to be their guide. "I haven't been paying attention," she said. "I don't know where we are, exactly."

In the distance, Jonathan heard the sound of approaching vehicles. If he used his imagination, he could see the distant phantoms of red and blue emergency lights. Staying put was out of play. He had to assume that the people in the chopper had weapons, and a stationary target would be their greatest gift.

"Okay, this way," he said. Relying on instinct and his memory of the map he'd studied on his GPS, he led them off in what had to be north. "Stay close to the buildings and move fast."

In the canyons created by the low-rise warehouse buildings, the chopper overhead appeared to be everywhere. The grinding hum of the rotor blades pounded the night from all directions.

The fact that the aircraft had had a chin light in the first place gave Jonathan hope that the flight crew didn't have night vision, but hope was a lot like prayer—always welcome, but rarely dependable for results. The chopper would find a place to set down soon, and in the meantime, the crew was no doubt working the radio to coordinate ground forces.

They needed to keep moving.

"Maria, is any of this looking familiar?"

"It all looks familiar," she said. "The buildings all look the same. It's been a long time since I've been here."

"What's the unit number again?"

"Twelve-seventy, I think."

"You think?"

"That's what I remember."

"Is that the number you gave to the FBI?"

"I think so, yes."

Jonathan felt a swell of anger, but he swallowed it down. What was it about civilians that once the tension ratcheted up, made everything become a question? No one was sure of anything anymore. Well, there was a solution for that.

Jonathan tapped the transmit button on his chest. "Mother Hen, Scorpion."

In Fisherman's Cove, Venice jumped when the Skys-Eye image refreshed and she saw the wrecked vehicle, the horror of the image made even worse by the fact that Jonathan hadn't checked in afterward.

She was just reaching for the transmit switch when her speakers popped. "Mother Hen, Scorpion."

Relief. She fought hard to keep the emotion out of her voice as she replied, "Is everybody all right? Looks like a bad wreck."

"We're fine, but we're in trouble. A little lost in the forest. Can you talk us in?"

Venice spun her chair a little to view a different screen. "Where are you exactly? I won't get another satellite image for two, almost three minutes."

A pause. "We're in front of unit seven-thirteen."

"Stand by one," she said.

"We don't have much more than one," Jonathan quipped. "The quicker the better."

Anticipating a challenge like this, Venice had called up a schematic for the storage facility over an hour ago. It appeared on her screen as checkerboard of north–south streets intersecting with east–west streets. Depending on size, some blocks had more units than others.

She keyed her mike. "From seven-thirteen, you need to go five blocks north and three blocks east."

"Roger," Scorpion said. "Keep an eye on the Skys-Eye feed. I know the bad guys are close, but I don't have a visual. We need to know where they are."

"Will do," she said.

Venice hated this part of her job—the passive watching and waiting while people she cared about fought for their lives. She knew they needed her—that the technology she tamed and interpreted was as critical to every mission as the weaponry wielded by the guys, but from this far away, the team felt very small and terribly isolated.

When her image finally refreshed, she used thermal imagery to find Jonathan and the team, and was pleased to see that they were making progress toward the target building. When she saw that the pursuing troops were taking the wrong path, she smiled.

The happiness evaporated in an instant when she realized what she was *really* seeing.

Jonathan's earbud popped. "Scorpion, they're trying to flank you on your right. It looks like they've figured out where you're going."

He and Boxers said it together: "Shit."

"What?" Tristan asked.

Jonathan keyed his mike. "Any chance we'll get there first?"

"They've got vehicles."

Not the question he'd asked, but it was an answer nonetheless.

Jonathan played the next few minutes out in his mind, and it all came down to a firefight that they couldn't possibly win. Surrender was not an option, so that left only a third alternative. If only he knew what it was.

"I'm open to suggestions, Big Guy," he said.

"I'm sure you'll come up with something, Boss. Meanwhile, is it your plan to keep jogging toward the ambush?"

Stopping made no sense. They had no defensive positions and they were outgunned. They'd lost the elements of surprise. So, what did that leave? If only storage units had secondary entrances.

Wait. That was it. "We'll go in through the back door," he announced.

Boxer gave him The Look. "What back door?"

"How much det cord do you have?"

The Big Guy beamed. "Enough to make a lot of back doors," he said.

Jonathan keyed his mike. "Mother Hen, I need the name of the street that runs parallel to the one with our target building."

Tristan was growing tired of the mysterious communications between Scorpion and the Big Guy. He got that they had somebody talking in their ear, but Tristan had a stake in this thing, too, you know? The least they could do was speak in complete sentences, or maybe even relay what it was they were talking about.

He was also tired of being the only one who seemed to struggle with the running. His lungs had burned before, but now with this huge bruise on his chest, the pain was even worse. The vest swung a little on his body with every step, and with each swing, it felt as if someone were poking a finger into the center of the sore spot.

And where were all the police and soldiers? Not to jinx anything, but after all that shooting, he'd have thought there'd be a little more hubbub.

Without warning, Scorpion and the Big Guy slid to a stop in the middle of the road.

"Okay, Tristan and Maria, there's been a change in plans."

Tristan felt something dissolve inside him. Every time Scorpion said something like that, life got a lot shittier.

As if to prove the point, the night became day as floodlights jumped to life from high atop God only knew how many poles.

The invaders' night vision was no longer an advantage. Palma felt proud that he'd thought of finding and throwing the main power switch that he knew had to be here somewhere.

The flanking maneuver was really just an extension of the strategy that Palma had put together to catch Harris and his team at Maria's house. Surround the one place they had to go, and wait for the prey to arrive. It was the most logical play, and therefore one that he had no choice but to deploy.

Because it was logical, and therefore obvious, he worried that his enemy would once again get a step ahead.

This time, he held back a reserve of eight men, two

each to cover the likely escape routes if the criminals tried to get away.

Meanwhile, Palma himself took Sergeant Sanchez and three of the surviving members of his original team and pursued his prey on foot.

Harris and company would have to be near panic now as they realized that they were being driven to a killing zone. Palma would enjoy watching them die.

He and his tiny squad moved carefully yet quickly as they pursued their targets north and east inside the storage compound. Hernandez had been very specific about the location of his smuggling tunnel. It was the single destination for Harris to target, so therefore it made no sense for them to lie in hiding along the way. As they got closer, he'd slow down.

On the other hand, if he heard shooting, he'd know that it was time to run in earnest.

Stealth no longer mattered. Bathed in light, their final advantage had been stripped away. From this point forward, survival was all about speed.

All they had to do was outrun a shitload of people who were all bent on killing them. Jonathan grabbed Tristan by the vest and pulled him close. "Listen to me," he said. "Do exactly as I say. Are you good with that?"

Tristan's eyes were twice their normal size and they showed terror.

"You can't panic on me, son. Do you understand that?"

"Yes. Yes, I understand."

"Okay." Jonathan spun him ninety degrees so that he was facing west. "You keep an eye on the end of the block. If you see a person—I mean, if you see *anyone*, shoot them. Set your selector on full-auto, and try to keep it to three-round bursts. A lot of them. Remember what we talked about. Keep the butt tightly in your shoulder, and get a lot of bullets downrange. Even if you don't hit anything, you'll keep their heads down. Can you do that?"

The kid nodded, and Jonathan needed to believe him. He turned to Maria, who'd overheard. "I'll watch the other end," she said.

Jonathan smiled. "Thank you."

While they spoke, Boxers took a pry bar to the hasp and lock of unit eleven-seventy, the storage unit that shared a back wall with their target building. Big Guy won the battle easily, stripping the entire assembly out of the corrugated metal door.

Jonathan wished he could let Boxers set the charges himself, and stay out here with the kids keeping cover, but setting the charges was a two-person job.

The interior of eleven-seventy might have been somebody's attic, stacked with furniture and toys, or, given that it was in Ciudad Juarez, a disguised meth lab and a few bodies.

Boxers tossed his ruck onto an old sofa, pulled open the top flap, and lifted a customized wooden spool wrapped with ten feet of plastic tubing stuffed with PETN—detonating cord. Also known as Primacord, it had been a staple in Boxers' rucksack for as long as Jonathan had known him. For all he knew, the Big Guy had taken a roll of the stuff with him as a Boy Scout when he went camping.

Boxers pulled the tactical light off the muzzle of his rifle and shined it on the back wall. Good news there: a concrete block wall, one of the most frangible building materials on the planet. "Cool," he said.

Boxers started to measure out a length of cord, and then stopped himself. "Screw it," he said. "We want a hole, so let's by-God make a hole."

"You're using the whole spool?" Jonathan's jaw dropped. Ten feet of det cord was, in technical parlance, a shitload of explosive. "You'll collapse the roof."

"But I can't mount it," Boxers countered. "I don't have epoxy, and even if I did, I wouldn't have time—" He stopped himself. "When did I start explaining explosive shit to you?"

Point taken. Boxers broke stuff, Jonathan negotiated stuff. That was the division of labor.

The Big Guy reached back into his ruck and pulled out yet another spool. "Cut me off fifteen seconds of OFF and connect it to a detonator."

Otherwise known as old-fashioned fuse, OFF was at once the most dependable yet imprecise way to set off explosives. Dependable because when the flame got to the ASA compound—a nasty mixture of lead styphnate, lead azide, and aluminum along with a tetryl kicker— it *always* went bang. Imprecise because a fifteen-second length of fuse might burn for ten or twelve seconds, or it might burn for twenty.

Jonathan eyeballed the length of fuse, cut it with his KA-BAR and pulled a detonator from his own ruck and married the two.

As he handed it to Boxers, the world outside the storage room erupted in gunfire.

* * *

Tristan was living the nightmare, the one where you spend the entire dream dreading that a thing will happen, and then, in the last instant before you jerk awake, there it is.

He'd been staring into the artificially lit night down the barrel of his rifle, waiting for and dreading the appearance of the people who'd been trying to kill them, and then there they were—a group of four of them. For a couple of seconds, he strained his eyes to see if they really were the people he feared. The one of them brought a rifle to his shoulder, and Tristan's finger took over for his brain.

He was pretty sure that he saw flashes from some gun barrels down there, but then the flashes from his own muzzle wiped all of those out. The noise, too. The gunfire in the canyon created by the buildings was deafening. The hammering bang of his rifle made his head feel like it had been stuffed with cotton.

It wasn't till the incoming bullets tore up the wall next to him that the true seriousness of his situation sank in. Christ, they were shooting back!

"Get down!" he yelled to Maria, but she was already ahead of him, having dropped to her stomach.

Tristan didn't pay a lot of attention to her. He had heads to keep down.

The soldiers at the end of the road had likewise dropped to the ground to shoot back.

He picked one of the four muzzle flashes, aimed at it, and took a deep breath, just as the Big Guy had instructed him to do. He let half of the breath out, and tightened his finger on the trigger. The rifle bucked against his shoulder. He counted three or four rounds—

it was actually hard to tell how many bullets were fired with each burst—and let up. Then he did it again. And again and again, until the bolt locked open, and it was time to fish another full magazine out of his vest.

He dropped out the old, slapped in the new, reset the bolt, and started shooting again.

Somewhere in the middle of the second magazine, he heard another long burst of rifle fire coming from above and behind. He assumed it was from Maria, but before he could turn to check, the Big Guy grabbed him by the back of his vest and lifted him as if he weighed nothing. The man moved with remarkable speed, carrying Tristan one unit *closer* to the soldiers he'd been shooting at, and dropping him onto the asphalt. As the Big Guy lay on top of him, he said, "Get down." As if there was a choice.

Three seconds later, the explosion was the loudest noise Tristan had ever heard.

If Tristan Wagner had been a better marksman, more people would be dead now.

As Palma crossed into the open from behind one row of buildings on his way to the row where he'd expected to engage the enemy, he saw the kid and Maria Elizondo by themselves in the alleyway. By the time he could react, the kid opened up on them.

Palma and his men dropped to the ground and returned fire, but it was all wild and unaimed, just as the incoming fire was.

The lull in the shooting told him that the kid was reloading, and that would be the best time—

Another long burst erupted from the shooter's location, and this one was both purposeful and effective, hitting Sergeant Sanchez in the head and killing him instantly.

Palma dared a peek and saw the enormous man— Lerner—dragging the boy forward to cover while Harris dragged the girl in the opposite direction, and both covered their protectees with their bodies.

That could only mean one thing.

"Cover up!" Palma yelled.

An enormous explosion destroyed the storage unit where the shooting had come from. The blast wave threw concrete and metal roofing up and out in every direction, and caved in the doors directly opposite the one they blew.

Even as the debris was still falling, Palma realized their plan. By blasting through the shared wall of the storage units, the Americans would have access to the tunnel entrance without exposing themselves to the troops that Palma had stationed on the front side.

Once inside the tunnel, Palma's tactical advantage would evaporate. Men in a single file, or even two abreast, can bring only one or two weapons to bear at a time—the same number as their opponents, who, in this case, had proven themselves to be outstanding marksmen. As the lead elements of a larger force are shot down in a tunnel, their bodies then serve as obstacles for the passage of others.

If Palma was going to win this battle, he was going to have to win it out in the open in the next few seconds.

Ignoring the concrete and dust and metal that continued to pepper the area, Palma rose to a prone shooting position and brought his rifle to his shoulder. With his elbows pressed against the littered asphalt, he sighted through the haze and saw all four of his targets arising from the ground.

The closest two—the big man and the boy—disappeared into the rubble before he could take a shot. Of the remaining two, one was wearing a ballistic vest, and the other was not.

Palma settled his sights on Maria Elizondo and squeezed the trigger.

CHAPTER THIRTY-FOUR

Jonathan felt the bullet reverberate through Maria's body, and just from the way she dropped, he knew that the bullet had clipped her spinal cord. He dropped with her, whipping his M27 to his shoulder and unleashing an entire magazine load down the street in the direction the shot had come from.

The sound of Jonathan's gunfire brought Boxers back around the edge of the shattered wall, and he added thirty rounds from his 417 to the fusillade.

Using Boxers' shooting as cover fire, Jonathan rose enough to heave Maria onto his shoulder in a fireman's carry, and from there, he ducked into the ruined storage unit. As he'd hoped, the back wall had been reduced to rubble, and the roof was gone, but the blast wave had not communicated to the front wall of twelve-seventy.

"What happened to Maria?" Tristan asked when he saw Jonathan with the girl draped over his shoulder. Outside, Boxers continued to keep people's heads down

"Shot," Jonathan said. "Bad, I think."

As he stepped across the new threshold Boxers had

just created, he thumbed his tactical muzzle light to life and scanned the floor. He smiled when he saw the raw hole that had been cut into the concrete. He shined his light down the opening and was even more pleased to see the stout ladder that had been mounted on the vertical face. He had no idea how deep it went, but the bottom was beyond the beam of his light.

"Big Guy!" he yelled. "We're in business! Let's go!" To his PC: "You first, Tristan. I'll be right behind you." Under different circumstances, he might have gone first to clear the way, but he wanted to get the kid below grade and under cover as soon as possible. "Use the light I gave you."

A shadow fell over Jonathan, and there was Boxers, towering over him. "Give the girl to me," he said. "You'll get a hernia." He was already lifting Maria from Jonathan's shoulder to his own.

"You go first, then," Jonathan said to Boxers. "Tristan, hold up. Let the Big Guy go, and then you follow. I'll cover from up here."

"Look out!" Tristan yelled, and he brought his rifle to his shoulder.

Jonathan spun around firing. With all the good guys accounted for, everybody else out there with a heartbeat was a bad guy. He actually didn't see any targets, but he wasn't going to argue with the kid.

"Hurry!" Jonathan said, but when he turned, he saw that Boxers was already shoulders-deep into the tunnel opening. He was carrying Maria like a child now, more hooked in his arm than slung over his shoulder.

As soon as the Big Guy's head disappeared, Tristan dropped to his knees and climbed backward into the hole.

A shadow moved inside the rubble of eleven-seventy. And then another. People were gathering for an assault. If they all rushed at once, he'd never have a chance. And if they all rushed before he and his team were at the bottom of the ladderway and had started moving horizontally, all the bad guys would have to do is stick a weapon down the opening and pull the trigger. If they weren't hit by direct fire, then they'd most certainly be torn apart by ricochets and fragments.

On the front side of twelve-seventy, people were working at the lock to the front door.

Jonathan fired a long burst through the sheet metal front wall to give them something to think about, and then he turned and fired another burst through the opening they'd blown in the back wall.

"We're clear!" Boxers yelled from the bottom. "Twenty-eight rungs."

As Jonathan backed toward the opening in the floor, he let the M27 fall against its sling and he ripped open two of the big flaps on the front of his vest. Each held a fragmentation grenade. He lifted one out, and in one continuous motion, he pulled the safety pin with a sharp twisting motion and tossed it through the hole he'd blown in the concrete. It incited exactly the panic he'd been hoping for, people yelling and pushing to get out of the way.

Out front, someone took a shotgun to the lock on the door as Jonathan dropped chest-deep into the tunnel entrance.

Compared to the other explosions of the night, the grenade blast wasn't much to listen to, but the effect of a bajillion high-velocity fragments on human tissue and psyches could not be overstated.

With a second grenade clutched in his right hand, the pin pulled but the arming spoon clamped tight, Jonathan waited for the tactical entry through the front.

As soon as they kicked in the door, he lobbed the grenade into the opening and dropped out of sight.

Captain Palma had never experienced this level of combat, never fully understood the level of carnage that a few people with weapons could inflict on greater numbers. In his experience, his opposing force caved at the mere sight of his soldiers. The few who dared to fire on him were quickly dispatched.

But this enemy—these men—were killing machines.

And the grenade had all but wiped out his force. It had landed in the perfect place at the perfect time. He'd just gathered his men to coordinate entry with the larger team in the front when the tiny bomb sailed through the blasted hole and skittered across the floor.

There'd been pushing and shoving, but when it exploded, it left no one standing, including Palma, though he was one of the lucky ones. Three of his men had literally been torn apart by the blast, in the process absorbing more than their fair share of the kinetic energy and fragments.

Palma himself felt burning stabs in his neck and face. While a wipe with his hand produced a smear of blood, and he could feel the torn margins of his skin in two places, he didn't believe his wounds to be life threatening.

He'd barely processed the fact that he was still alive when a second grenade ravaged the front entry team.

All around him, the world had devolved into chaos.

With his own squad too wounded and demoralized to continue, he could only imagine how little interest he could muster from the local emergency forces to follow these murderers underground.

If someone didn't follow, they would all get away.

If they got away, the life left for Palma wouldn't be worth living.

As voices around him called for doctors and ambulances, he realized that he had no choice but to follow on his own.

The air in the tunnel smelled like wet dirt.

Tristan fought the blooming sense of panic just as he fought the urge to run ahead. None of them knew exactly where this passageway would end, but the smoothness of the floors and eight-foot ceiling height spoke of impressive engineering.

He wanted to talk about it, to ask questions, but that would just be more noise.

Noise to cover the horrible sounds that Maria made.

The Big Guy had resumed carrying her over his shoulder, so since Tristan was second in line in this underground parade, that put her face just in front of his. She smelled of blood and vomit, and she begged to be left to die.

"Please," she whined. "It hurts so much." She made a raspy, gargling sound as she spoke.

Every time the Big Guy adjusted her on his shoulder, she shrieked in agony. And apparently, even somebody as strong as the Big Guy had his limits, because he was slowing down.

"We need to keep moving," Scorpion said from behind.

The Big Guy stopped and, as gently as possible, lowered Maria from his shoulder onto the ground.

"What are you doing?" Scorpion snapped.

"She's gonna die," Big Guy said, "unless we do something to stop the flow of blood. Look at me."

The front of his vest shimmered crimson from his shoulder down.

"We don't have time for this," Scorpion said.

"Then just leave her," the Big Guy snapped back. "Seems stupid to me to go through all this effort just to carry a corpse. Let's see if there's something we can do."

"There's a lot of ground left to cover," Scorpion said.

"My point exactly. Now give me some light." As he spoke, the Big Guy pulled up Maria's shirt to reveal a gaping hole in her midsection, where stuff that was supposed to be tucked in was hanging out.

Tristan looked away.

Maria was going to die. Jonathan hadn't realized that her wound was so extensive. Or maybe he had but hadn't wanted to believe it. Either way, they couldn't just leave her here.

"Thank you," Maria said. Her voice was a thready shadow of what it had been. "This feels much better."

"We're not done yet, Maria," Jonathan said. "We've still got a long way to go."

"Leave me," she said.

"We don't leave people behind," Jonathan said.

"Please."

"Absolutely not."

Her eyes had taken on the grayish hue that meant she was bleeding out. She forced a smile. "I am dying, am I not?"

It was a question to which Jonathan had pledged long ago to always give a truthful answer. "Yes."

"Then let me die here. This hurts less."

"This isn't a time for heroics," Jonathan said. He put his arms under hers to lift her, but she wriggled free. The effort made her yell, and Jonathan jerked away.

"I am not a hero," Maria said. "The Lord in Heaven knows that I am not a hero. I am a coward who fears pain. Please let me die here."

"But if Hernandez gets ahold of you—"

"Dead is dead, Mr. Scorpion," she said. "In Mexico or in the U.S. With you or with Felix. It really does not matter. I am already paralyzed. My heart is racing. It won't be long." As she said that last part, she winced against a slice of pain. "Could you leave me a gun though? Just in case. I seem to have lost mine."

Jonathan shot a look to Boxers. If they left her a weapon, she'd use it to commit suicide.

"It's not for me," Maria said, reading his thoughts. "But if they come, maybe I can spend my last moments fighting. I can spend them helping the people who tried so hard to help me."

Boxers cleared his throat. "She's right, Scorpion."

Anger flashed. He shot to his feet. "We do *not* leave people behind."

"She's not our PC," Boxers said matter-of-factly. "And if we don't listen to her, we'll unnecessarily risk losing the one who *is* our PC." He shot a glance toward Tristan.

"Oh, no," Tristan said. "Don't make this about me. Don't leave her to save me."

Jonathan wanted the answer to be different from what it had to be. "Tristan," he said. "Give your weapon to Maria, please."

"Like hell!" Tristan said. He wasn't going to have something like this on his conscience for the rest of his life. They'd all suffered through this together. He had no more right to live than she did.

"It's the only way," Scorpion said. "I know it sucks, but it's the only way."

"And we don't have time to dick around," Boxers said. "If you make me carry *you*, I'll do it, even if I have to knock you senseless first."

How could this be happening? How could it be right that out of all of his friends and the chaperones and now Maria, he would be the only one to come home alive? What had he done that was so important that he deserved that? What could he possibly do with the rest of his life to earn that kind of sacrifice?

Scorpion reached for Tristan's weapon, but the boy twisted away. "No!"

Scorpion reached again. In the wash of the flash-lights, there was tenderness in Scorpion's eyes as he reached to unclasp the weapon from its sling.

Tristan twisted away again. "No," he said, softer this time. "I'll do it."

He unclipped the rifle from its sling and knelt next to Maria. He laid the weapon on her lap. "Be careful," he said. "The safety's off." That done, he stripped four magazines from the pockets of his vest. "In case you need these, too."

Maria placed her hand gently on his cheek. "You're so handsome," she said. "Have a good life, Jaime."

"I'm Tristan," he said.

She smiled and took his hand in both of hers and kissed it. "Then have a good life *for* Jaime."

Tristan scowled. "Who's—"

"Gotta go," Jonathan said.

The familiar grip fell onto the collar of Tristan's vest, and he found himself being lifted away.

"Scorpion," Maria said in that fading voice. She beckoned for him to come closer.

Scorpion bent and brought his ear to her lips. He listened for a moment then turned to the rest of them. "Big Guy, get going with Tristan. I'll catch up."

Something awful snagged in Tristan's gut. "Why?" he said. "What are you going to do?"

"Come on, kid," Big Guy said. He gave a gentle tug on his arm.

As he allowed himself to be escorted along, Tristan pressed the Big Guy for insight. "He's not going to kill her, is he?"

"I don't know what they're talking about," the Big Guy said. "But I guaran-damn-tee you that it's not that."

Palma moved as quickly as he could in the darkness of the tunnel. Not wanting to reveal his location with a flashlight beam, he kept his left hand in contact with the wall and trusted that the floors would remain clear of obstacles.

He wished he could move faster, but he knew that the girl had been wounded, and that would make them move more slowly than they normally would. And since they were in the lead—and didn't know that he was following—he was betting that they would illuminate their way with flashlights. In this level of darkness, even the faintest light would shine like a beacon.

In fact, he saw that very beacon right now. It was more a distant glow than a light beam, but down here, it had to be man-made. The glow was projected from a source of white light, and it wasn't moving. It was distant, but in the darkness, it was impossible to tell how far.

Palma dropped to a crouch and brought his weapon to his shoulder. He sensed that he'd entered a trap. The classic booby trap involved an irresistible enticement to draw the victim in close, and an illuminated light seemed like just such a thing. Who would be stupid enough to sit still with a light on? For all they knew, there were dozens of armed men following them. The light only made sense as a trap.

Harris and Lerner had night vision. They wouldn't need light at all, would they?

Or maybe in the absoluteness of the darkness here in the tunnel, there wasn't enough light to amplify.

His nerves sent the sensation of a thousand ants crawling up his back and neck. This had to be a trap.

Yet what were his options?

He could risk it and perhaps meet his death, or he could abandon the chase and meet his death for certain, at the hands of Felix Hernandez and his torturers.

He advanced with excruciating slowness, doing his best to keep a low profile while remaining absolutely silent. He remained pressed against the left-hand wall, and despite his fear of losing his night vision, he kept his sights trained on the glow. If people were there, they would cast a shadow. Or the light would move.

But there were no shadows and nothing moved.

As he neared the source of the light—he could see the distinctive circular outline of a flashlight beam on the ceiling now—he slowed even more, to perhaps ten feet per minute. It took forever, but he needed to be sure this time. His prey had been one step ahead from the very beginning, and in here, there simply was no room to make a mistake.

Finally, he was near enough to see the silhouette of a person slumped against the wall. Closer still, he saw that it was Maria Elizondo, and she lay perfectly still. From ten feet away, even in the dim light of the flashlight, he could see the blood-soaked T-shirt.

Palma smiled. In fact, he nearly laughed out loud.

With Maria dead, he could now live. Felix wouldn't be happy about it—in fact he'd be furious when he learned that he'd lost his opportunity to torture her—but under the circumstances, given all the destruction, Palma would be able to make him understand. He'd decide later whether it would be prudent to share the detail that Palma himself had killed her.

He needed to be certain.

Palma considered shooting her again, this time in the head, but he decided not to. That much noise in such a confined space might push Harris and Lerner over the edge. Palma didn't care about them anymore. Maria was the key to his personal survival.

But he still needed to be certain.

And certainty came with risk.

Still moving slowly and silently, Palma slid his Mini Maglite from its loop on his belt. With his rifle at his shoulder and his finger poised on the trigger, he raised the light high over his head and switched it on. If Harris and his team were lying in wait, the bright light would wash out their night vision, and maybe, for a second or two, Palma would have the advantage.

But the light revealed nothing.

Then this made sense to him.

They knew Maria was dying, so they'd left her here. She was afraid of the dark, so they left the light for her.

Palma dared to rise to his full height now, and he approached Maria's body more easily.

She lay slumped to her right side, her face down and away from him. He tapped her nearest hip—her left— with the toe of his boot, but she didn't move.

He watched her chest carefully for signs of breathing, but again he saw nothing.

Still, he needed to be certain.

Keeping his weapon trained on her head, he reached out with his left hand and pulled her into a more upright sitting position so that he could check her pulse.

So young and so thin, her torso weighed virtually nothing as—

Maria had tucked the hand grenade in her left armpit, with the pin pulled. Palma knew what it was from the *ting!* of the safety spoon flying away and arming the detonator. When the grenade rolled between his feet, he turned to run.

It didn't matter.

CHAPTER THIRTY-FIVE

The explosion registered more as a thump than a bang, but it was loud enough to make Tristan jump and duck. "What was that?"

"Nothing for us to worry about," Scorpion said. "Keep going." Stealth no longer seemed to be an issue.

"It was an explosion!" Tristan said. "How can that be nothing for us to worry about?"

A look passed between the Big Guy and the boss. It didn't linger, but it was significant, and Tristan caught it. "What aren't you telling me?"

"Come on, Tristan," Scorpion said. For the first time, he appeared tired. Nearly spent. "Please just let it go and keep walking."

"I think I have a right to know."

"And I think you're wrong. Please, just—"

"Maria just blew herself up, didn't she?" Tristan didn't know where that came from, or how it had occurred to him, but he was certain that that had to be it. "Was that what she asked you at the end? For a grenade to blow herself up?"

Another look passed between the two men. Big Guy

said, "What can I say, Boss? The kid's good at connecting the dots."

Tristan pulled up short. "Dots! Dots? That's what
she was to you? She gets too heavy to carry so we just
leave her to die and then she gets reduced to being a
dot? Oh, my God." Out of nowhere, Tristan felt flushed,
like he needed to sit down. It was as if someone had
hacked away the final chunk of mortar in the dam that
held his emotions together. The reality of it all was
more than he could bear.

Suddenly, there wasn't enough air to breathe. He
sank to his knees, and pressed his hands to his face, a
last desperate effort to keep the tears from coming.

He saw Maria's beautiful face, so alive, and then so
agonized. He saw Allison lying dead on the floor of the
bus, and Mrs. James being forced to do such awful things
only to be shot down by the terrorist she'd obliged.

Sobs wracked his body as he heard a wailing sound
pealing from his throat. These were sights he'd see in
his mind for the rest of his life. How could anyone live
with that?

He thought of the man he shot, and of the excitement that gave him, and then he felt overwhelmed with
even more grief. Overwhelmed by shame.

"We don't have time for this," the Big Buy said.

"Yeah, we do," Scorpion replied.

Tristan felt a hand on his shoulder. It didn't comfort
him so much as steady him.

He knew he should be repulsed. These men were
trained killers—so used to it that they treated cold-
blooded murder as more of a business transaction than
the unspeakable act of violence that it was.

"Listen to me, Tristan," Scorpion said, his voice so close to his ear that it made him jump. "Maria wanted you to live, and in the end she was fine with dying to make sure that happened. When I went back to speak with her, she told me that you reminded her of her brother Jaime. He was about your age when Felix Hernandez's goons murdered him."

Tristan took a huge breath and wiped tears and snot from his face with a swipe of his arm. He knew that Scorpion was trying to comfort him, but how did—

"It was Maria's idea to booby-trap her own body," Scorpion went on. "She knew the soldiers would stop to check on her. That was the explosion you heard, son. That was Maria saving your life. Saving all our lives."

Tristan's world felt as if it had too many moving parts. They were out of synch, and nothing made sense. "What makes me worth all this?" he asked. There, he'd spoken aloud his worst fears.

Scorpion gave a kind smile. "Fifty or sixty years from now, when you look back over a whole life, I hope you'll be able to answer that question."

A few feet away, Big Guy shuffled impatiently, and Tristan got it. He'd have countless years ahead to throw pity parties for himself.

But here, they still had a job to do.

A miserable, awful freaking job, yes, but a job.

They had to go home.

When Jonathan saw the lights approaching from the other end of the tunnel, he knew their ordeal was over, but he wasn't at all sure what the initial meeting was going to be like. At the first sign of the glow, Jonathan brought his team to a stop.

"My name is Leon Harris!" he yelled. "I am with Richard Lerner and Tristan Wagner! We are heavily armed, but pose no threat to you!"

A voice called from the light, "Put your weapons down and advance!"

Jonathan yelled, "No! It's been a long day, and we will not disarm until we know that we are safe."

"Ballsy move, there, Boss," Boxers grumbled.

A long silence followed. Two minutes or more.

"What are they doing?" Tristan whispered.

"I have no idea," Jonathan confessed.

"Well, they're not shooting at us," Boxers quipped. "That's kind of a nice change."

Finally, the lights up ahead moved, and a dark form emerged from the glare, walking closer. There was a purposefulness to the stride.

"Hands off your weapons," Jonathan whispered.

"I don't have a weapon anymore," Tristan said.

"He wasn't talking to you," Boxers whispered back.

At the precise instant when Jonathan realized that the silhouette belonged to a woman, that woman's voice said, "Welcome home."

She walked directly to Jonathan and extended her hand. "Veronica Costanza," she said. "I'm with the FBI." She scanned the other faces. "You're missing one." Behind her, others approached.

"Maria didn't make it," Jonathan said.

"But she saved our lives," Tristan said.

Veronica looked for confirmation.

"Saved us all," Jonathan said. "A courageous woman."

The disappointment on the FBI agent's face was obvious—the United States' case against Felix Hernandez and Trevor Munro had just fallen apart—but there was sadness there, too.

Agent Costanza turned to Tristan. "You, young man, need to follow these agents out of this god-awful tunnel. We'll get some food in you and get you back to your family."

"I'm not under arrest?" Tristan asked. He looked shocked.

"We're in the process of getting that all worked out," she said. "Meanwhile, don't worry about it. I want you to go with Agent Purgo here."

A recent Academy graduate stepped into the light and offered his hand to Tristan. "You can call me Kent," he said. "Come on, let's go."

Tristan shook his hand and stepped forward. He looked to Jonathan and Boxers. "I'll see you guys in a few minutes, right?"

"Not if I see you first," Boxers said—but with a smile.

"We'll see you in a few, Tristan," Jonathan said, knowing full well that he'd just lied.

Agent Costanza crossed her arms. "Busy day?"

"A little bit," Jonathan said.

"You know, the Mexican government is calling you two terrorists."

Boxers said, "I can see how they might get that impression."

"The television pictures are pretty impressive," Costanza said. She clearly was marking time for something. A few seconds later, she cocked her head in the way characteristic of an incoming message in an earpiece.

Sure enough, she brought her hand to her lips and said into a wrist mike, "All right, I copy. Thank you." To Jonathan and Boxers: "My orders on you two could not be clearer. The essentials are this: You were never here. There's a guy out there waiting for you with a car. I don't want to know where you're going. Have a nice night." She checked her watch. "Oh, my bad. It's five a.m. Have a nice day."

"What are you going to do with the tunnel?" Jonathan asked.

"Use it as a bargaining chip, I hope. I figure we can make some people really uncomfortable on both sides of the Rio Grande with what we find. Now get out of here."

It turned out to be a longer walk than Jonathan had anticipated—every bit of a hundred yards, he guessed. He walked with Boxers in silence, doing his best to ignore the harm he had brought to so many families.

The tunnel ended at another metal ladder. This one emerged into the basement of a home whose owner no doubt had serious explaining to do. Jonathan spoke to no one as he passed a dozen or more law enforcement officers who'd obviously been instructed not to notice them.

The basement stairs led to a modest living room, and from there, the front door brought him back to the thick summer air.

"She said something about a car and driver," Jonathan thought aloud.

"I'm voting that it's him," Boxers said, pointing to a late-model Expedition, where Dom D'Angelo sat on the flatbed under the open tailgate, waiting.

"Well, well, well," Jonathan said as he strode across the grass to greet his friend. "What on earth—" The dour look on Dom's face froze Jonathan's words in his throat. "What?" That's when he noticed that his old friend was wearing his priest uniform, clerical collar and all.

Dom stood. "It's Gail," he said.

Jonathan didn't ask how Dom had arranged for the private Lear from El Paso directly into Scottsdale Airport. He was sure it had involved Venice and her access to his credit card, and all of that was fine. While he worked the phone, trying in vain to get meaningful information from a medical staff who feared HIPAA lawsuits far more than they cared about close friends and relatives, Dom and Boxers left him alone in the aft end of the plane while they clustered in conversation up front near the door to the flight deck.

Big Guy looked especially uncomfortable in the luxurious leather of the passenger compartment. He'd told Jonathan before that he hated the view from the cabin. "Who the hell cares where you are or where you've been?" he'd said. "I want to look at where we're going."

The flight was blessedly short, and since Scottsdale Airport specialized in executive charters, and therefore understood the peccadilloes of wealthy, busy people, the time from wheels down to having his butt in the seat of a moving car clocked in at something less than ten minutes. And nobody gave a crap about his filthy appearance or camouflaged clothing.

That would come when his driver whipped into the Osborn Medical Center's driveway and disgorged his passengers into the emergency department via the space normally used to park ambulances. He'd left his body armor and weapons in the Lear—all but his .45, which was legal to carry in Arizona, but he had nonetheless concealed in a high hip holster under the flap of his shirttail.

He strode to the triage station, and as he approached, he drew the attention of an armed security guard, who stepped forward to intercept. As he closed the distance, though, and got a really good look at Boxers, he seemed to lose some of his resolve.

"Can I help you, gentlemen?" he said.

Dom took the lead. "Good afternoon," he said. "Can you direct us to the trauma intensive care unit?"

The guard's shoulders relaxed a little. "Good afternoon, Father," he said. Something about that collar brought out politeness in people.

It was all Jonathan could do to endure the navigation instructions. He wanted to be with Gail, to see for himself what those animals had done to her. Having just navigated the length of a country and survived a running firefight, he was more than capable of finding a hospital room on his own.

A beefy hand landed on his shoulder. Boxers'.

"Hey, Boss," Big Guy said, barely above a whisper. "You need to take a breath and settle down. We got no enemies in here. Everybody's on Gunslinger's side."

Point taken. The main problem with adrenaline was that once it got into your system, it took its own sweet time going away. It was time to shift from war mode to peace mode, and he didn't have the luxury of his typical transition time.

"Thanks," he said.

Dom led the way from here. The walk turned out to be far shorter in execution than it was in description. Once they got to the door of the unit, Dom stepped aside to allow Jonathan to press the buzzer.

"I'm here to see Gail Bonneville," he said to the harsh voice of the woman who answered his push of the button over the intercom.

"She's already got one visitor," she said. "Only one more is allowed."

"I'm bringing my priest with me," Jonathan said. There wasn't even a hint of request in his tone.

The nurse didn't reply, but the lock buzzed and Jonathan pulled the door open.

He looked to Boxers. "Sorry, Big Guy."

"Don't worry about me," Boxers said. "I've seen plenty enough hospitals. I'm gonna go find the cafeteria and clean them out of food." He started down the hall without waiting for a reply.

Jonathan paused at the door and looked at Dom. "How bad?" he asked. Again.

"She's been shot, Jon." Dom's tone had a what-do-you-want-from-me edge. "Three, four hours ago, last time I saw her, she was still in the ER and they said they thought she'd live, but there were no guarantees."

It was pretty much what he'd reported the previous two times Jonathan had asked the question. Word for word, in fact.

Jonathan realized that he was stalling. He hated hospitals. He'd logged too many hours in them getting himself repaired, and he'd lost way too many friends in them.

The locked double doors led to an anteroom, and

from there to another set of double doors that remained closed but unlocked.

Stepping through those doors into the trauma ICU itself was like stepping back in time—into a past where you could bring modern technology along for the ride. In recent years, hospitals had undergone face-lifts that made them look like happy, inviting places, their hallways resembling high-end hotels.

In here, though, where life was as fragile as a single missed symptom, nothing counted but efficiency. Glasswalled rooms guaranteed a lack of privacy as mostly naked patients lay plugged in to more technology than a space shuttle. Swollen yellow bags of urine hung from every side rail, the specific color and quantity of their contents serving as important indicators of their owners' health.

Gail lay in the room that was directly diagonal from the entryway, requiring Jonathan and Dom to pass assorted victims of varied traumas. Most appeared to be unconscious, and of the two whose eyes were open, both showed no interest in the television that played in the bracket near the ceiling. Instead, they stared out through their drug-induced hazes into whatever images their brains had manufactured for them. At least they didn't appear to be in any pain.

Jonathan saw Irene Rivers in the chair at Gail's bedside before he actually saw Gail beyond the enormous wrapping that encased her head.

"You didn't tell me that Wolverine was here," Jonathan said sotto voce to Dom.

"She didn't tell me she was coming."

I wonder what that means, Jonathan didn't say.

Irene seemed to sense their approach and turned in

her seat to see them. She stood and extended her hand. When Jonathan took it, she covered it with her left. "I thought she deserved a little company," she said, answering the look she saw in Jonathan's face. "She's tough. I wish we still had her on the payroll."

Jonathan smiled at the compliment, then eased past her for a closer look at Gail. Her face was swollen and bore purple highlights, but he'd seen worse. He knew to look past the drain lines and the intravenous tubes, and was heartened to see that the dressings and bandages were pure white. That meant she wasn't bleeding and she wasn't leaking cerebrospinal fluid, both good signs.

"Shot in the arm, the chest, and the head," Irene said over his shoulder. "And she was still able to take out four bad guys."

Jonathan turned to face Irene. Again, his face spoke for him.

"We don't know the details," she said. "I'm not sure we ever will. A worker at the Crystal Palace heard noises in the stairwell and stepped out to investigate. He found a blood trail and followed it to Gail. The worker called nine-one-one from his cell phone, and thank God he did, because if he'd called on a landline, it would have gone to the same security desk that turned away the police that responded to my first call. Scottsdale Police and Fire responded and because I had been knocking around for information, they dialed me in, too. Our people followed the same blood trail back up the stairs, and we found the guys she'd killed."

Irene paused to make sure she had Jonathan's full attention. "Wait till you get this," she said. "Your girlfriend made it down eleven floors with those injuries."

She looked back to Gail. "One tough, tough young lady."

Jonathan had known that since the day they'd first met. But he'd known a lot of very, very tough people who'd lost their battles against bullets.

He moved back to her bedside and threaded his way through the IV tubes to grasp her hand. As he entwined his fingers with hers, he noticed traces of blood in the crease where her manicured nails met the nail beds.

Gail stirred at his touch, and he smiled, gently raising her hand above the bed rail and bending to kiss it.

"It's Digger," he said. "I'm here."

Her uncovered eye opened for just a second or two, and then closed. He sensed that the lid was just too heavy.

"Harriett," she said.

Jonathan scowled as he scoured his memory.

"I don't understand," Jonathan said.

This time, Gail didn't waste energy on her eyelid. "How is Harriett?"

Dom whispered, "Gail was trying to save her. She didn't make it."

"Don't worry about her," Jonathan said, stroking her hand with his thumb as his fingers gripped a little tighter. "You worry about getting well."

"She was my responsibility," Gail said. "Did she get out?" As she spoke, the rhythm of the blips on her heart monitor increased.

There were some things about which Jonathan could not allow himself to lie. "No," he said. "She was killed."

Gail's chest heaved as she took a huge breath. "My fault," she said.

Jonathan wanted to correct her, but didn't. If Gail

had not gone to the Crystal Palace, lots of people would still be alive. The fact that most of them deserved killing didn't remove the burden of the one who didn't.

"Digger?" Gail said.

"Right here."

"Kiss me," she said.

He leaned across the bed rail and did just that, pressing his lips gently against hers. She did her best to kiss him back.

As he pulled away, he stroked her hair. "I love you," he said. It was the first time he'd ever spoken the words aloud to Gail.

Gail winced. "I wanted to quit," she said. "You talked me out of it."

"That's because you're too good at what you do," he said. They'd had this conversation a thousand times.

"This time for real," Gail said. "I quit. I can't hurt anyone else."

"This time, I won't say a word. You do what you need to do."

Gail nodded slightly, but even that tiny movement seemed to hurt. "More," she said. "I need you to quit, too."

Jonathan didn't care all that much about the details of what became of the Crystal Palace Cathedral, but from what he'd gathered from the news, Jackie Mitchell and her executive committee would spend the rest of their lives in prison if they didn't end up on the wrong end of a needle in the death chamber.

The government's case against Felix Hernandez—

and, by extension, their case against Trevor Munro—died with Maria Elizondo.

And without a case against him, Munro still remained poised to advance within the Agency. It was the nature of their business in Langley to cross ethical lines. Convincing people to betray their own country to provide intelligence data was a dirty business—certainly no dirtier than abetting a drug trade in return for special favors. Besides, Uncle Sam had the ATF and the DEA to take care of drugs and weapons. And occasionally the Army.

The levels of cynicism and general dysfunction within the U.S. government had sickened Jonathan for years. Over time, he'd learned to look away, wrapping himself in his own cloak of cynicism. It's the way of politicians and bureaucrats to feed on the blood of others in order to advance their careers. He'd learned to live with it.

Until now. Until Trevor Munro. He was a peculiar brand of mass murderer who killed randomly and efficiently without ever pulling a trigger or throwing a bomb. He did it with full deniability.

His bosses in Langley had the power to stop him, but instead chose to promote him. Soon he would be the third-highest-ranking spook in the CIA, with a bloated paycheck that was financed by honest Americans. It wasn't right.

Jonathan had never done well at managing anger. Some injustices were so out of proportion that he couldn't live with the imbalance.

Over the years, Jonathan had seen too many of his Special Ops pals slide the slippery moral slope toward hired killer, and he'd vowed to himself and to God and to everything holy that he would never become an assassin. It would just be too easy a line to cross, and once crossed, there could be no return.

These thoughts—this rage—tormented him as he sat in Trevor Munro's rigorously neat living room with its clean lines and right angles, awaiting the man's arrival home from work. He told himself that justice and assassination were two different things.

Tonight would be all about justice, meted out by the subsonic rounds he'd loaded into the suppressed .22-caliber pistol in his lap.

The living room wall hummed as the garage door opened.

Jonathan waited until the overhead door rumbled closed again, and then he stood. He didn't make his move, though, until he heard the interior garage door open and close and the sound of mail slapping down on the table.

Jonathan stepped into the foyer, and from there straight into the kitchen.

Munro actually made a yipping sound as he sensed Jonathan's presence, and he whirled to face his attacker.

The man Munro saw was dressed all in black, and his face was covered by a black mask.

"I hear you've been looking for me," Jonathan said. He smiled at the sight of the spreading stain in Munro's trousers. "Well, here I am."

ACKNOWLEDGMENTS

Family is always first. Thank you, Joy, for always being there, and always understanding. I love you.

Chris, you rock. I'm so proud of you.

I owe special thanks to a couple of genuine war heroes who invited me into the world of U.S. Navy SEALs for a couple of days and let me see stuff and play with toys that I would otherwise never have had access to. Steve "Dutch" Van Horn is a terrific tour guide for the SEALs compound in Virginia Beach, and the hour or two I spent on the shooting range with Stephen "Turbo" Toboz as my instructor was truly special. I shot the HK416 (Jonathan Grave's M27), the HK417, the sweet little MP7, and the granddaddy of the day, a .300 WinMag sniper rifle. Great day. Thanks, guys.

Jackie Mitchell gave a generous donation to the American Heart Association for her name to be included in this book. Having just had dinner with the real Jackie Mitchell for the first time, I can assure you that in reality she's a very nice lady—far nicer than her fictional namesake. Thank heaven she has a sense of humor. Thanks to her for giving to such a good cause.

Trevor Munro made a donation to the Recycling Research Foundation in return for having a character named after him. I assure the world that I borrowed only his name. The fictional Trevor Munro bears no resemblance to anything but my imagination.

Many people touch my life on a regular basis, and all of them make the journey more valuable. I can't possibly name everyone, but I'd like to call out a few in particular: Jeffery Deaver, Pat Barney and Sam Shockley, Bob and Bert Garino (I miss you guys!), Ellen Crosby, Donna Andrews, Alan Orloff, and Art Taylor.

The folks at Kensington Publishing continue to amaze me. Michaela Hamilton is simply the best of the best when it comes to editors, and I'm sure it helps a lot to be surrounded by a terrific team. Adeola Saul is a terrific publicist whose heart and mind are always aligned on the books she manages, and Alexandra Nicolajsen is wonderfully persuasive in dragging analog writers into the digital world. None of that would work, though, without the passion of publisher Laurie Parkin, who is empowered by the great guy in the big corner office, Steve Zacharius. Thank you all for everything.

Last but Lord knows not least, thanks to my agent and great friend, Anne Hawkins of John Hawkins and Associates. She's been there through all of it.

Turn the page for an exciting preview of John
Gilstrap's next exciting thriller
starring Jonathan Grave

HIGH TREASON

Coming from Pinnacle in 2013

In all his seventeen years with the United States Secret Service, Special Agent Jason Knapp had never felt this out of place, this exposed. The January chill combined with his jumpy nerves to create a sense of dread that rendered every noise too loud, every odor too intense.

Rendered the night far too dark.

With his SIG Sauer P229 on his hip, and an MP5 submachine gun slung under his arm—not to mention his five teammates on Cowgirl's protection detail—he couldn't imagine a scenario that might get away from them, but sometimes you get that niggling voice in the back of your head that tells you that things aren't right. Years of experience had taught Knapp to listen to that voice when it spoke.

Oh, that Mrs. Darmond would learn to listen to her protection detail. Oh, that she would listen to *anyone*.

While he himself rarely visited the White House residence, stories abounded among his colleagues that Cowgirl and Champion fought like banshees once the doors were closed. She never seemed to get the fact that image mattered to presidents, and that first ladies had a responsibility to show a certain decorum.

Clearly, she didn't care.

These late-night party jaunts were becoming more and more routine, and Knapp was getting sick of them. He understood that she rejected the traditional role of first lady, and he got that despite her renown she wanted to have some semblance of a normal life, but the steadily increasing risks she took were flat-out irresponsible.

Tonight was the worst of the lot.

It was one thing to dash out to a bar on the spur of the moment with a reduced protection detail—first spouses and first children had done that for decades—but to insist on a place like the Wild Times bar in Southeast D.C. was a step too far. It was five steps too far.

Great disguise notwithstanding, Cowgirl was a white lady in a very dark part of town. And it was nearly one in the morning.

Knapp stood outside the main entrance to the club, shifting from foot to foot to ward away the cold. Charlie Robinson flanked the other side of the door, and together they looked like the plainclothes version of the toy soldiers that welcomed children to the FAO Schwartz toy store in Manhattan. He felt at least that conspicuous.

Twenty feet away, Cowgirl's chariot, an armored Suburban, idled in the handicapped space at the curb, its tailpipe adding a cloud of condensation to the night. Inside, Gene Tomkin sat behind the wheel, no doubt reveling in the warmth of the cab. Bill Lansing enjoyed similar bragging rights in the follow car that idled in the alley behind the bar.

Typical of OTR movements—off the record—the detail had chosen silver Suburbans instead of the black ones that were so ubiquitous to official Washington, specifically to call less attention to themselves. They'd driven here just like any other traffic, obeying stoplights and using turn signals the whole way. On paper that meant that you remained unnoticed.

But a Suburban was a Suburban, and if you looked hard enough you could see the emergency lights behind the windows and the grille. Throw in the well-dressed white guys standing like toy soldiers, and they might as well have been holding flashing signs.

In these days of Twitter and Facebook, when rumors traveled at the speed of light, all it would take for this calm night to turn to shit would be for somebody to connect some very obvious dots. While the good citizens of the District of Columbia had more or less unanimously cast their votes to sweep Champion into office, they'd since turned against him. It didn't stretch Knapp's imagination even a little to envision a spontaneous protest.

Then again, Cowgirl was such a media magnet, he could just as easily envision a spontaneous TMZ feeding frenzy. Neither option was more attractive than the other in this neighborhood.

The Wild Times was doing a hell of a business. The main act on the stage was a rapper of considerable local fame—or maybe he was a hip-hopper (how do you tell the difference?)—and he was drawing hundreds of twentysomething kids. Within the last twenty minutes, the pace of arrivals had picked up—and almost nobody was leaving.

From a tactical perspective, the two agents inside with Cowgirl—Peter Campbell and Dusty Binks, the detail supervisor—must be enduring the tortures of the damned. In an alternate world where the first lady might have given a shit, no one would have been allowed to touch the protectee, but in a nightclub situation, where fans paid good money to press closer to the stage, preventing personal contact became nearly impossible.

For the most part, the arriving revelers projected a pretty benign aura. It was the nature of young men to swagger in the presence of their girlfriends, and with that came a certain tough-guy gait, but over the years Knapp had learned to trust his ability to read the real thing from the imitation. Over the course of the past hour, his warning bells hadn't rung even once.

Until right now.

A clutch of four guys approached from the north, and everything about them screamed malevolence. It wasn't just the gangsta gait and the gangsta clothes. In the case of the leader in particular, it was the eyes. Knapp could see the glare from twenty feet away. This guy wanted people to be afraid of him.

"Do you see this?" he asked Robinson without moving his eyes from the threat.

Robinson took up a position on Knapp's right. "Handle it carefully," he warned. More than a few careers had been wrecked by YouTube videos of white cops challenging black citizens.

As the kids closed to within a dozen feet, Knapp

stepped forward. "Good evening, gentlemen," he said. "You know, it's pretty crowded inside."

"The fuck outta my way," the leader said. He started to push past, but Knapp body blocked him. No hands, no violence. He just physically blocked their path.

"Look at the vehicle," Knapp said, pointing to the Suburban. "Take a real close look."

Their heads turned in unison, and they seemed to get it at the same instant.

"If any of you are armed, this club is exactly the last place you want to be right now. Do you understand what I'm saying?"

"What?" the leader said. "Is it like the president or something?"

Knapp ignored the question. "Here are your choices, gentlemen. You can go someplace else, or you can submit to a search right here on the street. If I find a firearm on any of you, I'll arrest you all, and your mamas won't see their boys for about fifteen years. Which way do you want to go?"

Simple, respectful, and face saving.

"Come on, Antoine," one of them said. "This place sucks anyway."

Antoine held Knapp's gaze for just long enough to communicate his lack of fear. Then he walked away, taking his friends with him.

"Nicely done, Agent Knapp," Robinson said.

They returned to their posts. "Every time we do one of these late-night OTRs, I'm amazed by the number of people who keep vampire hours. Don't these kids have jobs to wake up for?"

Robinson chuckled. "I figure they all drive buses or hazmat trucks."

With the Antoine non-confrontation behind them, Knapp told himself to relax, but in the world of gang-bangers, you always had to be on your toes for the re-taliatory strike. He couldn't imagine that Antoine and his crew would be in the mood to take on federal agents, but you never knew.

He just wanted to get the hell out of here.

"Look left," Robinson said.

Half a block away, a scrawny, filthy little man was doing his best to navigate a shopping cart around the corner to join their little slice of the world. The cart overflowed with blankets and assorted stuff—the total-ity of his worldly possessions, Knapp imagined. Aged somewhere between thirty and eighty, this guy had the look of a man who'd been homeless for decades. There was a hunched movement to the chronically homeless that spoke of a departure of all hope. It would be heart-breaking if they didn't smell so bad.

"If Cowgirl sees him, you know she'll offer him a ride," Robinson quipped.

Knapp laughed. "And Champion will give him a job. Couldn't do worse than some of his other appoint-ments." Knapp didn't share the first family's attraction to the downtrodden, but he admired it. It was the one passion of the president's that seemed to come from an honest place.

Knapp didn't want to take action against this wretched guy, but if he got too close, he'd have to do something. Though heroic to socialists and poets, the preponder-ance of homeless folks were, in Knapp's experience, nut jobs, harmless at the surface, but inherently unstable. They posed a hazard that needed to be managed.

He felt genuine relief when the guy parked himself on a sidewalk grate and started to set up camp.

Knapp's earpiece popped as somebody broke squelch on the radio. "Lansing, Binks. Bring the follow car to the front. Cowgirl's moving in about three."

"Thank God," Knapp said aloud but off the air. Finally.

He and Robinson shifted from their positions flanking the doors of the Wild Times to new positions flanking the doors to Cowgirl's chariot. He double-checked to make sure that his coat was open and his weapon available. A scan of the sidewalk showed more of what they'd been seeing all night.

When the follow car appeared from the end of the block and pulled in behind the chariot, Knapp brought his left hand to his mouth and pressed the button on his wrist mike. "Binks, Knapp," he said. "We're set outside."

"Cowgirl is moving now."

This was it, the moment of greatest vulnerability. Ask Squeaky Fromme, Sara Jane Moore, or John Hinckley. These few seconds when the protectee is exposed are the moments of opportunity for suicidal bad guys to take their best shot.

Robinson pulled open the Suburban's door and cheated his body forward to scan for threats from that end of the street, and Knapp cheated to the rear to scan the direction of the homeless guy and the real estate beyond him. He noted with some unease that the guy was paying attention in a way that he hadn't before. His eyes seemed somehow sharper.

Knapp's inner alarm clanged.

Ahead and to his left, the double doors swung out, revealing a unmistakably unhappy Cowgirl , who seemed to be resisting her departure. She wasn't quite yelling yet, but assuming that past was precedent, the yelling would come soon.

Movement to his right brought Knapp's attention back around to the homeless man, who suddenly looked less homeless as he shot to his feet and hurled something at the chariot.

Knapp fought the urge to intercept the throw, and instead drew his sidearm as he shouted "Grenade!"

He'd just leveled his sights on the attacker when an explosion ripped the chariot apart from the inside, the pressure wave rattling his brain and shoving him face first onto the concrete. He didn't know if he'd fired a shot, but if he had, it missed, because the homeless guy was still standing.

He'd produced a submachine gun from somewhere— a P90, Knapp thought, but he wasn't sure—and he was going to town, blasting the night on full-auto.

Behind him, he knew that Campbell and Binks would be shielding Cowgirl with their bodies as they hustled her toward the follow car. In his ear, he heard Lansing shouting, "Shots fired! Shots fired! Agents down!"

Once Knapp found his balance, he rolled to a knee and fired three bullets at the attacker's center of mass. The man remained unfazed and focused, shooting steadily at the First Lady.

Body armor, Knapp thought. He took aim at the attacker's head and fired three more times. The attacker collapsed.

But the shooting continued, seemingly from every compass point. Had passersby joined the fight? What the hell—

Binks and Campbell were still ten feet from the follow car when head shots killed them both within a second of each other. They collapsed to the street, bringing Cowgirl with them. She curled into a fetal ball and started to scream.

Past her, and over her head, bullets raked the doors of the follow car. Going that way was no longer an option.

Keeping low, Knapp let his SIG drop to the pavement as he reached for his slung MP5. This wasn't time for aimed shots; it was time for covering fire. At this moment, the First Lady of the United States was far more important than any other innocents in this crowd. He held the weapon as a pistol in his left hand as he raked the direction he thought the new shots were coming from.

With his right hand, he grabbed Cowgirl by the neck of her blouse and pulled. "Back into the club!" he commanded as he draped his body over hers.

To others it might have looked as though she was carrying him on her back as he hustled her toward the front doors of the club, past the burning chariot and around the body of Charlie Robinson, who'd been torn apart by the blast.

Knapp was still five steps away when searing heat tore through his midsection, driving the breath from his lungs and making him stagger.

He'd taken that bullet for Cowgirl. He'd done his job. Now he just had to finish it.

He had to get her inside.

The next two bullets took him in the hip and the elbow.

He was done, and he knew it.

"Inside!" he yelled and he pushed the first lady as hard as he could.

He saw her step through the doors the instant before a bullet sheared his throat.

John Gilstrap is the acclaimed author of eight thrillers: *Threat Warning*, *Hostage Zero*, *No Mercy*, *Six Minutes to Freedom*, *Scott Free*, *Even Steven*, *At All Costs*, and *Nathan's Run*. His books have been translated into more than twenty languages. A safety and environmental expert and former firefighter, he holds a master's degree from the University of Southern California and a bachelor's degree from the College of William and Mary in Virginia. John has also adapted four books for the big screen: *Red Dragon* (uncredited) from the Thomas Harris novel, *Word of Honor* from the Nelson DeMille novel, and *Young Men and Fire*, from the Norman Maclean book. He lives in Fairfax, Virginia (near Washington, D.C.). Please visit www.johngilstrap.com.

More Nail-Biting Suspense From Your Favorite Thriller Authors